ABOUT THE AUTHOR

Marianne Rosen is an emerging author of contemporary family saga. A former interior designer, she is inspired by the many stunning homes she has worked in and writes about the longing for home and the drama of family.

She is a member of the Hay Writers' Circle, has performed at Hay Festival and is winner of the Richard Booth Prize for Non-fiction in 2018. *The Lights of Riverdell* is the third of the four-book Riverdell Saga.

For release updates: www.mariannerosen.com

CONTENT WARNINGS

This book includes scenes of a sexual nature, discussion of abortion and infertility, mention of childhood abuse, gender dysphoria, loss of a loved one and homelessness caused by war.

If you wish to have more information to make an informed choice please view the author's website:

www.mariannerosen.com/content-warnings

THE LIGHTS OF RIVERDELL

MARIANNE ROSEN

ORIELbooks
www.orielbooks.com

THE LIGHTS OF RIVERDELL

ISBN 978-1-8380810-6-5

First published in Great Britain
in 2021 by Oriel Books Ltd
Copyright © 2021 by Marianne Rosen

Front cover design Amanda Hillier
Copyright © 2021 by Marianne Rosen
Incidental illustrations by Amanda Hillier
Copyright © 2020 by Amanda Hillier
Printed and bound by Clays UK

❀ Created with Vellum

For Great Aunt Alice,
no longer breathing.

A Guide to the Characters of the Riverdell Saga

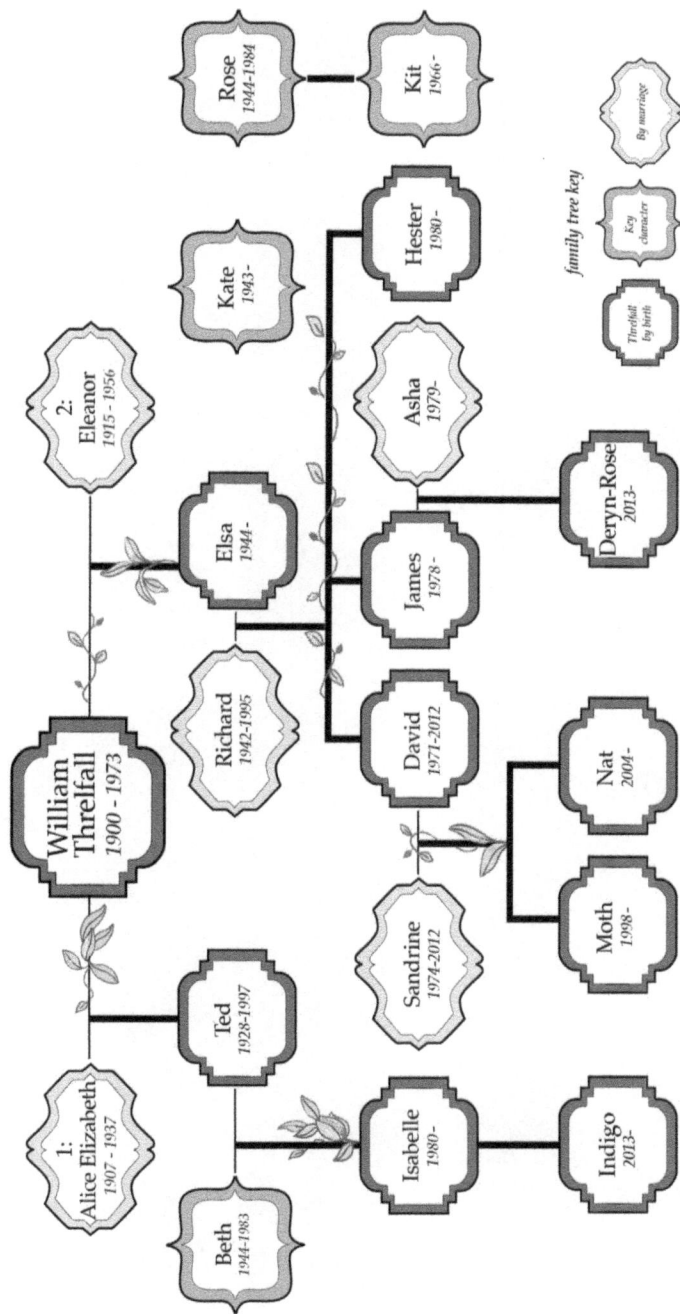

family tree key

- By marriage
- Key character
- Threlfall by birth

William Threlfall 1900 - 1973

1: Alice Elizabeth 1907 - 1937

2: Eleanor 1915 - 1956

Ted 1928-1997

Beth 1944-1983

Richard 1942-1995

Elsa 1944-

Kate 1943-

Rose 1944-1984

Kit 1966-

Isabelle 1980-

Indigo 2013-

Sandrine 1974-2012

David 1971-2012

Moth 1998-

Nat 2004-

James 1978-

Asha 1979-

Hester 1980-

Deryn-Rose 2013-

1

Oh, I am spiteful today. A week sitting through that nonsense has turned me sour.

Life never fails to disappoint me. You'd think it would at least try, for the sheer hell of surprise. But no. Same old, same old.

You didn't come.

He claimed it wasn't logistically possible.

Who uses such a pissant phrase about someone they love? Not logistically possible. Are you his wife or a bolt of cloth to be transported? Would it have killed anyone to delay the funeral a few more days? It's not as though he was rushing to the death bed of the old bastard. All the dying was already done!

I don't believe him. He did it to hurt you. To hurt us. He did it to prioritise himself. What man bloody doesn't?

Still, result's the same. You didn't come.

And we were all expected to be understanding about it. Elsa clucking about distances and transport and difficulty. She's barely left the bloody county she was born in, yet she understood all about the impossibility of locating a person from one part of India to another to relocate both to England. I could have slapped her. I would have managed it. You get on a plane, find the person, put them on a plane. It's hardly rocket science. I mean we're talking Delhi to London, not the sodding moon. And Kate... ugh. She's always been soft where it comes to the Threlfall men. Father figures the lot of them. That's exactly what led her into that disastrous mess with that ruddy leprechaun she married. Why do women abandoned by their fathers always end up turning back into little girls the moment an older man shows them some kindness? Thank Go– Hera for Granny, else perhaps I'd be the same? Kate's granny was an old goat to let her be sent away to boarding school. I hope she dies a vile and twisted death to match her bleached soul.

Though, I guess, without her, I'd never have met Kate.

Oh alright, a vile if not twisted death. Let the old goat have her dignity. Her loss is my gain. I wouldn't be without Kate, even if I can't stand her around the Threlfall men.

Well, one's dead and the other can sod off back to India and I'll have my Kate back. I do miss her in London. I spent the years she was there longing for a bigger flat, even the space for two beds, but as soon as she left the flat felt cavernous.

I'm glad to be home. I can feel the crawling skin on my back settling into place again.

If it weren't for Richard, I'd have stood up in the church and called Ted a lying, selfish bastard when he spoke about your fond memories of William. Elsa weeping while I made fists. At least Richard understood. Elsa might have been born with a silver spoon in her mouth (and who am I to criticise that) but she struck gold when she went digging for a husband. He grabbed my hand and held it the whole way through Ted's ridiculous bloody eulogy. Pretending his father was a wonderful inspiration to him, a second father to his wife. Oh please. They could barely sit in the same room together and his wife wasn't bloody there. There's no space at Riverdell for two men. It's like watching two cocks square up over the hens. I hope Elsa has nothing but sons and grows old watching them fight over the scraps of their beloved estate.

Hah, if you could only hear this. Shush, Rose, don't be unkind, you'd say.

Oh alright.

I hope she has nothing more but daughters and gets to endow them with a house each before she dies. She doesn't realise how lucky she is that Ted ended up in India. It's all hers now, and she'd have had nothing if he hadn't fallen out with his father. I hope she doesn't decide to do something stupid and give it back to him.

There, that's the moment I missed you most. I can see it now.

Not when Ted came back, or even during the funeral, but that moment yesterday, when we went with Elsa to the study. Ted wouldn't even go in there, jealousy probably, and it took her three days to face the moment. It was Kate who made her in the end.

'You can't ignore it for ever. Might as well get it done, Queenie.'

The three of us, pushing open the door as we had all those times before, except it should have been four.

Yes, that's when I could have wept. Watching Elsa sit in her father's chair, opening the drawers, trying to adjust to the other side of the desk, grief and responsibility. Kate and I sat in the chairs by the fire. Kate knew. She could see it in me. There was more than one ghost in the room.

I miss you. Still. And you didn't come. How could you not come?

The blossom is in the cherry trees outside the windows. This street has wealth even in its branches. Why can I not appreciate the blossom without wondering what grimness planted it?

You always loved spring. New life coming. William couldn't have picked a worse time to die for me, Riverdell with the magnolia flowering. I can still see the flower you picked for me. Wobbling on the old wall in the courtyard as you reached for the higher branches. The back of your knees as your skirt slipped upwards. Desire exploding, fully formed and clutching my innards. How it aches, still. I could be sick with the longing.

'I love you, Rose, like the tree loves the blossom. You'll always be first.'

No. Stop this.

Don't go back. I can't keep doing this to myself.

Would I be arrested for hacking down the old cherries of Bristol?

What if I hired someone to creep out each night and cut all the fresh blossom off the branches?

A pox on Riverdell's magnolia, I hope it withers and dies.

I can hear Kit in the kitchen. He's quoting Shakespeare for cake. Hang on, yes, Hamlet.

He's glad to be home too. Perhaps Riverdell without William will lose its charm? He's always been over fond of the place. If it weren't for Granny, I think he'd up and move there.

I was beyond proud of him. It's disgraceful. This fierce surging joy and smugness that comes with parenthood. Well, in brief surges anyway, when I don't want to scream in his face. But not this visit. He was perfect. David squealing as usual. God–ly Mother, I hate how that child squeals. At least Kit will throw a proper tantrum, not this whining nonsense. I'm sure dogs in the town cringe and hide when he sets up. Elsa better hurry up and have another sharpish, it will do him no favours to have his mother to himself for too long. Kit seemed to grasp the importance of the moment. To understand that William was gone. The old man with bad breath and scraggy hair, leaving him with a fist too full of sweets. He was quieter than I've ever known him. What utter comfort to have his little hand in mine when I wanted to scream with outrage at them. Hard to throw a parental strop when your child is behaving perfectly. It was harder to resist those cuddles at night, even though I know I should foster independence. Another awful, sodding phrase. Which heartless old goat came up with that? He doesn't need another drop of independence, he's got it in ocean loads. Unlike David. Kit loathed him. I could tell. How a seven-year-old can do disdain, I have no idea, but he managed it. I must be less proud. I'll raise him to be another bastard if I don't give him some sense of self-doubt. How I still wish he'd been a girl. There's this hideous social edifice of masculinity to constantly counter with a boy. A girl I would have made unstoppable.

Enough. I've written it out. My grief, which was never for William, is released.

You didn't come. I should have tempered my stupid hopes in the first place.

I promised myself I wouldn't be that lovesick Rose anymore.

2

M oth tracked his way back toward base. The low rising sun teasing across his shoulders, shining down into the alleyways as it drew up over the tents. It was only the thirteenth but warmer than April could ever be in England.

The fleeting charm of the Akcakale refugee camp, squatting on the northern edge of the southern Turkish border town of the same name, a stone's throw from Syria, rose with its residents. The clamour of early morning breakfast preparations. Freshness caught in the brief cool of the morning. He enjoyed this brief window of optimism before it slackened into that dull hunger zone that dragged its dusty feet all the way to lunch. Nothing to do but wait for arrivals of food, and trade what essentials their neighbours had stockpiled. Mattresses turned out and flung over sagging canvas to air the stifling interiors. A dull hum of chatter from the thousands of people spiked by the drone of vehicles down the wider tracks. An odd silence at times settling, impossibly, across the entire fluttering canvas town, until someone broke the tension and the low drone returned.

As he walked past, the women checked their face coverings, turning away from him. Men sat on their heels, watching. Watching the women. Watching him.

Moth hated how they watched the women. He knew they weren't all the same, but it was hard to remember that after a night spent sitting outside toilet blocks trying to protect women with young children who couldn't make it through the night. Knowing he could only be in one place at a time. Hard to remember some of them were just bored. Or depressed. Or watching their wives. Or praying for a future behind the silence and the stares. Wondering who this towering white foreigner with the apricot hair was.

Moth knew he stood out. That he was a good head taller than most men. That his hair was long enough to scrape into a knot on his head but was left uncovered. It had been four years since he had left England and, despite his more frequent communications, he knew his family back home would struggle to recognise him. Moth would be a match for his uncle, James, now. Height, shoulder breadth, perhaps not muscle set. Not yet. He had some more growing to do before he could match James at rolling bales into place for cattle or throwing grain sacks around like chocolate bars. Had the same feet though, size fourteen. Though at least he hadn't ended up with the same carrot topping. Kit had jokingly called his hair apricot, to provoke him, but here in Turkey the colour had taken on true meaning where the fruit was a daily staple. The knife cut across his left jaw line had left a white crevice between the stubble growth that was still softening into a scar. He shaved daily, to rediscover its sharpness against his tanned skin. Liking the contrast.

Liking the glory, you mean.

He stopped for all the children. Hoping for treats from his pocket, knowing they had long since run out. Giving a smile or a hand instead.

He was tired. Hungry. It had been a long night.

There better be some food left when you get back to base.

Base. The tangled compound of huts, containers and tents that made up the centre of this transitory, dirt track world that he had fallen into late in the summer of 2014 and here he still was, nearly two years later in 2016.

A young teenager who would normally have come forward to beg for a sweet, held back, watching her siblings. Her mother called her name, she looked downward, scurried backwards. Moth felt his heart drop another notch. Another one lost. Either to puberty, or a nightly visitation he hadn't been able to stop. Moth watched her retreat in embarrassment.

Maybe she's just being modest?

It was hard not to read the world through his own eyes. To remember that the violence and abuse he'd known himself as a young boy, both from his father and while travelling solo through Europe, was not everyone's experience. Harder still when he saw or heard too much evidence on a nightly basis to confirm his worst suspicions.

He felt a hand tug at his, looked down into the dirty face of a child. Shook his head and passed his hand over the long hair. When he looked back up, the older girl had retreated into a tent. Her mother glaring at him from the opening. It hurt to see that distrust on her face.

You can't blame her.

No. No, he couldn't. He'd learnt that his own distrust of men was nothing compared to what women must feel.

Though he loved the evidence in the rough mirrors of the washrooms that he was no longer a boy travelling through Europe, that the arsehole who had raped him there would think twice now, he hated seeing himself as a man in the eyes of women. It was hard not to stop, not to ask for trust, to implore that he was different. That he wanted to help. But what did his one difference make in the sum of their experience. Moth turned away from the glaring woman.

He needed food. Sleep. To rest up for another night. At night he might make a difference. That was all he could hope for.

At least you've got no bruises this morning.

It had been a long night but less damaging than others.

Bonn, his sort-of boss, had kept him away from the northwest quarter for over a month after the incident with the knife.

After you got your gargantuan arse kicked.

But the bruises and cuts had been worth it. He'd returned to his patrol with some respect to match the scar. Moth ran his hand lightly down the ragged skin on his chin. He liked the feel of it even more than the look. Though he did make sure to let the stubble grow before he Skyped home. His younger sister, Nat, was easily spooked, and Isabelle would do that crease between her eyes in concern that told him she was trying to be the responsible older relative but hated interrogating him. And as for Luca, his...

Your...

... well, Luca would have an epic fit if he saw it. He didn't need to know that Moth had been lucky not to lose an eye. Only the angle of the blade catching the moonlight had made him pull his head back in time. Allowed him to jump back from the second slash aimed at his ribs and plant a boot firmly enough to convince the wielder to back off. But Luca being able to see the scar was not about to happen any time soon.

Luca was in Geneva. At long last. Having finally harassed the United Nations to give him a job and left the small-town café where he and Moth had met in Italy. And, though Moth had not managed to make it into Asia, coming hard up against the exploding wall of Syria, Turkey was far enough away from Luca that they might not meet up again. After all it had been three years, almost to the month, since…

Since…

Moth flexed his hands into fists deep inside his pockets. The stiffness from the night chill easing out with the sun. He cricked his neck, left, right, left, rolled the right shoulder to grind the knotted muscles out, stretched his back. Bed. Bed would be good. After all those miles of sleeping on the ground in the bike tent, a canvas frame bed was a luxury. He would sleep the heat away, wake up hungry, surer of a meal than anyone else he walked past, and head back out to do his night patrol.

Moth focused on the dust kicked up by his tired feet. Geneva was a long way away. As was the time he and Luca had spent together in Italy. Whatever they had been to one another was surely going to be lost in this new phase of Luca's life.

He hasn't forgotten in three years.

Moth still couldn't fathom why anyone would wait three years for him to keep a promise, let alone Luca, who wouldn't need to wait more than three minutes if he just looked up in the street. The weight of three years pressing down on that promise had become too hard to resolve. It was easier to focus on what was right in front of him.

The streets nearer the base were wider, more organised. Satellite dishes appeared, puddles of children spread around them. Here, the oldest members of the camp resided, those who had been stuck in limbo long enough to be making a living from it. Negotiators with those who came afterwards. Controlling the who, where, when of supplies and communication. Moth noticed the minute details of superiority. Water containers, electric cables, brooms, washing lines, books, shoes, fatter children.

He kept his head down and sped up. Here the men watched him even harder. Calculating if he was a threat to their order. This odd man who didn't wear the blue cap or medic badge but lived in the base camp and patrolled their alleyways and latrines at night. Bonn had tried to send him home after the attack, accusing him of taking up precious medical resources.

Jacques Bonnier's a manipulative bastard.

Bonn was many things. Mostly what he needed to be as the shitty circumstances dictated. He'd given Moth a bed and food since he'd edged into the base asking for advice on getting through Syria. Bonn had promised him help and kept him busy, then found out who he was by the end of the first week and made uncountable efforts to get him packed home. They had been in a cat-and-mouse game of helping and hindering each other ever since. Maybe Bonn had even encouraged the attack, as a taster to dim Moth's resolve. Even if it had gone a bit haywire, he could believe that would be exactly the camp chief's style. Forty years of UN service had made him what he needed to be, rather than what he might want to be. Single, living from one crisis to the next, going where the winds of hell took him.

Luca's going to end up the same.

Luca couldn't end up like Bonn if life threw a thousand refugee children at his feet on a nightly basis. It was more probable that Luca would end up crushed in the process and realise he was a better barista than he would ever be a human rights campaigner. Bonn was hard on the inside, paunchy on the outside. Living from one meal to the next and imposing a routine on his days no matter what trouble came through his container office door. Breakfast at five, lunch at twelve, dinner at seven. Work in between. Standing when others fell. Screaming orders when others wept. Idealism dead on the blood-soaked ground of Cambodia, where he'd served his first posting at the land bridge refugee camps. Luca was soft on the inside, despite all those planes and angles on the outside leading the eye where the eye didn't need to go.

Yep, sure as hell don't look that long at Bonn.

Moth flicked the thoughts away. Luca was in Geneva. He was here. Right where he needed to be. And he wasn't going anywhere looking at anyone's bones. Not unless they were dead in a grave and needed pissing on, as he had promised himself to do with his father's, or exhuming for human rights investigation, as he had begun to consider doing for a career.

He left the last tents behind, walked through the ragged gates of the base, past the steel walls and into the inner circle.

Friends called hello as he made his way to the washrooms.

Do these count as friends?

He didn't know yet. Circumstantial associates probably.

'Moth,' Aidan called across from the canteen. 'You're still alive.'

'You're still talking,' he called back. 'I'm coming for breakfast.'

'Breakfast is gone, Bonn took your share.'

'Greedy bastard.'

'Nah, he's got it for you, up top.' Aidan threw his eyes skyward, to where the containers were stacked three high, giving a command view out across the camp. 'Said you need to go see him if you want it.'

'Great.'

'Yeah, knew you'd appreciate it.'

Moth flipped him the finger, grinned as Aidan caught it and made an obscene gesture. All the world in chaos and the Irishman making jokes of it. Maybe that was all you could do. Cope in your own way. Aidan with his crude jokes and insults. Bonn with his food fetish. Moth with his night patrols. He hoped Luca did leave the UN. It was no place for a good person.

Showered, his clothes brushed down for another day, damp shoulder-length hair dampening the neck of a fresh T-shirt, he climbed the steps to Bonn's nest. Wondering what mind game he'd have to play today. When would Bonn realise the harder he tried to send Moth home, the more determined he became to stay?

He tapped on the door, drew a breath and went in. The room was a huddle of activity, people arguing with the man at the middle over who had the greatest priority. Jose was there, venting about the medical supplies. Maria, raging about sanitation. Jonah, talking about staff. Yves, from the nearby transit camp. Dimitri, transport. Eba, ante natal. The list went on. It reminded him oddly of the family all together at Riverdell. The room ripe with irritation.

He let the heavy door click into place behind him and waited. Bonn caught his eye and nodded him over to a desk. On it, a plate waited for him. Moth sidled round the full room and pulled a chair out. They all ignored him. They had more pressing things to worry about than Bonn's pet shadow. Though Jose had complained about the treatment he'd received for his cuts.

And Jonah looks through you rather than at you to make sure you know you're not really staff.

He didn't blame them. They had their ways too. The camp's chief doctor, Jose, was a meticulous record keeper. A place for everything and everything in its place, and Moth fitted neither. And Jonah, the HR lead, handled the weight of his responsibility with intense attention to the mental health of his team. Moth had told him often enough to shove his concern up his own arse and refused to do the medicals, that Jonah had no choice but to cut him off. He wasn't staff, he didn't get paid. Except in food and shelter. Begrudged medical attention. And perhaps Moth, dripping with blood on the night he had been attacked, swearing at Jose that he could keep his plastic-coated hands to himself or lose them, had told all they needed to know about his mental health.

From his chair, Moth watched the solid core of a man stood in the centre of the storm. Bonn was listening, nodding, negating, swearing. He held them together as he did himself. With efficiency, not affection. Khaki combats, a grey turtle-neck beneath his padded gilet coat, pockets bulging with essentials. Both the padding and the bulges helping to disguise the heft they covered. Blue badge shining on the cap he held in one hand, flicking the weight of it against his other while he digested all the day's info and made the hard choices. Bonn was a man used to disappointing people, and indifferent to their bad opinion of him. Knowing it changed from day to day and decision to decision. He stood solidly between his team and the powers above. Every political mishap between the host country and the NGOs was Bonn's to resolve. Letting his team bring their troubles to his door, keeping his own locked firmly away. Moth tried to ignore how often the blue eyes, strangely attuned to the shade of his UN cap...

... probably had them lasered to match the sodding corporate colours...

... landed on him. There was a gleeful light in them. Bonn took a perverse delight in the inevitability of conflict. That glint rarely meant good news. In keeping his own eyes elsewhere, Moth found them pulled to the view.

Three containers height might not sound much for a lookout, but when the city surrounding it was no higher than a tent, it gave an unnerving vision of vast unrooted permanency tied down with pegs and flapping continually in the breeze. An oak tree clinging to life with the roots of a daisy.

Life on the bike had been clearly rootless, a freedom he had planned, lied and stolen to achieve. Life at Riverdell dug so deep into the ground it resembled a grave more than a home. Akcakale Camp wasn't freedom, and it wasn't home, it was a vicious staging post between neither. Rippling an aged dirty latte against the darker baked earth. Further in the distance, he could see the valley fields beginning to hint at green. This was deep rural country, a place of farms and productivity. But not for the people in the camp. Spring in the tent camp was hard, stuck between the dirt roads and boredom while the valley floor began to flower and come to life. You could look out and see there was a better life, suggesting you should be trying to move toward it.

It's about time you moved on yourself.

Moved on where? There was nowhere to move to. After leaving Luca in Italy, he had taken his time touring Greece. Time to find his strength, recover his courage. Time to get over sleeping in the tent at night, jumping at every sound. Time to stop waking up in the thick of night shuddering from nightmares. Time to stop telling himself to go back to Italy and Luca. He'd pushed on into Turkey late in 2013, encouraged by the thought of warmer nights as winter came on. But his plans to keep moving south had been overtaken by the war in Syria. He'd made his way along the unravelling Turkish/Syrian border, bloated with human flood, struggling to hold onto his bike, his belongings, only to find the borders in Iraq and Iran even stricter. By the time he'd ridden up through Georgia and Armenia, to find the two countries in panic alert between Russia and the war they were shouldering into, Moth had faced he was stuck.

Right in the bloody middle.

Couldn't go forward, wouldn't go back.

He'd drifted, until he ended up in the camp. Moth chewed on cold, dry toast and contemplated the same problem that he woke to each morning.

Where the hell are you going?

Emails from Luca and Isabelle didn't help. Evidence of their own developing lives and infinite questions about his plans defining the emptiness of his horizons. And now, he was an adult. Which meant Bonn was under even greater pressure to get rid of him. He remembered the desperation he'd felt on his fifteenth birthday. That email in Rochenau, Austria, on the morning of his fifteenth birthday, Kit tempting him to Italy. He'd wanted to turn sixteen more than anything, become a man in the eyes of the world. Now here he was, less than a month past his eighteenth birthday and the world didn't give a shit about him. Along with the other kids who found themselves passing eighteen in the camps.

No longer unaccompanied children. Now adults in the meat-grinding shit storm of Syria.

Moth refocused on his food.

Food. It all came down to food. Bonn knew the truth of it. It wasn't greed that made him a religious eater, it was gratitude and memory. You couldn't watch people starve to the brink of life and slip silently across it without learning that neat fact in your bones. He wondered if Luca had learnt that truth at UNGO yet or was enjoying himself in the cafes of Geneva instead.

Does it matter?

It didn't. Luca could do as he pleased in the sodding brothels of Geneva for all he cared. And preferably stop sending lengthy emails about the intricacies of his new life, his sewer-grade job, his boss constantly misnaming him, his shared flat with three other lads, and all that optimism shining through his delight that he finally had his dream job.

Not so optimistic last time.

Moth grinned as he ate the final forkfuls. Luca's boss in the logistics department had appointed him chief coffee maker for the department, based on his barista skills. Luca hadn't been too happy about that. Hardly the job he'd dreamt of when he joined the High Commission for Refugees.

'What are you smirking at? Nothing much to laugh at out there to me.'

Moth wiped the smile. Damn it. Bonn didn't miss a shit in a crap house.

'I wasn't smiling at the outside.' He turned away from the window. Jose was pulling the door to. He'd not even heard the meeting end.

'Ahh, feeling happy on the inside,' Bonn smirked at him. 'Perhaps it's not what you are thinking about, but who?'

'You wanted to see me?' Moth put his knife down and pushed away from the table, turning the cheap plastic chair round. Straddling it to enjoy the thin plastic barrier it left between them.

'Ah, evasion,' Bonn grinned at him. 'So, you were thinking about someone.'

Moth stared at him, a set smile on his lips. He would not be provoked.

'Well, keep your lovely secrets to yourself, my frigid friend,' Bonn spoke the words with a warmth like the rustling of dry sand moved by a snake, a hypnotic French accent soothing the danger. Moth tensed himself. 'Orders have come to close the transit camp.'

They looked at one another. Moth wouldn't give him the satisfaction of a swear.

The transit camp on the edge of Akcakale town. It had been threatened for over nine months. It would mean an influx of more bodies. Refugees and workers. Into an already overcrowded site. Everybody not needed would be purged in advance. The under-18s travelling unaccompanied would be rounded up and relocated. The ones skipping out of that category would be herded together or pushed out. Anyone not justifying their bed in the compound would be gone.

And that includes you.

'You get that bike fixed yet?' Bonn asked him.

The bike was in pieces, part propped against the tent wall, part stuck beneath Aidan's bed. Mostly reminding him every day he got up that his life plan was in just as many pieces.

'No, not yet.'

They sat in silence, Moth focused on the floor between them.

'You get any more emails from home recently?'

Moth was damned if he was going to make this any easier for him. He'd earned his place.

'Maybe you should check, huh?' Bonn's accent remained under the sandstorm of influences he'd picked up from a life on the move. Home was a hastily thrown pitch on sand, or mud, or forest floor. 'You don't want to end up like me, Moth. We all need a home.'

'You don't.' It sounded petulant, even to him. Moth groaned and hung his head over the chair back. If anyone could make him feel inadequate, it was Bonn. 'I don't want to go home, I want to help here.'

'If you want to help, go home, get an education, come back stronger. I told you before, peacekeeping duty will get you killed. And I can't get you in the door anywhere else if you have no education, no language skills.'

'I have a friend who thought that, speaks sixteen sodding languages and has a Master's degree in international bullshittery. Making coffee in Geneva HQ right now. Probably taking dictation notes across the desk too.'

Bonn huffed, half-amused, half-needled. Global reports of sexual assault by UN peacekeepers had hit them all hard. Moth was finding a sense of humour about his sorest subject helped bring it into the light. He could see through the shame that tried to keep it silent. He knew the exact shape and shade of that place. It was narrow and dense, like a coffin. Prying the lid open came easiest one quip at a time.

'I'm not the best person to advise, maybe,' Bonn did a Gallic shrug that reminded Moth of Leon, the French farmer he had spent a summer working for when he first left England, 'but I wouldn't want to see you end up the same as me.' He slapped the blue cap against his own chest and threw it onto the nearest table, leaning back in his chair. As central to the room as he currently was to Moth's choices. 'There are people in your life Moth. You've been here long enough this time. Go home, rest, let me see what I can do to get you a place, officially. The transit camp staff are joining us, I must make space for them and my hands are tied. It won't be long before one of them starts asking questions and Jonah is looking for any excuse to get rid of you.'

Moth thought about the people in his life. Nat in Swansea, sending him emails about her new high-school friends and clubs. Isabelle at Riverdell, raising a daughter he'd never met. Luca in Geneva, making coffee and taking orders from his dismissive boss. He looked out of the window at the camp. How did you go home from this, knowing thousands of those you left behind would never find home?

'Don't think about it,' Bonn advised him. 'Make yourself a home and go there, regularly. You'll be a better aid worker for it. If that's really what you want to do with your life.'

Is that what you want to do with your life?

In the late hours of day, the hour when he gathered his courage and went back out into the camp for the night, Moth often asked himself. The still intensity of massed humanity close upon him made him long for the bike and the open road, made him pull the map out and wonder if he should try another route. Perhaps head back into Europe, cut north round the Black Sea, through Russia toward Asia. The world seemed on fire and there was no safe place to travel. He could head back west, tour more of Europe. But here he was, in the thick of it, contributing, helping, instead of thinking about himself. He would fold the map away, ignore the disjointed parts of the bike and head out into the dark camp.

And are you doing that for yourself? Or to prove yourself.

Padding out the content of his emails to Luca with a sense

of worthiness. Or to convince Isabelle he was too busy to come home. Or to resist the pull back into Nat's world, a western civilised world he despised but didn't want to take from her.

'You're still thinking too hard,' Bonn told him, standing up. Moth knew that signal. It was the end of their chat. 'Go, sleep, check your emails. The camp will be closed at the end of May, you have a little time left.'

End of May. It was the thirteenth of April already.

'But Moth?'

'Hmm?'

'You must decide soon, or the decision will be made for you.'

Moth stood up to leave, tucking the chair beneath the desk and heading for the door.

'Don't ignore me,' Bonn told him.

'I'm not, I get it.' Moth turned to look at him. 'Go home or get lost. One or the other, right?'

'No.' Bonn scowled at him. 'Take the time to make a better decision. You've done good work here, Moth, now you have a chance to choose how you can do better. Don't waste it, ignoring your choices until it is too late and getting stuck with no choice at all.'

Bonn picked up his cap and smoothed it over his head. His eyes brightening toward it, pulling the man and the cap together. Moth could never see himself in the blue cap. Kit would tell him it looked hideous with his hair for one thing.

And you'd only be doing it to make Luca jealous.

Go home. Get an education. Be a good boy. Become a better man.

Always people telling him what to do. How to live.

Eighteen or not, some things never changed.

Moth pulled the door shut behind him and started down the steps. It was time to look at the bike.

'I'M LATE,' Asha announced the obvious as Isabelle opened the front door of Riverdell.

Behind her cousin-in-law's head bowed over the huge bag of supplies she rarely had the chance to sort through, Isabelle could see the first flower on the magnolia unfurling in the morning sun, the shape of its petals a blur in her short-sighted vision. She'd been waiting for them. Counting the days as their furry buds bulged, burst and began to peel back-wards. She would write in her diary later that day, 13th April 2016, the first magnolia flower came.

'You're always late.' Isabelle smiled at Deryn as the two-year-old girl pulled loose from her mother's hand and slipped past her through the doorway into the house.

'I've got to dash, sorry,' Asha added.

'Don't be, there's no need.'

'I've put the bottle feed in, and I've mashed a pot of...'

Isabelle listened with one ear to Asha's morning list of parental anxieties while enjoying the sunshine.

'... and don't forget her phonics.' Asha drew breath and looked up, holding out the worn copy of *First Phonics are Fun* with a determined set to her jaw.

'We won't.' Isabelle refocused and took the book from Asha. 'We do it with our lunch. Kate's brilliant at it.'

Asha let an inch of tension out of her breath-trapped, button-bursting chest and took a step back toward the lip of the grandly columned porch that nestled in the crook of Riverdell's wings. It was a playful morning, light bouncing along the dewy plants of the border, glinting on the open gates in their stone archway, gilding the dirt that lay up the side of Asha's car. Asha stood beneath the shade of the porch with a frown stuck in the creases at the side of her lips, in the dip between her eyes, in the gleam of sweat that sat in her philtrum. Asha was not in a playful mood.

Isabelle took in her creased suit struggling to stay in place between the splurge of hips and bust that Asha hadn't managed to get rid of since pregnancy. The hair scraped back in a ponytail with a half-inch of roots showing where she hadn't had time to dye them. The fringe cut to mitigate the impact and struggling to stay straight from lack of styling time. The lipstick smudged from kissing James a distracted goodbye. Time was not Asha's friend and playful was the thing she found hardest to do as a parent.

'You should go, you're only going to get later. Don't worry, we'll be fine. See you at teatime.'

Asha took another step back, peering behind Isabelle to see if Deryn had paused to say farewell to her.

'Indigo is making breakfast with Gosia, she's probably gone to help.'

Asha manoeuvred her facial features like gears from "stressed with life" through "pained disappointment her daughter hadn't so much as looked backward" to "sagging relief a fellow Polish woman was part of her daughter's haphazard day care" that Isabelle felt sorry for her, stepped forward and gave her a quick hug.

'Go, work, stop fretting. And when you pick up tonight, you're sitting down for a cup of tea with me. I want to hear all about your day.'

Asha gave her a quick squeeze and a wobbly smile before running across the gravelled courtyard. Isabelle noticed the mud that had spattered up the back of her trouser legs to match the car. As the image dissolved from her short-sighted view, Isabelle didn't have the heart to call out to her. It would only add to her stress level and besides, they lived in the countryside. Asha's clients should see the mud as evidence of her presence on their estates not just in the office, as much as evidence of her trying too hard to be everything to everyone and not enough to herself.

Isabelle watched the car circle the magnolia tree and head out of the gates. In its absence the light returned to playing with the courtyard. She stood and savoured the beautiful morning. Watching the plants hovering over the stone path, the castle walls disappearing as the sun peeped over them, the sound of the town echoing down to her, the wind rushing in the trees that lined the path up the steep castle hillside. It still caught at her that this stunning home belonged to her. She had been used to so many years of coming home to stay with her closest family, never knowing that Riverdell would pass to her. It had been four years now since her eldest cousin David had killed himself and his wife in a drink-driving car crash, since his orphaned children Moth and Nat had come to live at Riverdell, since her aunt Elsa, Asha's mother-in-law, had dropped the bombshell that the house and estate would pass to Isabelle, not her own children, and then retired to Swansea. Passing through the long hallways and forty plus rooms of the old stone house, Isabelle could still find herself tripping over the reality that her life had become.

She thought of putting on a coat and walking up Climbing Jack to High Vinnalls, making herself sweat with the effort, to stand in a stiff breeze and look down over the valleys, resting at the top on her mother's memorial bench. She looked at the magnolia and wondered where Moth was on this gorgeous morning. Everywhere at Riverdell held a memory she could catch of him. Standing together on this doorstep and watching Elsa leave for Swansea seemed only a moment ago, not four years. She wanted to linger and bring his form firmly back to mind. But it was hard, the confident emails and Skype calls from Turkey blurring with the brutally attacked young man she had last seen in Italy. Thinking of Moth always released a tangle of emotions. Anger and grief over what she had learned of David's abuse that had driven Moth away from them, gladness that she had been there in Italy to help him recover from another assault, happiness that he was living his own life, an abiding ache that he was missing from theirs and the constant wish that he would walk into her workroom again, strike up a conversation and make her feel more at peace with herself than anyone else had ever managed. It was selfish she knew, yet she so wanted him to come home. He had only ever been at Riverdell for five precious months, and still the house felt like it was waiting for him to return.

From the kitchen windows she heard a muffled crash and closed her eyes in despair. They never lasted, these brief moments of respite. Parenthood was an unravelling. A complete unpicking of life. A sprawling disarray of all the components of what had once made sense and been functional, into a never-ending interruption at her best efforts to remake it into something complete.

As she turned away from her tranquil moment and closed the door, she held the odd conflict of thoughts. Moth, still absent. Herself, a mother. Isabelle looked up at the high coloured lights of the leaded window on the half-landing, at the open door to the drawing room, the dusty surface of the grand piano, the large sofa that sat in front of the fire and was draped with clothes, bags, toys and blankets. Riverdell was no longer the immaculate five-star B&B business that it had been under Elsa's care. It had become a home again, sprawling, never tidy, all its people and contents drifting toward the hallway and resting there. She crossed the hallway, her sock-clad feet feeling the flattened fibre of the old rug, pushed open the kitchen door and walked into the eye of her own storm.

It hadn't been an outright lie. Gosia Wisniewski, her weekly housekeeper turned daily sanity-keeper, was making breakfast. And Indigo was helping make breakfast. They just weren't doing it together, or in the same kitchen. Gosia was downstairs, making breakfast for Kate's guests in the basement kitchen. Indigo was upstairs making breakfast in Riverdell's main kitchen with Kate, and now Deryn.

The two girls were stood on chairs at the kitchen counter with their backs to her. Indigo in the same outfit she had worn obsessively for the last three weeks. The velvet hem of the patchwork pinafore apron curled with the impact of nightly hand-washing and swift drying on the boiler, her jersey T-shirt and leggings crumpled and grubby, one foot only socked, her blonde curls scraped into odd angles with an assortment of clips too big for her head and secured with the ineffective enthusiasm of a two-year-old's hands. Deryn had a perfectly ironed cotton dungaree suit with embroidery that matched on the buttoned, collared shirt underneath. Matching socks. Dark hair brushed and secured to the side with a firm hand and a single clip. They stood at the same height, to within an inch, despite the five-month age difference and the fact that Deryn's father James was a Threlfall in height. Both children dwarfed by the lofty ceilings and grand proportions of the huge room. The three arched windows that looked over the courtyard, the observatory-sized window that sat behind the long run of countertop and sink, pulling the gaze out over the gardens toward the weir. The Aga next to the girls sitting into the corner of the room, nestled in front of the large chimney breast, alongside the oak dresser whose grand span of shelves sagged with age. The girls' legs were jumping up and down on the chairs with excitement, bottoms wiggling from side to side like eager puppies. Deryn's padded with a nappy. Indigo's unpadded. Isabelle's sole parental achievement, and the one she had learned never to crow about. She might have failed on breastfeeding, sleep routine, eating habits, co-sleeping, even early phonics, but Indigo had been out of nappies from her first birthday. One of the reasons she didn't gloat was knowing that it had more to do with her child's staggering need for independence than her own abilities as a parent.

Kate's head appeared from the floor area behind them, rising to find her watching, dustpan and brush in hand.

Isabelle moved forward and took in the details.

'It's fine, no one was hurt.' Kate pre-empted her comments and threw the jingling contents into the bin.

'How about the china?'

'Great news, we're getting through it slowly.'

Isabelle looked at the dresser. Another majolica plate was missing. 'You know that's a valuable family heirloom,' she scolded with a grin.

'Utterly priceless,' Kate retorted.

There was less than half of the original majolica service on the shelves these days. Once Asha had started smashing it to demonstrate her ire with the family she had only recently married into, the step from there to regular use had been a

swift one. Majolica did not suit the dishwasher, or little jam-
slippery fingers, or regular use.

'You will leave me at least one piece, won't you?' Isabelle
moved toward the girls, grabbing a pinny from the back of a
chair. 'I have fond memories of that china.'

'What?' Kate asked. 'When on earth did you garner
those?'

'Moth and I used them that holiday Elsa first went to
Swansea,' Isabelle said.

'And that overrides the time Asha used them as frisbees?'

'Uh-huh.'

Isabelle stood behind the girls and looked over their
shoulders. They were making potato cakes, their hands
covered in flour and mashed potato. Indigo looked up at her
as she sucked the mash from her fingers before plunging
them right back into the mix. Beside their bowls were a
mixture of terracotta spice jars, covered in mashy finger-
prints. The jars weren't keen on the dishwasher either, but
Isabelle had a simple rule; if it didn't survive the dishwasher
it didn't belong at Riverdell. As she was confident Chinese
Five Spice, oregano and saffron did not really belong in
potato cakes either. She pulled the sleeves of the pinny onto
her hands, slipped Deryn's mucky hands in hers and pulled
the pinny over Deryn's hands and up her arms, pulling it
tight over her clean clothes to tie it at the back. She had tried
giving Deryn her own set of clothes, but Asha had found out
and got territorial. In desperately trying to keep Deryn's
clothes moderately protected, Isabelle had accidentally
developed a range of vintage-appeal pinnies that she was now
selling through her Etsy shop. She gave the girls a kiss apiece
on their heads and turned to look at Kate, catching the edges
of a frown compacting her lips.

Kate trying to frown had once made her nervous but had none of the scary impact that Asha's did. When Asha frowned you caught the oncoming draft of a locomotive of married irritation looking for a destination. When Kate frowned it was a cloud on a spring day with a swift wind behind it. Moving on as rapidly as Kate did in her slipshod shoes. Retirement had been a soon-discarded deceit. The rush of a new home, a new focus, a new idea catching hold and pulling her on to a new venture with the same vigour and fun that she had always invested into life. Isabelle took in the slightly longer hair, cut into layers and mussed with a quick hand and a squirt from a can, silver, amber and honey highlights cutting through the darker grey flicks and waves. More laughter lines pulled at the corners of her eyes now, but the eyes shone with a vivid blue spark that could quieten the most enthusiastic of Indigo's behaviour. If Kate's life had become fuller, it had also become more relaxed. Less focused on the details of perfection that had held her bistro together. Kate was still as swift, as enthusiastic, as demanding, but she had softened into more fun with the new business and the new family life, and her frown had lost its razor-edge. These days it was Asha's frown which made Isabelle squirm.

'What?' Isabelle asked with blinking innocence.

Kate gave her a look. A look that encapsulated a question never asked, a concern all too often expressed. Isabelle was used to the look. Used to evading the curiosity. She was weary of the one unspoken undercurrent in their life and preferred to hope her continued refusal to be provoked on the point would allow it to slip forever into the background.

'Nothing.' Kate turned her attention back to the potato cakes and the girls. 'I think that's enough saffron, else your poo will turn orange and Mummy will be complaining,

Deryn. How about you make coffee?' she tossed over her shoulder to Isabelle.

'Deal.'

Isabelle went to the new machine. It's blue enamel curves still thrilled her. There had been a heart-stopping moment last November when the old espresso machine had given up the ghost and she and Kate had momentarily faced a future without one. A five o'clock wake up with Indigo, combined with Kate no longer having the bistro to be able to get a deal for them had been a rough start to that day. It had been the only time in the last three years that she had heard Kate call Kit and demand his assistance. A week later a van had arrived, and the customised Sanremo had been installed with them both clutching inadequate coffees and watching in amazement. Kate had set to using it and told her to ring Kit to thank him.

'You ring him, it's your fault in the first place we're all addicted to proper coffee,' Isabelle had protested.

'I'm making the first proper coffee we've had in a week, you ring him.'

Isabelle let the milk fizz, thinking for the umpteenth time she should give up milk altogether and shift her own post baby-weight remnants. She kept those thoughts to herself, knowing she was still slimmer after having a child than most women were before pregnancy. She'd mentioned it to Kit once, thinking he was one of the few who wouldn't judge, but even he had said she looked healthy for the first time in her life. It wasn't the annoyance of the added pounds, it was the loss of clothes she had worn since her teenage years. Fabrics that had memories of her life and had carried her through all the years of working in India. These days she felt even her clothes pinned her to Riverdell.

Listening to Kate talking to the girls, Isabelle glanced over at their serious faces taking in her instructions, sucking their fingers and adding more seasoning. Kate was the ultimate in childcare. In the absence of real grandparents regularly present in their lives, Kate had absorbed that honorary power over the girls. She was their Guru, their God, their Fairy Godmother. They adored the way she skidded into their lives and swept them along in the rush before depositing them back on the kitchen table like empty bowls and disappearing to the next challenge, the next class, the next influx of super cool retirees clutching copies of her latest book on living the life in your seventies. As she pooled warmed milk into the cups, she could hear Kate's phone pinging in her pocket. Notifications the new theme tune of her life. Alongside the slapping of potato cakes in flour and onto the plate.

'Right, to the table,' Kate told the girls in a fierce order. 'Away from the oven until you're how old?'

'Five,' they piped up together.

'And wash your hands. No, not with your tongues, with water and soap. Knives and forks at the ready. Isabelle, clear some space at the table.'

Isabelle looked at the table and exercised an unparalleled level of self-control in not answering Kate back, shovelling the spreading tide of crap back to the middle, making space at the edges. The table was another of her parental failures. A fact reflected in Asha's face each time she walked into the kitchen and looked at it. With not a single word she could tell Isabelle that all her potty-training smugness counted for nothing considering the mess her kitchen table was. She hadn't seen the glorious golden oak, herringbone surface of the round table from the day it had arrived, ordered in a fit of pique after Hester had leant on the table that had formerly been there and told her she had no right to be a parent.

Isabelle could recall sitting uncomfortably at the head of that traditional rectangular table, where they had all seemed to acquire set places, being forced to account for her life choices and telling them instead about the secrets Moth had run away from rather than admit. Watching as she told Elsa her eldest son had abused her grandson, seeing the contempt in Hester's eyes that she dared pretend she belonged in that chair at the head of the table and telling herself, while the family descended into chaos, that she would replace the table at the first opportunity for a round one, where everyone belonged and was equal. Despite her fine intentions and the best efforts of Gosia, the shiny new table had stood no chance against Indigo and Kate, who seemed to view it as the centre of all their complex machinations.

It was at this table that Kate had written her book *Uninvisible Me*. It was where she had decided Isabelle's hopeless efforts at fostering her supposed events business was better faced than ignored and negotiated a deal to rent the lower ground floor ballroom from her along with the use of the entire garden. It was here she had budgeted the five-day gardening and lifestyle courses she ran for women refusing to grow old and invisible. It was here she had negotiated for Gosia to clean the five rooms on the second floor flat as guest bedrooms. It was here, basically, that Kate had decided the shape their new life was going to take. And it was here that Indigo pooled the results of her collecting instinct as she trailed around the house passed from one adult to the other as they all tried to do their business.

From one day to the next Isabelle never knew what would be added to the pile. A letter from another newspaper asking for an interview, or a drying collection of petals from the garden. A sample box of age-defying products Kate was being beseeched to promote or a bowl full of self-mixed bathroom products that would lead Isabelle to a sticky source somewhere else in the house. A box full of promotional material or a wobbling tower of all the dusters in the house. Toward the middle of the round table, a precarious stalagmite of seed catalogues, *Saga* and *Shropshire Life* were supporting a woven fabric basket with a nest of dead daffodils and hyacinths in the centre. Round the edges she had crafted twelve dips by plaiting and curling the fabric. In four of the dips were the neatly folded squares of golden foil that had housed the eggs of the Apostles. Eight chocolate eggs remained hidden somewhere in the house almost two weeks after Easter. Considering Indigo's delight in hiding in the most impossible to find corners of the house, Isabelle had seriously overestimated the search and locate capacity of her child. While the state of the table was far from perfect, its fit in their life gave her comfort every time she sat at it.

She watched the girls climbing onto their chairs and held her breath. Kate glared at her from the frying pan, daring her to go and help them. She sipped her drink and watched them successfully make the ascent. Indomitable and adored, that was the official policy. Kate had told her from day one she would not tolerate Indigo becoming an over-indulged, over-protected first child like David. Indigo, and by default Deryn who spent at least two-thirds of her life at Riverdell, were to grow up learning the knocks the hard way. No safety catches, no safety gates, no idiotic conversations about the safety concerns of an espresso machine, no booster seats on the chairs, no bibs, no baby monitors. A vast ocean of love to wash away the bruises. Kate put the first cakes to cool on the side as she made the rest, talking ten to the dozen to the room, holding the girls' attention.

'So,' Kate deposited their food at the table and sat down on the other side of the girls, hands fluttering round them in encouragement, 'what's your day hold?'

Isabelle tried to pin that concept down. The long trajectory of the hours ahead. The even longer list of all that she needed to do. The indescribable mess two children could make of a soft poached egg. She looked at the egg on her own plate and felt her appetite wither.

'I've got orders to finish and a load to pack up for the post tomorrow.'

'The Ludford still going strong?'

Isabelle loved that Kate always started with business talk. In the grind of holding her head above parenting waters it helped to have a woman who always put her business first. She grimaced and nodded. Of the three designs of vintage aprons she sold, the Ludford was in her opinion the least effective. But it best resembled the cross-strapped linen lines of an apron most mothers dreamt of wearing. It was hugely wasteful of fabric and a bore to sew, carefully cutting the single shape piece out and sewing the straps into their neat folds. The only excitement to be had from the Ludford was selecting the fabrics she used. Her favourite apron to sew, and least ordered, was the one now covering Deryn. The Whitcliffe boasted three-quarter puffed sleeves, a crossover back with no fastenings to fumble with and deep pockets that lay on the inside. She found the front-loading pockets of the others tended to end up full of food waste. The Whitcliffe took longer to make and had a higher price tag. But it was the doyenne of pinnies in her household. The humble Dinham was the plainest of the designs. A simple A-line shape made from thick plain linen in a variety of soft tones.

'Well, you know what they say.' Kate leant over Deryn and tapped Indigo's fingers with the handle of her knife to remind her to stop playing and get eating. 'Concentrate on your best-sellers.'

'I wouldn't mind the chance to concentrate on anything for more than ten minutes,' Isabelle said, glad her own fingers were out of the way of Kate's knife.

Since having Indigo, she had begun to recall the smaller details from her own childhood that had slipped away. Growing up in this same kitchen, buffeted between the love and care of both Elsa and Kate, like sisters who had lost sense of who the children really belonged to. She would catch Kate mussing up Indigo's clothes, hitching one sock hem lower than the other, rolling one sleeve up, grabbing a smear of food and dirtying up her face and feel a shiver of memory across her back. When she was wrung out in the afternoons from not getting her tasks done and Kate would sweep in, pick up a whingy Indigo and disappear to give her a few hours, she remembered the long walks she would return sleepy from that Kate had taken her on as a child. The fishing for fairies in the weir that Indigo would tell her about. The searching for will-o'-wisps in the mossy dark holes of the waterfalls on the Breadwalk. Watching Indigo suck her rapped knuckle with an egg encrusted mouth she remembered Elsa scolding Kate for doing the exact same thing and Kate winking at her behind Elsa's back. She'd spent her whole adult life dreaming of the missing details of her mother, forgetting the myriad ways in which two women not her mother had raised her. In the mix of these moments Isabelle felt a crushing combination of grief for what she should have known and overwhelming gratitude for what she had been given.

Motherhood was like that, Isabelle thought, as she snuck her own egg onto Indigo's plate. A slippage in and out of time and consciousness, emotion and reason. People were forever telling her that the time flew, but she felt that time had changed. It existed in a different realm from the years when she had passed between England and India, home and work. Time now tasked her with the impossible job of raising another person and remaining herself. When she reached for the threads of time and tried to weave them, they unravelled into a slippery yarn in her hands. Four years since she had last returned from India. Three years since she had last seen Moth in Italy. Two years since she had become a mother. A year since she had set up her new business and given up on being a venue host at Riverdell. None of these dates made any sense. Any more than did the thirty odd years between her own pre-memory childhood and Indigo's. Or the eternity since she had been other than the owner of Riverdell, other than a mother, other than a woman with a basket full of dead flowers on top of her messy kitchen table.

'And what social plans do you have for this weekend?' Kate caught at her drifting attention with a question that sucked her stomach into a knot. An emphasis on the word social which caught the attention of both girls and turned their eyes to her. She looked beyond the girls to Kate, watching as their eyes turned to follow. They could sense a big question a mile away, even when they couldn't understand it. 'Hmmm?'

As Isabelle tried to summon something that would satisfy Kate, her phone rang. The ring tone telling them both who was phoning. Isabelle watched the breath get punched out of Kate's sails.

'Well, it's time I got on, my class will be late.' Kate stood up and took her plate to the sink while Isabelle reached for her phone. 'Girls, I'll see you at lunchtime.'

She deposited kisses on the girls' heads and moved for the door, glancing back at Isabelle and saying, 'We'll finish that conversation later.'

'Can't wait,' Isabelle lied. She pushed away the remnants of her breakfast with relief and answered the first distraction of the day. 'Hi, how are you?'

Kit's face appeared on the screen, surrounded by a swaying mass of blue glass baubles decorated with downy feather angels. His brown eyes sparkling, his smile cutting a swathe across his smooth-shaven chin and her screen, lighting up the kitchen.

'What are we doing for Christmas?'

'What?' Isabelle asked. 'You are joking? I haven't even found all the Easter Apostles yet, I can't possibly think about... that other thing.'

'Well, you need to, I have to make decisions about the lights, the tree, the who what when.' His face shimmied in and out of focus.

'Kit, it's not yet nine o'clock on a Thursday morning in April. Are you joking me? Where are you anyway? The line is terrible.'

'Japan. This place is blow-your-mind stunning in April. Blossom as far as the eye can see. Look.' The phone swung round to show her a swathe of blossom in the distance that made her magnolia tree seem desiccated. 'You should see the colours, Isabelle. You'd love it.'

'Why on earth are you there?' Isabelle looked out through

the window into the courtyard, struggling to see the blossom she had spotted earlier. 'Have you heard from Moth at all?'

'No, I bloody haven't. He's ignoring me. I'm buying Japanese origami and glass baubles.'

'Doesn't he know that's not allowed?' Isabelle toyed with her knife, keeping the phone held out at the edge of her vision where Kit's determined use of Face Time for all his calls couldn't overwhelm her. She avoided glancing at herself in the top right corner. When Kit had started it, in the sleepless, car crash days and nights of early parenthood, she had thought it an intentionally spiteful form of torture. That he would call her, looking as perfect as ever and show up the hollowed-out eyes and pasty cheeks, pregnancy flattened hair and vomit-catching scarf permanently draped over her shoulder. Now she knew he did it to feel good about himself, not to belittle her. Kit looked amazing on screen, any screen. If she thought the previous three years had been a time slip, they had slipped right over Kit. 'I thought Hester did all your Christmas stuff now?'

'She does mostly, but I wanted to do a paint research trip. The palette out here is giving me so much Zen, and I thought why not look at the Christmas market. Did you know they make origami angels and donkeys? I'd given up on him until I came here.'

'Oh, you must get some, the girls will adore them.' She glanced at the girls who were getting fidgety. She wondered how long she had left before they tried to sidle their way out of the kitchen. 'Why "until you came here"?'

'It made me realise, we need to give him a reason to come home.'

Isabelle felt her toes curl at the statement. It was a statement that had all the hallmarks of a Kit rollercoaster.

'We need to get the family together at Riverdell for Christmas.'

'Eh, what?' Isabelle asked.

'It's partly my fault, after all, I'm always too busy at Christmas to think about my own family. But this year, with Hester in charge, I'm changing that. We shall have a proper Christmas at Riverdell for the girls to remember, and it will be a reason for Moth to come home. We'll get Elsa and Nat there for him, he'll come back to see her. It will be epic.'

'Ooookay.' Isabelle held the image of Kit arriving, with a fully-fledged Christmas tucked in a sack thrown across his shoulder and thought the girls would probably pass out from excitement. That Asha would either be thrilled someone else was finally making an effort, or furious she had competition. That the family had not been together at Riverdell since Hester had stormed into the house after finding out Isabelle was pregnant and caused a monumental family melt-down they were all still recovering from. When Kit said "family" did he mean Hester too? She thought about telling Kate the big idea of that event and, finally, she thought about Moth, feeling the pressure to come home for such an event and knew he would hate it. 'Maybe we could think about it a bit closer to the time?'

'No, that's exactly the problem with you.' Kit's voice wavered down the line and came back, his face peering close into the camera as if he could reel her in. 'If I don't set it in stone now, you'll wriggle out of it. You're turning into a total mom-cluse these days.'

'A what?'

'Mom-cluse.' Kit told her, turning away and muttering in the background to someone else. 'Reclused in your mom-

world and ignoring the rest of life. When did you even last get dressed up, go out on a date, get laid?'

Isabelle looked at her daughter. The last thing she wanted to talk to Kit about was the last time she'd had sex. That was the one conversation they all picked their way around and which she studiously ignored.

'This family's been too scared to get together since Elsa dropped her bombshell about Riverdell.' Kit rushed on through her silence and Isabelle decided not to argue over the exact point at which the family had realised they were better apart. After all, Kit hadn't been in the kitchen to hear Hester's bitterness. 'We're not going to heal the rifts by ignoring them.'

'I didn't realise you were worried about the family.' She tried to keep up with the twists and turns in his conversation. She could sense a trap being woven in the air. 'Though it's lovely that you are. I'll email Moth to see what he thinks and have a chat with Kate.'

'You're not being very enthusiastic. Are the girls there? I want their opinion on these baubles.'

'There is no way I'm showing the girls where you are. Two-year-olds don't have quality opinions on baubles, Kit, they go for quantity, and they'll think Chr– the big event you're planning is next week. You're going to have to give me some time to think about this.'

The door to the kitchen opened and Gosia walked in. Took one look at the scene and puffed out disapproval, waved her hands at Isabelle in dismissal and set toward the girls who squealed in excitement. Isabelle stood up from the table and moved back to the coffee machine. She had two hours to herself before she had to take over from Gosia. With about six hours work to manage. Christmas would have to wait.

'Fine,' Kit said. 'I'll take that as a yes and we'll talk in more details when I get back.'

'When do you get back?'

'Two weeks. Ade's got a new dance opening, I promised to be back for it.'

Isabelle tied to imagine his boyfriend, Adele, swallowing Kit's sudden enthusiasm for a big family Christmas at the ancestral pile and found herself wondering what madness had truly gotten into Kit.

'Did you talk to Adele about Christmas?'

'Yeah, I'm going to tell him when I get back.'

'So, you didn't talk to him?' She had a grubby leg hug from Indigo as Gosia chased them from the table, held her head against her thigh and curled the hair round her ear, smiling encouragement down at her. The balance between fierce independence and sudden insecurity in her daughter was as thin a line as Kit's attention span, and as wearing to cope with. 'Shouldn't you discuss it with him first?'

'He'll love it.' Kit frowned at her. She was obviously being a dullard. 'He'll be thrilled someone else is sorting it. If he doesn't, he can always not come.'

Isabelle watched him dismiss Adele's feelings with a hand swat across the screen and felt for him. Kit's life, between home decor, Christmas and now a paint emporium, had grown erratic at best, anarchic as standard.

'Well, I have to go and work.' Isabelle said. 'We'll talk again.'

'I'll make you love the idea, you watch.' Kit zoomed his phone on to some intricate paper ornaments and back to his happy smile before cutting her off.

She finished making her drink and made her way out of the noisy kitchen. She couldn't help thinking that she stood

as much chance of getting Kit to stand still for ten minutes, or
Indigo to stop disappearing into the void that was Riverdell,
or Kate to stop nagging her to get a boyfriend, as she did get
Moth to come home for a big family Christmas. But none of
them compared to her inability to make time fit her life.

KIT HELD his finger relentlessly on the door buzzer and
turned to look at the drive as he heard the vans pull up.

The vision of loveliness they presented made him swell
inside, competing with a shiver from the onset of the chilly
evening and causing a frisson of pleasure as the security
lights clicked on, sensing either the onset of dusk or the
arrival of brilliance, Kit couldn't decide. His low-slung BMW,
nine months old and still giving joy, commanded the wide
space, its spotless black paint gleaming in the sunset and the
sparkle of lights from the house. Kit admired the view of the
driveway from the recessed porch.

When Jay had bought the house, in the years before they
were friends, he'd hit gold. A virtually derelict 1930s' large,
double-fronted house with a huge attic studio, the house was
a white elephant on the market. Not old enough to be period.
Too small to be luxury. Too close to the outskirts of Woking to
be rural. Set in nearly an acre of garden shrouded by mature
trees growing a canopy so dense only grass could compete
and protected by an insane tree preservation order,
prohibiting anyone from knocking down the ridiculous
house and building a modern mansion on it like all the
neighbours. Woking Golf Club stretching out from the back
fence. It was a fluke really, how Jay had managed to find it
and buy it.

The bare branches of the smugly preserved trees were

swaying across the blushed but cold sky in a firm breeze. It was a cute sunset for the beginning of December. Setting orange and rose hues to dance across the grey vans as they rocked to a stop, catching the trims on the opening doors as his crew piled out and making Kit wonder if he'd got those exact shades in his paint catalogue yet. He lifted his shades to get a true sense of the colours and then dropped them back over his eyes as he felt himself squinting at the bright patch of sky.

'Tell me this isn't some twisted way to get us to do more work?' Lou asked as she stepped out, whipping her neck from side to side, emphasising the shaved sides of her head with her hair pulled into a ponytail now they were away from the clients. Cracking her knuckles as she stretched her hands out. Appraising the front of the tall house as though she was already planning how to hang lights off its ugly arse. 'I thought we were done today?'

He thought about telling her to stop moaning, snatched the words back by their tail end and narrowly avoided dragging himself into another argument. Every minor disagreement funnelled them the same way these days. Lou claiming he was jealous she'd taken some of his queer turf and always trying to assert his authority. Lou flexed her new inclinations like a converted smoker, and it drove him nuts. He wanted to point out that, technically, she could be bisexual but, as he couldn't stand the whole label business anyway, and, as Lou wasn't even dating anyone, he struggled not to win every argument by telling her it was all highly theoretical and to just shut the hell up. And after all, perhaps she was just moaning about the fact that their Christmas season 2016 had been nearly double the year before. They were all exhausted.

'You could festoon some fairy lights across that doorway

for sure,' Fred added with a grin, leaning against the front of the van.

Kit wanted to tell him to lean a tad more lightly. He was worried about Fred's constant leaning damaging the bonnet, convinced he could see a Fred-sized dimple emerging in the metal. But that would only set Lou telling him he was fatphobic. And if he pointed out he loved Fred's fat, that fat alone could move more than all their muscles put together, he'd be accused of reducing Fred to an animal.

'Nah, you want to wrap those trees,' Ed got out of the far side of the second van and stepped toward the garden. 'Oof, this must take some mowing.'

Kit snatched back the retort that all he thought about these days was his garden. A postage stamp affair that had turned Ed into a garden-centre junky. Tempted to tell him the kid they were brewing would tear the shit out of his curated lawn by the time he was twelve months old. Tempted to buy him a puppy that would piss all over it, knowing Ed couldn't resist a dog. But it would upset Ed, who was precious about his new house and defensive of his property ladder ambitions and bring accusations of racism from Adele on Ed's behalf. Because Kit's new love interest was so racially sensitive about dating a white man that he looked for evidence of Kit's assumed racism everywhere. And Kit had learned not to claim having black people in his team was evidence to the contrary because, Jesus Fucking Christ, that had been a long bloody argument in their early days.

He watched Vee, the latest member of the team step from the van she had shared with Fred and look round. Vee had joined them at Henri's behest. He'd pulled her CV and job application off the internet and made it clear to Kit they were not discussing adding to the team. Even with Hester now in charge of the Christmas decorating market and Henri running his design business, Kit was stretched with the marketing and development of the Maison de Lavelle paints. With contracts with all the major designers, he was often getting on or hopping off a plane, leading to a greater need for delegation that made sense but felt itchy. Vee tucked a loose wisp of hair behind her ears and smiled at him without meeting his eyes.

Kit wished she would say more. He could cope with the complaints about his lesbophobia, his fatphobia, his racism. He could cope with all the complexities of this crazy family he'd pulled to himself. Especially when they arrived looking this cool, as though they'd stepped out of a *Fast and Furious* movie, his car the central beast in the set up. He could cope with being too exhausted to sleep. He could even cope with... well, no, he could ignore, pointedly bloody ignore... Isabelle and the fiasco of Christmas. But he wished Vee would express herself more. Perhaps it was her self-consciousness about her accent, which had a strong Czech tinge to it despite more than a decade living here, but he couldn't get a handle on her when she was so quiet.

'Is anyone even home?' Lou asked, joining Fred in his lean on the bonnet.

It was as though she knew exactly how to wind him up. Kit turned back to the door and leant on the buzzer again. He'd been there five minutes before them. Five whole minutes of extra time, that was what £98K for his car had given him. Five minutes to stand here leaning on the doorbell at Jay's house, thinking he'd kick his arse when he finally opened it.

'Doesn't look like anyone's in.' Ed glanced up at the top floor as he moved across to the curving bay window of the ground floor, peering inside at the Christmas lights. 'You sure he's not gone on holiday?'

'Great, another idiot who decks their house in lights, plugs it in to the grid and buggers off to Dubai for a month,' Lou complained. 'Don't these people care there's an environmental crisis?'

'No.' Ed, Fred and Kit all told her together.

At least they agreed on that one. Lou's environmentalism was seriously at odds with their commercial interests. Not to mention irritating as hell, making them feel guilty. Fred with his constant plastic Coke bottles. Ed with his incessant lawn mowing. Kit with his 4.4 V8 engine. He wondered what Vee thought about Lou's green superiority. He didn't know. That was the thing. It was what you didn't know that left you vulnerable. She only seemed to get on with Henri, their European background a common point. But if he mentioned that, he'd be pulled up again. Brexit spat out on the carpet like a furball and the team all dodging the clean-up. The world was getting too bloody sensitive. And if he pulled his own sexuality to his defence, which he'd never felt the need of before, it would be hollers of tokenism.

'Ground floor is rented out,' Kit told Ed. 'He's on the top floor.'

He took his hand off the door buzzer. If Jay were going to answer he'd have irritated him enough by now. And the sodding key was back home in Bristol. From the days when he'd had to call in and check on Jay's dog, Uggs. But that wouldn't be happening anymore.

'Maybe he wants to be left alone?' Lou suggested.

Behind the vans another car came humming off the busy road and into the driveway, sounding like an irritated bee. They all peered to look. The drive was big, but they'd fully commandeered it. A Citroen the size and colour of a rotten lemon edged its way alongside Ed's van and pulled up tight to the grass edge. A tall thin bloke unfolded himself from inside it. Kit took him in; neat suit, trouser legs a tad too short; smart satchel, leather a smidge too shiny; rented posh house, life goals overly aspirational; ethical car, budget a mite too small.

'Can I help you?' the man asked. Looking at the crew with various degrees of concern that deepened into a frown when he saw Ed straightening up from the front window. He shut the door, locked the car with a click and walked toward the front door and Kit with an attitude of ownership.

'Hi.' Kit saw Fred and Lou clock the attitude, roll their eyes at each other and lean some more. 'You must be the latest tenant, I'm Kit de Lavelle.'

He saw Lou smirk behind the guy's back and grinned at her. Crazy they might all be, but no one got to judge them, bar him.

'You wouldn't mind letting me in, would you? Jay asked me to stop by but he's not answering, and I've left my key at home.'

Kit didn't admit that it had been November when Jay asked him to stop in. Right after Trump got elected. When he'd texted that the world might as well end and would he like to come to his end-of-the-world celebration because 2016 had proven to be the biggest shit show of his life. Except Kit had been too busy in November with fairy lights to give a shit about Trump. And now it was December and Jay wasn't answering his phone and he'd gotten that call last week from the vets, because his number was down for an emergency contact, saying Jay hadn't answered their calls to collect the cremated remains. Then he'd known Jay wasn't answering the phone to anyone. And why.

The guy pulled himself up to his full height and stepped up beside Kit. Kit gave him a broad smile, eyeing him up from slicked-back hair down to gleaming shoes. A glance that took in every detail and left a lingering suggestion in the eyes and a pout on his lips. It was the easiest thing in the world to discomfort a straight bloke. You just had to hold their gaze for the right length of time. Kit moved a little closer.

'Have you seen him recently?' Lowering his voice, pulling the guy into his confidence to make up for the snub. So, what if he was renting a life he couldn't afford to buy. He didn't need to know that he was paying for the life Jay could afford. He needed to know not to judge his crew. 'Have you spoken with him?'

'No, our work hours differ. I haven't seen him in…' Kit watched the guy trying to remember the last time he'd actually seen his landlord. 'Well, it's probably been a few weeks, maybe a month.'

Kit stared at him in disbelief. 'Heard him coming and going? The water being used, the toilet flushed?'

'It's a substantial property, we respect each other's privacy.'

'Uh-huh,' Kit nodded at the man while frowning, creating that exact balance of "I'm listening and not hearing because I don't want to embarrass you" that dispatched his clients' more idiotic ideas. 'I'm worried about him, since the dog, you know. Be a brick and let me in?'

The guy blinked. It was a lot, to come home, expecting to toss up a quinoa salad, and find the combined mass of Kit de Lavelle's workforce taking over your drive, asking to be let into your house.

'No?' Kit sighed in mock despair. 'Well, can't blame you. I'd do the same. Never mind.' Kit stepped down from the door and made to walk toward the van. 'Fred, find a big spanner or something. We'll have to smash the back window in. I'm not going until we know he's not here.'

'You can't smash the window,' the guy said.

'Why not?'

'It's called breaking and entering, I shall call the police.'

'Very upstanding of you,' Kit told him. 'Make it a fucking big spanner, Fred. Jay likes his security glass. Stairwell at the back, door at the top. I'll wait for the police out here. If he's topped himself on my watch I am going to be so pissed.'

'You think he might have?' Ed asked, lingering in front of the big bay window.

'It's been a pretty rough year. What's he got to live for other than the sodding lawn and his caring tenants?' Kit opened the door of his car and got in, keyed the engine, put his hand on the horn and blasted it.

The tenant managed to nearly not wince. A bare flicker of discomfort jangling his keys.

Kit leant out of the car and hollered.

'Jay, answer the fucking door you prick.'

He leant on the horn again and let it blast a tad longer. He could see Fred switch elbows to lean the other way and Lou check her nails. Why, he had no idea, they were too short for storing dirt and she too damn clean to catch any. Probably wondering what colour to paint them for the weekend.

'JAY!!'

'Well, if he ain't dead he should have heard by now,' Ed mused to the tenant, still trying to decide whether to go in or to refuse any entry. 'Did you see him going away, did he let you know he was leaving at all?'

'I hope he hasn't hung himself,' Kit leant out of the car

again. 'That makes a mess, they shit themselves. Fred, where's the damn spanner?'

'I'm going, I'm going.'

Fred eased himself from the bonnet, hitched his sweat-pants up and ambled to the back of the van which had pitched sideways with the absence of his weight on the front. Kit resented those sweatpants, the boiler suits had looked so much better. There was nothing, but nothing you could creatively do to improve dark grey jersey merle. But Fred had outgrown the biggest of boiler suits and Ed had refused to wear one if he was on his own.

Kit smiled warmly at the tenant sweating on the front doorstep, he just needed a little extra push. A bit more noise, a bit more swearing.

'Did you call the police yet?' he yelled over the door of the car as he hit the horn again. 'Maybe an ambulance too?'

'Nah, don't,' Ed suggested. 'We don't want to get done for wasting emergency services time. Police can use a body bag.'

'Alright,' the tenant said. 'I'll let you in.'

'Good choice,' Ed told him, stepping up to the doorstep.

Kit got out the car and headed for the house. 'Vee, Fred, you stop here. Lou, Ed, with me.'

The tenant opened the door and stepped into the hall, looking up the wide stairwell with discomfort. Probably rethinking his aspirational housing interests. Inside , the house felt less grand, it was certainly no Riverdell. In fact, it was paltry compared to the houses Kit and his team worked on. But Jay had done well for himself, putting all his experi-ence at renovating pubs and restaurants to use in converting the property into two luxury apartments. The ground floor hallway was a mutual entryway with strict rules. Pegs for wet coats. Racks for dirty shoes. A barren umbrella stand. Otherwise, strictly to be left empty. All bar one of the original doors had been removed and the hall reduced, maximising the space on both floors. Kit took the stairs two at a time, to prove he still could, curving round the half-landing to hammer on the half-glass door that fronted the wall that sealed off the top floor.

'Jay, buddy, please open up.'

Kit was beginning to feel a shimmy of guilt. The great ship of his self-assurance looming toward an iceberg threatening emotional carnage. The immensity of his Christmas carnival strung out along the rigging, rattling in the breeze of danger. He didn't think Jay would top himself. It was totally not his style. Way too dramatic. But it had been a tough year. His long-standing girlfriend Lydia dumping him on Valentine's Day in spectacularly public style. Brexit in June which had sent him into a political frenzy of anger. Trump getting elected. And Uggs, bloody Uggs dying, which he hadn't even known about until the vets called and asked that the cremation be paid for. Uggs had died in September and Jay hadn't even let him know. Which was the point at which the hull would be breached, Kit could tell. That the dog had died, and he had been too busy to know about it.

He stared petulantly at the glass door, the reflection of his shades shimmering in its coloured lights. Kit pulled them off in irritation.

Did Jay not even give a shit about him? Did he not realise how hard 2016 had been on him too, avoiding the entire world finding out it was his fiftieth year? Which seemed all sorts of vain and insecure to him, and which he knew Kate would mock him for while she made a fortune from kicking the ageist butt of society, but in his luxury design world, age mattered. His appearance had to be as carefully curated as his paint collection and design portfolio. To speak of gravitas and elegance, without being outdated. It took an extraordinary level of effort to stay looking as he had in his forties. The blond lowlights now doing battle with the grey on a fortnightly basis, the obsession he had developed with sunscreen and mois-turiser, the cost of a wardrobe that had to work extra hard to keep him looking sharp. He'd had to switch up his gym schedule to include yoga, a task so dull as to make him hate it, but without which he couldn't maintain the muscle definition he wanted while also protecting his back and joints from the weightlifting. His face no longer suited even the slightest of five-o-clock shadow and, having dallied with a beard over the last few years, he'd ended up arranging his appointments for the morning, when his jaw was smoothest. Not to mention having to carry a pair of tweezers everywhere with him because stray hairs had started sprouting from his ears, nose and eyebrows with sly disregard for the morning mirror. And the hardest thing to manage had been his diminishing eyesight. Stuck between the options of contacts and glasses, Kit had opted for prescription shades, which he wore even in winter, despite mockery from the team. At least they also protected his eyes from sun damage, and the thought of having to take contacts out at night was as appealing as the thought of having to put false teeth in a glass by the side of the bed.

And it wasn't just the taint of vanity that made ageing so tedious, it was living up to the needs of everyone else in his life. To stay cool enough for his effortlessly gorgeous boyfriend who was not only eight years younger than him but had the physique advantage of being a professional choreographer. To keep Fred from eating himself to an early, arterially clogged grave over depression that his brother was moving away from him in life. To keep Lou pinned down enough to be functional while she tried to get laid. To stop obsessing over the idea that Henri was, rather than being his most steadfast employee, planning to leave and seducing half his design clients. To stop himself from wanting to have the almightiest strop at Isabelle who had ruined Christmas. To resisting, every damn bloody morning when he woke up, from looking at Kate's Instagram page for the chance to see her. From failing, every damn bloody morning, staring at her latest photos and trying to drown out the incessant query of what had happened to them. From feeling a creeping discomfort that he was somehow cheating on Adele as he failed the same test every damn bloody morning, which made him more acquiescent in the relationship than could ever feel comfortable.

Honestly, Kit thought, flicking his hair into place and putting his glasses back on. Was it too much to ask that his best mate hadn't topped himself and left him the biggest fucking mess to clear up, and a guilt trip the size of an Alaskan oil spill to cope with?

'That's a pretty door to break,' Ed mused as he arrived at the top of the stairs.

'Yeah, those leads will be a twat to replace,' Lou added, coming to rest at the other side of him. A light hand on his shoulder. 'Chill boss, he never seemed the type to do himself in.'

Kit held back the comment that you could never tell what someone would do under extreme heartache. Lou had the T-shirt and the scars on her wrists to prove it.

'I have a spare key,' the tenant called nervously up the stairs.

'Honestly, I'm going to bash him,' Ed muttered under his breath. 'He tells us when we're at the top of the stairs?'

'Wonderful!' Lou called back, squeezing his arm before she let go and went running back down the stairs.

Ed and Kit stared at the flickering glass lights of the doorway, listening to her get the key and come back upstairs. It was the original front door of the house, moved up here to create a barrier between Jay and his tenants, replaced downstairs with a solid door of security rigour. Behind the primary shades of the 1930's lights, Jay had sealed himself away into a life which only a privileged few pierced. Paid for by a business his father had been ashamed to see him run. Kit knocked one last time on the door. Jay had been a complex knotted mess before Lydia tangled him up and drop-kicked him.

Lou passed him the key with a tight set to her lips.

Kit unlocked the door and pushed it open. Stale air and the smell of a greasy spoon cafe greeted them all with the force of an unlocked tomb.

'Ugh,' Ed muttered.

'Chilly kebab, gross,' Lou waved the air away from her nose.

'At least someone's been eating,' Ed said.

Kit only noticed the absences. Uggs, with his huge bulky head held low, waiting to see if he should attack the intruder or not. Absent from the hallway. Light streaming in from the facing doors that lined the length like dancers and which Jay had always left open. Absent from the hallway. Music drifting down from the upstairs attic dance studio. Absent from the hallway. A dead body hanging from the ceiling. Mercifully absent from the hallway.

'This is all shades of wrong,' Kit muttered as he stepped

inside. 'Ed, check upstairs. Lou, let's check these rooms.' If Jay had hung himself, it would be upstairs from the rafters of the attic. The mortgage loopholes they were jumping through meant Ed owed him a big favour.

There were six rooms on the first floor. Large sitting room and master bedroom to the front, with the bay windows. He and Lou stepped up to the first doors and opened them with a nervous nod at each other. Jay's slick living room was empty, the wrap around cream sofa and deep pile rug, the precision aligned pictures of trees bringing the outside of the big bay window into the room, the two slender bookcases with their colour arranged spines, the curled, crisped leaves of the tall potted plants, the 52" screen with a dull layer of dust on it.

Dust. Jay. The guy was minimalist to a degree that dust didn't dare visit, let alone assume residence. Kit felt his shoulders rippling with discomfort and flexed his hands. He glanced across at Lou, she shook her head from the bedroom. Upstairs Kit heard Ed open the doorway into the studio. He held his breath, looking at Lou. No shouts of horror came back down the curving stairwell. They moved down the hallway.

'Ever get the feeling some psycho is going to jump out the next door and kill us all with a cheese grater?' Lou asked as they came to the next doors.

'No one could kill you with a cheese grater,' Kit jibed back. They opened their respective doors. Lou into Jay's office, Kit into the bathroom.

Kit glanced inside, it was empty. But used. An odour of urine rank in the air. He went and opened the window. Took in the dried, cracked soap on the vanity basin, the dull ring of water etched at various lines up the innards of the bath.

'No blood-filled bath with a corpse then?' Lou asked from the doorway.

'Will you shut up?' Kit asked. 'You're not helping.'

'Office is empty, dust all over the keyboard. Not been used in a month or more, I'd say.'

Ed came down the hallway from the stairs. 'Nothing up there but dead moths and dust as thick as the grave. I'd say it's not been used in years, let alone months.'

Not since Valentine's Day probably. Kit would kick Lydia's cheating pert butt from one side of the dancefloor to the outer realms of Siberia if he came across her again.

'What's left?' Lou asked, jerking her head down the corridor.

'Kitchen and spare bedroom,' Kit replied.

'Face it boss, he's gone on holiday somewhere,' Ed told him, leaning against the wall and watching as they moved to the final doors.

'I'm making it a new rule we don't lean,' Kit told him. 'On anything. Why are you all permanently propping yourselves up?'

'Because we're all knackered?' Lou suggested as Ed heaved himself away from the wall and followed Kit. 'Because working for you will put us in an early grave?'

'Employing all you will put me in an early grave!' Kit retorted as he opened the kitchen door.

The final colours of the sunset streamed in from the big window overlooking the golf course, dazzling him with golds and oranges that he wanted to try and name. Catching his eyes with envy as he desperately tried to hold onto the palette, oh but what glorious colours they would add to his paint range.

'Jeeeesuuuuus,' Ed murmured beside him.

Kit blinked his way out of his latest craze. It was exquisite torment, capturing colour and pinning it down to a shade card. It was insatiable, pulling at him in the least opportune moments, like when he should be focusing on conversation, or on sex, or on compassion. The state of the kitchen impinged. The yards of black marble stacked high with food containers, pizza boxes, milkshakes, drinks cartons. The congealed contents stretching onto the high bar table in the middle, teetering off chairs, creating pathways on the floor.

It looked as though Isabelle's old downstairs workroom had gone on a bender with the kitchen chaos she and Moth had created at Riverdell, hooked up with Ozzy Osbourne and rocked up to a BTS after party. It stank like an unwashed teenager. Wafting out to meet Kit and Ed, pushing them back into the hallway to escape. Kit put his sleeve up to his mouth and went over to open the window. The doorway onto the fire escape steps and Uggs' penned area lost behind high-stacked mouldy food containers.

'How many Just Eat deliveries has the guy downstairs not noticed?' Ed asked.

Kit moved back to the doorway and saw Uggs' food bowl. Piled high with dried biscuits, overflowing across the floor. It pulled him up short and he knew, just knew, Jay had topped himself. His best mate had called time and he'd not even noticed.

'Boss,' Lou called from the other room. Her tone too quiet, too calm. That voice that told him disaster was threatening but the client didn't need to know about it.

'Fuck,' Kit said. He was never going to get over this moment. It was going to haunt him through every happy hour for the rest of his life. Snatch his appetite whenever he tried to eat takeout again. Stare him in the eyes at whatever shitty funeral he would have to pull together, watching Jay's mother and sisters crying their eyes out. Christ, it would be awkward. 'Fuck, fuck, fuck.'

He walked past Ed and into the last room of the house. The spare room he had occasionally stayed in. The curtains drawn tight, the air suffocatingly dense with human smell. His eyes blinking in the dark so that he had to take his glasses off to see. Lou was stood five feet into the room, staring into the corner. She moved aside as he came up to her. Kit took a shallow hard breath and tried to see what was waiting for him.

In the corner of the room was a nest. A dumping of duvet, sheets, pillows and clothes. Mounding up into the angles of the walls. Forming a barrier around a solid lump. He moved forward, heard Ed go to turn the light on and Lou say sharply, 'No, don't.'

He turned to look at her, but she had her hand out to stop Ed and was shaking her head. He looked back at the mound. Nothing inside him wanted to see what was inside. He stepped forward, felt clothes crush under his feet and odour rise to meet him. Leant down and with trembling hands peeled back the wall of fabric, swallowing dread as he did.

Hair met him. Dark long hair with glints of grey and waves in it. He pushed the bedding further aside. Found the hair was a head, bent onto arms, folded across knees. Stilled to a point of distress.

But not dead.

Kit reached out and laid a hand on the arm, aware he was trembling. Guilt slipping into relief, sliding sideways into anxiety, rising toward anger.

'Go steady, boss,' Lou said behind him.

'Hey, buddy.' Kit crouched down in front of Jay and

reached out to smooth his hair back. 'You scared the crap out of me.'

The head burrowed down, arms clenched in, and Jay retreated from the touch. His voice came rasping out of the depths of his body.

'Can't you take a hint you selfish bastard?'

Kit grinned at the mess in front of him. Now this, this he could cope with.

'Nope, it's not my strong point. I'm not going away so you might as well look at me.'

Jay shuddered and swore into his arms.

'Don't make me throw a bucket of cold water over you,' Kit threatened.

The hair moved, the head rolled up and Jay appeared. Jay with a full beard. With about a stone more weight sitting on his face. With rank breath, bloodshot eyes and despair as deep as a mine shaft staring back from the brown pupils that Kit could hardly see in the gloom.

'Just fucking go away,' Jay told him.

'Yeah, no,' Kit said. 'That is not what's going to happen here.'

Jay stared back at him, his face puffy with entrenched misery.

'Go away and leave me alone.' Jay rocked his head back against the wall.

'Or, instead, this is what's happening.' Kit put his other hand on the crossed arms. 'You are coming home with me, you are getting a bath and a haircut, and you are not leaving until I see that crazy arse smile back on your face and some sanity in your eyes.'

Jay closed his eyes and banged his head against the wall, three thuds of refusal and rage.

'I know about Uggs,' Kit added.

The thuds stopped.

'I'm not leaving you here, buddy.' Kit stood up and took a step back. 'Either you stand up and walk out, or I'll get Fred to carry you out.'

Kit held out his hand to the lump on the floor. Jay opened his eyes, staring at his hand through a wash of tears. Kit struggled against the lump in his throat. Love, seriously, what a mess it made of life. He offered his hand closer, watching in relief as Jay uncurled his hand and stretched it out to him.

Kit took it and squeezed comfort into it, offered the other hand and pulled Jay up out of the corner nest.

'Jesus, you got fat,' Kit said as he grabbed an arm round Jay's waist and pulled him close. Jay had always been taut with muscle, slender and powerful at the same time. 'You can work that off too, we'll get Fred to keep you company.'

Kit started walking toward the door, nodding at Lou to go ahead. Ed had already disappeared. He listened as Lou strode out of the flat and went ahead to clear the way. Her voice brooking no argument with the tenant.

As they got toward the end of the corridor Jay stopped and looked back, twisting against Kit's shoulder. Breath shallow in his chest. Panic kicking in. Kit looked down the hallway, saw the wrong sort of absences all over again.

'This isn't about the dog, you know that right?' Kit told him.

Jay turned away from the hall and let himself be pulled over the threshold. When they got downstairs, the hallway and drive were devoid of folks. Kit put Jay in the passenger seat of the car and shut the door, went back into the house to find Lou in the hallway waiting for him.

'You head home,' she said. 'We'll do what we can to tidy up and see you tomorrow.'

He surprised her with a big hug and stepped back. All her grouchiness was the biggest cover for a heart as wide as an ocean and as bruised as the dusk falling over the drive. Only Lou could have cleared that pathway as swiftly and quietly to save the tattered pudgy rags of Jay's pride.

'Love, Jesus.' Lou shook her head in annoyance.

'Yeah, you remember that,' he told her and headed out of the house.

He got into the car, shut the door and looked at Jay in the passenger seat, staring out the windscreen at the house.

'You ready?'

Jay looked over at him but didn't respond. Kit reversed the car out of the drive and pulled away. As they headed down the road lined with tall walls, mature trees and high-browed double frontages, he could sense Jay watching him.

'Kit?'

'Uh-huh?'

'Are you wearing makeup?'

3

The mess that men leave behind them. I am so mad at Ted. At myself.

How I wish I could drag back time, that I had not left so soon after William's funeral. I was so upset that you had not come home, I couldn't wait to get away. I never imagined Ted would linger on. What a fool I was. Without the old antagonism between him and his father to drive him back to India, of course he lingered. And I wasn't there to protect Kate from his arrogance.

I will never, never, thrice never, raise Kit to be a man who assumes his needs and opinions exceed others. That women are lesser creatures confined to be mothers, whores or cleaners for bloody life. I could snarl at Elsa as soon as stab her vile brother or slap her spoilt little son. Dear Mary, save my temper. It's as though the entire women's liberation movement bypassed Elsa's happy little bower of privilege. Does she even turn the news on? Or is it limited to Richard's reports from the farm. How is David ever supposed to grow up to be a modern man with his mother to set him an example of womanhood? She is forever springing up to do something for him when he is perfectly capable of learning himself. Even Richard tells her to stop hovering over him. I do wish he'd hurry up and get her pregnant again, but she says she is reluctant to lose this magical bond with her firstborn.

Yes, she used that expression. Firstborn, the mythical heir of the kingdom.

Even Kit tried to trip him up the other day. David went squealing to his mother's skirts (don't get me started on Elsa's dress sense, it's never been great, and her widening hips seemed to have inclined toward the comfort of tweed) and telling tales. I didn't have the heart to tell the truth, that Kit was sick of playing with him and tripped him up to get rid of him. My son is not always perfect, well, he's far from perfect, he's a provocative little rat, but at least he doesn't snitch. Whatever mess Kit gets into, he gets himself out of. Or lies trying.

Children are a mirror. I watch him and see all my habits condensed into a cipher. Not always the most comfortable of feelings.

I told him off, of course I did. And at night we cuddled up in bed and talked about how to deal with people we don't get on with but are forced into company with. I told him he had to ask himself why he was in company with them. Was it through association? It is abhorrently possible to loathe someone who is loved by someone we love. This took a bit of explaining. I used his teacher, Miss Morgan. An insipid snip of primary vacuity I cannot bear to see, let alone converse with, dress sense as mediocre as Elsa's. (If I had to list the ways in which I miss a co-parent, the endurance of school-teachers and their progress reports would be high on the list. I would never attend another such day. Every time I attend the school I go home and look through the Steiner brochure but can't find the heart to tell Granny we must move away.) But Kit adores her. I mean, he dotes on the dullard. We talked about this and how Elsa and Richard love their son, even though we don't, but we do love them.

Next, we talked about whether the connection is useful in any way? Did the tolerating enable a longer term, bigger picture goal? I hate my boss passionately but the organisation we work for is something I will stand up for all day long. One day they will recognise his inferiority and promote me over him, and I shall order him to make the tea. Though it shall be coffee when I am in charge, and I might ban his sodding Earl Grey altogether. Kit suggested I order the best biscuits too, and I agreed. We compared biscuits to choose a winner. He chose a Custard Cream, and I selected a Jaffa Cake, which we argued over as we always do. By the time we finished we were hungry, and I had to sneak downstairs to get us a midnight snack.

Riverdell at night is a strange place. Full of the shadows of its long life. I want to creep about and peer through all the doors to see what lingers behind them. I felt the urge to turn all the lights on and stood there half-tempted, thinking I heard someone's ghostly footsteps creeping in the upper hall, but it was only Kit, too curious to stay in bed and wanting to help me. We had a fit of giggles trying to keep quiet on our way to the kitchen. This house is too vast. A child could get into all sorts of trouble before you had a chance to catch them out. Perhaps it is small wonder Elsa is such a fussy mother.

I wonder what else I would value about a co-parent. Someone to get up and make coffee in the morning? No, I'd never cope with the mornings I'd have to make theirs in return. Regular sex, but no, that would get tedious far too quickly, and I wouldn't care to miss out on these nights with Kit, not while he is young. Men are always jealous of the love we feel for our children. Resenting the child suckling at our breasts when they crave us to be sucking on their dicks. I am glad to have had him to myself as a child. I love his delight in talking long into the night about things he has no real comprehension over, valuing the chatter because it is time we share together. I wonder how much he will remember. He lies asleep now, twisted in the sheets and tossed about the bed like a boat in a storm. His hair is catching the soft light, it has grown as pale as mine is dark. I wonder who his father was, that night is such a blur. There was a blond one, I believe. Who cares? He is mine anyway, all mine. And his hair is gorgeous. Long enough to see the curls, to feel them slide through my fingers as I smooth his head to help him sleep. I am grateful for the genetic donation, it reminds me of you, and I imagine the soft golden hair is yours.

But tonight, he drifted off quickly and I am here, restless, writing, looking out over the river dancing in moonlight. This was always our room. Though the twin beds are gone now, replaced with a vast double. Kit has a small bed settee set up. Elsa trying to sort my life, improve my parenting, encourage me to find the fitting companion. She has been hosting parties. One for my birthday, and one for the hell of it, so far. And more to come apparently. Dear Virgins queer and Virgins great, the woman is a boring host. How many twinsets and tweeds can one room decently hold before wilting into irremediable tedium? While she parades the single balding men of this puckered up town in front of me. I don't deny I'm bored enough to take a dozen to bed for the sake of my sanity. But Kit drops off to the sound of my comforter a treat, and I'd rather pleasure myself than shock the bachelors of Ludlow by telling them their sisters are prettier and their idea of sexual gratification is as dull as their politics and dress sense.

A month at Riverdell, what was I thinking? A summer here will only ever hold painful memories. We only ever used one bed in this room, though Elsa will deny the truth before her eyes if it does not sit with her ideals. I am glad to have Kit with me, he chases away your ghost with his snores and burps. And he is glad to be here again, though I was reluctant to come. But Elsa was desperate our boys become best friends, (no chance there, if we go the summer without Kit drowning David in the river, I shall count my parenting irre-proachable) and worried enough about Kate to ask me to come.

Two things I have concluded in the week I have been here.

Firstly, Elsa must give up David to Richard if the child is to grow a backbone. My own dislike aside, and I recognise I like no child but my own, the boy is not all bad. He is bright and can be clever, and when he laughs, truly laughs, not for his mother's attention, there is a wonderful joy in him. Plus, Kit says he has a fascination with how things are built. Always piecing stuff together, books, glasses, cards. And when Richard is here, he stands taller, acts sweeter. But Richard is not always here, he leaves early and returns late from the farm. The boy is left entirely with Elsa and will not be parted from her at this rate until he goes to school. I shall speak with Richard and push for them to spend more time together.

Secondly, Kate must get over whatever idiocy she contrived last year and pull herself together.

I should never have left so soon, I knew she was in a

fragile state. She adored William. Elsa and Ted's father was the closest thing she knew to one herself and Ted stepped straight into his father's emptied shoes. I can't fathom it, what idiocy he suggested for those four weeks, as though he knows anything about her work. He is a textile merchant not a publican, but despite the lack of credentials she listened to him, and her business has stuttered and stumbled ever since. William knew her far better. He trusted her enough to give her the money for the deposit, he knew she would manage it quite perfectly. Perhaps Ted was jealous of the money his father gave her? Perhaps being at Riverdell all those weeks made him realise what he had lost after all? It's one thing to face your disinheritance in theory half a world away, another altogether to see your redundancy after the will is read. Richard would have stopped him from interfering with Elsa but who was there to protect Kate? She has forgotten her own strength and believes she needs a man in her life. Bemoaning her own ideas, her own dress sense, her own worth. Makes me want to slap her. And stab Ted all over again. I feel so violent tonight. I hope he is a better husband and lover than a friend. For he has been no friend to Kate.

Bloody men and the havoc they wreak.

There, that's what kept me awake and brought me here. I could never co-parent, especially not with a man. What damage would they do the child? Even if I have a permanent lover, a life fixture, I will always be the only parent. The things we love the most cannot be shared. My child is my own. As Kate's business is hers and hers alone. I should never have let you go so easily, that was youth, the power of social pressure over my own conviction. Us women putting the men and their needs first, again.

We must stop this nonsense that men are the rightful answer.

Only we know ourselves best. Only we can craft the vision for what we love the most. She has forgotten herself and I must remind her exactly what she is capable of. That marriage did not and never will suit her. That whatever nonsense Ted told her about his business will not work for hers. Grief for William, wrapped up in too great an admiration for Ted, have dulled the sharp edge of her own brilliance. Three more weeks and clear tasks ahead. Save David from a watery death, get Elsa out of tweeds, engage Richard in parenting, shake Kate out of her misery and back into herself, and, with a bit of luck, find myself a summer fling to ease the tedium of Elsa's excruciating parties.

Dear Freya, if I end up screwing a balding, boring solicitor to save my sanity, please don't judge me.

4

Three weeks after Bonn had told him he was running out of time, Moth climbed back up the stairs to the camp commander's office resenting every tread. The bike would not be fixed, Jonah was moving through the compound like a dose of salts and tension was stalking the rows of tents as the influx of another 4000 bodies threatened the fine line of control.

He paused outside the door and cast an eye over the enclosed space of the compound. He could see the sparkling mess of the bike on the ground outside his shared tent. Upside down and with the wheels still spinning where he'd thrown down the spanner and sworn in defeat, leaving with a rough hand on the flat rubber as he answered Aidan's call that Bonn wanted him. Accompanied with a lewd hip gesture that didn't soothe his mechanical strop.

'Screw you, Aide,' he'd called after him.

Aidan pointed to Bonn's container in response and made the gesture of a dick going into his mouth.

Perhaps he should consider it. Maybe it might increase his options.

That would involve you making a decision.

From his vantage point, Moth lifted his eyes beyond the rippling tents to the far hills beyond. That was a decision that he'd avoided since Venice.

Yeah, when you made that stupid promise.

He lowered his eyes from the hills to the heat haze rippling along the main road that linked Sanliurfa, or Urfa as the locals called it, in the north to the border town of Akcakale. The dust stirring as cars and trucks went past the perimeter gates. Venice was a watery dream in comparison to this place. The salty breeze across the bay, the sense of fluid grace that seemed to bind the town and Luca in his memory. Luca should have been Venetian, the place had suited him well. It's narrow canals and back streets catching at the angles of his collarbones and limbs, the constant dazzle of water on stone and marble reflecting in the brightness of Luca's eyes or the shine of his hair as he flicked it back into place. The sunlight sharp enough to make him look transparent and Moth want to stop him floating away.

Moth would give his next hot meal to be near the sea again, not facing the summons on the other side of the door. In three weeks, he'd made zero progress and Bonn was going to extract that truth like a rotten tooth with no anaesthetic.

Stop dreaming about the sea and get on with it.

Moth took hold of the handle and gathered his breath. This, he could deal with. Luca, not yet. He ducked his head and stepped inside. Bonn and Yves looked up from the table full of data they were consulting.

'Ah, Moth, at last.' Bonn straightened and turned toward him.

Yves frowned and pulled away with irritation. Moth sensed he, rather than the paperwork, was the cause of that frown.

'I can come back if you need more time?' he suggested.

'No, I need you now. Yves and I have an offer for you.'

Moth watched Yves cross his arms over his chest, stand a little taller and tighten his jaw. It was a remarkably square jaw to begin with. Irritation turned it into a tank. Whatever was brewing, Moth suspected it had little to do with what Yves wanted. He grabbed the nearest chair and sat down. A little less height offensive could only help.

'Three weeks left until the transit camp staff join us. I'm sure you've seen how tight space is. How's the bike coming along?' Bonn asked, turning his back and stirring papers on the desk.

'Great, coming along good.'

Moth stared at his back, out through the window, past the sunlight glaring through the thinning top of Bonn's greying hair, down the length of his own legs, anywhere but at Yves who stared at him the whole time. Yves, another Frenchman, had little in common with his boss. Bonn was all strength and light, frown and laughter, steel and padded gut. Yves was square. All over square. Square shoulders, square arms, square attitude, even his knees were square. Possibly even his balls were square.

And you look like a round bloody peg to him.

Moth gave up avoiding and looked up into Yves' eyes. He didn't smile, there was no point. Both knew whatever Bonn decided would be what happened. If he couldn't get the bike fit and get out before it happened, Bonn would be telling him which direction he was walking in and how fast he was going.

Yves looked back at him with the same sour level of irritation Moth felt with the bike.

He was not part of Yves' plan.

The busted bike was certainly not part of Moths.

Busted in so many interconnected and niggling ways that were going to get it about out through the gate but not far enough to avoid the bungee cord twang of Bonn's reach. Despite a patch up in Venice, the age of the frame and his collision with an earthen bank had begun to tell. It was old, older than new parts wanted to fit, older than mechanics could really be bothered with. He'd fallen for the gleaming polish the bike shop had given it and missed to notice that the kink in the frame had been knocked into line and the cracks filled and now was about to snap in half. The bike had had enough. And Yves had had enough. And he'd had enough of waiting for Bonn's provoking mind games.

'You giving me marching orders or what?' he asked Bonn's back boobs.

How do you end up getting fat on your back?

By not moving often enough, that was how. Even Luca would be putting on weight, sat twiddling fancy pens between his bored thumbs in Geneva. The thought of Luca ending up with flabby back boobs cheered him up a little.

'Well, that's your choice.' Bonn turned to face him, leaning back against the desk. Yves breathed out through his nose, barely covered resentment. Bonn's lips tweaked in the corners. 'Yves is having trouble persuading the transit refugees to move.'

'Anyone would have the same trouble.' Yves tilted his tank jaw up an inch to defend himself.

'You know the story,' Bonn sighed at Moth. 'The Turkish government wants them out of the local town where they're a strain to the economy and into the official camp at Suruc where they can regulate their movement. At Suruc they'll be a minority group. Our own HQ has decided the staff are to lodge here and work between us and Suruc, making them even more vulnerable. Understandably, they are anxious, many are hoping to come here if they resist the move long enough.'

'They'd probably be less keen to come here if they heard how the refugees here talk about them.' It was hard to get used to the snobbery that existed between families, ethnic groups, camps. Moth tried not to judge. He remembered when the bike had been his life. The less you had the more you fought to hold onto it. The transit camp refugees were seen as minority refuse by the residents here. 'Why can't some of the staff go to Suruc to help ease the transition?'

'Heaven forbid the logistics teams at UNGO pay us a visit and realise what looks good on the map and in the spreadsheets contributes to ethnic carnage on the ground. We wouldn't want them getting their pretty shoes all dusty.'

Moth blinked as multiple bits of information slipped sideways in his brain. Luca worked in logistics at UNGO, the Geneva office of the UN. 'Is that what logistics do?'

'What?'

'The maths stuff.' Moth had caught Bonn off stride. 'I thought logistics was transport.'

'Dimitri is transport,' Yves said, trying to grasp the conversation and realising how inadequate his comment was. 'Obviously.'

Moth and Bonn both stared at him, long enough that Yves tried to tilt his jaw even further up and found his neck couldn't oblige so pushed his shoulders back instead.

'Merde,' Bonn muttered, picking the cap up from his desk

and slapping it in his hand. 'Dimitri is transport, here. Logistics is transport, yes. Transport is logistics, yes. Is transport just logistics, yes. Is logistics just transport, no. What idiots am I dealing with?'

'I know someone in logistics, in Geneva. I didn't realise what that was.'

'You thought it was transport?' Yves asked with curdled contempt.

'You want them to pay a visit?' Bonn asked.

'No!' Moth protested. 'You wanted them to pay a visit.'

'No, I didn't, I want you both to stop talking about the bloody transport.'

'I wasn't talking about transport, he did.' Moth pointed at Yves.

'Merde,' Yves echoed, dropping his shoulders and unlocking his arms. Letting the tank lower.

'She got pretty shoes?' Bonn asked, giving Yves another moment to chill. 'Eh? Pretty shoes with high heels?'

'No, she's not...' Moth thought about Luca. His slipping trousers, his skinny hips and smart shoes tapping their way round the streets and bridges of Venice. Now was not a time to get into the details of Luca's shoes with Bonn. 'What did you want me for, anyway?'

'He wants you to come with me,' Yves told him. 'He thinks you might be able to help.'

'Help?' Moth looked from Yves to Bonn. 'Me?'

'We have a high proportion of unaccomps,' Yves explained. 'My team are focusing on the families to persuade them to move. Most don't want to know. They simply won't move, and we don't have enough time to work with the unaccomps. We are going to lose a lot.'

'Where will they go?'

'Nowhere.' Bonn flicked his cap like a cat's tail. 'They will slip into the cracks of nowhere. Try to move into the town. Or make it up the road to Urfa before the army find them. Try to move closer to Europe. Try to live in the hills. The normal stuff. Anywhere other than a camp with another ethnic concentration. And I'm getting nowhere with the imbeciles up top, either in this country or at HQ. There isn't anywhere else for them. They go to Suruc or end up nowhere, unprocessed. Turkey is running out of empathy, space and money. And Europe is tightening its borders.'

Silence filled the room. Making it cramp down and warm up. Moth felt Bonn tugging on that string. He should have shouldered the bike and walked out of the camp a week ago. He'd seen enough young men do it. Teenagers, younger than him. Tired of being the punch bag in the shared youth tents. Or pushed out of the tents by bulging families and violent fathers. Eyeing him up at night as they lingered outside the toilet blocks, hoping to steal enough money to eat the next day. And it wasn't just the boys, the bravest girls left too. Watching their older sisters shunted into corners and straight into marriage with widowers twice their age. Disappearing in the night, leaving their mothers to face the brunt of the anger in the morning. Some of them he was glad to see go. Some of them he knew wouldn't survive a month. He sat forward in the chair, bending his legs and resting his forearms on them, examining his nails. Moth knew exactly what it was to be underage, unaccompanied, travelling through Europe. He'd made it further than most. And he'd had a head start of money, health and language they didn't.

'Shit.' He broke the silence first.

'I want you to go with Yves, work with the minors. I'm going to try and extend the closure date as much as I can by protesting our readiness. Suruc is doing the same. Meanwhile, do what you can. I'm giving you transport. You are to move between the camps, the nearby towns and here. Build bridges between them. Get contact numbers, get info, anything to help us track them. Do anything you can to tighten the gaps to nowhere. Do you understand?'

Did he say transport?

'How the hell am I going to do that?' Moth asked. 'I don't even know the language.'

'That hasn't stopped you here.' Bonn looked across at Yves with a sly grin. Moth tried not to curl his lips. Damn Bonn, he'd told Yves about his clubs. The early afternoon gatherings he facilitated with the young teenagers to help give them a sense of identity away from their family. Sharing information and technology to try to build a sense of hope.

'I can't do that in this timescale,' Moth protested. 'It's taken me a year here to make headway, you know that.'

'I know that.' Bonn let his smile broaden, turning it on Moth.

'Don't give me that encouraging grin, you can shove it,' Moth told him. 'I can't build that level of trust overnight, they'll know you've sent me. It will make matters worse, not better.'

'That's what I told him,' Yves added.

'Do you think I don't know that?' Bonn snapped in a blaze of heat.

Here we go. You're still missing the main point though.

Bonn was flicking from suave man in charge, to seductive ego-soother, to desperate guerrilla fighter. Moth had watched him do it often enough to know the impact. Yves barely managed to not wince.

'Do you think I don't know we don't have enough time?

Or enough space? Or enough money?' he demanded. 'And while you two stand here whining like little boys with their first stiffy, do you know what is happening to those kids we are letting slip away?'

'Oh, stop with the horror stories,' Moth said. 'Yes, I bloody know, and I don't need you turning it into a guilt trip. What's the point here?'

'I don't care how much you achieve.' Bonn threw his cap on the table in emphasis and leant, a hand each side of its message. 'I care that we try anything we can for as long as we possibly can. That is the point here. If you save five from disappearing into hell, five is enough. If you save none, but you tried, that is barely enough. If we do nothing and blame the powers above, that is not enough.'

'So, three weeks. Maybe a little more?'

'I'm hoping we can delay another month. Eba is working with the antenatal clinic at Suruc, and the late pregnancies have complications which make the closure date impossible.'

'That's convenient.' Moth didn't believe it was the pregnancies so much as Eba and Bonn conspiring. 'Let's hope logistics don't pay a visit to the antenatal clinic.'

'It is necessary.' Bonn brushed away the lie as he would a fly. 'Moth, pack your essential gear. I want updates every three days from you. In person. Here. Do you get that? I need to know where you are. I cannot afford to have you causing trouble with the Turkish authorities. Yves, he stays in the camp, not the compound. Make him as safe as you can but make it clear he's not one of yours. Give him all the info and contacts you can. Moth, get to know them. I'm not expecting miracles. Even if you have built a bridge, if they won't move, you may be able to help us keep track of them. When they get desperate, they'll use whatever they have.'

'You know you might as well have given me the trafficker's job description,' Moth pointed out. 'Make friends, take details, give them a fragile hope for when life gets harder.'

'Oui, and I'm sure you won't be the only one doing the same. We need time, to either move or help process them. Focus on the youngest first. Do you have any questions?'

'You're accepting complete responsibility for his safety?' Yves demanded. 'I don't agree with this, another minor on my hands is the last thing I need, and you may cause more harm than good with this hare-brained scheme.'

'I'm not a minor,' Moth butted in, 'and he doesn't have responsib–'

'I accept complete responsibility.' Bonn held a hand up to stall Moth's attempt to protest. 'Moth can look after himself, and any trouble he brings will fall on my desk.'

'I want that in writing,' Yves pointed his solid, square finger at the desk. 'I'm not being pulled up in front of some tribunal in ten years' time because you decided to go off-piste and his body gets found in a shallow grave.' The square finger swung round to face Moth.

'You worry too much about tribunals.' Bonn said.

'You don't worry enough about anything,' Yves retorted.

Moth ducked his head to hide a smile. Yves was like a younger version of Bonn, not that he'd admit it. Give him two more decades and enough new camps with the same eternal problems, and he'd be the one ignoring the rules to get things done.

But perhaps not with fat on his back. Can we get to the point yet?

'Moth, any questions?' Bonn looked at him.

Well yes, there is one. Isn't there.

'You're giving me transport?'

Bonn smiled at him. A broad, smug French smile. The sort which Leon gave at the end of a gruelling day, with all the lavender boxes packed and the staff heading in to cook, the sun lighting up the tip of the Mont as it set behind his fields. Bonn picked up a set of keys from the desk behind him, hefted them and threw them across the room to Moth.

'Yes, my gargantuan little friend, I am giving you transport.'

Moth caught the keys. A weight in his palm. A shiver of excitement and fear running through him as he closed his hands around them. Keys. The first keys he had ever held. A first as Luca had been a first. Moth let his palm warm the cool metal. Life held an infinite number of firsts. Luca had taught him that that in Venice. You could make however many you wanted. No one got to take that away from him.

'And if you lose or damage it, I will extract a leg in return.' Bonn promised.

'YOU ARE JOKING?'

Aidan grinned from one ear to the other, enjoying Moth's sense of outrage. 'What did you expect, a Bentley? With your silver spoon already packed.'

Moth held onto his retort. Then refused to let his tight jaw stick out. Remembering Yves the day before. Aidan would be able to see the nark as well as he had.

'At least a candelabra,' he said instead.

'Yeah, I bet.' Aidan blew smoke out, shifted his feet and resettled.

You wouldn't think a grown man could lean against a tent, but Aidan had perfected the art. If Luca was skinny, all bones and limbs and eye-grabbing angles, Aidan was lanky. Hair lanky. Bone lanky. As though the long strands of indifferent hair that gusted past his face or got scraped back into a limp ponytail were the final indication of a lank inner growth. Melding into the tent material in a pose that would hurt normal bones. The only time Aidan got inspired was in the pursuit of cigarettes which he never ran out of. 'Should have known Bonn would save the best for you, lucky bastard.'

'This is the best?' Moth asked, pointing at the bike in front of them.

They looked at it together, Aidan squinting through the smoke and past his bad eyesight to take in the battered, rust-bitten, stand-wobbling bike. Moth wasn't sure it would even take his weight, let alone carry him the dry distances between Akcakale and Suruc.

'You won't be saying that once you've had it snatched out of your hands and been beaten into the dust for it.'

Moth looked at the keys in his hand. He'd had higher hopes for this particular first. Maybe anticipation didn't make things sweeter, maybe it made disappointment inevitable.

You should try setting a time limit on your anticipation. Give it a fighting chance. Like maybe not three years.

'Are you trying to comfort me?' he asked Aidan.

'Not really.'

'Good, because you're failing.'

'Well, it's a step up from that wreck anyway.' Aidan nodded at the upended bike stood two feet away. 'At least you can scrap that bitch now.'

Moth didn't want to have to consider that. Where he was leaving the bike. As he rode away on the new one. It was a betrayal. Abandonment. And how could he convey that the battered frame of the bike he'd toured Europe on was more familiar to his body than anything...

… or anyone…

… else.

Moth looked at the motorised version. Whatever model it had once been, had been worn away by a life too rough. Moth had only been on a motorbike once in his life, and it had looked entirely different to this. A shiny red sports model Luca had hired for the day to take them away from the coast and up into the hills above Venice. Moth had begged Luca to let him have a go and he'd refused.

'Why are bikes always female?'

'Seriously?' Aidan asked.

'Seriously.' Moth walked over and spun the unhappy back wheel of his old bike. 'I don't get why transport is always female.'

Aidan threw his fag end on the ground and crushed it into safety. He scooped the stub up and stuck it in his pocket, scooping his bones out of the fabric hollow they'd made. Bonn went mad if he found stubs littering the compound. 'Anyways, at least you have transport. It's a long walk to Suruc otherwise. You do know how to ride one of these, right?' Aidan asked.

Moth wasn't sure one half-day's ride as a passenger counted as experience, but he wasn't dumb enough to pass that on to Aidan, who would pass it straight on to Bonn.

'Of course.'

'Right then, I've got work to do, have fun packing.' Aidan set off toward the mess tent.

'Cheers.' Moth watched Aidan walk away. 'Aide?'

'Yeah?' He turned to look at him but kept walking.

'Save me some breakfast.'

Aidan chucked a curious look at him, raising his eyebrows as understanding kicked in. The moment Moth left,

their routine changed. Perhaps he might be back for breakfast one day, perhaps he might not.

'Sure thing, Moth.'

Moth watched him wave and turn away. Aidan had been
cooking for NGOs since running away from a speeding ticket
in Dublin at nineteen. One that came with striking a pedes-
trian and evading arrest. He'd made it through ten years of
not being able to go home by never saying goodbye. Moth
wondered if he'd end up the same.

You should get packing. You haven't long.

Yves was heading back in an hour and Moth was meant to
be going with him. He turned away from the new motorbike,
grabbed hold of the rhombus of his old bike and flipped it
upright. Carried it into the tent.

Six double bunks laid out along the sides. His was the top
at the far end. Here, where heat warmed the top bunks to
growing temperatures, the least important member got the
top bunk furthest from any breeze that might seep through
the door. He would miss this bunk. It had felt safe. Where he
went next would not. The thought rippled through him,
shuddering across his shoulders. He lurched with it, leaning
against the solid metal frame of the bike.

You've forgotten what that means.

Not knowing what tomorrow brought. Yes, he had
stepped back from that. But forgotten it? No. He'd never
forget it. It had been the only constant in over three years of a
life shifting past him. The bike solid in a way life was not. He
couldn't forget that. He had a month, maybe a little more, of
using the motorbike, buying himself time. He would need to
find supplies, use what little spare time he had left to rebuild
the bike. Get the tent patched up again.

Moth put the bike back against the far wall of the tent,

tucked as far into the corner as its gangling frame could go. It had been hard enough to protect it when he was here all the time. How would it fare with him gone for days? Looking even more wrecked for his efforts at reconstruction. He didn't trust Jonah not to have it hauled out and flattened into a saucepan.

He pulled the bag and panniers out from under the foot end of Aidan's bunk. The contents of his life spilled on the floor. The tent was thin with use, and he knew it had holes and fraying edges he needed to get patched. His clothes were a mismatched grab for whatever was going spare that had a remote chance of fitting. The padded jacket that had kept him alive through four winters. The dented can of the stove. It all looked battered and small, a life he had once fitted and had forgotten how to fold himself into.

Moth ignored the tightness across his shoulders as he repacked it. The tent had been made for James, a man whose shape he had grown into. He was more than capable of fitting back inside that tiny world.

He pushed the bike panniers and tent back under the bed. He'd have to hope Aidan would keep an eye on them, not sell them and blame someone else. Sat down on the floor with the rucksack on his knees and what was left spread out in a drab rainbow. Sitting on the lower bed would have been rudeness. In this world the only thing you counted as your own was the bed you could come back to at the end of a shift. Moth looked up at his top bunk. It had become a great luxury, that too short bedframe and its thin mattress. He wondered how long it would take Jonah to give it away to someone more worthy.

The rucksack was worn too. The colours faded, the straps ragged. He had felt naked to begin with. Walking through the camp without it stuck to his back. For all that time on the bike it had been the only thing he never left behind. Here, he'd learnt a bag made him a target. He'd fared better in the camp when he went with nothing to show.

He moved two sets of clothes and a water bottle to the side and contemplated what was left. He leafed through the notebook he'd tracked his days in. Filled until it could be filled no more, ending three weeks after he arrived at the camp. Untouched since. The café business card that Luca had given him when they first met holding the final place, worn and fraying round the edges with how often Moth had held it and twisted it in the darkness of a wakeful night. The cigarette case he had stolen from Riverdell, cradling the needle he had taken as a reminder of his time with Isabelle and the brittle sprig of lavender that reminded him of his mother, home, France and the friends he had made there all in one whisper of fading scent. The bulging postcards in their protective bag. He opened it, the plastic rustling in his hands.

Folded round the cards were printed emails. Nat's excitement popping up in the voice he heard growing up over the phone. Elsa and Hester visible in the outlines of her latest achievement. Isabelle's voice was quieter. He imagined her sitting in the study, snatching moments to herself, drifting into the reverie he recalled from when she worked. He had to recreate the house anew from her descriptions. The workroom moved upstairs, the old one converted to a ballroom that had only hosted one wedding. Filled instead with Kate's reincarnation as a gardening celebrity. Indigo, the baby he had never met, growing from Isabelle's arms to her first independent steps to a habit for getting lost in the big house that terrified them all. He stared at the photos with fascination, trying to make this child feel real. The wild waves of pale hair, the dimpled cheeks and fat wrists. Belonging to Isabelle, being part of Riverdell. Shorter messages from Kit, inventing paint names for his new business an obsession that spanned the ins and outs of his love life. He refolded their voices and stacked them, turning his attention to the cards. At the bottom of the pile, the two he held most dear.

Guethary, with Beau and Mila sat outside their refurbished restaurant. The old woman who had rescued him from despair in France and the young woman who he in turn had rescued and sent to France. Living and working together to keep Beau's old restaurant open. Mila had won the local council over, and the photographer, and the town, from what he could work out. She had a residence certificate now and was seeking permanency in France. Moth consumed their faces, how they had changed since he saw them. Mila filling out into a beauty, no wonder the town had welcomed her. She was stunning. Even he could see that. Her hair flowing over her shoulder in waves, no longer split-ended and dull. Her face heart-shaped and chiselled, her mouth a full bow of red lipstick. Beau, older, more wrinkled, sitting straight in the chair, her hair curled for the photo, a glass of red wine in her nail-painted hand. A bright dress sitting across bony shoulders. The same slick of lipstick stuck in the lines of her lips. They looked invincible, refreshed with the same bright shade of red that painted the restaurant windows, refreshed the old check tablecloths. He tucked the postcard behind the last one. Glad for its reminder that he had done right by them.

The final postcard he cradled in soft hands, hunching over its perfection. St Mark's Square, from the canal front. Filled with puddles and shining in the sun. Luca had laughed at him for getting a British postcard, all rain and gloom. But he remembered the weather in Venice more than he did the architecture. How it had been watery in all ways possible, the sea, the canals, the rain. He remembered them sheltering from sudden drenchings in covered bridges, doorways, churches. Tucked together and letting it pass, full of startled breath and closeness. Eating crepes on stone steps as they dipped bare legs into the waters. Walking the long edge of the pier away from the crowds and out into the park at the furthest northern tip of the city. Every view of Venice had served to frame Luca. If he hadn't looked overwhelming enough in the cafe in Male, where the surroundings didn't reflect his brilliance, Venice, all her marble, water and picturesque alleyways and bridges, had made Luca positively shine. Moth had watched others watching Luca, women smiling at his passing, men staring in envy. How their eyes slipped to his own presence and slipped away.

You weren't at your best, remember.

He had been overwhelmed by Venice. A scraggly, ugly tourist who didn't fit its demands for grace and beauty.

You fit right in here.

He did. He felt comfortable here. Walking the narrow pathways between cramped tents, lost among the thousands of bodies, grateful for his height advantage.

Luca on the other hand, would not fit in here.

Luca would stand out like a lost fashion model here. He belonged in Geneva, or Venice, or Milan. Somewhere, somewhere...

... glitzy.

Moth let his fingers run across the surface of the postcard. Three years ago. It didn't feel that long. He could hear the calls from the gondoliers, the cry of seagulls, the wind slapping the waves in the bay. He could hear the morning bells waking the town. While they stirred awake in their darkened hotel room. The mornings in Venice. He would never forget those. The high walls of the narrow streets keeping the room dim long after light reached down the alleyways. He would lie awake and listen to Luca stirring. Waiting for his hands to reach out. Moth shuddered at the memory. The scent of night-warm skin, the dimness of sight, the intensity of touch, the warmth of breath.

He pushed it away. Reached for the emails to wrap up the cards. He had too much to do to go back down those memories.

And Venice was gone. Memories captured on a postcard and stirred by early morning light. Puddles and an unbroken, unfulfilled promise.

ISABELLE LOOKED DOWN AT DERYN, the dimpled cheeks and tear-streaked eyes of the child asking for reassurance and tried to put a convincing smile on her face as they both stood on the porch step and watched Asha drive out of the courtyard. Listening to the car accelerate hard up the narrow hill.

Figuring her way between the breath-taking final shot of guilt trip Asha had delivered as she'd abandoned her child, and the decimated plans she had had for her day. Plans she had been carefully nurturing as she crossed the hallway toward her workroom and got caught by the unexpected squealing arrival of tyres on the gravel. She had opened the door half-expecting to see Kit. Not a fuming Asha practically throwing her child at her, along with a healthy dose of her irritation.

Isabelle breathed out and reminded herself that Asha was right, if not kind, in how she'd delivered the truth. That it must be hard for anyone looking in from the outside to see it any other way.

It's not as though you need to work, Isabelle.

Which was strange because all she could think of as she looked at Deryn was that her only dedicated workday of the week had just been sabotaged. From 8.30 am when Kate dropped Indigo at nursery, the sole external childcare they had, all the way through to teatime which she was excused from, and bedtime which was Indigo's favourite of the week, as she shared it with Rob. She need not emerge from her working, routine-free cocoon until the moment when Rob tapped on the door and dragged her into the study for a glass of wine and a long chat. Those had been the clouds of happiness she was drifting across the hallway on, two minutes earlier.

'It's not my fault, there's no one else I can ask,' Asha had explained as she hauled a crying Deryn out of the car. 'Your bloody cousin can't think beyond the farm. It's supposed to be his day and he's booked the contractors.'

'But Indigo is at nursery.'

'I know, but I have back-to-back appointments and a sale to finalise that's going to pay our mortgage for the month.'

Isabelle felt the beginning of the guilt wedge in those words. She took in Asha's own tear-streaked face, her impossible task of trying to work full time and raise Deryn, her need for perfection and hatred of failure, her crushing sense that she was letting her child down and the financial weight of the mortgage which she herself had asked Isabelle to saddle them with. She tried desperately to think about her orders, her calm and restorative day, the precisely stacked arrangement by which others were working to give her this chance about to be stolen by Asha.

'And it's not as though you need to work, Isabelle.'

The delay in her thought processes gave Asha time to push the thick end of the wedge in.

'I'll make it up to you, I promise.'

No, she wouldn't. Asha didn't have time for what she needed to do, let alone for catching up on favours. She squeezed Deryn's hand and picked her up into a cuddle, wiping away the tears staining her cheeks.

'Well, this is a surprise. Indigo is going to be so jealous. Let's get some snacks and decide what we're going to do.'

She carried Deryn through to the kitchen and narrowed in on her options for rescuing the day and her workload, reaching for bread, putting it into the toaster.

'We're going to have to think of what to do with ourselves,' she talked in a soft rolling tone to the child on her hip, soothing her with a confident voice if not words. She glanced out of the window down to the garden. On the patio below, where they had held Kate's housewarming party, the current group of guests were gathering for their assessment meeting. Day four of the week. Taking stock of where they'd got to. By the end of the day Kate would have them picking out the one thing they wanted to focus on first. By tomorrow morning they would be working on an action plan.

An action plan. Focus. Those were things she could do with herself. But Kate's classes were strictly for older women struggling with the slide into invisibility. They didn't cover young mothers whose life had been put on hold. Isabelle got the strawberry jam out of the fridge. Deryn needed comfort food, cuddles and a dose of happy confidence to restore her.

'I don't think we're going to be welcome in the garden today,' she told Deryn. Despite the warm weather and sunshine, which would have helped to cheer Deryn up, the garden was going to be full of small focus groups, hunched over their planning. Not the place for a young child, who would remind them all of what they'd given to others already. Plus, Kate would be fuming that she'd let Asha sabotage her working day.

'So, that's the garden out and the workroom out,' she told Deryn, handing her a square of sticky toast. 'Which means we'll have to find another task to do before Rob gets here.'

She had Gosia there from 4 pm when she picked Indigo up until 5 pm when Rob would appear from his early finish at work. That meant she had lost seven hours work which she would have to make up that night. She thought about missing out on her and Rob's evening chat, got another twinge of guilt, thought about curtailing it, felt even more mercenary. Added another two hours of unavailable time to her schedule. She would be working into the small hours for the next few days, and she'd still miss the deadline on at least half of those orders.

Isabelle ate a piece of jammy toast. Deryn wasn't the only one who needed comfort. She pulled her phone out and flicked it to her notes section. Kit had got her into this. A way of keeping track of the scattered thoughts which she struggled to keep together, and a way of tallying the promises she failed to keep to him about managing Riverdell better. Her day was undone, but it wasn't as though there weren't other pressing jobs she could turn to. They're just pinnies, she told herself, handing Deryn another piece of toast. She could hear Moth's voice telling her to get perspective. It's not war and famine, no one is going to die if their pinny arrives a day or two late. She thought about her response time and delivery ratings and winced. It's just pinnies. She scrolled down her list of notes. She needed a job she could do with a disappointed child.

Call the builders about the chimney repointing.

Kate had vetoed the suggestion. Scaffolding in her garden as she was launching her new business? Tell Kit to get lost, the damp patch in the unused bedroom can be repainted. If Isabelle ever has any guests.

Get the contractors in to landscape the access to the new building site.

Her toes curled at that. The thought of beginning the project across the way from the gates to Riverdell, developing the old barn and land into the exclusive houses they'd been granted planning for. Eco-friendly and flood plain resilient. She'd had enough of selling property and managing projects from the first year she had been left in charge of Riverdell. She'd used the excuse of a baby to postpone the plans. And Kate had insisted it not be done until winter because she needed the car parking space through summer. Kit had complained that winter was the worst time to start a landscaping job. Isabelle had avoided stepping into the argument long enough, she wasn't about to start today.

'Anyway, I don't need to begin a job that's going to take over more than today, do I?' she asked Deryn, swaying her on her hip.

She scrolled further down. Get the workroom walls stripped of their old paper and redecorated.

Unnecessary. Only she went in there and she was too busy to notice the old yellow damask wallpaper from Elsa's decor scheme.

Get the stairwell carpet replaced.

She supposed they could walk into town and look at carpets. She glanced at Deryn's sticky fingers. Without Indigo,

her concentration in the carpet shop would be too short-lived
to allow Isabelle to make a decision.

Replace the kitchen table.

Well, at least she had done one thing on her list. The
reclamation guy had practically passed out when she called
him and offered him the old table. A thought which
reminded her that the very same happy tradesman had also
asked her out for a drink, and she had never responded.
Isabelle pushed aside the uncomfortable thought and
focused on the table which gave her strength. The tweaks of
guilt she had once felt at changing things about Riverdell had
gone with that old table. It was as though it had held all the
bad memories of Hester's hatred, all the solid outline of what
Elsa had taught her. The round table pulled her new, peculiar
family together, small and intimate, close enough that she
could see them all clearly.

It was not a table that was going to host a family
Christmas dinner.

Isabelle frowned at the thought. Kit's ideas were seeping
into her mind. Possibly because he had rung her near daily to
remind her of them for the last month. Until the words were
beginning to build a storm in her head where she was trying
to keep them from Kate.

Kate, who was adamant that Kit had gone to Japan for
the sole purpose of getting pictures of the blossom, which
had no relevance to either Christmas decorations or paint
charts. That "outdoors" was her thing. That he'd broken the
rules of engagement in their Instagram battle. Kate, who had
stood outside inspecting the limp magnolia with Martin as
though both the tree and the gardener were personally
failing her. The solitary bloom that had unfurled had curled
and wilted overnight, watching the other buds crisp and die

without opening before itself falling to the ground. Isabelle had felt sorry for the tree. And for Kate. Though she no more understood how this rivalry had become fierce between them than she did the long, inconclusive conversation she'd had with Martin about the tree. Might it be dying? Might it merely be sick and recover next year? What did a tree sicken of? Apart from overwhelming expectations of its blossoming capacity.

No, Kate did not need to know about Christmas. She would outright declare Kit was taking advantage of Riverdell and encroaching on her territory. Kit, who appeared in their lives with no warning and left before they had the chance to catch a breath, arriving laden with gifts for the girls and disappearing without stopping the night. Kit who had all but disappeared from their lives, taking Hester with him. Kit who had thrown her the hideous idea of a family Christmas and dressed it with the irresistible bow of tempting Moth home. She tickled Deryn beneath the chin until a tentative smile appeared. Deryn was a quiet child, with watching eyes and a slow smile, growing up between two households and two languages. Isabelle could relate to her reserved watchfulness, even if it was a little unnerving. One sight of Indigo could change her, out would come the smiles and excitement, the happy Deryn with a warm giggle that stuck in her throat. Isabelle felt nervous. Seven whole hours with a child not her own.

'You'd like Moth,' she told her, smoothing Deryn's immaculate hair. Even in a panic Asha had got her child presentable. 'He looks a lot like your daddy. But he's quiet and serious like you. Right now, he's in Turkey, helping people who don't have a home. Sometimes I think he's forgotten he has one of his own.'

Deryn held up a sticky hand and began to suck jam residue from her fingers.

Right, she told herself, walking to the sink to find a cloth. 'Get a grip and find a job. Or you'll be doing first phonics all day long.'

She looked back at the table, she could try clearing that lot. Kate would have a fit if she moved all those magazines. If they did have a family Christmas, she was going to have to get the dining room ready. As well as the spare bedrooms languishing in their spare-furniture-filled hinterland.

'The dining room.' She looked down at Deryn. 'Even Kate will be happy if we tackle that. Though she'll probably only fill it with more catalogues. Come on, let's go have a look.'

She walked out of the kitchen, the quietness of the house rising up the stairwell. She opened the door to the dining room and stood looking inside. Deryn taking in the contents with her.

'I used to come in here to get away from everyone,' she told Deryn. Her voice coming up short and hollow against the stacks of furniture and filled boxes. 'A mouse couldn't get lost in here now. Goodness but your granny had a lot of furniture when she was here.'

'Granny,' Deryn echoed, looking over her shoulder.

'No, she's not here. Probably a good thing. She was never any good at getting rid of stuff.' Isabelle walked into the small pathway that snaked round the table. Its surface piled high with boxes made the kitchen table look spruce. 'Maybe this is a bad idea. It might be easier to simply clear the kitchen table.'

Isabelle visualised telling Kit they would have to use the kitchen for Christmas and got a clear image of his disdain filling the phone screen. He was probably right, she really ought to start well in advance. There was certainly enough to do. Upstairs only two bedrooms were available to sleep in, and even they looked more like school dorms than bedrooms. And she couldn't really claim Indigo's babyhood as excuse anymore for the chaotic state of her house. And, after all, it wasn't as though she needed to work.

'Okay, let's do this. Christmas or not.'

'Christmas,' Deryn repeated.

'I never said that. Don't you tell Kate I said that.'

'Christmas.'

WITHOUT INDIGO there to lead Deryn astray, Isabelle was finding a soothing aspect to Asha's daughter. She was quieter, more contented than her own child.

Perhaps it was the five months age difference but when she gave Deryn a box and put her in the middle of the hall to empty it, Deryn would stay there and do it. Giving Isabelle the chance to go and find another box and slowly make her way further into the dining room. If it had been Indigo, by the time Isabelle made it back to the hall, she would have lost her daughter.

By lunchtime, when Kate came upstairs to escape her groups for an hour, expecting the kitchen to herself and Isabelle in the workroom, she was pulled from the kitchen by the sound of Deryn chattering to porcelain statues she'd lined up on the sofa. Each on their own cushion. Isabelle walked through from the east corridor with another box in her hand to see Kate stood in the kitchen doorway, mouth agape at the ungodly mess a nearly three-year-old can create in three hours, a storm forming in her eyes.

'I know what you're going to say...' Isabelle headed it off.

'... this is supposed to be your...'

'... but perhaps you could save the lecture until later?' Isabelle cocked her head at a listening Deryn.

Kate drew her lips into a tight line of stifled irritation, sucking in the reprimand.

'Christmas.' Deryn filled the silence.

Isabelle made a careful point of not blinking and put the box down, treading carefully through the maze of ornaments, china, books, photo albums and lamps that Deryn had left across the floor.

'What on earth are you doing?' Kate asked.

'Emptying the dining room.'

'Why?'

'I couldn't think of anything better to do, under the circumstances.' Isabelle glanced at Deryn, with an emphasis on the last word of her sentence.

'This is completely unacceptable.'

'I know it's a mess, don't worry, we'll get it sorted.' Isabelle straightened from putting the box down. In four hours Gosia would be back, she could only imagine the uproar that would cause.

'I wasn't talking about the mess, Isabelle.'

'I know that too.' Isabelle looked back at her. 'What could I do? She has to work, apparently I don't.'

'Is that what she said?'

Isabelle stared back, still stinging from the morning comment. Kate's irritation sagged from her taut chest in a frustrated huff and she moved into the hallway toward Isabelle, looking about at the scattered contents of the boxes.

Kate picked up a china owl and scowled at it. 'Elsa had the most hideous propensity for knick-knacks. You should pack it all up and send it to her. The fact that I don't have to work has nothing at all to do with the fact that I need to work. No one gets to tell me what I do and don't need to do. Now, you keep walking straight past that sodding dining room and into your workroom. Deryn and I shall have lunch together. You've got an hour. I'll bring you coffee and a snack.'

Kate handed her the owl as they met in the middle of the mess.

'But I've started this now,' Isabelle said.

'Yes, and it will take a month of sorting, there's nothing lost by doing an hour's work in the middle.' Kate gave her a hug, speaking close to her ear, 'If anyone told me the same, I'd stab them in the foot with a gardening fork. Your customers are as valued as hers.'

Isabelle hugged her back, the owl held out at a distance. 'But I don't have a mortgage to pay.'

'No, but you've got a bigger bloody house to look after and a child to set an example to, same as hers.' Kate pulled back and gave her a tough grin. 'That was a mean comment, she better not say it again. No go on, you work. Deryn, darling, come make toasties with me. Shall we bring some of those with us?' Kate didn't even try to fight Deryn clutching two figurines in her hands. She simply hoisted the child, the porcelain and the tail end of a cushion onto her hip and headed back to the kitchen. 'I think you should take those home with you, Mummy will love them. In fact, I think we should pack a special box full of them for her.'

Isabelle set the china owl down on the table and went to her workroom, ignoring the open dining room door and the dust swirling through the air in the sunshine.

. . .

BY THREE O'CLOCK her patience was wearing thinner than her
jeans. The dining room was empty of boxes and somehow
fuller of furniture. You couldn't safely walk through the
hallway without risking an ankle injury and Deryn was quiet
to the verge of tears. Isabelle scooped her up from clinging to
her leg, made them both cocoa and retreated to the study
where she made a nest on the sofa with blankets and tried to
read to her. Over an hour left until Indigo came home.
Isabelle tried not to think about how tired Indigo was on a
Thursday afternoon, or that the girls would barely have time
to adjust to each other when Asha arrived in a rush to collect
Deryn, or that it would probably leave Indigo in tears, just as
Rob arrived. She pushed away the desire to pity herself as
Deryn snuck from the sofa for the third time and walked
toward the far shelves filled with the neat lines of old diaries,
finding her courage to tuck her fingers into their slim spines
and peeling them from the shelf, unsuckering the well stuck
together leather covers. Isabelle retreated to her desk and
looked at the current copy, phone in hand, needing help and
stuck on a choice.

Ring Kit and admit she was making a start on sorting the
house and ask him to sell the redundant furniture.

Or ring Steve, the reclamation guy whose drink offer
she'd never replied to, and ask him if he was still interested in
buying her rejects.

Stuck between the gloating look on Kit's face and the
heap of coal she would add to the furnace of his plans, having
not yet told Kate. Or the sparkle and smugness on Kate's face
if she invited Steve back into the house again. Because Kate
did not miss a whisper.

When Indigo had been no more than two months old and
permanently leeched to her side, Isabelle had had a great

excuse to decline, worn out with the failure to get Indigo to sleep or feed, disbelieving that anyone would ask her to dress up and go out socialising when she could barely get a brush to her hair or keep her breath fresh. She'd mumbled her excuses, promised to think about it and ignored the house full of unwanted furniture ever since. For a swift delicious moment, she considered putting all the boxes and furniture back, refusing to do Christmas and evading the whole issue for another few years.

Glancing out of the window she saw the ailing tree in the courtyard. Its leaves curled and warped at the edges. She couldn't ignore life forever. Hiding in this bubble of motherhood. Deep inside, she knew it was unhealthy. That she had a life to get back to.

She flicked open the MacBook, watching Deryn making piles from the old diaries. Dust gusting out from between their pages, surfing across the top edges with the delighted puffs of a child's breath. Isabelle pulled up her inbox, scanning it.

Nothing from Moth. It had been weeks now. She wished he would come home. Or that she could take Indigo and go see him. Sit and talk. Really talk. About where he was, what he was doing. Though even as she looked for his name and felt a hollow pinch inside at its absence, she knew the questions that haunted her were about her own life. Where she was, what she was doing. Questions that Kate and Kit both snuck in round the edges of their conversations about work, child, home. Little pokes at the quiet and happy muddle that her life had become. These notions that she should be somewhere, doing something grander than managing as she was.

The emptiness of her life showed in the steadying decline of her inbox. Her colleagues in Bollywood had dropped her name from their lists. Her friends in that world had become clearly work associates, their friendship a smokescreen of regularity and proximity. Moth's emails had reduced to ever shorter snippets as he swam into the larger waters of life with almost a job. Luca had emailed her. She opened it to read of his latest frustration with work. The feeling that he'd entered a job believing it was a stepping-stone, to find himself on a ducking stool instead, persistently pushed below the lesser waters of administration work. Asking always if she'd heard from Moth, what were his plans? She could feel his loneliness in the constancy of his emails. Holding his hopes together with outward effort. Weren't they both waiting for Moth to come home and give them meaning and purpose? What if she could tempt Moth back, invite Luca to join them. Her heart thrilled with the idea of seeing them both again. Of seeing Nat finally reunited with her brother. Indigo finally meeting the missing man in their lives. A thrill that fuelled the desire to ignore her immediate hurdle. Damn Kit, he knew exactly how to tempt her to action.

She couldn't call Kit, not yet, not without talking to Kate first. And Steve couldn't have possibly remembered her for over two years. He wasn't the sort of man to wait that long on a promise. What man was? Other than Luca.

She glanced again at Deryn, her clothes now dusted with a shade of grey that reminded Isabelle with a shudder of the endless dust that the alterations on the house had stirred. Kit's promise that it would be swept away had been false. Th house still had a habit of depositing sudden falls of the stuff in unequal measure in the oddest of places. A handrail thick with grime, a shelf coated above one immaculate. It drove Gosia mad with inconsistency. Isabelle pulled her phone out and found the number, took an encouraging breath and rang Steve.

'Whorled Reclamation,' a woman's voice answered. Isabelle's heart leapt with hope.

'Hi, I was wondering if Steve was available?'

'He's with a customer, oh, hang on... can I ask who's calling, please?'

'Isabelle Threlfall.'

She heard her voice related at a distance, then the woman's voice came back. It sounded young and vibrant. Chirpy, Kate would call it. Watching Deryn bang diaries together to raise bigger dust devils, Isabelle felt far from chirpy.

'Hi, he's not able to come to the phone, can I take a message?'

Isabelle wondered if he was engaged with a customer or returning her indifference for two years. She felt an odd mix of guilt and gratitude in the dismissal. Perhaps she could get rid of the furniture and have evaded the date.

'Yes, please. Could you tell him I'm finally getting round to clearing out and I'd like him to come and take some furniture, if he's still interested.'

'Can I take a number please, I'll get him to call you back.'

'Of course.' Isabelle gave her phone number and put the phone down, feeling dissatisfied with the inconclusive result. Now she was waiting for him to call back and unable to call Kit in the meantime and make progress. She glanced at the clock on her phone. Forty more minutes to go. Downstairs she knew Kate would be trying to squeeze each drop from the clock. Here she sat with time on her hands, praying for it to slip away.

. . .

AT HALF PAST eight that evening, Rob walked into the work-room with a glass of wine in each hand. Isabelle let out the caged breath she had been sewing at high speed on and tried to let go of the hope she might finish one more pinny. He'd given her an extra fifteen minutes already.

'Right, where do you want me?'

'Pardon?' Isabelle asked with a laugh as she swivelled on the stool away from her sewing machine, pulling a Ludford out from under the foot.

'You need some help to make up for Asha's inroads into your time today.' He put his glass down on the mantelpiece and looked round the room, ankle deep in fabric cuttings for a safe place to put hers. She held her hand out for it, took a sip and popped it on the stack of drawers to her right, away from all the fabrics. 'I'm not saying I can sew a stitch, and I strongly recommend against arming me with scissors, but I have a Christmas degree in packaging. Where are your finished orders?'

'You want to help me pack?' Isabelle asked in disbelief.

'Don't you trust me?'

'Not trust you. Are you kidding me? You're one of the few I do trust.'

Rob had done the impossible and turned their night of drunken stupidity and morning-after embarrassment into a friendship that she would be crushed to lose. Released from his withered marriage to Hester, he had grown younger, dapper. Perfectly fashionable in his combination of dead men's clothes and vintage tweed waistcoats. Worn with an air of unexpected, mid-life liberation that spruced up his greying hair and made it look suave. His single lifestyle had taken a taken a stone of weight and the crush of an unhappy relation-ship from him. She remembered the day, shortly after she returned from Italy, that Rob walked into her study with a bunch of flowers, an abject apology for his foolishness and a promise to be a better friend to her, if she could find it in her heart to put the past behind them. She had held her breath on the disbelief it would work and watched him become her staunchest ally. There with Kate the night she went into labour. There for Indigo at every major event since, birthdays, Easter, Christmas. Part of their haphazard family life at Riverdell.

'Though I might dispute your wrapping skills,' Isabelle contended. 'They're a lot more enthusiastic than effective.'

'Well, they're the only ones you're being offered. Show me the way.'

Isabelle stood and moved to the table. On it were completed orders, stacked high, with their order sheets leaved between the fabric. She demonstrated to him how the Ludford folded one way, the Whitcliffe another. How the tissue paper had to be placed to minimise the creases. The shallow boxes they were packaged in, the plastic outers encasing them. When he had done one successfully with fumbling fingers three times slower than her own, she returned to the machine.

'You know I'm hopeless at small talk when I'm sewing, right?'

'Thank God for that, I've had my fill of waffle this week. I'll talk, you can companionably ignore me.'

She half listened as he packed with slow but precise concentration, fine tuning with contented hums as he got more confident. The boxes shuffling in a soft slide across the calico tabletop as the hour passed, listening to his week's news. The latest efforts of the partners to bully him into working five days a week. Rob stopped over on a

Thursday night, stayed for breakfast on Friday mornings and left at lunchtime to do a half day at work. A choice that seemed to suggest he wasn't taking law seriously enough for his new role as partner. Rob thought they were all serious enough and should work less. That vexation released, Rob moved on to tales about the daggers lurking in the chess committee meetings as he attempted to encourage widening the circle to mentor younger players. As he settled into complaining of his ambitions to climb the mountains of Europe with his rambling club that never amounted to anything more than a different path up Cadair Idris, Isabelle interrupted him.

'Rob, do you think I'm drifting?'

'Hmm?' he looked up from his packing, conversation stopped in mid-flow. 'Drifting in what way?'

'Through life?' she looked out of the darkened window across the river to the woods. 'I fear I've lost my way a bit.'

'How so?'

'Um, I don't know. It feels as though I ought to be doing more?'

'More than working at ten o'clock at night while raising a child and running a house the size of the Titanic?' he asked with a curious curl of amusement to his voice.

'Don't tease me. I mean, rather than working all hours, shouldn't I be working toward something?'

'Something with a capital S?'

'Yes, exactly.' She looked down at the ties she was forming and began sewing again.

'I might not be the best person to ask. Life got infinitely better for me the moment I decided to give up on those capital letters.'

'I think Kit and Kate feel I'm slacking a bit.'

'They both need to stop hiding their own failings in a work ethic that would leave the rest of us dead.'

'Asha thinks I don't need to work.'

'Yes, I heard.' Rob's voice tightened behind her. 'I should think she might want to avoid Kate for a few days on the back of that.'

Isabelle lifted the feed foot and flipped the ties around under the needle, clamping them back down and sewing along the other edge.

'You know she'll be happier once this damn vote is done,' Rob added. 'It's unsettling all of us, but it can't be easy for any European living here.'

Isabelle didn't respond. Asha's opinion of the Brexit vote was scathing. An insult not just to herself but her own child. The fact that she and Asha shared the same opinion was lost in the fact that all of Asha's clients with houses like Riverdell were all for the exit. It had become a wealth thing, this vote, and by extension Isabelle was complicit. There had been a deeper dig in the statement that she didn't need to work. A positioning.

'What sort of a Something are you feeling guilty over not achieving? Rob moved the conversation on.

'I wish I could put my finger on it.' She pushed the last bump of the gathered seams of the tie through the foot, reversed and disengaged. Pulling out the result with a sharp glance at the stitch line. 'Moth always had this immense sense of a plan for his life. I miss that. He gave me some conviction that I could find a purpose too, rather than swinging where the wind dictated.'

'I think you've taken other people's opinions too much to heart.' Rob's voice burred with irritation. She glanced up at him, but he was tussling with tape on the corner of a package and frowning in concentration. 'I thought we'd both managed to get rid of that burden. Do you enjoy your life, Isabelle?'

'Yes, of course.'

'But?'

'But...' Isabelle tried to capture that doubt pulled out by Asha's irritation, stirred by a day of emptying the dining room. A but that lay tangled between thoughts of Moth, Christmas and furniture. '... perhaps there's more?'

He tapped the package down with a final fumble and smiled at it before turning to catch her watching him. 'Addictive stuff this packaging, perhaps I should consider working for Amazon if the partners kick me out?'

She smiled at him, raising doubtful eyebrows.

'Your life is full, Isabelle,' he told her. 'If you think there may be more you want, perhaps you first need to consider making space for it?'

'How do I do that?'

'Well, perhaps think about how much you are doing for others rather than for yourself.'

It was as close to a criticism as Rob would come. Kate on the other hand would spend all weekend complaining she was too soft on Asha. Perhaps neither of them needed to hear about Kit's plans yet.

'How about you finish that one and let's have ten minutes sit down before we call it a night? You can get up stupid early and get back to it. I'll go refresh our glasses.' He patted the parcel in satisfaction, collected their glasses and left the room saying, 'Don't make me come and throw you out.'

It sent a shiver of memory through her. Moth had told her nearly the exact same thing the last night they spent in her workroom. Had she moved in a circle back to the same place of searching while others had moved onward to a place of conviction and purpose? She stood away from the machine and glanced one more time across the river, shimmering in the lights from high above the town. The sky full of thick dark clouds and threatening rain. She drew the curtains and headed to the study, glad for the break. Walked in to find the diaries scattered across the floor. She knelt and began to gather them up, piling them in front of the bookcase.

'Oh, dear Lord, what happened here?' Rob asked as he walked back in. Wine glasses and a packet of her favourite biscuits in hand.

'Deryn.'

'I suppose we should be glad it wasn't Indigo.' He put the glasses down and bent to scoop up diaries, delivering them to her growing piles.

'They all need putting back in order.' She began to search for the years on their spines.

'How about you do something radical and shove them all back on anyhow?'

'Robert Jameson, wash your mouth out with soap.'

'You kill yourself if you want to, I'm going to sit and drink wine and eat biscuits.' He moved away. 'I've got 1836 when you find 1835.'

She looked through the piles in dwindling enthusiasm and gave up, moving to his side on the sofa and taking a biscuit, adding the disarrayed pile of diaries to her list for the weekend.

Rob was flicking through the diary in his hand, frowning at it. She nibbled the edge of her biscuit, dipped it in the red wine and sucked the sour combination of chocolate and tannin.

'Well, well, will you look at that.'

'What?'

Rob had flicked from the end of the diary to the front and held it up with the inner cover opened. There was a stamped insignia on the inside.

'Do you know what that is?'

'No, should I?'

'The British East India Company.'

'Oh.'

'I suppose it should come as no surprise. Near every wealthy family in the country had their fingers in that particular pie.' Rob returned to flicking through the pages.

'Is that something I need to feel hideously guilty about?'

'There's probably worse skeletons in many old families if you look hard enough, Isabelle. Wealth comes to the few by way of the impoverished many. I should have guessed really, after all you've got old Clive of India's blood himself, even if rather diluted. You might want to consider letting a historian have a look at these, there could be some data in there of interest to an India scholar.'

She took the book out of his hands and flipped through it. The diaries came from a binder in Italy, courtesy of a running order that Elsa had left established for her. They had changed since this one, but the same shape and style of page echoed that which sat on her desk.

'I thought they recorded the same nonsense as I put in it. Birthdays, visitors, house damage, ill magnolias. I haven't got a clue what to put in there most days.'

She glanced at the meticulous handwriting, heavily slanting to the right. Wondering who had owned the house in 1836.

'Well, Clive's son married the Earl of Powis' daughter and took over the family seat himself. Their ailing wealth was refreshed by Clive's ventures in India. I think it was one of their younger granddaughters who married a Threlfall. The Company was still trading when your distant ancestor lived here. Look, that's a record of imports.' Rob pointed out the notes that looked like tangled yarn to her. 'Historical importance I'd say. Maybe don't bother putting them back on the shelves, see if the British Library might be interested. Clear yourself some shelf space into the bargain.'

'Shouldn't I read them first?'

'That depends on how brave you're feeling. You never know what you might unearth digging in old diaries.'

'If it's anything like I add in now, it will be nothing but yawn factor.'

'What's wrong with the magnolia?' Rob changed the subject.

'Martin doesn't know.'

'And what are you doing with the dining room?'

'Clearing it out.'

Rob raised an eyebrow at her too innocent voice. She grimaced at him.

'I was thinking about Christmas, that's all.'

'In May?' he asked. 'That's rather forward planning for you.'

She grimaced into her wine glass.

'What are you up to?' he asked.

She puffed out in tiredness and threw the diary down on the low table, sank back into the sofa cushions and tucked her feet up. 'Kit wants to organise a family Christmas at Riverdell.'

'How big a family Christmas?' he asked.

She thought about it, the quiet days she and Indigo had shared with Rob and Kate for the last two years. Asha and

James away in Swansea. Kit conjuring Christmas itself onto the exclusive streets of London. Hester kept firmly away with the workload. Moth travelling through Europe.

'I have no idea,' she admitted. 'Though knowing Kit, it will be pretty huge.'

'Intriguing,' he mused, sitting back into his corner. 'I wonder who you're doing that for.' His comment was a statement, not a question seeking an answer. It was the practised face and tone of a lawyer, she realised, and felt a rush of gratitude that he had produced it.

'THIS IS your room for as long as you're here.' Kit opened the first-floor doorway and let Jay go ahead. 'We're on the top floor and I've no other guests expected.'

Kit watched Jay walk toward the bed. It always took him back, walking into this room. To a place where he'd known only comfort and truth. It was hallowed ground, left undisturbed and safe for those rare moments when he too needed to wrap himself in a duvet and pretend the world no longer existed.

'This was my mother's room,' he told Jay from the doorway.

'It looks different to the rest of the house.' Jay took in the decor.

The old furniture, the faded wallpaper, the delicate desk in front of the window with its lockable drop-down writing shelf. Kit could remember waking up at night in the bed and seeing her sat there, staring out the window before scribbling with a pressure and speed that scratched the paper to a hum. Holding his breath so she wouldn't notice him, seduced back into sleep by the same noise that had woken him.

'Yeah, Granny's taste. A bit grim, I know, but it's my memory of them both.'

'And you're letting me stay in here?' Jay asked, running his hand over the plush eiderdown.

'Umm, I figured you'd have better manners than to kill yourself in my little shrine to my mother.'

'I'm not going to kill myself.'

'Glad to hear it.' Kit didn't believe him. Jay might not have known he was on the path to self-destruction, but in Kit's experience a person always rejected the truth with a high tone and Jay's voice could have reached the ugly three-lobed glass light fitting.

'What's this?' Jay had reached the far side of the room and was looking at the chest.

Kit had put it there, against the only spare wall, where it rather marred the feel of the room. Annoyingly adrift in the space between the desk and one of the elegant Georgian chests of drawers that sat either side of the bed, where it blocked the drawers from opening. Its only advantage was that he couldn't see it on his nightly visits to the door of the room, which he would open, breath in the air of history and close with a calmer mind. Only when no one was here though, Adele would think that all sorts of elitist white nostalgia. He stayed within the doorway, leaning against its solid edge.

'That's my mother's chest, apparently filled with her old diaries.' He scanned the room, checking to make sure it was acceptable. Old and outdated he could cope with. But he'd had to pick up the cleaners before on not keeping the spare rooms perfectly ready for guests. 'Elsa dropped it on me a few years ago and told me to read the ghastly things.'

'Did you?'

'Couldn't open it.'

Jay glanced at him with a frown. Kit could cope with that frown. It was a facial muscle away from the pit of despair he'd seen in the corner of Jay's spare bedroom.

'And no pulling the bedclothes into the corner,' Kit told him. 'You sleep on the bed, in the bed, under the covers.'

'And that stopped you?' Jay ignored his effort at distraction.

'Stopped me what?' Kit played annoying. If there was one way to engage Jay it was to act ignorant. He couldn't stand it.

'From opening it?' Jay asked.

'It seemed a good enough sign to leave well alone.' Kit shrugged. 'I mean, would you? Want to read your mother's diaries?'

'Hell yes, why wouldn't you?'

'I guess you didn't know my mother. I'm going to run you a bath.'

'What?'

'You need a bath, a proper long bath. I don't mind you slipping beneath my mother's covers, but you could at least do it without a three-week scum on your dick, or however long you were holed up in there.'

Kit had turned away when Jay asked, 'Is that your mother?'

It pulled him up, made him grimace. The portrait hung where it always had. On the wall opposite the bed, over the fireplace. One of only two pictures in the house that had not been sold to make way for Kit's own taste. Granny had been restored to the drawing room after redecoration. His mother's portrait had never been moved. It suited the time warp nature of the bedroom.

'She's stunning,' Jay said in his silence.

It was a rare and haunting image. His mother's face and cleavage filled the space. A solemn stare daring you to look away. Her hair gathered in loose chignons to each side of her face, her eyes, deep pools of shadow and query. A touch of blush in the glistening finish of her lips, parted enough to suggest she was about to speak. Soft velvet folds of dark purple draping down her shoulders. The dress still hung in the closet, a halter-neck affair that gathered to above the navel, slashed and flared from the hip. Kit liked to stand and look into her eyes on quiet nights of doubt. Making himself stronger in that gaze.

'Yes, she was.'

Kit walked down the corridor toward the grand bathroom. When he'd taken over the house and renovated it, he'd made the difficult choice about how best to update the bedroom and bathroom ratio. Most houses on the street had long since converted to all ensuite, as each owner came and went and upgraded it for the next price-grabbing sale. It was ridiculous how house values were notched up or down according to the balance between those rooms. A lucrative arrangement he encouraged all his clients to pursue. As he had no intention of ever selling it, Kit had resisted the loss of the elegant proportions and finer architectural details of the room.

He opened the door and called down the hallway to Jay, 'Bathroom's in here, we've got our own upstairs so it's all yours.'

The bathroom was a large and generous room with chairs beside the freestanding tub, a full ceramic suite and a mammoth walk-in shower. Kit put the plug in the jacuzzi bath and turned the taps to begin filling. He looked over the collection of bath salt jars, hand mixed batches from the boutique in Old Market. They cost him a fortune and ended up getting replaced, but Jay was in luck, they were fresh only a few weeks ago when he'd gone on a massive splurge to ease his irritation with Isabelle. Chamomile, calming and relaxing. No, he didn't want Jay calm. Calm was not his style. Lavender, tranquillity and pleasure. Hmm, maybe not yet. Rose petal, easing sadness and heartache. Kit reached for the blushed shade of the jar, scooped a generous mound into the bathwater with the wooden ladle and swirled his hand to dissolve the grit. The scent of rose lifted with the steam and eased into his nostrils. Sadness and heartache, that was the problem with Jay.

Kit walked over to the wide mirror across the sink and watched the steam start to rise from behind him as he checked his face. It had been a long day. A 5 am start to get to London and finish the final tweaks to the last customer's Christmas decor. The new Mrs Fforde had not been the easiest of customers. But it was never easy being the third wife for your first family Christmas. And if it had taken delicate extra handling and last-minute adjustments to the lights in the twenty-foot-high tree outside the Kensington mansion, who was Kit to judge? And now that he had finished Mrs Fforde and all his customers were happy in their Christmas nests, the month was empty. Stretching ahead of him all the way to the end of the year. Boredom held at bay by Jay's crisis, but what after that?

Kit massaged the skin up his cheekbones, away from the edge of his eye socket. The problem with phone filters was they made it harder to accept reality. Half a century's worth of lines were being skilfully underplayed by following the YouTube Asahi tutorials that Kate raved about, encouraged with a slight touch of makeup. A flash of eyeliner here, a flicker of colour there. A gentle hint lifting everything upwards. Enough that his customers would notice and wonder, not enough to discomfort them, finely tuned to stop them from staring at him and counting the years in his lines like the innards of a cut tree.

'Is that a bathtub or a swimming pool?' Jay asked from the door. 'Did I disturb your admiration?'

Kit turned from the mirror, 'Agitation more like.' He leant against the edge of the marble vanity counter, noticing Jay's shoeless feet, which had whispered down the hallway and under the sound of the running water. 'I find new lines in every mirror.'

'Stop looking in mirrors?' Jay suggested.

'Come on, in you get.'

'I don't swim too well.'

They stared at each other across the oak floorboards. Original ten-inch width. Lifted and replaced on top of the snake's wedding of plumbing the bathroom had needed. Kit kicked his own shoes off.

'You aren't expecting me to share that bath?' Jay asked, glancing from Kit to the bath and back.

'Why, would that make you uncomfortable?'

'No.'

Kit grinned as Jay's voice went higher again.

'I'll go get snacks, you get in.' Kit walked toward the door and paused, glancing down at Jay's folded arms, how they sat on the expanded waistline. 'Healthy snacks.'

WHEN KIT GOT BACK to the bathroom, tray in hand, laden with the platter of meat, sushi, olives and salad, glasses, bottle of wine and hand baked oat biscuits, he paused a moment outside the closed door and listened for the swirl of water. Inside he could hear Jay, deep breaths and long sighs interspersed with silence and the pulsing rhythm of water. He opened the door and walked in. Locks were not his style. Hence, if they were someone's style, like his mother for instance, best to respect the warning.

'Don't you knock?' Jay asked, sitting up in the bath from where he'd been floating toward the top. Kit watched his dick disappear beneath the waves, followed by the bulging stomach. Upright in the bath, clinging to the sides, Jay retained the physical neatness he'd always had. The muscled shoulders and arms, the taut pecs. Kit had caught him just in time. The weight had only spread across his stomach, hid below the beard on his jawline. A month of redress and there was a chance it would all be gone.

'In my own home?' Kit put the tray down on the table beside the bath. 'With a potential suicide in my bath large enough to drown in. No, I don't knock.'

Before Jay could draw breath to protest, Kit pulled off the gown he'd changed into and stepped into the bath. Watching Jay stare pointedly away and scurry his legs backwards. Yep, uncomfortable as hell, that was what male nudity did to Jay.

'You won't mind if I join you?' Kit asked as he settled into the water with a happy sigh.

'Do I have a bloody choice?' Jay asked, avoiding him until the water had settled round his chest.

'I need to make up for lost time.' Kit passed him a glass of wine. 'I've been a crap friend.'

'I can cope with the disappointment better than the apology.' Jay took the glass and pulled into his corner.

Kit stretched his legs out into the warm water, feeling the swirl of bubbles inside and out.

'What is this stuff?' Jay looked at his drink with distrust and a sour twist to his face.

'Riesling Sekt,' Kit told him. 'I thought the bubbles went with the bath.'

'You don't have beer?'

'You're banned from beer. Along with burgers, chips, kebabs and whatever other poison you've been putting in your system for the last few months.'

'I want to go home,' Jay complained.

'Not until next year.'

'I have work.'

'No, you don't. You obviously haven't worked in months, probably since Uggs died. You aren't going home, or back to work, until I'm confident you're back to the miserable, cranky, fit-as-fuck Jay I know.'

Jay pursed his lips and tightened his jaw.

'And definitely not until you can hear Uggs' name without wanting to punch me.'

Jay glared mutinously at him from the far end of the bath.

'Drink up, buttercup.' Kit emptied his first glass and reached for the bottle. 'Sushi or olives?'

'Neither.'

'Fine, have salami-wrapped rocket.' Kit held out the tempter with a pair of baby silver tongs, which Jay ignored. 'Don't make me drop it in the tub and go looking for it.'

Jay ratcheted in his lips another notch and took the meat roll out of the tongs.

'How bloody civilised.'

'I'm glad you approve.' Kit topped up his glass and sat back. Jay put the roll in his mouth without a bite and flickered his eyes to the plate.

'Surely, you have other more important people to boss

about at this time of year?' Jay asked. 'You aren't serious about me being here until next year?'

'My plans got downgraded when I found you in the corner of your room.'

The door to the bathroom opened again and they both looked up to see Adele in the doorway.

'I thought I heard voices!'

Kit felt his stomach clench as it did every time Adele entered a room. Aware that he was staring and unable to look away. It had been the same since they bumped into each other at a party hosted by the Kagalovsky family in London. They'd both attended aware that an invite wasn't really an invite. Kit downplaying to the irritated Adewale Ogunleye how well he knew the family, avoiding mentioning that he'd worked for them and innumerable associates for the last fifteen years, while trying to grasp the nuances of his mouthful of a name. Agreeing that yes, taking money from the Russians was both a social sin and probably a political crime, and no, the fact that the Russians were bankrolling his latest dance show was not a form of artistic commercialism. By the end of the evening Kit had taken even more of a mouthful and realised he was smitten with the incomparable physique of the guy while feeling permanently half a step behind him.

'Jay? Is that you behind that beard?' Adele walked into the room and let the door swing shut behind him. Homing in on the snacks. 'What's for supper?'

'Yes, it's him. Hors d'oeuvre only, I haven't thought any further. Jay's come to stay for a while.' Kit offered Adele his own wine glass. 'Here, borrow mine.'

'What are we drinking?' Adele threw himself in the chair

nearest Jay, where Kit had full view of him, and grimaced disappointment from behind Jay's back.

It wouldn't hurt Adele to cope with guests. There were times when their shared living arrangement sometimes felt a shave too close to domestication. It was part of them both being too busy to play the game. Kit had been used to turning up at all hours and pleasing himself when he ate or slept. Adele was used to a London lifestyle that paid lip service to his bachelor flat. Whenever they ended up in Bristol, Kit was expected to assume the domestic role. Which he hadn't realised he didn't enjoy when it was expected of him. Any more than he enjoyed Adele coming and going as he pleased while Kit felt judged for not being there when needed. That was the problem with age, Kit realised. It made you insecure. It made you do things you wouldn't have contemplated twenty years younger.

'Long day?' he asked Adele. Watching as he tipped his head back and necked the wine. Watching the shudder of that defined lump in his throat, the thought slipping below the neckline of Adele's v neck T-shirt with it. 'Are you joining us?'

That was also the problem with a younger lover, the inability to take his eyes away. The physical seduction of it catching him at such odd moments. He watched Jay tense at the idea of more naked men in his bath and tried not to smirk at him. Adele naked was a sight to make any man feel insecure and that was without the specific nature of Lydia's humiliation to consider. Adele considered, looking like he wanted to get in the bath but not share it either.

'There's steak in the fridge, how about we cook steak and frits?' Kit suggested.

'I'm trying to persuade him to turn vegan,' Adele told Jay.

'Do you have any idea how damaging meat is to your libido. Fries your dick. All he ever wants to eat is steak.'

'You're talking to a man who ate kebab for a month,' Kit retorted, noticing that the suggestion they could cook together had been ignored.

'How's life anyway, Jay?' Adele asked. 'We haven't seen you for ages. Where you been?'

'Taking some time out,' Kit responded. 'And now he's come to stop for Christmas.'

'Great, you can help me weather the strop,' Adele told Jay, who was twisting his head to look over his shoulder at Adele while trying to keep as much of himself submerged in the bath as possible. 'He's been vile ever since Isabelle rang him.'

Kit smiled as Jay looked at him with a raised eyebrow. He would have preferred to keep that to himself. He was trying to prove to Jay that he was being a good friend.

'Well, as you're not getting in, how about I get out and we go sort some vegan dinner?' Kit stood up from the bath, the water noisily revealing himself and splashing up Jay's face. Adele's eyes trailing downwards. Kit knew his body was stir-ring. Jay looked pointedly at the most boring detail of the tile work on the far wall. A smile crept into the corners of Adele's eyes and Kit felt more accommodating. He could cope with vegan dinner. And the bad mood would soon be gone. Adele stood up and grasped a folded towel from the rail, wrapped it round his torso as Kit stepped toward him. Close up, the irri-tation dispersed.

'Yes, it was a long day,' Adele admitted.

'Well, let's do something about that,' Kit said, kissing the side of his neck, watching Adele close his eyes in pleasure.

'Yes, why don't you two go and do something about that,' Jay said from the bath. 'I'll look after the snacks.'

Kit went and picked up the plate and took it away. 'You've had enough snacks. Dinner will be in an hour, come hungry. And lose the beard.'

'Oh, come on,' Jay complained. He picked up the wine bottle before Kit could and swished to the far side of the bath. 'I'm at least keeping the wine for company.'

'Ok, you keep the wine.' Kit grabbed Adele's hand and headed for the door. 'I've got company enough.'

5

I don't know whether to cry, scream or howl.

Will he end up hating me or forgiving me? Damn these vile decisions I must make, wondering if I will be right in the end or have traumatised him beyond recovery.

He resisted the school move from the day I told him and refused to speak to me as I left. I came home in floods and Granny got out the vodka, gave us both a shot and left me with the bottle. She was subdued. I know she feels guilty, but she shouldn't. When my tears are over, I will make sure to comfort her too. She struggled on for the last two years, but it was too much to ask her to hold the fort and keep him in check. It was either give up the job and come home to be a proper mum or send him away to board and save my career. And Granny made sure I knew that was the choice, she didn't butter up the options one jot.

Damn this love that burns me up. Damn it to hell and three times back. What did I ever think would happen to me as a mother but that I would be chewed up and spat back out? He hates me for sure and I hope he gives the masters merry hell. Will Granny end up right or will I regret listening to someone else, again, as I do whenever I think of you?

I wish you were here, that you could help me with these choices. You always were the anchor to my thoughts.

He was not challenged enough at the local state school, bored stupid, riling his teachers and the children. I'm not convinced he'll be any less bored at public school but perhaps the challenge of competing with other boys who think themselves above him might help. Kit will never be bullied, at least I know that much. He'd punch first and ask forgiveness later. Not give two damns if he didn't get it and burn the house down as he left.

And now I'm home, free to do as I please for the next six weeks. Mother to a child at public boarding school. Paid for by the trust fund from my father. Who I've not seen since the day he left me here, hiding his disgraceful bastard with his divorced mother. How wonderfully sodding upper class I have become.

I even have the portrait to prove it. A gift from Granny at Christmas last year. It hangs above the fireplace in my room, staring down at me while I write. Granny gave the artist a photo from a party. My hair is up and my neckline plunging. I am amused to admit I find the rendering of my own cleavage arousing. Kit reckons it is a perfect fit for me. I look like I'm about to stab the viewer. There is so much pent-up aggression in my face, and my lips halfway to a frown yet my eyes are filled with longing. Is this the way the world sees me, or do I see myself at last instead?

Oh, it's to be tears. Damn them, wretched useless things. What bloody point this maudlin? I made my decision. I always promised I would not ask for help from anyone. Nor seek approval. My wild bold boy was too much for the likes of Miss Morgan and her contemporaries.

To hell with the lot of them. I shall try it for a year. And if he hates it at the end and me with it, I shall change the decision and make him love me again.

I told him about sex. Before he left. You would not think it so difficult to tell your own child about the basic facts of nature. To consider whether I put a conventional slant on it or tell him my own version of the birds and bees? Kit asked why it was called the birds and the bees, as they can't mate. I told him because people are generally idiots and make up all sorts of polite nonsense rather than tell children the truth. And promptly proceeded to tell him all sorts of half-truths and evasions myself.

I told him that sex is one way we find joy as adults. It's a bodily pleasure, same as eating, kissing, cuddling. I asked him how he felt about those things, and he said it depends on what you're eating, or who's kissing you. Which is how sex feels. It all depends on the circumstances, what you're doing and who with. I told him people say too much about what you should be doing because they're scared to explore what they could be doing. And that if anyone ever tells him what he should be doing with his own body that he's to tell them to sod off. His body is his own, and he is master of it. And that rule applies to others too, he must never tell someone what to do with their body or force them to do something they don't want to. Granny says I told him too young. Is nine too young? But I couldn't bear the thought of him learning a load of messed up twaddle from another kid at school.

Six weeks now to myself. I feel anxious, as though I have mislaid my purse. Even in London I am used to thinking that I must be back. That the hours I am there must be filled relentlessly to make space for the days I have to be home. Now, what seductive vastness lies before me. I can go to the flat for the whole time and not be back until his first break. This absence of child is a recreation. Nine years I have forgotten this bliss. Perhaps now I might be able to look up that career ladder rather than clinging to the lower rungs with my bloody teeth.

What else?

Come on, I must look forward, the bottle is nearly empty.

I shall fill my empty bed with a new lover each week. There, that is a challenge I can rise to. What do you say to that?

I shall peel the skin from their bodies with my teeth. I shall make them call my name and beg for mercy. I shall deflower a lesbos virgin on the benches of the Commons. Do you recall the chapel at school? How we lay naked on our piled clothes on the freezing floor behind the altar and took it in turns to rouse one another? Our new breasts bared to God while we scorned his name. You said he would damn us, and I swore I would never pray to him again.

I am flooded with the thought of it. How swiftly my tears dry, and desire stirs.

What else?

I shall take two at once. A man and a woman. Preferably in love with one another. I shall show them how to love each other better. I shall teach her how to demand her pleasure first. I will make them watch me with the other until they both hate me.

I shall mount a man as they love to mount us. Turn his face to the pillow and make of him a hole for my lust. Slide my strap on inside him.

Do you remember.

No?

I shall remind you.

Those long weeks on the way to India and idiocy.

How we lay together as the ship swayed and I slipped inside you. The perfect breathless 'O' of your mouth, your teeth gleaming, the moistness of your tongue as I slipped a finger inside those lips. I longed to be a man. The desperation of it, to be giving you pleasure and longing to put myself, that false part of myself that was rousing you, inside your mouth where my fingers knew the heat of your tongue. I can remember it vividly, it builds within me now. It takes but two fingers and I am bursting with the thought, even all this distance apart you own me. Ragged and breath spent and longing for your lips.

Why do I write these things to you? Scraps torn from my notebook. Will I rip this out, send it, as I have others? Will I write more? Tell you how I long to be pulled inside another body? The thoughts I dare not write anywhere but here, dare I write them to you? If I did, would it help? Would it make any difference to this confusion? Have you become like all the rest, who would read and be horrified? Or are you yet my Beth? That told me what I told Kit, there's nothing unnatural that's given freely between two people. Do you know that I ask the same question of all my lovers, the one I asked you? And that I ask it because I seek the same answer. My desires have grown, not lessened. Our memories taunt me.

Do you know what I desire right now?

To take a man. To be a man and take a man.

Are you shocked?

I write this to shock you. To dare myself.

What cowardice in me.

To be a man when I despise them so much?

What drunken nonsense and self-pity.

I will not send it. There is nothing here but bitterness, and you would see straight through it.

I shall write you a more decent letter. Tell you how I have sent Kit to boarding school to save my career. That Granny grows slowly older, and I have determined to drown my guilt in a new lover each week. The rest shall stay here, where it belongs, unfit for other eyes. Locked in the chest I brought home with me. One day I shall burn it, a huge bonfire of my own vanities. When I am old, grey-haired and slack, and desire is a spent thing that no longer torments me. We shall do it together, before we die.

Now the bottle is empty, and I need a shag. Or another bottle. Either will suffice.

6

Aidan was leaning against the wall to the compound when he arrived, talking to the gate guards. Moth noted their uniform, Turkish army. Something had changed. It was past eleven. The camp brooding and inert. The curved rows of the tents he'd passed shone like silver bows in the clear night.

'I swear you're getting later.' Aidan threw his glowing stub on the ground and didn't stoop to pick it up.

'What's up?' Moth asked, idling past the guards with a nod, into the compound parking spaces. Turning off the engine and stretching his back as he got off.

'Why should anything be up?'

Moth watched the gates being closed behind him. The guards staying on the inside. Something was up. Aidan had never stayed up to greet him before. Moth glanced across to the stairs that led to Bonn's nest. The railings at the bottom were empty. He looked to Aidan who was looking only at the ground.

'I don't normally get a welcome committee.'

'Nah, just the mess of trying to fit all these extra bodies in. Come on, I kept your supper. Come eat. You'll have to crash on the floor in our tent tonight. There's no bed for a cockroach let alone your giant legs.'

Moth followed Aidan to the food hall. The compound at night would normally have a quiet buzz to it. People taking an hour or two to catch up on jobs, share news with each other, call family. The doors to the tents were closed. The storerooms, medic centres and containers all dark.

'Looks different around here.' Moth tested the waters from behind Aidan's back.

Irish shoulders shrugged indifference, 'Yeah, tension between the newcomers and the residents. Orders to be extra careful.'

'I guess it doesn't take many when the space is already full, huh?'

'Huh,' Aidan huffed agreement. 'Grab a seat. I'll get your grub.'

Moth pulled out a chair at one of the long tables. Dotted about the big space he could see a dozen heads, some together, some apart. Phones and tablets glowing in front of them. Laptops even. He wasn't sure he'd even seen a laptop in here before. Aidan came back with a tray. A large plate of spiced stew, flatbreads, dates, tea. He reached for the mug of tea first. Chased away the dusty road with it.

'Laptops?' Moth nodded across the room. 'That's new.'

'Yeah, the mess tent got designated as out of hours space. Otherwise, all spaces are closed past 10 pm. Folk trying to keep in touch with family. There's a shit load of upheaval going on. Turkish government got all tooty about the delay to the transit camp closure. How'd your trip go?'

'Trip? You make it sound like a fishing jaunt.'

'Sorry, how'd your dumbass ride through the hills in search of last hope city go? Better?'

'Much.' Moth grabbed a flatbread and dug it into the shimmering oily surface of the stew. 'Please, tell me there's no lentils in this?'

'There's no lentils in it.'

'You're lying.'

'People need to be more grateful I'm able to get lentils to up their calorific and protein intake.'

'I'm always grateful for food. I'm never going to like lentils.' Moth forked the food apart, pointing at the hidden grains within.

'Stop moaning and eat,' Aidan stepped back from the table, 'I'll be back in five. Don't choke on the lentils, medic tent is closed.'

'What?' Moth paused at that. 'Medic tent was always open 24/7. That's the point of it.'

Aidan shrugged again. 'Like I say, don't choke. Things have changed.'

Moth watched Aidan between forkfuls. The food was twice reheated and stuck to his teeth, but the closest to a meal he'd had for three days.

Bonn had stayed true to his word.

For now.

Though he knew that was getting harder. As the weeks ticked by, the nudges by which he was removed increased. His bunk had been taken. His bags stored in the staff locker room. His bike leaning against Bonn's metal stairs when he arrived home...

Home?

... back, one day. Chained to the railing. He'd felt the chains harder than anything else that had happened.

The rootless shifting between three camps, a persistent piece of refuse thrown out that kept boomeranging back to base, that he could manage. Yves abandoning him the moment they left Bonn's circle of influence. Sleeping on the ground in his tatty old sleeping bag beside the bike. The fights he'd had to hold onto the sodding bike. The bike, stuttering its way along the long bleak road to Suruc. The grimness of life on the edges of Akcakale as the transit camp was bullied by Turkish troops. The slow mizzling away of faces he had come to know. The sense of despair and failure. Being hungry, cold, too hot, too tired, his knuckles bruised from fighting and chapped by the wind.

All of it, the surreal way in which he'd survived the seven long hours of that first abandoned night, to the seven painful days of that first long week, to now, a whole seven weeks later, wind-chilled fingers aching from the long ride down the E99 from Urfa.

He'd done more travelling in the last seven weeks than he had for a year.

To arrive precisely nowhere.

He hadn't told Bonn about Yves. About the lack of water or food or sleeping facilities. He made a religious appearance on the third day at Bonn's camp and made sure he crammed enough in the rucksack to get by on. Three weeks into the campaign of contempt he'd experienced at the transit camp, Moth realised Bonn must have heard about it. Eba had appeared, looking for him, shown him to an empty tent near the staff compound. He'd thanked her, spotted Yves watching from a distance and, as soon as Eba was called away, walked in the other direction. He'd survived three weeks without any support, Yves could get stuffed if he was going to take a helping hand now.

He hadn't told Bonn about the fights. About spending that first night holding onto the bike by the skin of his knuckles.

And the night after. Oh, and the night after that too.

By the third night they'd grown tired of trying. So desperate, they lacked persistence. Or perhaps they'd realised the bike wouldn't take them anywhere without the fuel they couldn't afford to buy. Perhaps the brighter ones realised he might be useful, by the time he'd gone to Suruc, Urfa and back in the first week. Arriving back even more bruised than when he left to sleep on the ground beside the bike outside their tents. Offering more than a bike now. Offering knowledge. Options. Between the poor English, the cagey communication, the parental concern and the cultural fear.

There were only five days left. Three days ago, a water cannon truck had moved up to the perimeter. Eba had turned up the following day with a truck and begun moving the pregnant women and new-borns. Too many families had refused to be separated, dragging postnatal women from the medic tent clutching their bellies and tiny rags of babies. Ethnic fear of reprisal and separation greater than the fear of infection or death. Eba's lips setting in a twisted knife line.

Moth had left during the middle of it. His latest messages tucked up in his bag. He'd become an errand boy. Carrying messages between camps, between families, between groups of teenagers living rough on the streets. Akcakale town the last place anyone wanted to end up. Over-patrolled, over-controlled, stripped of safety by its border proximity. Three of the transit camp unaccomps had already turned up in ditches. Too many more had disappeared, with no contacts to where they were going. Moth looked for them in the bigger towns, tried to keep tabs, ask questions. Avoiding getting too close to the soldiers himself. He took one person with him on the way north. Dropping them into the outskirts of Suruc, giving them directions, hoping they wouldn't get picked up by the traffickers first. More than once fighting off another last-ditch attempt to steal the bike from under him. He was big, and they were weak. It never left him feeling good though.

All this he hadn't told Bonn during his three-day interval breakfast reports, but he had kicked off about the old bike chained to the steps. Bonn had born the rage with a raised eyebrow, asked 'You done?' and told him to be grateful they'd found a chain when Jonah had tried to hurl it into the camp.

Sitting watching the quiet interior of the mess tent and eating his food, Moth remembered his anger at it being chained up with a grimace. How he would like to see it still there, now he had no idea where it was. Whatever was happening here, he needed to get out. Find a base. Maybe Urfa, maybe one of the quiet spots he'd clocked in his triangular trajectory around the countryside. It was warm enough now, he could live in the tent.

You could go home. Real home.

Moth scraped the last forkful of food up and sat back in the chair with his flatbread. His options were getting thinner. He didn't have time to answer emails, let alone think about the options. Home seemed further away, not nearer, with starving lads hanging in doorways and giving favours down alleyways to survive the next day.

How was he supposed to go home from this? To England? Riverdell? Isabelle fretting about her home. James worrying about the farm. A country pulling its feet away from the grim tide of humanity trying to reach its shores. Or Geneva? To resolve what he'd left undone.

There was nowhere called home. He might as well stay here and help the other homeless as run away to nowhere.

Moth felt tiredness from the long trip tighten up his back against the plastic chair and wriggled to ease it off. He was glad not to be powering the bike himself. It had been too long since he rode daily. Getting back on the bike would be a shock.

If the bike is still here.

He had at least found a bike repair place in Urfa.

If you can afford to pay the bill.

Discomfort crept up his back and across his shoulders. He watched Aidan go across to the table with the laptop. People he didn't recognise. Aidan smiling, nodding, grinning at what he heard. Shrugging shoulders in an appearance of sympathy. Since when did Aidan make conversation? The guy existed on a fag and a shag. Moth chewed the dry last corner of tough doughy bread and washed it down with the dregs of his cool tea. Wondering if he would get any takeaways for his backpack. As he put the empty mug down, Aidan came back carrying a laptop. Putting it at the table and pulling a chair out.

'Any chance of another cuppa?' Moth asked before he could sit down.

'Yeah, I'll get one myself.' He pushed the laptop toward Moth. It was a battered old thing, with a pixelated line across the dead centre. 'Here, check your emails while I get them.'

'Na, I'll do it in the morning, I'm too tired.' He pushed it back to Aidan. 'You use it.'

'Moth.' Aidan pushed it firmly toward his hand. 'Check them. Bonn insisted.'

'Now?'

'Yes, now. Do you want this tea or not?'

'Christ, you're grumpy,' Moth told him with a grin.

'You going to check them or what?'

'Yes, yes, fine. I'll check them. Make it a big mug.'

Aidan took his tray away, leaving a space that Moth couldn't readily avoid filling with the laptop.

You're avoiding it.

Yes, he was. Avoiding having to admit to Bonn he had emails to respond to. Avoiding what lay in his inbox, demanding attention. What news from Nat, from Riverdell, from Luca? It was easier not to hear it. To not hold the normality of their life against the trinity of his own. Long roads, lonely nights, skies clear all the way to the stars.

You need help to get the bike fixed.

Moth flicked the chrome page up. Pulled up his email. Fists forming in front of the keyboard, lines cracking in the chapped skin across his knuckles. In the top corner he noticed the owner's avatar. Clicked on it. The pc was Aidan's. How come he was lending it out? In the twelve months he'd known Aidan, he'd not known he had a laptop. Now here he was running a virtual library on it. He loosened his fists as the highlighted list appeared. Seventeen emails. His weeks had passed so swiftly.

He opened those from Nat first, one after the other. Snippets. Names. Her life a list of friends he'd never met. Her language was excitable, her mistakes fewer each time she wrote. She was a different sister to the one he'd left. He sent her the news he always did. Towns he'd seen, places he'd been, highlights of an older brother travelling abroad. Suruc, Urfa. Mountains and stars in between. He left out the Turkish army patrols, the beatings, the camp closure. Mentioned he was borrowing a bike from a friend while his was fixed. Eight emails left.

Two from Kit. One telling him all about his boyfriend. All about his work projects. Colour names. Titian Blue or Titus Sky. Fondant Flush or Boudoir Blush. There was an edge of suggestion to the names that made Kit appear, full-bodied and with a scathing look of interior disgust, standing beside him at the table as he looked round the tent. The second email, following an hour on from the first, full of questions about Moth.

Yeah, he realised what a selfish arse he was in the first one.

Moth scratched at his chin and sent a two-word email back. Apricot Fuzz.

That left three apiece from Isabelle and Luca. He glanced up again. Aidan was in the kitchen, taking forever with his tea. The people who he'd claimed the laptop off had left without his noticing. He clicked on Isabelle's emails. Scrolling through the lengthy details. Indigo and Deryn searching the house for Easter eggs. Kate's Instagram war with Kit. Kit's attempts to coerce a family Christmas out of her at Riverdell. Rob's plan to construct a palatial Wendy house in the old Chestnut tree. Asha's terseness and anger provoked by Brexit. Her own work frustrations. Snippets from diaries she was reading. He noticed three mentions of India across one email and found it hooking at his mind. Was she thinking of visiting India? He could imagine her sitting on the high stool at her table, writing them. The fire crackling behind her in the great hearth.

It doesn't look like that anymore, remember.

It was hard to remember Riverdell except as he'd left it. It was a different place now. Isabelle's, not Elsa's. A private home, not a public business. She had moved out of the basement where they had spent so much time. He wrote back.

All good. India sounds good, are you thinking of going? Bike bust. Borrowing one from a friend. Tent needs patching. Send needle and thread. Thanks for keeping in touch with Nat. Tell Indigo the Wendy house should be bigger.

There was nothing left but Luca's emails. Moth rolled his hands into fists again before flexing them out to open the first email. His fingers shook as he raised them over the touch pad.

This is ridiculous.

His knees jiggling beneath the table brought that long ago table in Italy back, the café where they had first met. The embarrassment he hid beneath its surface. Moth opened the email and began to read. Each word leaping from the scene as Luca recreated his life in Geneva. A life as rich in thought and culture as his was impoverished. Luca was full of the meetings he got to attend. Full of the tangible joy of at last being where he had longed to be and worked toward. He spoke about committees, debates, memos with the same passion as Bonn negotiated his morning resource scrum. Moth withering beneath the weight of their differences. Alongside a stinging reality that their lives had grown further apart. Luca sent photos. Of his desk, his work colleagues, his shared flat, the parties he went to. They left him numb. Aching over an image of the lake strung out in the background of a swimming party. Luca huddled beneath a massive towel with the arms of friends joined together, smiles and laughter. Lakes and Luca belonged to him, not those nameless bodies in the cold sunrise of an early swim.

He scrolled to the next email, full of the same. Luca making a life, finding a place. Onto the last. Less enthusiastic. He'd been put on a two-week stint of archiving by his boss. Came back to find his desk given to someone else. Himself moved to a lesser one, closer to the coffee machine. He wrote about taking a trip into the mountains on his own. Driving for the day, following thawing roads on winding views, thinking about where Moth was. Asking when he might visit Geneva? Why hadn't he written? Was he well? How was that promise coming on? Was he lonely? A list of hurts in the questions that made Moth twinge with guilt and doubt.

Aidan came over with two big cups of tea, sat down opposite him. Moth ignored him a moment longer, focused on the email. He had to respond.

Tell him you broke that promise.

Except he hadn't.

Tell him you're going home to Riverdell.

But he wasn't.

Tell him anything, just get over it.

'You done?' Aidan asked.

'Yeah, I'm done. Nothing that couldn't have waited until tomorrow.' Moth closed the emails without responding, shut the laptop down and pushed it across the table to Aidan. 'What's the rush?'

'You'll see.'

Luca's unanswered emails niggled him, but he needed more time to think. He'd reply next time he stopped in. 'You lending out your laptop to the whole camp or select individuals.'

'Bonn asked me to, can't say I'm thrilled about it.'

'What's going on here, Aide?'

'Told you, the Turks got all strong arm on the NGOs.' Aidan slurped from his cup, slouching in his chair.

Moth stared across the table at him. Silence deepened between them. Aidan slurped again. Silence stretched. Moth sank into it. He was used to silence. It was spatially deeper at night, sleeping rough in his sleeping bag, the stuffing escaping as he moved on the hard ground. Aidan was used to the camp, the compound, tight-packed bunks in a tent. Keeping a whisper was beyond him.

'Alright,' Aidan glanced sideways. 'Bonn's being moved. He told me not to tell you. Most of the staff don't know yet.'

'Moved? Where?'

'Zaatari, Jordan. I think. South somewhere.'

'Shit.'

'Yeah, tell us about it. The Turks put pressure on him for delaying the transit camp stuff. They might have had a snitch feeding them information. HQ had to soothe them with a change of management.'

'So, what does that…'

'I don't know anything more,' Aidan held up his hands to forestall the rush of questions, 'before you start bothering me.'

They both sat in the hush that followed. Moth listing the concerns in his head. His next meal. His next bed. His bike. His gear.

'Bonn suggested you might want some stuff printing off.' Aidan nodded at the laptop.

'I normally do that in the mornings in his office.'

'Yeah, well. He said if you need anything printing, forward it to me and I'll do it for you.'

Forward his personal emails to Aidan? Moth would rather walk naked through the camp with his hands tied behind his back. Bonn must have known him well enough by now to know the idiocy of that statement.

'I told him you wouldn't,' Aidan took another glug of tea.

'Nothing I need this time. Thanks for the offer.'

'Right,' Aidan picked up the laptop and stood up. 'Let's get some sodding kip. I've gotta be up at five.'

Moth watched him walk toward the kitchen, giving a heads up to the few people left. He watched as they scraped back chairs, walked toward the exit. Glancing his way in curiosity. When Aidan turned the lights off in the kitchen and moved back toward him, Moth stood up and followed.

'Who's coming in to replace Bonn?'

'Already here,' Aidan muttered. 'You'll see soon enough. Bonn wants you in the office at nine.'

'Where's my bike?'

'Padlocked up out back, getting in my bloody way.'

'I owe you.'

'Too right. Here.' Aidan passed him a key over the table. 'Make sure you give it back to me. Jonah's counting ever sodding pin that leaves the stores.'

MOTH WOKE at five the next morning, when Aidan stepped over him. Aching from the hard floor and the restless night.

He lay there, listening to the soft rustlings as Aidan dressed. The sound of pants being pulled on, soft jersey pulled over hair. The gurgles and bone creaks of a body waking. A belt being done up. Shoes pulled on.

Aidan put a hand on his shoulder as he left, ducked low to whisper, 'Grab an hour in my bunk, see you later.'

The draught from the door opening and closing reached across the floor to encourage the idea. He moved, in his bag, folding his bones onto the soft give of Aidan's warm bunk. The scent of his pillow rising beneath his head. Lay, waking, listening to the sound of sleeping men. He reached a hand into his bag, closed his eyes. Thought about water. Lake sides.

Bodies pink and curled over their cold. Luca's muscled calves below the towel. The curve of a shoulder as weak morning light from the Venetian sunrise came through thin curtains. Sucking in air as the wave of release swept out of him, clamping his teeth to stop it from waking anyone.

You're as stuck between that promise and courage as you are between these three crappy towns.

He felt the moment's bliss swing toward disgust and caught it. Closed his eyes and lingered in the thoughts. Focusing on Venice. Luca by the ferry terminal. Saying good-bye. Pleasure rippling through his body as he remembered, pushing back the ugly thoughts.

'You won't break that promise?' In the darkness behind his eyelids, Luca's voice was as close as Aidan's had been. Strung out with his Italian accent, hushed between sad lips.

Moth would never look at his lips in the same way after their last night. Going as far as he'd been able. Hanging onto the image of those gates shut by Isabelle on the past as Luca gave him his first blowjob. Holding back the images that threatened to ruin the moment. Fingers clinging to Luca's thick wavy hair. It was hard to focus, out in the daylight.

'I won't break it,' he said.

'You don't regret it?' Luca's eyes searching his.

Regret it? That first of the night before. Fear turned to ecstasy as he realised, he could still make his own firsts. 'No.'

'You know you could come stay with me for a bit,' Luca had asked, reaching for his hand. 'You don't have to leave.'

Moth looked away, out toward the other waiting foot passengers. Seeing their eyes flitting away as his scanned over them. He didn't know what he would do if Luca kissed him. He didn't know how to manage this yet. In the privacy of their room last night, a single lamp throwing Luca's movements into relief against the wall, the unexpected pleasure, the teeth-gritting urgency of wanting more, he'd found a happy, brave place. Out here, beside the sea, the ferry huge and looming as it lowered its ramp, the day felt overwhelming.

'I'll come back.' He squeezed Luca's hands, pulled his fingers away, fussed with the bike.

He tried to ignore the flutter of Luca's eyes. The silence as he tightened the pannier straps.

'You're ashamed of me,' Luca said in a hushed tone.

Moth straightened up and looked at him, reddening.

'Out here, around people, you're ashamed of us?'

'I'm not ashamed.' Moth looked down at Luca's feet, his smart leather shoes against the line marked tarmac. When he looked up at Luca's face, there was defensive disbelief etched across his ridiculous cheekbones. 'Not of you. I swear.' How could anyone be this handsome and have insecurity? He reached out and touched the leather thong where it dipped below the neckline of his top. Pulled it out to see the roughened silver bead that hung at the base. He had felt that silver bead trace its way down his body, across his chest, over his stomach, between his thighs. The feel of it in his hand shook him. 'But I'm not confident either. Not like you. And I'm ashamed of that.'

'Then you'll come back?' Luca asked. 'And keep that promise?'

Moth smiled at him. For one moment forgetting the ferry, the eagerness to be gone, the crowds. He leant close, foreheads touching, eyes closing. Trying to be brave and own that one last moment, tucking the silver bead back inside the shirt.

Moth had opened his eyes. The world reduced to Luca's

brown irises with their amber streaks you could only see close up. The long black eyelashes with their curving tips.

'I'll keep it.'

In the sharp taut morning of the tent in Turkey, Moth felt the pleasure end, opened his eyes to see the dip of humanity curving the mattress between the bowing metal slats of the bunk above him. Hand warm and heavy over his shrinking dick as he focused on the day ahead.

If you go back.

He filled the time before his meeting with Bonn. The first thing he did was find his bike. Tied up next to the stinking bins out the back of the kitchen. It looked even sadder than it had tied to the railings. He had to get it to Urfa. He still had no other option than to get it fixed. Money or no money he couldn't do anything with it here. He went to see Aidan. He was busy making breakfast, yelling orders at the volunteers on their shift. Moth had done his share in the kitchen. Aidan was cranky in the mornings.

'You got any deliveries coming in from Urfa?' Moth asked.

'Yeah, later today. Fehran's due in. Why?'

'Can you lend me some money?'

'Not a chance. Why?'

'You really want to know?'

Aidan paused in flipping flatbreads on the grill, glanced over at him. 'No, not really. And don't miss your meeting with Bonn, he'll have my hide.'

'Yes, Grandpa.'

Aidan flipped a finger at him in response.

'What time is that lorry coming in?' Moth asked.

'About two, normally. You can help me unload in return for lunch.'

Moth grinned and gave him a thumbs up, went looking for his panniers. Avoiding Jonah among the hectic morning criss-cross of staff in the compound. Noticing the presence of more Turkish guards than he'd ever seen. He dropped in at Eba's clinic, passed on messages from two pregnant women who had moved with their families to the shacks popping up round Akcakale town.

He climbed the stairs to Bonn's office at two minutes to nine. Feeling the sun strong on his back as he went. Edging into the full room when he opened the door. Finding a space to lean against the wall. Watching reality unfold one terse statement at a time. Noticing how Bonn ignored his presence. A tidy man in Turkish uniform stood at the edge of the circle, scrutinising everything with a line of irritation stuck between his eyebrows, threatening to crease his face in half. Brown eyes flicked his way, dismissed him, went back to watching Bonn.

It was the normal crowd. Jose, Maria, Jonah, Dimitri, Eba. All quieter than normal. Some faces he recognised from the transit camp but didn't know. A fractured line of tense space between the two groups. And, in the middle, hearing reports, making decisions, giving orders. Yves. While Bonn listened, the blue cap crushed into a tube and being pulled slowly through his coiled fist.

Ah, shit. You're stuffed now.

Yves was in charge.

How the hell had that happened. Moth thought back over the terseness between them. Bonn dragging his bureaucratic feet to slow down the eviction. All the while Yves watching and waiting. He'd never warmed to Yves.

Now you never will.

The wanker had stabbed Bonn in the back. Now they were all going to suffer. Moth thought about sneaking straight back out the door. Shuffled his feet with the thoughts. Bonn looked dead at him, blue eyes pinning him down.

Missed your chance now.

He settled back against the wall, looked at the ceiling and listened to the tone of Yves' management. The sullen cloud of the Turkish uniform dampening down the habitual releasing of tension that Bonn had always allowed. The team were wound up tight. Unable to vent. That was going to be Yves' style. Closed compound, working hours, guarded gates, guarded opinions. It couldn't have been more different to what they were used to. One by one the room emptied. The door snapping closed behind each terse exit. Until he was the fourth man in the room and all eyes bar Bonn's turned on him.

'You,' Yves demanded his attention.

Moth raised his eyebrows.

'What is your business here?' the Turkish man asked in perfect English that skipped along the syllables with distaste.

'He has none.' Yves stared straight at him.

Bonn spoke over Yves. For the first time. 'He's here on my business.'

'You have no business that is not in the interest of our government,' the Turk countered in crisp enunciation.

It was weird, Moth thought, how speaking a language so perfectly could reduce it to words without weight.

Moth watched Yves lean back in his chair, his jaw tightening. One day he hoped someone would shatter that jawline. He kind of hoped it might be Bonn. Moth had never hated a man's jawline before. It didn't even have a right to be that clean shaven. Not here, not amongst all this.

'As far as I'm aware, UNHCR works with your government, not for them.' Bonn stood up and slapped the cap in his hand. 'I believe you have an inspection to carry out?' Bonn stared at Yves. 'Nine-thirty on the nose, you can't expect respect if you miss your own deadlines.'

Yves stared back. Bonn raised his eyebrows, slapping his cap in the deathly silence.

Yves stood up, snatched a clipboard from the wall and walked to the door. He looked back at Moth. Raised a finger. 'One more week and your time here is over.'

The Turkish uniform looked at the door swinging shut behind him, across to Bonn, back to Moth. The frown deepening as he decided where his priority lay. Moth stayed leaning against the opposite wall. Bonn looked at the door swinging shut behind Yves and waited, slapping the cap leisurely against his palm. A loud damp irritation that echoed in the frigid silence. The man brought his eyebrows virtually together and gave up, walking to the door and pulling it open. Trying to redeem the moment with a final long stare at Moth before leaving.

'Wow, that was fun.' Moth pulled a chair out and turned it to face Bonn. 'Did Yves actually have a clipboard with him?'

'Oui, the idiot believes he can run a camp this big with a timetable and ticks.'

Moth thought about what he'd seen of Yves. As much as he hated that jawline, he had to admit the man had overseen the transit camp with diligence. 'It might work, you never know.'

Bonn scowled at him, sat down and leant back in his chair

and sighed. 'He will have the staff in the counselling tent by the end of the month.'

'There's a counselling tent?'

'There is now.' Bonn stared out of the window. Resentment etched across his face. Counting the tents and all the lives in them. Trying to say farewell to two years' work.

Moth wondered how it must feel. To fight day in, night out for the protection of people you never truly knew, to be pushed out, onto the next place. Wondering what mess you were heading into. Watching the terse muscle jumping in the turn of Bonn's neck he could feel the edge of what Bonn tried to warn him about.

'Zaatari, I hear?'

Bonn turned to face him. Nodded.

'Straight there or do you get a break first?'

'I fly to UNGO on Tuesday, debriefing, out to Jordan three days later.'

Moth tried to think what day it was. Thursday. It was Thursday. 23rd June. He had less than a week before Bonn left. One more triangle. One more refuel.

UNGO. Four letters littered across Luca's emails with as much enthusiasm as lentils in Aidan's cooking.

'Wow, three days debriefing. Not much of a break.'

Bonn didn't reply.

'You pissed with Yves?' Moth asked.

Bonn slapped his palm with the cap one last time and threw it down on the table.

'Oui. Non. Ah, merde, I pity the man. He's been put in charge with a leash. He'll find he's a puppet in a game. The Turkish government are playing long ball now. They need someone in charge who needs backup. So they can either claim his incompetence or control him to keep his job.'

'Long ball?'

Bonn looked out the window, 'See all those tents? They will be here in a decade. There is nothing for them to go back to. And Europe is tightening its borders. Look at your country. You think Brexit is anything other than a direct border tightening?'

Moth didn't respond. Thinking about Isabelle's email, Asha's irritation. All he knew about Brexit was European contempt from the non-British staff and the upper-class murmurs from a home he didn't count his own.

'Turkey is stuck in the middle, with millions of displaced people crippling their economy. That guy,' Bonn nodded out of the closed door, 'is not a soldier, he is economics department. They,' he nodded out of the window, 'are not people. They are numbers, on a piece of paper, in an office.'

'If Yves is here, who's looking after the transit camp?'

'No one. The Turkish government demanded the removal of all NGOs yesterday. They have two days left to disperse. It was decided that the absence of any staff would encourage the move. Improve their thoughts about moving to Suruc.'

Moth thought about the people he had left behind. Hundreds of families refusing to move to the bigger camp. Nowhere else to go but into the streets or hills.

'They won't move if they haven't already. Yves must know that. Didn't he try to tell them.'

'Don't waste your breath. It is done Moth. They will force them out. Don't be there when it happens or you'll end up on the inside of a Turkish jail, and I don't want to have to come drag your arse out, or worse, fail to do so.'

'You're telling me not to go back?'

'You won't get in. The Turks have banned the entry of any staff.'

Moth felt his teeth tighten against the images rising in his head. The water cannon truck, the increased troops. The people he'd left behind.

'There are pregnant women in that camp. Children as young as eight unaccompanied, babies, bedridden old people.' Moth stood up in agitation.

'Moth, I want you to come with me. To Zaatari.'

'But what about...'

'... Moth, don't ignore me...'

'... you can't expect me to leave them...'

'... there is nothing you can do, aren't you listening to me...'

'... I'm not staff, I don't have to do what they say...'

'... you are not fucking God either, you can't ignore the government or you'll...'

'... end up in jail. Yes, I fucking hear you.'

They both pulled back from the argument. Moth angered at how readily Bonn was accepting his dismissal. Running back to HQ like a good soldier. Off to the next battle. Moth didn't have those options. The only option he had was right here.

Bonn wiped a hand down his face, squeezed his jaw with it, rubbing a hand along the rough edge of his double chin, trying to calm himself.

'You taught me how to help,' Moth told him before he could speak. 'Don't ask me to stop because you have to.'

'I want you to help yourself too. Or at least let someone else do it.'

'I can take care of myself.'

'Oh, reel your bloody chin in, you look like Yves,' Bonn snapped. Moth turned away from him and went to look out the window, over the tents. His back rigid with frustration.

'It is hard, Moth. Always hard to leave. This is my job. I get sent one place, do what I can, get sent to the next hotspot. Nothing is ever finished. If you throw yourself to the lions, you will end up dead.' Moth heard him pause, holding a thought on his breath, then say, 'Come back to Geneva with me. I can pull that much off. Try to get you on my staff for Zaatari.'

Luca would be fuming if you got on a relief team.

Three days in Geneva before flying out to Jordan, maybe even a paid job. The lure of that thought snapped shut in Moth's mind. He turned to face Bonn.

'That's bullshit. You told me I have no qualifications, barely even for peacekeeping, let alone UNHCR.'

'Moth, I can't leave you here.' Bonn's voice bit into a growl. 'I can't go to Zaatari worrying about you the whole time.'

Moth stared at the floor. The truth echoing in his bitter French lilt. There was no place for him on the Zaatari team. That was a lie meant to get him away. Anger mixing with fear. The thought of being out there, on his own without Bonn in the background, scared him. Three years on his own and he'd managed fine.

You've grown soft.

'I'm not leaving, so you better stop worrying and cut the emotional guilt trip,' he told Bonn. 'Maybe your hands are tied, and you can't do anything. You gave me a job and I've done it. They'll be expecting me back. I have messages to give them. They have family and friends to find. I have to get back into that camp.'

'And what after that? If you manage to get in, give your messages, and get back out, what will you do next? You think Yves is going to let you stay here? Your bike is a UN asset, not yours to claim. Come with me to Geneva, let's see if we can set you up so you can do this work properly.'

'You want me to go to school? Join a training course? While you go to Zaatari with a clear conscience? Where the hell am I going to live in Geneva?'

'I thought you had a friend there. Can't you stop with her?'

Moth gritted his teeth. No, stopping with Luca was not an option he was ready to consider.

'You do have a friend there, don't you?' Bonn needled him.

'You can't organise my life for me.'

'I'm trying to bloody help you. Merde, you are stubborn. What about your aunt, back home, the rich one? Won't she help you?'

Trying to picture Isabelle as his rich aunt was more than Moth could manage. 'Christ, you have this all sorted, don't you? I'm your last problem. You tick me off and you can leave without a backward glance.'

Moth hurled the insult across the room at him with all the vengeance of a teenager and felt its meanness the moment it left his mouth.

'Shit, I'm sorry.' Moth threw himself back into his chair, folding over his knees in guilt and staring at the rough vinyl floor between his boots. 'I didn't mean that. I'm just mad.'

He glanced up to see Bonn staring at the table, shoulders sagging with the thoughts. He looked away. Waited to see if he'd burnt all his bridges. Trying to think about Geneva. Luca's face if he turned up. Facing that promise. Bonn and Luca getting him all set up and feeling good about themselves. No. No way.

He needed to go back on his own terms.

If you go back.

He might have made a promise to Luca. A dumb promise to give him first chance, once he was sure. A dumb promise he hadn't broken for three years. But he'd made a promise to himself before that. When he left England. To live his life his way. If he went back to Geneva in Bonn's tailwind, he'd be no better than when he left Venice. Held together by other people's help.

'I can't go to Geneva. I can't go back to England. And I can't come with you to Zaatari, we both know that. This is the only place for me, for now.'

'You can't stay here, where will you go?'

'Urfa.' Moth put a deeper tone of conviction into his voice. 'There are a couple of aid agencies there I can volunteer for. If I can get the bike there, I can get it fixed, sleep in the tent until I find a place, a job.'

Bonn had the grace not to poke holes in those huge optimisms.

'How will you get the bike there?'

'I'm going to try and get it on Aidan's delivery truck this afternoon. Though, I could kind of use a bit of cash, to bribe the driver. And can I use the motorbike until you leave? Can you get me into the camp one more time?'

Bonn stayed silent, motionless, poised to blow Moth's cards down.

'Please, Bonn. Give me one more trip. I'll bring the bike back, pick up my stuff and be gone before you leave.'

'You ask a lot.'

'You told me to give it all I could.'

'One condition.' Bonn stood up and slowly put his cap on his head. 'You'll have to find your own way into that camp, I can't help you there. And if you get stuck, don't think I will help you out either. I'll give you the money for the driver, and the next three days with the bike. In return, you must take the details of a colleague in Urfa, give me the name of your friend in Geneva, and I go ask her if you can stop with her. And your email address. You let me try to get you on a training course while I'm there. I succeed, you leave here and join up. I fail, you do what the hell you want.'

'That's three conditions, at least, I couldn't keep count,' Moth complained.

'That's the deal. You take my contact's details, give me your girlfriend's name, your email address and promise to join a course if I can arrange it.'

'That will give you peace of mind to go to Zaatari?'

Bonn nodded. Moth knew the chances of Bonn getting him on any course were negligible. He'd left school at fourteen and had no employment history. It would be stupid to hold onto that false idea for even ten minutes.

'Moth, if you don't agree, the bike stays here, and Yves will deport you tomorrow. You agree, three more days and I see you before I leave.'

Moth wanted to walk out, to resist even accepting this limit on his choices. But he knew Bonn was the only way he'd get back to the transit camp. 'Fine. Deal.'

'Your girlfriend's name?'

The answer wasn't what Bonn was expecting. Moth remembered his embarrassment, stood on the quay at Venice. Closing his eyes and leaning his head against Luca's skin.

Courage. He'd left to find his courage. Three years later he was no closer.

'His name is Luca. Luca Moretti.'

.   .   .

SHE WOKE to a smack across the cheek. The weight of Indigo stirring by her side as she tossed to the other side of the bed.

Isabelle stirred in the dark depths of her bedroom and tried to focus. Being woken by a kick to the ribs or a smack of a clenched fist was her least preferred way of coming to. She remembered being woken by Kit's mouth on her skin and shivered into further consciousness.

Another kick to the thigh encouraged her to move further over in the king-size bed. Indigo's ragged head of wild curls peeped from beneath the duvet. She would be too hot, that was what was causing the kicking. Isabelle peeled the duvet back further and smiled as her daughter's frown appeared beneath tightly scrunched eyes. It had been a rough night. She lightly stroked Indigo's hair until the frown lessened and sleep took over again.

Pulling herself up against the headboard, Isabelle gauged the creases of light peeping over the top of the curtains and creeping along the floorboards. It was too early to wake up. She had tried to put Indigo back in her own room three times last night and finally fallen asleep with her tucked in her elbow. The scent of a relaxed, sleeping child wafted up to her now, that precise combination of skin, warmth and dirt that made this child her own. Isabelle pulled the curls through her fingers.

It was impossible to fathom. This place she had finally come to, motherhood. The presence of a child who filled her with courage and peace, sitting alongside the memory of two pregnancies she had terminated before Indigo, the trauma they had caused in her life. Lying in the quiet moment of waking, when today was any day, no day, this day and her child beside her was eternal, Isabelle felt the stretch of invisible pressures pulling at her. Grief at what she had given up.

Guilt at the happiness she had been granted. Gratitude, sweeping, crushing gratitude, that she had been allowed the chance to have a child in a way that made sense to her.

In these lost moments between sleep and waking, the stillness of her life settled with a profound and endless depth on her. Reminding her of the oddity of her choices and how they suited her. In this bubble of life held back, beyond the bed, the door, Isabelle felt the intense joy of her choices. Rising from within and giving her confidence that perhaps she was missing some greater purpose but that she had found her own path and was on it. This quiet bliss was taken from her in steady increments throughout the day. By the constant rub of opinion that parenting was a pluralism. By Asha's niggling questions that kept the question of paternity forever high and present. Watching Indigo and worrying at what point she might become aware that her mother had cheated her of half her rights. By night, ragged with tiredness and a tempestuous child who wanted independence by the daylight hour and to sleep in her mother's own skin at night, Isabelle lost what final remnants of bliss she had.

Waking, they returned to her, and she pulled them close. She could feel Indigo's skin beneath her hand, living, moving, warming her own. The feel of skin on skin took her back. Three years. The overwhelming month that had been Kate's moving in party, the mess of emotions from that night which had sent her running to Italy and Kit's arms, the feel of Moth's anguish as it tore him apart to talk to her. Isabelle looked up at the distant ceiling. How was it possible that such a mess could have led her to this? She had been granted her own daughter, her own life. And, if she woke at times with her body longing for another touch, or sometimes wondered if she would ever feel the comfort of arms holding her, if she wondered one day what Indigo would demand to know about her father, she would leave all those queries the other side of the door to this bliss, this moment. Waking, her own soul a droplet curled at her side. Fists clenched, legs tucked up, hair frosting a face kissed with nightly dribble.

She clung to the thoughts as the day demanded entry. It was, what day, what real day was it? Oh. That day.

Isabelle watched her bliss slide through the cracks in the floorboard and settle into the dust below.

Friday. 24th June. 2016.

She glanced at her watch. Half past seven. Kate and Rob would be up. No matter what time they had gone to bed, waiting for the Brexit vote result while she retreated early, tussling Indigo into bed. She hadn't wanted to know. One more sleep she'd said, when she could go to bed with the optimism that the country wouldn't backslide into national-ism. Now it couldn't be avoided. She slipped from the bed and, leaving Indigo with the covers drawn well below her head, headed for the bathroom.

In the shower, waking up properly under the stream of warm water, the day encroached further. Oh, and that day as well.

She groaned beneath the water and wondered how it was that such disparate ideas could come together with such total inappropriacy. Perhaps he would cancel. Again. The furniture guy had called, casual, busy, maybe he would come. Set a date and cancelled twice while the furniture in the dining room gathered the capricious house dust devils to themselves in delight and Kate steadily broke her way through the permanent china jigsaw puzzle of the hall that had become Indigo and Deryn's favourite game. If he cancelled today, she would give up and call Kit to help.

Which would finally mean talking to Kate about Christmas.

Isabelle steadied her hands against the cold tiles and tried to suck courage in with the chill.

After all, it was her house. She was the one in charge here. And if Moth's increasing lack of communication was anything to go by, a reason to come home was needed. Rob's query danced a shiver down her spine. Who was she doing this for? Was it for Indigo, to enlarge her sense of family? Was it for Kit, who she missed in their lives? Was it for Moth, who tuned her loneliness like a fork on crystal? Was it for Elsa, to show she had chosen a worthy successor for the family as well as the house? Was it for Rob, to show the family he remained a part of it? Was it for Asha, to prove herself worthy of friendship?

Oh, and that day too.

Isabelle groaned under the stream of water and danced in frustration on the floor of the bath.

How, how, how had she arranged all this on the same day? And how the hell was she going to manage a dinner for Asha and James if the Brexit vote had gone against them.

Kate must help her cook. Rob must be coerced to come back and join them. She needed backup. Hell, she'd even welcome Hester there to share the brunt of Asha's irritation. She tried to picture that, Hester sat at the kitchen table now too small to hold them all, surrounded by the toys of the family children she hadn't contributed to, listening to Asha hold forth on the idiocy of the British character in general and the futility of farming in particular. With that sour edge of frustration that pushed James into silence. The thought morphed, into Christmas, with Hester watching Rob with

Indigo. Would Rob even come with Hester there? Isabelle wrapped her arms tight and hugged all the thoughts away.

Hester would not come. Not even Kit would persuade her to return to Riverdell, let alone for Christmas. Hester had walked out that long ago night and refused to ever come back. She was a disconnected voice occasionally found on the phone when Isabelle rang Swansea to speak to Nat. A name brought up by Elsa, by Kit, by Asha. It was a peculiar pain to realise she still missed their old girlhood friendship, lost behind the relief that the antagonism between them had been given space. No, there was no way to fix how broken their relationship was, and nothing at Riverdell that would ever call Hester back.

Isabelle stepped out of the shower and dried herself. Above the sink was the old mirror from her former bath-room. Same mirror, new light. It showed up the fuller cheek-bones, the line that had appeared beneath her jaw if she didn't hold her head up, painted on shadows under the eyes. Her breasts shrunken from the impact of failed feeding, her stomach creased, her hips that had refused to widen and her thighs traced with fine lines where she had put on weight and lost it. They were subtle changes. Easily lost beneath the linens and jerseys, all too soon shown in the jeans she had once adored. Subtle changes but they marked her. Older. 36 years of life peering back at her. More history. Fewer choices. She traced the rise of her stomach, it had never fully returned to the concave space where she had curled her legs up on a chair. Now when she did that, she could feel her body move aside in irritation. She pulled the damp hair back behind her ear. It was longer too, a shoulder-length bob now, not the sharp cut against the back of her head. Wavy where she left it to dry, mostly caught up in a grip.

Well, here she stood, avoiding the day again. She grinned at the reflection in the mirror. Some things didn't change.

SHE WALKED into the kitchen to find Rob and Kate nursing cups in an eerie silence at the table and felt hope grasp an impossible straw.

'You two look glum, tell me we voted to stay?'

Kate looked at Rob with a twitch to her lips and took a sip of coffee.

'I'm not sure if it's good news or bad news,' Rob told her.

'Well, it can't be both. Hang on, let me get coffee, I can't take this straight up.'

She moved to the espresso machine.

'You look as though you got dressed in the dark,' Kate said behind her back.

She felt the jug warm under her hand. 'Indigo was asleep, and I didn't want to wake her yet.'

'You lost again?'

'When don't I lose?' Isabelle agreed. She had given up caring about the co-sleeping. Sleep itself had become more important than where it was happening. And it wasn't as though there was anyone else sharing her bed to complain. But that was the exact point that Kate most detested, Isabelle's lack of love life. She could manage without a father for Indigo, but the absence of a body in Isabelle's bed, a male, adult body, was more than she could understand.

'Lose the battle, win the war,' Rob offered.

Isabelle pointed a latte spoon at him in emphasis. 'My exact thought.'

She joined them at the table and sat down. They looked exhausted.

'Do you have to go to work today?' she asked Rob. 'You look shattered, both of you. Did you stay up all night?'

'Pretty much,' he confirmed. 'We probably didn't help ourselves though.' He nodded at two empty bottles of wine standing on the counter.

'That was spectacularly stupid, you shouldn't even drive this morning. Why don't you stop over for the weekend? Indigo will love it.'

'Sly bitch,' Kate muttered. 'She wants you here for dinner, Rob. Asha and James are coming.'

'Does your head hurt?' Isabelle asked Kate, blushing. 'That's not the only reason, Rob.'

'Believe that if you need to,' Kate told him.

'I'll take any reason if it comes with dinner,' he reminded her, winking at Isabelle over the rim of the cup.

'Come on then, were you commiserating or celebrating when you got drunk in the early hours?' Isabelle asked, steeling herself.

'Don't be superior,' Kate told her. 'At least we stayed up for the historic moment.'

She looked from one to the other, her small glimmer of hope fading.

'Any idea?' Rob asked her.

'Stop dragging it out and tell me.'

They looked across the table at each other.

'We voted Leave.' Kate announced and frowned into her empty cup.

Isabelle felt the decision seep in and blot out the final hope she'd kindled. The drip-feed way in which anger and disbelief had accumulated since February when Cameron announced the referendum weakening into a numb grief and disappointment that this could have happened. That they had voted to leave a union they had spent so many years building themselves into. A union that linked her to the world outside this kitchen. A world where she could remember Moth, could visualise Luca. The shock of that finality curdling with shame, that she was part of a country that had taken such a decision. What would Moth say? He would surely hate it. She blinked in the fierce June light coming through the window.

'Ouch,' she looked out toward the withered magnolia, past it to the perfect curve of the arched gateway. What could persuade him to come home to a country closing their borders to the world?

'Indeed,' Rob agreed.

'Why aren't you two dancing for joy?' She looked from one to the other in confusion. 'Unless you really did party too hard last night, I thought you'd be thrilled?'

It was a subject they had been forced to agree to bitterly disagree on. This vote, dividing families across the kitchen table. For the first few months it had been a subject of intense discussion, even excitement. As unreal as the March sunshine. But as the weather improved and June crept closer, they had all faced the chasm between them. Kate, Rob and James had been for leaving, Isabelle, Asha and Gosia for remaining. They had all agreed not to discuss how they would finally vote.

'It doesn't feel how I thought it would feel,' Kate told her.

'The hangover or the result?' Isabelle asked.

'Don't be spiteful. You've nursed a few hangovers of your own in this kitchen, as I remember?' Kate threw back.

Isabelle refused to look at Rob, exhorting her cheeks not to warm through and resisted a retort. The hangover she had nursed after Kate's housewarming had been the one that had put her off drinking more than a glassful ever since. Kate's shoulders lowered a little.

'It just… I thought it would feel momentous,' Kate added. 'It doesn't at all. It feels as though we crested a mountain to see another mountain, and beyond that more mountains. And I can't imagine how on earth we are going to find our way.'

Isabelle looked at her with a mixture of pity and jubilation and held tight to the escaping tendrils of her wish to be smug. It was a sour victory, to be on the losing side and see no joy in the victors.

'It feels a lot like divorce,' Rob added with dejection.

She and Kate looked at each other, and back at Rob. Well, he should know.

'I need a sherry,' Kate announced. 'Do we even have any left in this house?'

'It will be in the dining room, under a layer of dust, if we do.' Isabelle watched her get up and leave the kitchen, reached over and grasped Rob's hand. 'At least we're only divorcing Europe this time, not Hester. Stay for dinner, please?'

He turned his hand under hers and squeezed it back.

ISABELLE SPENT the day nursing their wounded spirits and marvelling at the fact that their dejection made the loss more bearable.

Rob rang work to announce he was taking the afternoon off and heard from the receptionist that the partners had welcomed them all to work with champagne and had those who'd voted Remain in tears. He'd spent fifteen minutes speaking to all those who had been upset by the thoughtless celebration and threatened the senior partner to quit the firm before he put the phone down in fury. She'd sent him out to the river with Indigo to feed the ducks.

Kate returned from her classes at lunchtime and slumped in a chair with Indigo, refusing to make herself or anyone else lunch. Isabelle made them both an omelette and gave her an Irish coffee. Indigo was tearing the cold omelette into shapes when Kit's ring tone intruded into the kitchen, vibrating on the tabletop. Kate looked at Isabelle with eyes that had never looked so tired, a mouth twitching toward a smile and slumping in despair, a move as though to put Indigo aside before cuddling her closer. Isabelle knew that now was not the time for Kate to overhear any whisper of Christmas.

'I'll just take this in the study.' She moved to the door and into the hallway before Kate could complain. Answering the phone as she tiptoed round china and glass. 'Hey, have you called to gloat or weep? I'm not sure I can take much more of the despair.'

'Who's in despair?' He was in bed, yawning at her. His hair an unkempt mess, his chin dotted with stubble, his chest bare.

'Kate and Rob. Are you still in bed?'

'No, coming to bed.'

Isabelle saw the bed move beside him and Adele's naked shoulders appeared beside Kit.

'Hey gorgeous.' Adele twisted Kit's phone to include himself in the screen shot. 'What's news in Smallville?'

Isabelle grinned back at him. It was impossible not to. The man had a way of pulling happiness out of rainclouds. 'Did you two stay up all night too? Kate and Rob got drunk together and are both totally dejected over it all.'

'Well, it's done. No point in shutting the stable door now. I hope you made them feel hideously guilty.' He settled down into the curve of Kit's shoulder. She hadn't thought a man could get any more sculpted than Kit, but against Adele he looked almost pudgy. Kate complained that he'd chosen a black lover for the wow factor of how they looked on Instagram. Isabelle had been shocked. It wasn't like Kate to voice intolerance, even on the sly, and Isabelle couldn't work out where the spite came from.

'I don't think I needed to, they seem to have managed by themselves.' Isabelle walked down the hallway toward the study, trying not to stare.

'Stop leching over my boyfriend,' Kit told her and pulled the phone to himself. 'Whoa, wait one goddamn minute. What the hell have you done to the hallway?'

Isabelle tried to block his view of the hall with her body and moved determinedly to the study. 'Nothing. Well, not nothing. I was sorting through a few boxes in the dining room and the girls got hold of it while my back was turned.'

'Does this mean we're doing Christmas?' He turned his head to look at Adele, away from her. 'She's emptying the rooms! We're doing Christmas at Riverdell!' Kit punched the bedclothes in delight.

'Wait, wait, I never said yes.' Isabelle tried to reel him in.

'But you are emptying the rooms?'

'I made a start on clearing the dining room, that's all. I had Deryn for a day and couldn't work.'

'Yes!' Kit crowed at her. 'I knew you couldn't resist it. Did you email Moth yet? I'm going to do it. Right now.'

Isabelle watched him start to move and Adele's hand pull him back into the bed with a groan of complaint.

'Don't you dare.' She perched on the stool at her desk and pointed a stern finger at him. 'I have not yet agreed, and I will not make that plan this far in advance. I'm making some effort to clear the rooms, in case they are needed, not because.'

Kit sank back into the bedclothes where she could see his hair sinking into the pillow, Adele's hand stroking across his chest.

'Anyway, it's hardly the day to talk about Christmas. What about the result?' Isabelle tried to refocus him.

'It's going to double the price of everything by Christmas, which will work wonders for my business as I'll treble my fees.'

'That's all you take from this?' Isabelle prayed he wouldn't speak to Moth about the subject.

'Why's Kate down anyway?' Kit changed the subject. 'I thought she'd be dancing round the garden naked with flowers on her tits.'

She frowned at him. 'She's slumped in the kitchen, and I had to cook her lunch.'

Kit stared, taking in the unlikely image of Kate dejected, before waving a hand across the screen. 'Well, I have no sympathy with her, she bought it on herself.'

'I suppose we might be feeling the same if we'd won,' she said. 'Perhaps we might have a few doubts too?'

'He wouldn't,' Adele tweaked the phone his way with a grin. 'He didn't vote. Myself, I no longer have any doubts. We are a nation that is 52% nationalist wankers and 48% weak liberals with an unspecified number of lazy cowards.'

'Kit! You didn't vote?' Isabelle complained. 'How could you not vote?'

'I couldn't decide,' he moaned, mouthing an obscenity at Adele over the phone. 'And before you get all soap box on me, you wait. It's all about 52 and 48 and the Leavers will flash that card all the way to the bloody end. You'll see. History is written by those who don't speak. I'll bet you... agh.'

Kit's voice cut off with a complaint and his head reared up against the pillow.

'Ok, I get it. I have to go.' He grinned at Isabelle. 'Adele has my nuts in a vice.'

She blinked in the light of his obvious distraction. Kit in bed. She had forgotten how intense that could be.

'We'll talk about Christmas next time,' he said. 'Tell Kate to get over it and make a course from the disappointment. Au revoir.'

Isabelle was still connected when he tossed the phone across the bedsheets. She got a glimpse of skin. A naked swathe of skin. Tried to close her eyes while ending the call and managed to hear more than she wanted to.

The day did not seem to be getting any shorter and she missed the feeling of joy she had woken with. Reaching for her pen she wrote with care in her diary. Brexit Vote. Leave wins. Even the winners are stunned. On the corner of her desk lay three of the older diaries. She picked it up and flicked from page to page. Despite Rob's suggestions she had not been able to resist the urge to read through them. For the majority they recorded the same as her, small snippets of disinterest and tedium. She had jumped past Elsa's handwriting, feeling guilty about prying. Skimmed through the sharp lines of William's years. 1966. Heart fluttering when she saw her mother's name written there. Edward married Beth in Bombay. I fear for her happiness. Sold the shop in Wyle Cop. No confidence in the economy.

'What are you doing?'

Isabelle jumped at the sound, 'Oh, God.'

Kate had Indigo on her hip, a piece of dirt encrusted

omelette waving in each finger. 'See, I told you Mummy would be hiding in here.'

'I'm not hiding, I'm reading.'

'What are you reading? Kate walked over to the desk and set Indigo down on the corner.

Isabelle pulled the diaries out of her child's reach before the greasy fingers could reach the soft leather covers. 'The old diaries that Deryn pulled off the shelves.'

'Haven't you got anything better to do?'

'Loads, no doubt. But they're rather addictive.'

'Really?' Kate loaded her voice with doubt, keeping her hands on Indigo's legs to stop her falling.

'Umm, very Game of Thrones.'

'Is there as much sex?'

'Why would anyone record their sex life in their daily desk diary?'

'Rose used to,' Kate said. 'She put everything in there.'

'How do you know?'

'We shared a flat for years, she was always scribbling in them.'

'I wonder where they went?'

'Kit has them now.' Kate made a paltry effort at removing the omelette from Indigo and received a warning bleat of rage and fists crumpling tighter. That Kate hadn't simply pulled them straight out of her hands told Isabelle more about the impact of the hangover than anything else. 'Hopefully, he has the wisdom not to read them.'

'Wouldn't you be the least bit curious?'

'Curiosity about Rose would kill the cat for sure.' Kate held out her hands to Indigo with a stern look on her face and demanded the pieces of omelette. 'Come on, tiger, give up the dead lunch.'

'Was she a lot like Kit?'

Kate stared at Indigo until the child gave up, receiving a kiss on each cheek in return for the soggy, crumbling egg deposited in Kate's hands. 'Lovely, thank you.' She didn't respond to Isabelle's question.

It was strange territory the standoff between Kit and Kate. Isabelle couldn't work out the ground that lay behind this war they had. She had returned from Italy with so much to tackle herself she hadn't noticed Kit's long absence from their life, or Kate's habit of avoiding him in conversation until she realised one tired, early childhood day, that her questions were always turned aside. Awareness that had slipped beneath the waves of exhaustion and sleepless nights, until she surfaced again to discover their communication had dwindled to a ratings war on their Instagram accounts. And that she was required to get an Instagram account and tread a microscopically fine silken thread between them, cataloguing her likes and comments to each. Isabelle tried again, veering sideways.

'Do you ever wonder why Rose didn't come back?'

'I didn't used to much.' Kate glanced at her across Indigo's tousled head. 'You know I believe the past is best left alone. Whatever decisions we made shouldn't be second guessed.'

'But?'

'The last few years, perhaps I've had too much time. I think I know why she didn't come back.'

Isabelle couldn't imagine how Kate thought she had too much time on her hands. Perhaps like her own, in the sparse moments between day and night. When loneliness some-times sat on the end of the bed and looked at you. She waited to see if Kate would continue.

'The human heart can only break so many times.' Kate let

the words out as though each one had been dredged from the river, turned over and laid on the shore. 'She loved Beth, you know. Loved her like a sister, a kindred soul, a lover. I never understood it, not at first. But now, I can imagine what it must have done to her, losing Beth. It seems a sentimental truth but perhaps we only know the true loves of our life after they are gone.'

'But she had Kit to come home to.'

Kate plucked Indigo from the table and set her on the floor.

'Kit was seventeen when Beth died. It wouldn't have the same pull as a small child. Besides, love can make you act in reckless ways, even before it gets caught up with grief.' She looked at the greasy contents of her hands and sighed. 'Look at this mess, I need to go and wash up and get ready for the afternoon.' She moved toward the door and glanced back. 'Why don't you get Rob to help you cook dinner tonight? He's moping in the drawing room watching the news on permanent loop. No healthier than looking through those dusty tomes.' She nodded at the diaries. 'Look forward Isabelle, it's the only way you get to go.'

ISABELLE TOOK Rob and Indigo out shopping after lunch. She figured there weren't many woes that couldn't be forgotten by dragging an independent toddler round Tesco. She'd forgotten about Steve turning up to look at the furniture and arrived back on the driveway to see his van hogging the space in front of the door. Her guilt at forgetting him taking her stomach to her toes as he turned from standing on the lip of the porch step to watch her pull her car to the far side of the magnolia tree, parking alongside Rob's new Range Rover

Evoque. Rob and Steve traded glances that filled her with discomfort.

'Oh God, I forgot the furniture guy.' She pulled the hand-brake on with a crunch that made Rob turn back and wince. Having a car and getting used to driving it were not the same. A car that Indigo had trashed with food and dirt and which she had no energy to care about. 'Can you manage with Indigo and the shopping?'

'Of course.'

She gripped his wrist in gratitude and jumped out of the driver's seat.

'Steve, hi, I'm sorry to keep you waiting. I thought you'd decided not to come.' She walked across the crunching gravel aware of his silence and the look that lingered over her shoulder where she could hear Rob getting Indigo out. She walked straight past him and opened the front door, turned to face him and pulled a confident smile from her curling toes.

He looked as though he had been on his way back to the van and couldn't now decide which way to go. His hands stuck in the pockets of his loose jeans, a rough linen shirt rolled up and creased round his forearms. He took a step toward the door, another.

'Yeah.' He pulled his hands out, glanced back at Rob who was getting shopping out of the boot, one hand holding onto Indigo. 'One of those days. I got delayed.'

'I can understand that. Do you want to come in?' she gestured toward the hall. 'Or have I missed my chance, do you need to go?'

'Na, I've got a bit of time. If you're not too busy now?'

'Great.' She walked ahead of him into the hall and came up against the explosion of boxes, china and domestic detritus that had now been there long enough that even Indigo and Deryn were ignoring it while Kate muttered about how useful the back stairs had been for her business. 'Excuse the mess, I had to clear a passage to the furniture. This way.'

She walked down the corridor and threw open the door onto the dining room. The sunlight was spread thickly across the gritty sheen of dust, lighting up her domestic indifference with spite.

'It's a bit dusty,' she confirmed the obvious.

'Guess you have enough rooms to abandon a few, huh?' His voice close behind her.

Isabelle turned to find him peering past her with guarded curiosity. It wasn't the bright warm smile she remembered from the last time he'd been here. Filled with interest about the house and what he might find there. Protective and relaxed as she declined his invite to go out for a drink. His shoulders seemed to fill the width of the space that led back to the door. She should have realised it would be awkward, this two-year disappearance after declining an invite.

'It's been a hectic few years.' Isabelle moved ahead into the space that surrounded the furniture and went to open the window to stir the dusty air. 'I should have cleared this out before, I don't know where the time goes.'

'I hear kids do that to you.'

She smiled at his sideswipe.

'Thought you'd sold the lot to someone else.' He began looking at the furniture, pulling one hand from his pockets to lay it on the sideboard.

She watched him try to resist the lure of the furniture, finally pulling his other hand out of his pocket. When he crouched down to open the cupboard door, fingering the hinges and clasps, she could see the bulge of his thighs against his jeans. Her poor eyesight caught sight of a solid line above his ear, recognised it as a pencil, perched there hours before and forgotten from habit.

'What are you looking to shift?'

'Most of it if you're interested in buying.'

'Wondered if you might have gone back to India?' He glanced up at her. 'Used to work there, didn't you?'

'Yes.' She tried to recall those days. 'It's been a long while since I was in India. This place and Indigo have taken all my attention.'

'Indigo?' he stood up, closing the cupboard door. 'That your daughter, out in the car?'

'Uh-huh.'

'She's sure grown, last time I saw her she was a sleeping bundle in a sling on your chest.'

Isabelle blinked at the memory.

'That your fella?' He asked the question while reaching up to run his hands along the outer edges of the wall units. Tucking his hands under their curving skirts, tracing the line of the glass. 'Are you selling these?

'Ehm, yes. No.'

He turned from the wall units and threw a raised eyebrow her way.

'Sorry, yes, they're for sale. No, he's not.' Isabelle clarified.

'Still the single mum then?'

She nodded, waiting for a small comment that normally finished that sentence. The "can't be easy" or "wow, you're brave" or "I don't know how you manage" compliments that left her feeling diminished, not uplifted.

'Must suit you, you certainly look well enough on it.' Steve looked at her, an uncertain smile toying with the edges of his mouth.

Isabelle saw his eyes travel down her body and back up, before passing over her to the old study desk that was tucked in a corner by the window. He moved toward her, shoulders, thighs and rough cotton shirt narrowing down the space between them to a distance where her eyesight fully focused. He was a little broader than Kit, his physique more natural than the gym-honed curation that was Kit's. He looked the craftsman he was, strong and confident. Wide shouldered, with a chiselled face flaring to a solid jaw beneath the casual stubble. Rough hands, nails worn down and yellowed with wax, followed the curve of the table's edge as he approached her, running his forefinger down the line of the grain, his thumb caressing the underside. She pulled back to let him pass, caught a whisper of a smile cross his face as he moved past where she had been stood, his mouth a wide easy stretch of amusement revealing the dazzling neat line of his teeth. He pulled his phone from his back pocket and crouched down in front of the desk, close enough that she could see the jeans tauten around his buttocks and the shirt stretch across the solid, defined shoulders hiding beneath.

'Though I suppose you're not the average single parent. Mind if I take some photos?'

'Not at all.' Her grip on the conversation seemed to be sliding sideways into a too narrow space. He slipped from personal to business and back again, her answers leaving her wondering what she had given him.

She watched him flip round the desk that she had huffed and puffed over. Turning it about in the narrow space until he could get to the drawers, pulling them in and out to assess their ease. Caressing the old leather with a sigh of happiness. There was something both hypnotic and discomforting about his pleasure. The little touches with which he connected to everything.

'Are you sure you can use it?' She frowned at the desk. Now she came to be rid of it forever she wondered how many of her ancestors had sat in the nook of its wood and filled in the daily pages of Riverdell. 'It's rather old-fashioned.'

'I may not be able to do much with it but if I take the wood back, clean down the leather, it won't look so jaded. Someone will want it.'

He moved down the other side of the table, hands trailing over the curved backs of the chairs. The last time she had used this room had been the hideous Easter lunch when she'd met Asha. He stopped at the last chair, where Moth had sat on that day. Talking with more courage than she'd been able to muster herself. He slid his hands down the sides of the chair and lowered himself to the floor, a speculative murmur of appreciation rising where Moth had sat.

'Do tell me you're not teasing about selling this table? Its handmade, possibly yew, or pear. Interesting wood anyway. And a decent width of it, so we could use the wood, even if we discard the legs. Though actually,' he rubbed his hand slowly up the leg of the table, curling his fingers round the fluting, 'I think we could use these on something else too, gorgeous shape to them.'

'I think I need to keep the table, for Christmas and stuff, unless you can help me find a more modern look?'

'That what you're doing?' he nodded at the room. 'Modernising the place? Most families like yours tend to try and hold onto the family heirlooms. I'm normally reduced to begging for the meanest of trifles.'

'Families like mine?' There was an air of challenge to how he used the phrase, provoking her to respond. 'My family seem to have thrown me the keys and run for the woods. I'm not too inclined to hold onto their abandoned detritus. Besides, I loved the desk I got from you. It replaced that one.' She pointed at the old desk. 'A lot more practical.'

'That's the craftsperson in you.' He moved to stand back by the door. 'You still sewing, or did you give that up to look after all this too?'

'No, still sewing,' she tucked her hair behind her ears, resisting the urge to duck beneath its comforting cover. 'Set up a business making vintage-style aprons. It's a bit of a battle to keep on top of it, but I haven't given up yet.'

'That's the thing with making stuff, it's hard to stop.' He curled his hands round the chair she had last sat in. 'If you sell the table, I'll take the chairs off your hands as part of the deal. They'll be harder to sell, but I've got an upholsterer that might take them.'

'How long have you been doing this?' she asked him, moving back toward the door.

'I've lost track,' he said. 'Left college and moved to Glasgow, totally broke. Ended up scrounging in skips for furniture, it kind of grew from there. Been doing it ever since. Anything else you want me to look at?'

'Yes, please. I've got a couple of rooms upstairs in a similar state.' She led him out of the dining room and back to the main hall, starting up the stairs. 'What brought you to Ludlow, it's a long way from Glasgow.'

'Love, in the first place,' he told her. 'Then I fell in love properly, with the town and the way of life. When the girl I met decided she wanted to move up the social ladder and relocate to London, I couldn't bear the thought of going back to urban life, so I stayed.'

She made it to the first floor, conscious of his eyes behind her as she went up the stairs.

The upstairs floors had suffered the most from her neglect and she eyed the doors with weariness. Elsa's bedroom had been left in a sacrosanct void and there was the sole respectable guestroom which Rob used when he stayed. The hallway walls held their faint shadows of former portraits. Three bedrooms lay filled with unwanted furniture and upstairs, on the top floor which she shared with Indigo, one spare room was filled with her sewing rejects from the original workroom, the other housed the overbearing portraits and final spare furniture.

She glanced at her watch and realised she had less than an hour to get dinner ready before Asha arrived.

'Short on time?' Steve asked behind her.

She glanced back at him. 'I need to pop and get dinner started. My cousin-in-law is coming for dinner and she's going to be in a foul mood already, without me starving her for an extra hour.' She opened the door to the first of the stacked bedrooms.

'Wow, what did you do?' Steve looked over her shoulder. 'Use a shoehorn to ram it all in?'

'Don't, please.' She stepped back and moved across to the next door, opened it too. He grimaced as he saw the contents. 'I have a habit of avoidance, according to most anyone who knows me.'

'I'll say.' He looked straight at her as he said it and quirked his eyebrows. 'What's pissing your cousin-in-law off?'

Isabelle struggled to control the blush that was warming her stomach. 'She's Polish. Been fuming since they announced the referendum, today's result is not going to help her mood.'

'Hardly surprising, must feel a right kick in the teeth.'

'Exactly.' She stepped across the hallway to open the final door. 'Can I leave you to have a look while I go start my consolation dinner? I'll be about fifteen minutes.'

'Sure thing.' He moved into the first room. 'Promise I won't pocket any of the crown jewels while I'm here.'

THE TIME DISAPPEARED AS READILY as Indigo could lose herself in the house. Between trying to get her meal together, nudging Rob to clear the table, finding the decorative details that she had wanted to liven the kitchen table with for Asha, managing Steve moving furniture in the bowels of the bedrooms and getting herself relatively respectable, Isabelle battled to push back the moment she heard Asha's car pull up on the gravel. Parking solidly behind Steve's van and blocking his departure.

Isabelle opened the front door to ask her to move as James followed her arrival in the Land Rover, as Kate walked through from the kitchen looking for her, as Asha arrived on the porch with a crumpled work suit and a scowl as dark as the castle hovering over them, as Steve came downstairs dusting his hands across his muscled thighs, as Rob walked out of the sitting room with Indigo holding onto his hand. Isabelle fixed a smile on her face and tried to send it in all directions as she negotiated the moment. Everyone began talking at once.

'What on earth have you done to my catalogues?' Kate asked as Indigo slipped Rob's hand and ran to her. 'And something's boiling over on the hob. Oh, hello.'

'Who else is joining us for dinner?' Asha asked, glancing

back out at the van before turning to see Steve descend the final steps. 'Oh, hello.'

'Oh, no, Steve was just looking over the furniture.' Isabelle explained.

'That's a shame.' A sly grin broke the scowl on Asha's face. 'We could do with some company to sweeten the evening.'

'I'll say,' Kate added, picking up Indigo and staring down Asha's challenge. 'Neutralise the acid a bit. Do say you're staying?'

'I'll check the hob,' Rob disappeared through the kitchen door with a stiff glance at Steve.

'Sorry, no,' Steve replied to Kate. 'I'm just the furniture guy.'

'Oh, hello.' James appeared in the doorway holding a decidedly grubby Deryn, finding his wife's expression turn from glowing to glowering as she moved her head from Steve to the state of her daughter. 'I'm James.'

'I'm leaving,' Steve said.

'I'm tired,' Asha complained as Deryn reached for her. 'You're on duty until I've had a drink. I've blocked you in, are you sure you won't join us? Have you two known each other long?'

Isabelle gritted her teeth at Asha's presumption.

'At least stop for a drink?' Kate added. 'Isabelle owes you one, right?'

'I'll move the cars,' James told Asha. 'Here, take this, give me your keys, go get a drink.' He deposited Deryn in her arms, took the keys and left before she could complain.

'I'll go open a bottle,' Kate moved for the kitchen doorway with Indigo. 'Or two.'

'Apiece?' Asha followed her with Deryn shoved against her hip.

They disappeared through the door with the children, leaving Isabelle with Steve in the hallway.

'Sorry about that,' Isabelle said to Steve, the door open to show James reversing out the gates and across the road. 'You can see why I didn't want to be late with dinner.'

'Yeah, looks like fun.' He moved across the hallway and stood beside the door, unable to leave until James moved the second car.

The offer to join them hovering unwanted in the air.

'You're welcome to stop for a drink.' She looked at the closed kitchen door which was not holding the noise back and grimaced back at him. 'If you really want to.'

'As I recall, my offer came first.' He pushed his hands into his pockets and gave her an amused grin. 'And to be honest, I've got friends I'm not talking to over this vote, let alone facing that.'

'Probably a wise move.'

'So, how about it?' he asked. 'Or are you still too busy?'

Behind them James reversed Asha's Ford out the gateway. Isabelle could see him glancing through the windscreen at them. She really should have called Kit about the furniture. Steve rocked back onto his heels, watching her, waiting for a response.

'I didn't think you'd still be interested,' Isabelle stalled.

'Neither did I.' He ran a hand through his hair, dug it straight back into his pocket. 'Until I realised I was avoiding coming. Normally you can't hold me back from a house visit.'

'I didn't mean to not call,' she explained. 'Time rather slipstreamed.'

'Well, how about it?' He took two steps toward the door. 'Have a drink with me. Tell me about your last few years.'

Isabelle could see James dawdling back through the arch-way, dragging his feet.

'Promise I'll buy the furniture even if you say no,' Steve added.

'Ok.'

'Ok to the drink?' he asked. 'Or to my buying the furniture?'

James paused to look at the magnolia in deep concentra-tion, on the other side of Steve's van. She wondered if this was how James had felt, asking Asha out the first time. Awkward as it felt to be asked, she respected the courage that it took.

'Ok to the drink.' After all, a drink was only a drink. She didn't have to go again if she didn't enjoy it.

'Right, tomorrow night?' Steve stepped down onto the porch, moving backward to his van. 'Before you change your mind. The Brewery, seven o'clock?'

'Ok.'

He grinned at her response and turned away. She watched him reverse out, waiting for James to join her.

'Right,' he said. 'You ready for this?'

She grimaced at him as she shut the door.

'Not really.'

KIT WAS MAKING breakfast in the kitchen with gusto. In the gym he could hear Fred and Jay grunting and swearing at each other. The backdrop of their pain making him feel sublime. He'd breezed through his own workout that morn-ing. Outside, the rain was tapping with irritation at the wide bifold doors. The garden looking limp and indifferent in its gloom. Grey hung over everything. Offending him with its refusal to show even the glimmer of a blue sky, yet not heavy enough to promise a white Christmas. It was Saturday morning, four days since Jay had arrived and, with Adele back in London, the house was theirs for the weekend.

He turned the sausages baking in the oven, sliced the black pudding into fine circles and pulled the eggs out of the fridge to warm up. It felt good to be alone. Later, when he went to bed, he would feel the emptiness of the mattress. Kit wandered to the table and put out cutlery. It was an emotional seesaw, this living together. People had visited, yes. Kate, Isabelle, other lovers over the years. But Bristol had always been the home he came back to. The centre of his private empire. Being a boss, a lover, a friend, was different to sharing a life. Even a life that saw two homes in two cities shared for no more than three days a week.

There was an inconvenience at times to not doing exactly as he wanted. Or to soothing Adele's ruffled feathers simply because he'd done something he wanted without asking first. Like deciding they would have Christmas at Riverdell. Like bringing Jay home. Kit was glad to have Adele in his bedroom, less happy with the way he teased Jay in the evenings.

Kit paused, grimacing at the line of cutlery on the grain of wood and tweaked it into perfection. The teasing smacked of insecurity. Not what he'd seen in Adele's rippling muscles and superb career path. What did he have to be insecure about? If anyone had the right to insecurity, surely it was him. The older partner.

He moved back to the kitchen, opened the oven and breathed in the fumes of sizzling meat. A whole weekend to themselves. What on earth were they going to do?

His phone rang, Kit picked it up from beside the sink and

saw Henri's name, swiped to answer and put the phone on speaker. 'What's up?'

'Why must something always be up?'

'You only ever ring with problems.'

'That is my job, after all,' Henri said.

Kit almost responded. Drummed his fingers against the worksurface to distract himself. Gritting his teeth to hold back the comment that he had wanted to discuss for the last nine months. He focused on the noise coming from the gym. January, he reminded himself. They'd get through Christmas, give the team a chance to fully recover and then he and Henri would be sitting down for a chat.

'So, there is a problem.' Kit knew there was a problem. The problem was with Henri and the urge to say so was getting harder to overcome. He twisted the words in his head into a shape that fitted the moment.

'Vee's struggling to work with Lou.'

Kit pictured them, the quiet withdrawn Vee trying to find her feet in the team. Lou, the mother hen making sure she was coping. 'What? Why? Lou's been brilliant with getting her trained up.'

'Well, yes, in one way, no doubt,' Henri agreed. 'Vee's not making a complaint, she's just been talking to me a bit.'

'Well at least she's talking to someone.' Kit grabbed the frying pan and put a knob of lard to slowly melt. Handling Jay's withdrawal from the greasy food he'd been eating was a matter of replacing with healthier fats before reducing those fats altogether. Along with making him drink a glass of water between every coffee or glass of wine.

'Yes, I thought you'd be happy. I know you've been fretting about her.'

'I wasn't fretting about Vee,' Kit said, gritting his teeth to control the words as they came out.

Kit couldn't put his finger on when the change had occurred between him and Henri. For the first few years he'd been as thick as the rest of the team. Kit had believed in a gunfight they'd all go down together, dying in a glorious Butch and Sundance hail of bullets. Only recently, he'd begun to feel Henri was eyeing the alternative exits. Kit had always known Henri would move on, he'd been head-hunted himself, so the longevity of his commitment had always been questionable. What really bugged Kit was not knowing the exact point at which Henri had begun considering his options, or the specific why of it. There were subtle pauses in their conversations where both left things unchallenged. He'd seen this slow break down of honesty in a relationship enough times to know where it ended. But extracting a lover from his life and extracting his business second-in-command were two entirely incomparable levels of delicacy.

'If she's not making a complaint, what is the problem?' Kit asked.

'It's a bit more delicate than that.' Henri had switched into his best customer accent. Kit felt his back flicker at the tone. He stretched it out slowly as he peeled the bacon from its pack, as his back therapist had taught him to do. Ease out the warning signs, miss the crashes. 'She is uncomfortable working with Lou.'

'Why?' Kit asked.

Henri paused on the phone.

'Oh, spit it out Henri, it can't be that bad.'

'Lou is overwhelming Vee with her... intimate preferences, these days.' Henri said it in a way that Kit could almost see his subtle shoulder shrug, the one that told customers of course he would listen to their choices, but he would not take responsibility for them.

'You are kidding me?' Kit held an ambient egg in his hand. 'She actually said that?'

'I'm precising the conversation for you, boss.'

'Why wouldn't she talk to me?' Kit broke the egg one-handed against the pan.

'I think you're expecting too much, she's a bit in awe of you.'

'Rubbish, all the team talk to me. We're practically family, Henri, how can I look after everyone if I don't know what's going on with them?' Kit picked another egg up, they felt like fragile bollocks nestled in his hand. 'I've never had a staff member this uptight before.'

'She's young, boss. And new to us all. I guess we should try and see it from her perspective. We might be a little more overwhelming than we realise.'

'Overwhelming? Did she say that too?'

'No, no.' Henri used his soothing voice and Kit felt his own testicles tighten. 'You're taking this too personally.' He hadn't been, right up until that moment. 'She is an employee finding her feet. She does have a point after all, Lou has been a bit ardent in her conversion. She's a bit... antagonistic toward men these days.'

Kit looked out toward the glass windows, the rain was hitting harder now, clouding the view down into the city. Turning the world outside all shades of sludgy indifference. Henri's suggestion irked Kit. It was one thing for him to have doubts about Lou, it was another for anyone else to voice those thoughts.

'We're a tight team, Henri,' Kit said. 'I'm not going to start a process where one member complains about another, and we have to start keeping them apart. Maybe Vee's not cut out for us.'

'I don't think you can fire her for feeling sexually uncomfortable round a team member.'

'She's twenty, Henri.' Kit glanced toward the gym, time to wrap this up. 'As far as I'm concerned, she's an adult. If she feels sexually harassed, she should make a formal complaint. If she's being homophobic, she can fuck off elsewhere.'

'So that's your official position on it?' Henri asked slowly. 'We ignore her discomfort and don't change the rota?'

'Did you have an official chat about it?' Kit asked. 'Or was it a personal discussion?'

Henri paused in his response. At the same time, the rain changed direction and stopped hammering the window. Jay and Fred came out of the gym together, dripping with sweat and stripped to their shorts. Fred's black skin folding over the top of his waistband, his shorts bulging fit to please an army. Jay's brown belly widened to the point of wanting to fold but stopping short of the commitment. They looked ragged from effort and full of satisfaction. A streak of vicious winter light lit up the raindrops on the windows and came into the downstairs room with crisp clarity. Kit realised the exact point that things had changed between him and Henri, the moment Adele appeared in Kit's life. However this conversation had arisen between Vee and Henri, it had been needed on both sides. Kit switched off the speaker and picked up the phone.

'If she's unhappy with any aspect of the job, tell her to come and talk to me.' Kit had about two seconds before the boys' ears tuned in to his conversation. 'You should know us well enough by now, Henri. We work together or we don't work together.'

Kit hung up and put the phone down on the cold granite,

the thrill of released pent-up irritation warming him, and looked across the room. 'You two look toasted.'

'You're killing us,' Fred complained, grinning, wiping the sweat from his neck with a towel.

'You're bloody loving it. Look at you both, all those pores oozing the poison out of your system.'

'Do we get a day off tomorrow?' Fred asked. 'I've got some poison to put back in tonight.'

'Nope, I don't care how hungover you are. I've already let you out of tonight's run. Wait until you see next week's plan.'

'WHAT'S NEXT?' Jay asked over the remains of breakfast after Fred had left.

Kit turned from looking out the window to see Jay watching him.

'Sorry?'

'What are we doing for the rest of the day?' Jay glanced at the vile weather. 'Or are you going to make me do some hideous run in this?'

'Nah, you're safe, I hate running in the rain. I won't make you do what I wouldn't myself.'

'Another one of your life rules?' Jay teased him.

'Definitely, it leaves me free from the risk of being judged a hypocrite.'

The quietness of the kitchen settled into the space of the table. Kit looked back out the window. He should get up, clear the table, get Jay ready to go shopping. Henri's conversation was lingering in his mind, taking the motivation out of him. Already making him doubt the moment of clarity that Henri had changed since he got with Adele. The doubt chewing away at him until he grew irritated. Annoyed by how his convictions, which had always felt absolute, had begun to wobble like a flat tyre, pulling him up. Doubting himself was a new experience and Kit hated it. Hated the way it had come on like a warning light with Moth, slid into his romance with Isabelle before crashing into his relationship with Kate and leaving a permanent oil drip that couldn't be fixed. All the while taunting him that maybe it was the untouchable impact of age affecting him mentally as much as it had begun to show physically. Yes, he could maintain the same outer appearance. But there were all these internal tweaks that needed added, unseen input to keep the slick-looking show on track.

'I'm not used to seeing you this chilled out.' Jay pushed back his chair and relaxed into the back of it. Letting one foot come up to rest on a knee, giving him a quizzical look that held a shadow of the smile Kit remembered. Jay always lit up when Fred was here, but it ebbed as soon as Fred left. Etched on his face, not rising from his heart. Still, even the reminder of how to smile would help bring back the reality of it. 'Makes me nervous, like we might actually relax for an hour.'

'Maybe we should,' Kit told him.

'Stop it, you're freaking me out. Surely you have the day planned out. Shopping, art, lunch, club?'

'Are you calling me predictable?'

'No, exhausting.'

'It takes me a while to slow down.' Kit shrugged, realised he had gathered the habit from Henri and pushed his shoulders down, his neck forward. What was a shrug after all, but a continental screw you?

'What happens when you do?'

Kit pursed his lips and thought back to the last time. March 2014. About a month after he and Kate had given up trying to rekindle their relationship. He'd hit a slump of boredom that had ended with six weeks in rehab clinic in Japan, but that might be more than Jay needed to know. Lou had covered him for that one, not even the rest of the team knew. And even Lou didn't need to know how close to bankruptcy that little habit had brought the business. At least it hadn't left him in the corner of a dark room though. 'I get hideously bored and start picking at life. It's not pretty.'

'Best not let that happen,' Jay said. 'Fancy watching old movies? Doing Tai Chi?'

Kit blinked at him. It was mildly irritating that everyone assumed he would always know what was happening next on the odd occasion he didn't want to tell everyone what to do.

'Tai Chi?' Kit asked. 'Are you kidding me? Have you seen how slow that stuff is? I fall asleep watching the videos. How about a massage?'

'What?' Jay asked, his foot slipping off his knee. 'You want us to go for a massage?'

'Well, no. I was thinking we could give each other a massage. I have a proper table.'

'You have a massage table?'

'Doesn't everyone?'

'No, Kit, not everyone has their own massage table.'

'Really? They should. Adele and I use it all the time, it's great for relaxation.'

'We are not giving each other massages.' Jay sat upright in his chair.

'That makes you uncomfortable?' Kit asked with a quirk to his lips. 'Which bit? Me and Adele massaging each other, or me massaging you?'

'You permanently nudging my boundaries makes me

uncomfortable,' Jay tossed back over the greasy plates. 'Especially when you're bored.'

'I'm not bored...'

'... yet!' Jay finished for him. 'I reckon this rehabilitation mission is sticking in your teeth a bit. Or is it that you got dumped by Isabelle when you could have taken on another client and made more money? I'm not sure.'

'Oooh, you go,' Kit taunted him. 'Isabelle did not dump me, she got waylaid. And I don't need to make any more money. I need to spend time with my friend whose company I have missed, whose life got screwed sideways by a lying bitch and a dead dog, and who's avoiding a challenge to his masculinity by being angry instead.'

Jay blinked at him, sat back in his chair, sullen.

'You are not strong enough to cross swords with me yet, buddy,' Kit told him. 'Ok, no massage. What *do* you want to do today?'

Kit picked up the remnants of his coffee and drained it. He watched Jay staring out the window, thinking, retreating. This weather was enough to depress anyone. It was hard to remember how dull December could be when you spent all of autumn turning the world into Santa's Grotto. Maybe old movies weren't a bad idea. They could close the curtains in the drawing room, make a buffet lunch... no, that was no good. Exercise and movement were what Jay needed, not food and inertia. By the end of his stay Kit might even have got him dancing again, let alone smiling. Now, that was a goal to aim for. Jay hadn't danced since Lydia dumped him on that Valentine's dancefloor. Left him standing and walked out with a black salsa champion she'd been shagging for six months on the side. Kit hadn't been there, but he'd heard about it from mutual friends, it had been intensely public. Jay looked back and caught him staring. Kit smiled over his coffee cup and watched him squirm, refusing to come up with a solution to their wet day. Jay needed motivating, not mollycoddling.

'I want to open your mother's chest.' Jay announced.

Kit realised he was now blinking. 'Oh, that's just mean.'

'There's no way I accept you can't open it,' Jay told him, the shadow of a smirk lurking in his face. 'There's nothing you can't do if you want to. I think you're scared of what you might find.'

Kit thought about what his therapist had found lurking in the corners of his mind and thought most people ought to be more scared of what they could discover. Getting himself back on track had gone quicker once Kit realised they were only scratching the surface. No thank you. Some edifices were better left intact behind a fresh facade than scraped back to the original bones.

'I told you, I don't have the key.'

'Then bust it open.'

'That's wholly disrespectful,' Kit told him.

'Aren't you even a tiny bit curious?' Jay asked, leaning forward onto the table. 'And come on, what else are we going to do but go outside and get soaking wet while you complain about everyone's crappy and inadequate Christmas decorations?'

'We could put our Christmas decorations up?' Kit suggested.

'What?'

'Well, I have all these decorations at the lockup. We might as well put them up, now we're spending Christmas here.'

Jay could not have looked any less enthused.

'Yeah, I feel you.' Kit admitted it felt half-hearted. 'How

about we go dancing instead?'

Jay sat back in his chair and folded his hands over his chest.

'What's it like?' Kit asked, leaning forward himself. 'We never talked about it, you not dancing. Don't you miss it? How do you move on from that?'

'I don't know, Kit,' Jay said. 'How do you move on from a disappointment like that? Why don't we talk about you and Kate?'

Kit sat back with a frown. Jay might not know about the habit that had landed him in the Japanese clinic, but he hadn't missed the U-turn in Kit's life that had kicked off that process. That was the problem with making big statements, like taking Jay to mingle with the family at Kate's housewarming. That had been a stupid arse big statement, after which life had begun its determined slide sideways.

'What's to talk about?' Kit gave a dismissive shrug, which tickled its way down his spine. 'We fell out, I moved on.'

'And that's all there is to it?' Jay asked. 'You're still not talking about it?'

'Hey, I told you. She didn't come to Italy and when I asked her why, she said she couldn't tell me.'

'And you couldn't cope with that secret.'

'There's no need for secrets if there's trust.' Kit resisted the urge to push his empty plate away from him. Curbed the urge to twist his watch. Reined in his toes that were threatening to jiggle across the floor beneath the table. Held his fingers away from feeling the edge of the thick wood between him and Jay. He felt every part of himself itch as Jay stared hard at him. Itch like he needed a hot shower, itch.

'Bollocks.' Jay scowled at him across the table. 'It's not the secrets you know about that cause the problem.'

'How the hell do you figure that out?'

'If a person trusts you, they'll tell you they have secrets and can't share them. They trust you to respect them.'

'Buddy, I appreciate your concern, but, honestly, you're digging over dead ground. I told you, I've moved on.'

'Uh-huh,' Jay said, with an understanding nod that Kit struggled not to frown at. 'Did you tell Adele about Kate yet?'

'Never tell your current lover your past affairs.'

'And that's not keeping secrets?' Jay asked. 'Sure as hell sounds like it to me.'

They stared at each other over the leftovers, both refusing to budge an inch over the dirty crocks.

'We're going to fall out if we end up stuck in this house all day together.' Kit sat back. 'I say Christmas decorations.'

'I say your mother's chest.'

'Both,' they said at the same time.

'Right, you're on sunshine.' Kit stood up. 'You clear up the table and go see to the chest. Good luck opening that ugly old thing, have you seen how solid it is? I'll go get the decorations from the lock up. You want me to bring a sledgehammer back?'

'No need.' Jay sat back with a look so smug Kit felt his shoulders creeping upwards. He watched as Jay reached into his pocket and pulled out a key attached to a faded gold, silken key tassel.

'You are shitting me?' Kit looked at the key with distrust. He'd been assuming Jay would fail miserably and baulk at outright destruction, which was not his style at all. 'Where the hell did you find that?'

'You left me alone for three days while Adele, how shall I say it, took your attention? That's how I found it,' Jay told him.

'We're going to talk about your issues with Adele,' Kit told him. 'But that's not...'

'... I don't have issues with him...'

'... the point.' Kit stared at the key in distrust. 'Is that seriously the right key?'

'Yup, I checked.' Jay held up his hand as Kit went to protest. 'No, I did not open it, I checked it unlocked the mechanism. I wasn't going to open it without your permission.'

'And where did you go rummaging to find the key?'

'I think the real question is, as I found it so easily, how did you not?' Jay asked. 'Are you sure it's *me* who's avoiding their issues.'

'I have unbelievably happy memories of my mother,' Kit told him. Well, right up until she left, anyway. It got a bit murkier after that, according to his therapist. Right about the point where they'd started talking about Kate. Which was the point where Kit had left the couch and found another solution. 'Perhaps I didn't want to disturb them.'

'So, don't you?' Jay dangled the key by its tassel.

It wasn't that Kit hadn't looked for it. Of course he had. Not long after Elsa gave him the chest, after the sideways shit slide caused by him and Kate falling out, after coming back from Japan. He'd been in the house by himself too much. Single. Bored. Restless. Battling addiction. He'd tried every key on it that Granny had left him. He'd checked all the drawers in his mother's bedroom, opened the closet and rummaged in the pockets of the clothes she'd left. Pulled out the crumbling top hat and stood naked in front of the mirror with it on his head. But it had taken him too close to those memories he'd left on the therapist's couch. He'd gone to sleep on her bed, woken up feeling hollow. Empty. Abandoned. Remembered his childhood waking up knowing she was there for him. An ache inside deep enough to terrify him. He'd thrown himself into work to make up for the damage he'd done to the business, met Adele not long after and forgotten about it. Until now. With Jay sparkling with smug delight. Kit would shove him on the top of the Christmas tree if he didn't stop it.

'Where was it?'

'Strapped to the back of your mother's portrait.'

Kit sat back in his chair and resisted the urge to barricade his chest with his arms. 'Huh.'

'I figured you must have altered most of the rest of the house over the years. It had to be either in her room or lost for antiquity.'

'And you just popped the picture off the wall and there it was?'

'Uh-huh.' Jay's smile began to bloom, the smile Kit was trying to rekindle.

'Alright,' Kit snapped. 'Don't be smug about it.'

Jay deflated like a popped balloon. Kit could growl. There was nothing more he wanted than to see Jay find his feet, but why did it have to be this one thing he'd fixated on? That fixation was both Jay's superpower and his Kryptonite. The focus that made him invincible at both his job and his dancing. The obsession that couldn't let go of Lydia. It was going to be a long trip to get him to move on. To refocus.

'My mother was an... interesting person.' Kit tried to temper Jay's enthusiasm. 'Liberated, defiant. You might be shocked by some of the stuff you find in there.'

'Is that why you don't want to read them?' Jay asked.

'Perhaps. A little.'

'What about if I read them and only relay the good bits?' Jay asked.

'What if there are no good bits?' The words were out before Kit could stop them.

'Everyone has good bits about their life,' Jay softened his tone, surprised by Kit's.

'You'd hope so, wouldn't you?' As Kit spoke a shudder rippled across his shoulders. He forced it down, the sensation clenching his guts, tensing his butt, flinting his jaw. The thought that there might have been no good memories, that she left because she was running away from a life she hated, a son she didn't want, that was the thought that had sent him from her bedroom. The therapist's suggestion that all his good memories with Kate were no more than a desperate effort at replacing his mother. It was a shudder that seemed to have the capacity to dislodge not only his innards but the foundation of the house, bringing the chest crashing through the ceiling, all the way from the bedroom, down through the drawing room and into the belly of the basement kitchen. Controlling that shudder took all the gym-honed muscle he had and flicked out a spinal flexor muscle that was his weakest pain point. Kit grimaced, trying to keep it under control.

'Hey, you good?' Jay asked in concern, reaching forward over the table. 'We don't have to do this, I guess I got a bit obsessed.'

'You?' Kit laughed. Carefully laughed, holding his muscles against the threatening flexor. 'Obsessed, really? Who'd have thought.'

Jay sat back in his chair. Leg crossed onto his knee, hand twitching a dance across his thigh.

'Oh fine, let's do it.' Kit knew he would end up regretting this. 'But you're helping with the decorations in return.'

7

W hy does Riverdell draw me back when so often it repulses me? I sometimes wonder if I will ever escape the bond we made there, returning like a ghost to haunt my past happiness. This time I return home fresh with understanding. Renewed with hope.

Elsa is swollen with the baby. You should have seen David's face. He is wretched with misery, lurking in corners, refusing to go to his mother. She is distraught with guilt. Richard has finally taken charge and, adding to the boy's misery over the impending arrival of a sibling, he now goes repeatedly to the farm. I think even Richard knows David is more likely to be an astronaut than a farmer. Still, he takes the boy, and insists on giving Elsa space. She has no more than six weeks left to go. I wonder what it will be this time. Perhaps a girl would be best, to soften the brunt of David's dislike. Or would he be kinder to a brother, a fellow playmate?

Kit was the sweetest. Considering he can be a merciless little bastard at times, he has enough charm to steal even my breath. He spent the entire journey there berating me for school, telling me how much he hates it, accusing me of abandonment and tormenting me with the notion of running away. The moment he walked through the door of Riverdell, he was adorable. Attentive to Elsa, playing with David, even going to the farm with him and Richard to soothe the irritation. It took me three days to relax into the change, I kept suspecting him of planning to blow us up in our beds while we were being seduced by his consideration. Elsa was totally taken in, she kept on and bloody on about how successful the school change is until I nearly decided to pull him out... oh... the conniving little rat.

He knows me too well and plays me like a fool.

Yes, my son has all the educated ways of public school now and, yes, I hate it and see its usefulness. I am a wallowing hypocrite. Damn it, this is not the clarity I came here to write about. I must not lose focus. Form, form, I shall come back to it, but let me chase this down first...

Kit put on a show to impress Elsa to irritate me into regretting educating him to fit into Riverdell. There. Now I see it. I shall murder him at breakfast while Granny struggles to eat her toast.

How, oh how, to counter his machinations? He plays the psychology trick with an edge sharp enough to cut himself on.

I'm amazed he has stuck it this long. I guess I see each year he boards as a chance to maintain the balance of our lives. What do I do if he leaves? Will he be old enough to take himself to and from school without Granny's help or do we up and move to London and leave Granny with a carer? The last thing I want is Kit in London. Especially now. And I can't bear the thought of Granny on her own. No, this is our

home. It has been my only home, though Elsa yawns on
about Riverdell being home to all us girls (privileged
wallowing whale, she is enormous with this child, I'm
amazed it's not twins). And Kit would not leave Granny
either. For all his contempt between here and Riverdell and
back, he is as devoted to her as he was at Riverdell. There is
kindness in him. Though he hides it under a sharp tongue
and a cockiness I loathe, he can see other people. Much
more than I ever have. He sees Elsa's guilt about her pregnancy and David's distress. He sees Richard's sadness that
David can't stand the farm (a boy for Richard, dear Freya, if
you please, and let it be a boy with Richard's charm too). He
sees Granny's tea stains on her starched blouse, her shaking
hands rattling the cup. There's a balance, between under-
filling it and making her feel belittled and overfilling it to a
point she can't cope. Her pride lies in the millimetre of
space between those two tea lines, and he knows it. Whereas
I get brittle with irritation if she tuts at me, he hands her the
cup with chatter and laughter to distract her and softens it
all with a plate of biscuits. He is extraordinary, this boy of
mine.

There, I have admitted it again. This parental idiocy, this
blind pride. But he is extraordinary, and I both admire and
fear him. He can switch between emotions with a speed I
cannot match. When he loses his temper, he's unafraid for
the world to see it, not clenching in his fists like I do. And he
is growing strong. Not tall, David is barely inches shorter
though there are five years between them, but Kit is broader
in the shoulders. And he has strong thighs and a good
solidity to his whole frame. He will be handsome, I think, and
seems already inclined to cultivate that. But agh, I ramble on
tonight, I must get back.

How to keep Kit at school? How to convince him to stay? Granny. That is it.

He must see by the end of this Christmas break how it only works for us to stay with her if he is away at school. I must emphasise her frailty, perhaps talk to him about the options for her care. Oh hell, what a vile and manipulative parent I am. Pray Hera, he never finds these diaries and reads this. But, yes, if he can play the game, so can I. I shall include him in the decisions, make him take responsibility. Fingers crossed he doesn't out dance me and throw her in a home and decide we should move to London. That won't work at all.

Now, back, to Riverdell. Yes, I gravitate back to Riverdell. Granny didn't want to do Christmas and Elsa was delighted to have us.

Do you have many friends I wonder? My ability to grow friendships seemed to end when you left. I have more acquaintances and lovers than can comfortably fit into a banquet hall together. But friends? It is still Elsa and Kate, and Richard, of course. Going back this time was a joy. Kate was delightful company and, somewhere between her and Elsa, I seemed to find the answers to the questions that have tormented me these last years.

Let me start with Elsa. Huge, and mooning with it. Her breasts gorged, her legs spread to ease the weight of it all. Honestly, if she had been a cow, I think Richard would have been concerned and confined her to a stall. How she will ever pass it is beyond me. It reminded me all over again of pregnancy. I hated how people looked at me as though I was fulfilling the destiny of my kind, the epitome of flowering womanhood. Elsa carries the same smugness, it positively overflows with the caresses she gives her belly all the time.

I went into retreat during my pregnancy, practically hibernating. The strange alienation from my own body. The obsession with what was growing inside it. The relief when it was freed from me. The aftermath. That slopping flesh of my belly, the gaping wreckage when I touched myself, the attachment of a child to my nipples. I couldn't bear it, poor boy, he was formula fed and I loved it. Him snuggled up against me and sucking on the bottle, us tucked together into bed at night.

Elsa's unbridled body brought it all back to me. And her delight. Her utter overwhelming joy with the labour of creation. I felt entirely cut off from it. Watching from the side with Richard, calculating the labour risk and the impact on David. And the relief. The swamping gratitude that it wasn't me. It kept catching me, hurtling down the halls and smacking me in the back. Thank every Goddess that ever lived, it wasn't me. This act of ultimate womanhood and I am horrified by it. I realised it wasn't Elsa, or pregnancy, it was femininity itself. This incarnation of gender that sits on her body like a fine calf glove of her mother's, has always been a misfit to mine. I wear the shape and fashion of it and love the dynamics of that act. I love the colour of my wardrobe, the styling of my clothes, the way I can command a response with the attire I choose. These aspects of my identity bring me joy and pleasure, as does the body itself. But inside, there is another part of me that I lock away. There is a repugnance with myself and a fascination with the other. I watch Kit's growing body with jealousy. I see his changes, the deepening of his voice, the way he notices people, (oh my wild and spiteful Goddesses, I think he has a crush on Kate, I must come back to Kate, my mind spins too fast for the pen tonight), the way he refuses to talk to me about sex. I am fascinated to know if he is masturbating and what he thinks about to arouse himself.

What is wrong with me?

There is no space out there for this tumult. I feel I could fly when I write, all the truths I hide are freed and carry me far aloft and away. And where is this place I seek to be free? And what is this body I seek to find? For it is not this.

It is not this.

There, that is what I learned at Riverdell this Christmas.

I am not this person.

This effortless grace and elegance that other people admire. It's far from effortless. It's carefully constructed, manicured and maintained. Perhaps other women find their true selves through denying fashion and beauty, but I can no more bear their hairy legs and pits, their trousers held up with a man's belt and hair unkempt and frizzy than I can the idea that beauty and fashion are the end of my ability, the aim of my life. No, I shall be both graceful and great. I shall follow Granny and take my tea in china cups and have my thinning hair coiffed weekly while reading the Times and telling my hairdresser the PM is a spunkless plebian. But that is not enough, that is not all I wish to be. There is more, much more and I see it nowhere out there so believe it should not exist in me. But it does. It does, it does, and I am filled with hope. The desire to be other than I am captured in the space between Elsa and Kate, showing me what might lie beyond them both. The turmoil tossed aside in this possibility. That I can find a way to be more.

My portrait, that I always thought miserable, shows me a new truth. That I am there, within, longing to come out into the world. And the frown is my frustration that I am barred within. Longing to smile, as Kate does with such ease and confidence.

Kate. Yes, darling Kate. You should see what she is doing with her business. You would be so proud of her.

Whatever poison Ted put in her veins has been drawn. Kate has found her feet and they are firm and lithe. Her bistro is a delight and packed to the gunnels. She has this thing, she explained it to me, about the colour blue. She says it makes her feel invincible and has taken it to herself, in her decor, in her clothes, in her thoughts. She found her way back to her own ideas through realising that she loved the old blue door of her business, the thing that Ted told her was giving all the wrong impressions and needed changing. She couldn't bring herself to do it and the moment she realised it, she was snapped out of her self-doubt. Now she uses blue as a lucky charm and she is invincible. Rushed off her feet and laughing with joy at it all. She says she is lonely but does not have time to think about it, and she is thrilled with Elsa's pregnancy. Hugging her as though she were a fat Buddha and taking in the fecund airs from her oozing pregnancy, before tossing it off and haring back to her own life. Kate is her own version of femininity, and it is robust and loud and unapologetic. She glows with the rush of her life and made me feel a carefully wrapped veneer of my own, not the essence of it. She has taken to wearing trousers all the time, saying skirts irritate her, yet she looks more feminine in them than Elsa does in her elasticated tweed A-lines (honestly, only Elsa could have found a shop that stocks wartime style in pregnancy fit.) Kate looks sexy. She looks wild and alive and untameable, as though she might skid out of her shoes at any minute and crash land. Kit could not stop staring. He even blushed when she ruffled his hair!

She made me jealous. Yes, and proud. I am beyond proud of what she is doing. Writing a column for the papers too and getting a head of steam behind her ideals. Oh, I was jealous and proud and sick with longing for an ounce of what she has.

But seeing it has restored me. And I can at last write with an open heart again. And I shall write you. I have been vile for too long. Wrapped up in confusion and doubt and longing and anger at you. I believed it was your fault, that you took the best part of me with you and kept it for yourself. But I have been lazy. I have given up seeking that part of myself.

There is more to me than I yet know. These troubling longings I have are troubling only to others not to myself. What am I? Destined to be a man? It is possible... it is possible.

The freedom of these words, to write what I have banished from my own mind. It makes my pen jump and scratch in shock to see them.

It is possible to be anything I wish. To change this form I was given, to find that which feels true. Others have done it, why not I?

I was never afraid before, I would try anything if I believed it suited me. When did I grow timid and fixed? Elsa makes no apology for her nature, nor Kate for hers, why should I?

I feel desire when I watch my child grow into his nature, I feel it in myself, this longing for a form I have told myself to loathe. It is the social display of masculinity I despise, its peacock-strutting arrogance, not the form itself.

I am rushed with relief and desire writing this. Intoxicated with this truth I have denied.

I can say now, I long to make love as a man. I am filled

with desire for a man. I am ruptured with the pleasure this gives me, hidden no more. Have I always loathed men because I had to be a woman with them? The thought of penetrating a man leaves me ragged. Faint with a level of desire I had no idea existed in me.

Whatever I truly am, I have yet to experience it. No more politeness. No more veneer.

The New Year is hard upon us, and I am ready for it. I have tried to tame myself to fit the world, now the world will have to fit me.

When I am done, will you welcome me?

Shall I ever have the courage to find out?

8

The truck swung to a stop outside the battered roller shutter door. As Moth climbed down from the passenger door, he saw it begin a slow rattling shuffle upwards. The shuddering sound grating down the dimness of the pre-dawn street.

Moth moved to the back, waiting while the driver climbed down. Listening to the stirring sounds of the city. Muezzins calling prayers. Birdsong rippling through the streets before the traffic took over. Voices calling greetings in a triad of languages. He stood and let the sounds wash over his tiredness. Urfa was a city of contradictions it was easy to like. Especially in the mornings when it was not yet awake enough to overwhelm him. Sitting on the bisection of major roads that ran almost true to the compass points, Urfa was a cultural crossroad on the way to greater places. After the long time he had spent in Bonn's camp only 50 kms down the southern road, it was a strange dose of normality he could not adjust to.

'Mothy!'

As the driver, Fehran, joined him and lifted the tailgate of the truck, Moth caught his amused roll of eyes as a sharp voice of concern greeted them from the building. Moth turned to face the owner.

'Dilru, hey,' he smiled back at the woman looking at him. Her pudgy hands planted without a hint of softness on her hips. A scowl of irritation on her face. A washed-out scarf wrapped round her head, its softened black emphasising the lines on her face. The grey wisps escaping around her ears. Her lips set in a tight line. 'I'm back.'

'Five days.' She set her ankles a little further apart on the pavement. Behind him he heard Fehran suck in his breath and jump up to busy himself in the back of the truck. 'Five days ago, I sent you to Suruc, you were supposed to come back the next day.'

'Yeah, sorry, I got a bit caught up.' He shifted the backpack on his tired shoulders, trying to find the energy for the argument brewing on her face. 'Fehran said you weren't happy.'

She sent a withering look toward the back of the truck, switched to one of her three native languages and hurled some contempt Fehran's way. Moth had to guess it was Turkish. Dilruba Kaya Yildirim spoke Turkish, Kurdish and Arabic, plus English with a French accent that baffled Moth. If there was a city determined to defeat him linguistically, it was Urfa. The Kurdish he had begun to learn in Akcakale had been demanding to grasp but at least consistently used. Here, he'd entered a city that backflipped through languages from one sentence to the next, each person able to speak at least two of the three equally present languages and changing as necessity demanded.

Dilru stepped forward three sharp spaces, grabbed his chin and pulled his head down to her level.

'Ow, Dilru, that hurts,' he tried to speak. She had his jaw clamped in her pudgy, iron grip. His words came out garbled.

'You stay away that long again, and I will spank you so hard you will weep like Halim.'

'Oww, Jesu—' she squeezed harder as he began to swear. 'Dilru. Halim is five. He cries if his milk is cold.'

She pulled his head even closer to her level, all five foot two of grim determination and oceanic compassion.

'You think I won't do it?'

Fehran went past with the first sack truck full of boxes.

'Let him go woman, he's only trying to help.'

Moth felt his head twisted toward Dilru's torso as she turned to follow Fehran with another scathing eddy of verbal abuse. He closed his eyes. Dilru's bosom, amplified by nurturing seven children, was way too close for comfort. She would have him in a squishy headlock in a moment.

'Dilru, I'm tired,' he pleaded. 'And hungry.'

Through his uncomfortable position, head pulled down, back bent, trying not to lay hands on the woman, he could see Husnu and Inci watching the scene with big grins.

'Hey,' he mumbled at the twins. 'Help me?'

'No way,' Husnu said as he walked to the back of the lorry. 'She's been busting us sideways for three days worrying about you, you take your turn.'

'Anne,' Inci murmured at her mother, 'leave him be, you will break his stupid long back.'

Moth felt the grip lessen a bit, but only to have himself hauled into the putty emotional mass that was her body as she began muttering at him in Arabic. Arabic was good. Arabic meant he was forgiven. She always muttered her happy in Arabic. His head was stroked, his face soothed, her voice crooning concern. He tried to smile at her. His back screaming. Sleeping rough in Suruc for five nights was not appreciating being bent over double, even if his head was resting on a plush pillow. She must have smothered at least three of her dead children in there. Dilruba, mother to seven living children and five passed, grandmother to fifteen, divorced and widowed, head of the Urfa Voluntary Kitchen of fifty-seven volunteers, chief pain in the arse to the town's efforts to ignore the refugees living on their town limits, and, as far as Moth was concerned, his only option.

You should have known Bonn would stitch you up good and proper.

He longed for Beau and her singsong French. At least Beau had not tried to smother him in broody tit. There had been a French elegance to Beau's care, even as old and impatient as she was, that was a dim memory in the overwhelming bosom of Turkish maternal instinct. He felt the pressure releasing, managed to straighten his back without grimacing and adjusted his backpack and pride.

'How am I going to tell Bonny I let you get killed on the streets of Suruc, eh?'

'Don't tell him anything. And I wasn't in the streets of Suruc.'

She stepped toward him with another frown. Moth took a hasty step back and held his hands up.

'Anne,' Inci muttered and stepped forward, pushing her mother aside. The youngest of Dilru's children by ten minutes after her brother, and holding the title of the child who broke their mother's legendary womb, pulling its twisted mass out with her as she left its confines and necessitating an emergency hysterectomy, Rahim Katili, a nickname that had taught him never…

… NEVER…

... to enquire about the origins of a nickname again, took hold of Moth's arm and led him past her mother. 'Can't you see he's tired. When did you last eat, Moth? Can you use your jaw or has my mother's hand broken it?'

They left Dilru yelling at the men outside and moved into the building.

'Thank you,' he told her. Inci was a finger's width taller than her mother and a slimmed down, brightened up, taut perspective on how Dilru must have looked at her age. Though, as her mother never failed to mention, she'd been married with three children nourished at her breast and two in the ground by twenty-five.

'We have been worried. You know she will not forgive herself if anything happens to you.'

Moth followed Inci to the kitchen at the back of the warehouse. Past the long tables where scarf-clad women packed boxes of essentials. Inci left a hand here, a smile there, a murmur of approval wherever she went. The men unloading the goods from the lorry and doing the heavy work, lowered their heads as she passed. All eyes followed Inci, ignoring him. He was a piece of gargantuan dross towed along in the tailwind of her beauty. Even the women stared after her.

Yet you feel nothing.

He felt gratitude. He was one step closer to being fed with each step they took across the rough concrete floor.

'I didn't ask her to take responsibility for me.'

'Bonny did.'

He would never get used to hearing Bonn called that. It both conveyed a Scottish twang and a note of happiness that Moth could not put with the stout Frenchman who'd abandoned him.

He didn't abandon you. He got shafted, remember.

It was hard to remember much at all about the last three weeks. Being thwarted in his attempt to get back into the transit camp. Nearly arrested. Loitering near the wire fences, passing messages through late at night. Waiting in the outskirts of Akcakale for two days for the few who left and came to find him. Afterwards, helping those who had escaped and were trying to walk to Suruc and Urfa, tagging from group to group on the bike. Limping back into the base on fumes, four days after he'd left. Bonn already gone, packed back to Geneva two days before he was expecting. Leaving Moth to be balled out by Yves an hour later with his panniers on his back. He'd stared up and down the long road between Urfa and Akcakale and wondered which way to go, crouching on his haunches as the overwhelming isolation of his life impinged itself on him.

Aidan had found him there ten minutes later, breathless with dodging his way out of the compound and down the alleyways where Yves couldn't see him. Giving Moth an envelope with a name and an address written in Bonn's hand. Dilru's kitchen, where his bike had been sent by lorry. Not knowing, when he handed over the envelope two days later after walking to Urfa, that Bonn had put a note inside asking her to keep an eye on him until he could send a ticket home. Trying to extricate his arse from Dilru's care was beginning to feel like trying to remove a bail tracker from his ankle. Except it had Dilru's teeth marks holding it in place. Three weeks later, with the mid-July sun baking the afternoon streets, they'd heard nothing.

'If she keeps shoving my head in her tits I won't come back again,' Moth muttered behind her. Inci turned and grinned at him until he could begin to feel his face warming. 'You have no idea what that feels like.'

'Are you kidding me?' Inci demanded. 'She breastfed me and Husnu until we were seven! She couldn't bear the fact we would be her last children.'

Moth shuddered and held a hand up to stop her. Feeling sorry for Husnu to be left with the memory. Husnu was as gorgeous as his sister, and as committed to chasing women as she was determined to push marriage away.

Yeah, but he wouldn't hold a candle to Luca.

Husnu had Inci's same small stature, big eyes and curving chin. He was pretty, trying to be tough. Working out to put muscles on his small frame. Attractive in a way that made Moth cautious about staring. It amused him. Moth was watching one twin and being watched to see if he was watching the other.

'You should be grateful she loves you,' Inci turned and pushed open the door into the kitchen. 'Who else is going to feed you, huh? Where else are you going to get work?'

Moth pulled a chair out from a table, slipping his backpack from his shoulder to the floor as he sat down. Inci had her back to him as she opened the huge vats of food kept warm all day long. The kitchens ran a constant supply of hot food to feed its volunteers through shifts that started at 4 am and finished at midnight. He wasn't sure work counted as a description for what he had been doing for three weeks. Packing and being fed in return, going out into the hills, villages and towns looking for more holed up homeless refugees they could help.

'You know you have no visa. If the police find out, you will be deported immediately. The people won't care if you are Syrian or English if you take work from their children.'

She grabbed a plate and began to ladle puddles of food round the edges. Small mounds of texture and taste that she pulled together. Her voice was clipped English, the well-studied precision of an accent trying to be perfect and made adorable by its imperfections. The too hard vowels and struggling th's. Moth pulled the notes from the top of his bag and tidied them up on the table in front of him. It wasn't much to show for five days work. Inci flickered a look over her shoulder, her scarf swishing with the flick of her long-plaited tail.

'How will Bonny find you if you are in the depths of a deportation unit in Istanbul? You have no money, and my mother can't afford to bribe your way out.'

She came back over to the table and stood looking at him, his hand over the pile of paper scraps.

'I can look after myself,' he muttered.

'This is looking after yourself?' she mocked him. 'You have no visa, no home, no job, no money. And you need a shower.'

Moth grinned up at her. 'I have a bike.'

'It is broken, you English idiot. It wouldn't make it to the end of the road.'

'I could try, if your mother would give me half a chance.' He pushed the papers toward her. She scowled at him, holding the plate of food out of reach. Moth's shoulders stiffened under that glare as he tried to hold his pride up.

She knows you're stuffed.

He couldn't afford to get the bike fixed. It was as simple as that. Dilru had given him food in return for work and a place to store it. Beyond that she would not risk the repercussions of helping him. She claimed the local police would shut her kitchen down if they found her harbouring an illegal. With the refugees adding to the economic pressures of their city, she was weaving her wide hips along a line too thin for her stout ankles. Taking Moth into her home was beyond her ability. He slept, if he was blessed, on the floor of Fehran's third floor apartment, grateful for a lukewarm shower. If Fehran wasn't there, he went with anyone who would take him. There had been nights when he'd walked out of town and slept in the fields. The bike would help. If he could earn enough money to get it fixed. He'd seen enough places he could set up for the night.

Earning money means getting a job.

Getting a job was impossible. There were already too many people competing for the illegal jobs he could get. And if he took one, it meant another refugee might go hungry or sleep in the streets.

You need more money, or you're stuffed.

Moth squirmed on the seat in front of her gaze, feeling the limits of his options. Narrowing down to a call. The choice about who he had to ask for help. What they might ask in return. His stomach churned at the thought.

Inci relented and put the food down in front of him and sat down opposite, pulling the paper toward her. Eyes scanning the messages, a dimple between her eyes deepening and fading as their contents dictated. Moth focused on his plate. He knew Dilru would send him packing if she even thought he was looking at her unmarried, youngest daughter. He didn't want to get into trouble for nothing.

She never seems to notice you looking at Husnu.

Inci could even make mass-produced curry look delicious. She had put the piles of coloured stew, vegetables, rice and baked cheese in a light shaded array, each choice measured out in equality to the next. He hadn't eaten hot food for five days. His stomach contracted in joy as the scents rose to meet him. He picked up the spoon.

'Thank you, Rahim Katili.'

She smiled at him, dimples flowering, eyes sparkling.

'You are welcome, Moth. Thank you for these,' she raised the papers. Nodded at his plate. 'Eat, come on.'

He made a careful, focused start. Inci was portion savvy, it was not an excessive amount of food, but it was rich and full of spice. His stomach rollicked and rolled, shy and eager. He remembered Male, hurling in front of Luca. He ate slowly enough to savour each mouth full, to give his system time to adjust. She frowned at him, eating each different pile one at a time. This was not how you did it. You mixed a little together, causing variety with each mouthful. That was how they ate. He ate as a child would, in their eyes. Except he left the worst to last, so he could leave it if he had to. Slowing down as his system crashed with the sudden spike of calories and carbs.

'You must check your emails.' Inci put down the bits of paper. 'You've been gone a while, Bonny might have sent news.'

No, he won't. He's got no news to send.

'Okay.'

There could be more emails from Luca to ignore though.

He'd never replied to the last one. There hadn't been time in the rush of change.

'Perhaps your family have been in touch.'

Moth forked the last few bits of his meal, felt a weariness in his stomach that battled the desire to eat. He put his fork down and sat back in his chair.

'How long since you saw your sister?' She was poking him, no doubt under orders from Dilru.

'Not since the last time we talked about this.'

'I'm sure she must miss you. Aren't you curious to see her?' Inci put on her tough face. The one without the dimples, her pupils contracting in determination. 'I couldn't imagine being apart from Husnu for four months, let alone four years. She will forget who you are.'

'She's happy, she's a school kid. After half an hour with me, she'd be bored and go back to her friends. One day you'll be glad to see the back of Husnu too.'

She drew a breath to speak, but kept it in. Let it out with a shallow sigh. Chewing the edge of her lower lip. Thinking of another angle to try. He grinned, waiting. Hands folded over his gurgling belly, trying to resist tiredness. Watching Inci put on her sweet face. The one with the fluttering eyes and softened pupils, the little 'O' she made with her lips. She put on her faces in the same way another woman might use makeup, selecting according to the occasion. Even the face she showed the world, concerned and encouraging, was a choice. He preferred her family face, the one where she laughed with Husnu, or teased her mother.

'Well, could you get your family to help you with a visa, get a work permit?' Her fingers tapped the dirty creased papers. 'I'm sure my mother would let you stay with us if you could get a legal permit.'

'They're not going to give me a permit when I'm already here, illegally.'

She began to curl the 'O' into a quiver.

'See this is why I don't want to go home,' Moth laughed at her. 'Have my sister trying to wrap me round her finger the way you do.'

Her mouth stretched out into a line, a kink of disappointment in her chin. Whoever she did end up with was going to have a tough time holding onto his own ideas.

'Moth, why won't you let anyone help you?'

'I don't need help,' he said, nodding at the paper. 'They need help. Turn your charms on them.'

'How come I can't make you see sense?'

'Because it's only your sense. I'd rather hold onto my own, thanks.'

'There isn't a man out there who wouldn't lick the floor clean if I asked them.' Inci pointed toward the door and the warehouse beyond.

'I can't imagine the weight of that power.'

'But it doesn't touch you. You don't look at me beyond the plate of food I bring you.'

'What can I say? I'm always hungry.' He shrugged.

'You might as well be my brother!'

'Maybe that's how I see you,' he agreed. But he blinked, thinking of Nat growing into this sort of power. Becoming a woman, being watched in the same way Inci was watched. Perhaps he frowned too because he looked up to see Inci with a calculating squint between her eyes and a quirk to her upper lip.

You've blown it now.

She looked down at the paper, the intelligence she hid behind her calculating faces shining through.

'So many boys on their own,' she said with slow concern.

Moth felt tension grab his full stomach and twist. Inci was beautiful. She was wily and manipulative. But beneath all the games she was bright, educated and sharp as a night-time rock between his shoulder blades and a thin sleeping bag.

'It worries Anne. What future do they have? No family to support them. No income. How will they find wives when they are nothing?'

He stayed as focused and immobile as it was possible to do in front of a stalking lion.

'But I worry about the others.'

Moth raised his eyebrows, refusing to engage.

'There is talk about what Isis are doing to the... other boys. Anne refuses to hear it, of course, my mother is of her generation. But I wonder, why there are so many single young men, prepared to risk their lives to escape?'

She stared at him, pulling the power of silence back to herself.

You're on thin ground.

'I guess freedom is tempting when you're being forcibly conscripted into killing your own people,' he offered.

'Perhaps.' She shrugged. 'I tried to talk to Husnu about it, but he got angry. When I asked him why he was so upset, he squirmed. I wonder if he's not trying too hard to be the man he thinks he should be. Mothers can't see what they don't want to but women, we see straight through that, you know.' She stared straight at him.

He was about to say there wasn't a gay hair on Husnu's too short head. For as much as Moth couldn't help but stare at him, Husnu barely knew Moth existed.

But she'll ask what makes you so sure.

Moth kept his mouth shut and avoided the trap. Inci wasn't questioning her brother's preferences.

'And if they escape persecution there, they'll find it no easier here. Refugees are a plague to our country. Even the ones with family, with prospects. Boys living on their own, or worse, together, they're inviting trouble.' She tidied the pile of papers in front of her on the worn table, squaring up their ragged edges. 'Last year's pride parade in Istanbul was dispersed with violence. Tear gas. Rubber bullets. Water hose. And Urfa is not Istanbul. These boys,' she tapped the paper, 'they need to be in Europe. Where it's safe to be gay.'

'You can't be sure they're gay,' he protested. 'That's making a big assumption.'

'I'm not a fool, Moth, don't treat me as one.' She looked at him with sharp eyes, her covered hair making her gaze more intense. 'I had a friend at school who was gay. Raif would spend all his time with me, walk me home from school, come to visit at weekends. Anne got suspicious of him. I was fifteen and she wanted me to think about marriage, badgering me about Raif's family, whether they were good enough. Drove me mad, until I told her, he spends all this time with me because of Husnu. He's not into girls.'

'I bet she loved that.'

'She banned him from the house,' Inci said. 'Went and told his parents what I'd told her. My mother is charity itself, until you threaten her sense of natural order.'

Moth tried not to breathe. Courage, he'd come away wanting to find courage.

'What happened?'

'I don't know,' she said. 'I never saw him again. Raif was pulled out of school, sent away to family in the East, where they are even more strict. When I tried to ask his sisters, they wouldn't say a word, not even mention his name. I think his father beat them all senseless to avoid any shame on the family. Shame that might affect their marriage chances. Damage his business.'

He pulled his toes closer to himself, scraping his knees along the underside of the table. Wishing he were smaller, less visible. Knowing how he stood out as a foreigner and now wondering if he stood out in other ways.

Size is a good thing.

He looked too big, too blokeish to look anything other than straight. And here in Turkey, his height was freakish, connecting him to men like Fehran. Big, tall, manly men.

That Anne protected her daughter from him was a good thing. Not everyone was as watchful and observant as Inci.

'You know, there was an honour killing in Istanbul.' Inci looked him dead in the eyes. 'A man killed his son for being gay. Shot him in the street outside his house. The family never claimed the body.'

Moth could feel the skin of his arms on the surface of the table growing clammy, making him itch to put his hands together. He focused on the knuckles of his hands folded against the split and stained Formica.

'It was the first public honour killing of a gay boy in Turkey. He came from Urfa. My mother knew the boy's father. All the elders, they didn't feel shame at what happened. Just annoyance, that Ahmet's father made it public. You kill a daughter for honour, you tell the world to cleanse your name. You kill a gay son for honour, you never speak of them.'

Inci spoke softly. Telling the story same as she would dictate the contents of the latest boxes. In the calm voice he could feel the pressure of daily reality. Conversations spoken round the dinner table. Families rejecting what was distasteful as they fed their children.

'I wonder sometimes if that was Raif's fate. All because I told my mother about him.'

They heard Dilru's voice cracking its way down the tables, an octave higher and a salt-cellar less sweet than her daughter's. Inci stood up and took his plate, picking up the papers.

'I know why you don't look at me, Moth,' she stepped back, lowering her voice, 'and I'm glad. Raif spent time with me because he liked me, same as you. But, if you see any of these boys, tell them to get to Europe as fast as they can. Tell them they're no safer here than Syria.'

Tell her Europe isn't that much safer, either.

'And Moth?'

He raised a guarded eyebrow in query.

'Check your emails, get some help from your family or friends. Please?'

Dilru swept through the door and took in the scene in one glance, her face puckering into a scowl that might once have had the grace of her daughter's but now favoured a sundried peach. As furry as it was wrinkled.

Inci held up her bits of paper and grinned at her mother.

'Look, Anne, Moth has found more children who need your help. Struggling on the streets of Suruc.' She put the plate down in the sink and danced toward her mother, whose face was creasing inward with concern. 'And he needs to check his emails, surely Bonny must have sent news by now. We should leave him.'

Inci gathered her mother up and pushed the papers into her hands, turning her and pushing her straight back out the door, nodding at the old communal pc set up in the corner. A relic from another century, let alone decade.

You need to get that bike fixed.

And he couldn't do it alone. If he could get it fixed, he could live out in the country between here and Suruc. He'd checked enough places out as he hitched lifts between the two towns. There were two or three quiet spots he could set up the bike while he figured out what to do next.

But only until winter. Then you'll need a visa and a work permit and a house.

But that was months away. And too many issues to focus on. Right now, he needed money to fix the bike. Then he could consider his options.

Family or friends. Who did he ask?

. . .

Outside the large and noisy venue, pretending that the warm summer night was affording her a dose of fresh air, Isabelle heard a train slowing to a stop at the station.

Looking through the straggling, summer-weary buddleias that framed the high, metal railings and drooped over the parked cars, she could see the tracks flickering as the train passed over them in a blur of windows and shapes. Though she couldn't see the station, Isabelle felt a rush of memory bring the small space acutely to her mind. She had come home to this station once or twice a year since she was a young woman. Stepping from the same train and wondering what awaited her. Moth had left from that platform, kissing her an awkward goodbye and running away.

Isabelle turned away and entered the large arched glass doorway of the Brewery. How things could change in three swift weeks. Walking through the groups back to the table she felt irritation that she had believed it would only be a drink. She could see Asha and Kate sat close on the sofa, talking together. They were watching Steve. Beside them, perched on the arm, James looked lost. Pint glass in hand, ears reddening as he tried to avoid listening to whatever they were saying.

Asha had not given up playing a heavy hand on the post-Brexit bitterness card. An anger fuelled by finding out that James had abstained as a way of trying to conciliate their differences on the matter. Isabelle was tired of the subject. Tired of the way the attention of the country had shifted a microscopic step from the if of leaving Europe to the how. She felt nothing but disbelief that it was all happening and had retreated from it. From the way it seemed to push Moth even further apart from them, stuck inside a Europe they were keen to ditch. Kate and Rob had thrown themselves into this new stage with vigour. A victory soured was to be reclaimed by the means. As she approached, she saw Asha and Kate glance at her and shift away from their close chat, moving to make space between them for her to sit.

She didn't need to ask what they were talking about, they had talked about nothing else since the night she first went for a drink with him.

'Who's empty?' James stood up. 'I'll get us a top-up.'

Asha held out her glass without looking at him and made Isabelle want to wince. Her bad temper was heartlessly public.

'I'll have another glass of wine, thank you James,' Kate passed her wine glass with a sympathetic smile.

'Isabelle?'

'No, I'm good thanks.' She watched him walk away and turned to Asha. 'How much longer are you going to punish him for?'

'Until I stop being mad at him.'

'Oh, let's not start that again,' Kate waved it away. 'We want to know if tonight's the night?'

'Yes, let's talk about you,' Asha agreed.

'Let's not,' Isabelle countered and wished she'd stayed outside.

'Surely you must be a little bit excited?' Asha pushed.

'Are you sure it's not you?' Isabelle retorted. 'If you two stare at his arse any more he might decide to take one of you home instead.'

Asha and Kate both looked back at Steve. He was stood with his back to them talking to some mates at another table. There was no doubting it was a spectacular view of him. She couldn't decide if he was talking with his back to them to prevent the chance she might send him an irritated glance, or because he knew it emphasised one of his finer assets.

'He can take me home any night,' Asha told them.

'Get in the queue, you already have one to warm your bed.' Kate sat forward from the deep sofa and wagged her finger across Isabelle at Asha.

'He's getting nothing out of me,' Asha retorted with a scowl at James, stood three deep at the bar. 'Besides, I can dream safely, I'm married.'

'Who wants to dream safely?' Kate asked. 'It takes far too long to get a drink in here, I'm sure James has spent most of the evening at the bar.'

'You're not at work anymore,' Isabelle reminded her.

'You're distracting us.' Asha poked her in the ribs. 'So, are you two, you know...'

'... you know?' Isabelle asked.

'Oh, come on,' Kate nestled into the deep cushions and cuddled up to her left side. 'At least let us live vicariously through you, darling. You're the only one with a bit of excitement.'

'So, I should shag him to give us a topic of conversation at the breakfast table?'

'No, you should just shag him,' Asha said. 'How long has it been?'

'Do you mind?' Isabelle protested.

'You're nervous,' Kate decided, sitting back up again. Twisting on the sofa and looking at her in surprise. 'What on earth for, the bloke is adorable.'

'And fit.' Asha was still staring at Steve. 'Really, really fit. Like he makes Kit look a bit jaded.'

'I'll tell Kit you said that,' Kate told her. 'Stop staring at him, you'll drill a hole in his back.'

'Like you're not staring at him,' Asha tossed back. 'Besides, that would involve you speaking to Kit.' Her eyes sparkled over her empty wine glass at Kate who huffed back.

'Why are you nervous?' Kate persisted.

'I'm not nervous!' Isabelle said.

'You're certainly not exuding confidence.' Kate patted her knee. 'And you do like him, don't you?'

'You've been out on quite a few dates if you don't.' Asha investigated the progress of their drinks, watching James shift on his feet at the bar. 'Why does he have to look so glum?'

'Maybe because you're giving him hell?' Kate suggested. 'Well, Isabelle, don't you fancy him?'

'Yes, I do. I think. I don't know.' Isabelle wanted to go back outside, walk toward the station and get on the first train. 'I just...'

'... just what?' Asha and Kate asked at the same moment.

'Don't you ever wonder if it's all a bit rushed?' Isabelle had to twist her head from one side to the other to see their faces. It was as though they were blinkering her, to look outward, where they thought she should be looking. 'You date a person a few times and straight in the sack?'

'It's supposed to be the fun part,' Kate scolded her. 'And, trust me, the options aren't permanently open.'

'And it is fun, but I want to know someone first. I feel a bit pressured, that's all.'

'By Steve?' Kate asked.

'By everyone!' Isabelle protested. 'I like my life the way it is. I'm not sure I want to change that. And I'm not the best person at standing up for myself.'

'You don't say,' Kate muttered.

'We've only been out on a handful of dates, that's all.' Isabelle curled her hand round the stem of her glass. She had been drinking with care. Aware of how easily the drinks were brought and flashed about. She looked past Steve. The place was buzzing, full of a good mix of people. Kate had come out of curiosity for the venue as much as from Steve's invite. Asha had come to get away from the farm. Rob was at Riverdell, doing double babysitting duty. She didn't need to look far to remember the powerful consequence of getting overly drunk in her life. 'I've always known the people I slept with really well before I got into bed with them.'

'I slept with James after two weeks,' Asha told them. 'After that hideous Easter Sunday lunch when I first met you.'

'And you a Catholic, shocking,' Kate teased her. When Asha bristled, she added, 'Oh reel it in, I was raised a Catholic too you know.'

'Catholic or not, I need to know the man in my life is going to do right by me in the bedroom.' Asha looked over at James. 'Even this mad at him I know it's only a matter of time before I want him again.'

Isabelle tried not to think about James. She could feel her toes curling on the floor as the conversation edged her and Asha closer to that mutual experience. James had been a considerate lover. But Kit had blown him out of the water. As for the brief night with Rob, she would never admit to the fact that she could remember nothing of it. Apart from waking up with him. Running away from him. Back to Kit in Italy, and then... well, after then, there hadn't been anyone else.

She looked past the pretty girls and their bright laughter, feeling out of place. She was a mother and she couldn't connect to their easy banter, their flirting and ready friendship. She couldn't connect to Steve, at least not yet. When he walked her home and held her hand or kissed her on the porch at Riverdell, looking into the house on the hope of an invitation, she felt expectation, not desire or pleasure or excitement.

'Well, give the guy a chance, that's what I say,' Kate gave her another pat on her knee. 'He's kind and genuine...'

'... and fit,' Asha added. 'Has he asked about Indigo yet, you know...'

'... and he obviously likes you, darling.' Kate pushed on over Asha's question. 'Don't throw the chance away. I know you're happy, but loneliness will seep in eventually. You can't depend entirely on your family to fill your life.'

James had made it through the crush and was returning their way with drinks. Isabelle was glad to see him.

Asha sighed as she looked at him and sat forward. 'Damn him, I actually feel sorry for the bastard. Excuse me, I need to go to the toilet and find my bad mood again.'

'You'll forgive him,' Isabelle told her.

'We'll see.' Asha stood up with a scowl at her, pulling her dress into place and moving away, she added, 'If you tell Steve before you tell me, I won't be happy.'

James arrived back as Steve returned from his group of friends, protesting that James had beat him to it and trying to repay him. Isabelle withered inside, hoping Asha had not been overheard as she left.

'Kate,' Steve held his hand out to her. 'Can I borrow you for a minute to meet a friend of mine? They've read your books and I want to show you off.'

'You can show me off anytime.' Kate let herself be pulled up. Passing James, she grasped his knee and whispered, 'There's a chink of light in that Polish tunnel of yours. Ask her outside and bloody kiss her before she changes her mind.'

James looked bewildered and glanced at Isabelle as Kate and Steve walked away.

'Go ahead, I'm good,' she reassured him. 'Plus, Kate's right, the drink has helped mellow her.'

James looked across to the toilets and picked up Asha's drink before walking away with a lift to his shoulders.

Isabelle pulled her phone out of her pocket. Alone on the large sofa she felt too visible. There were photos of Indigo and Deryn from the birthday party. Deryn had turned three over a week ago and Asha had done a tea party at the farm. Elsa in the background. The girls sat in the strewing's of a pinnata they had been too young to understand let alone smash. James victorious with bat in hand behind them. It was odd how few photos of her daughter alone she had. They were growing up like sisters. She envied Deryn her midsummer birthday. It was impossible to distinguish Indigo's from Christmas the day before, it had been the worst sort of planning. Isabelle grimaced. Looking at Indigo, her eyes drawn to her own child, away from the party girl, Isabelle gathered strength from the fact that her worst mistakes in life seemed to have created her greatest moments. She just wished people would stop asking awkward questions about it. Restless, she moved screen, opening her emails. Wondering if Moth had written. She jumped when a body landed beside her.

'Alone at last,' Steve quipped, a hand snaking along the back of the sofa and onto her shoulder.

Isabelle put the phone away and repressed the shock of disturbance that wanted to ripple across her shoulder.

'You did invite them,' she pointed out.

'And I'm glad they came, your family are fun.' He nodded over at Kate, talking to a group of younger women. 'They bloody love her. She's a local legend. Everyone misses her at The Door.'

'I wouldn't call her that to her face,' Isabelle warned. 'She's not overkeen on the moniker, says its ageist.'

'Thanks for the heads up.' Steve pulled his arm tighter on her shoulder, leant forward and kissed her.

It came as such a surprise. This public act of affection. She froze, was swamped with guilt, responded in delay. He cupped his hand to her chin and followed the curve to her neck, pulling her in closer. His tongue pushing against her teeth. Beer sour on his breath. Isabelle pulled back and smiled. Brittle and uncertain.

'Oh, sorry, bit too public?' Steve asked with a smile.

'I'm a bit, eh, well...' she blustered, her face smothering with heat, struggling with his relaxed gaze.

Steve leant back into the sofa and squeezed her shoulder.

'Can't be easy, single mum and all. Must be weird to think about yourself for a change.'

'Takes a bit of getting used to.' Isabelle felt the lie sting her.

'Shame Rob couldn't join us,' Steve looked away from her. 'Must be nice having a guaranteed babysitter though. How lucky are you?'

'Very.'

The noise of the room grew. Huddles of people with drinks and ever louder conversations to make themselves heard over the music and general banter. The gleaming vats of the brewing process gathering the sound and hurling it back. It made her realise how much she missed Kate's bistro. How they had always been blessed with their own private family venue to socialise in. She watched Kate drawing a large crowd to herself, her hands expressing, her hair glinting as she moved and spoke. It had always been natural for Kate, to create a centre and pull the world to her. As much as it had been in Moth's nature to keep to the sides, to stay on the outside, watching.

'You're deep in thought.' Steve took a drink from his glass. 'What's on your mind?'

She turned away from Kate, smiling at him. 'It's been a while since I saw Kate out. I forgot how charming she can be.'

'I'll say,' he frowned slightly at her glass, removing the arm from behind her shoulder and shifting slightly to give the space between them it needed. 'You're on the same drink, are you not enjoying yourself?'

He wanted more. She could sense it. More communication, more sharing, more intimacy, more fun. She felt a twinge of guilt and tried not to let it slide under her skin.

Isabelle reached out and put a hand on his knee. 'Not at all, I'm feeling a bit quiet tonight. Besides, I'm not a big social drinker, never have been.'

He took her hand, lifting it from his leg, squeezing it and replacing it higher up his thigh, his own hand keeping it weighed down there. Isabelle couldn't decide if it simply felt more comfortable there or was closer to what he really wanted. Knowing that if she moved it away now, he would take it as dismissal.

'How about we walk home?' he suggested. 'You don't need to be a party animal, Isabelle. I want you to enjoy my company, not theirs.' He nodded at the room full of people.

'I do,' she said. 'But the others are enjoying it, I don't want to curtail their night.'

'They're old enough to find their own way home, I'm sure James can handle two women without us.'

James was far from capable of handling his own wife, let

alone Asha and Kate drunk and high on company. But she did want to go home. To see Indigo in bed and sit with Rob in the study. Longings which rubbed against the man beside her as much as their thighs touched. It touched her, that he would consider her own needs, as well as his wants.

'If you don't mind, I would like that.'

'No problem, come on, let's escape.' He stood up and put his unfinished drink down on the table, offering her his hand.

'Shouldn't we tell Kate?'

'If you tell her, I'll have to say goodbye to the lot of them and we'll be here for hours. Let's sneak out and give James the mission.'

She let him pull her up from the sofa, a guilty glance at Kate. Kate wasn't looking at her. She was perfectly content where she was. She picked up her jacket and followed Steve out the door. James and Asha were at the far end of the patio, Asha sat on his knee, their heads close together, his arms holding her in place. James glanced their way and gave a subtle thumbs up to Steve's man signal for "you're on your own." As they walked away from the noise, down the access road toward the station, Steve took her hand in his, leading the way. They turned right to walk between the two super-markets and down to the traffic lights. In the late summer evening, the ski slope roof of Tesco was shimmering in the reflection of a dying sun bouncing against high clouds. She went to cross the road, head up the hill toward the castle and market.

'Let's go this way,' Steve pulled her back to the pavement, continuing down the road and turning right, tugging her over the road and toward the old churchyard. 'I love this back route round the Linney, hardly ever get a reason to go this way.'

She followed, a half pace behind him as they entered the archway. They wove through the graves, cast into deep shade beneath the sprawling yew trees. The path reduced to a void beneath her feet. It had been the route she and Moth took to the station. Why did this evening insist on reminding her of Moth? Was there news from him waiting in her unopened emails while she followed Steve, a firm shape ahead of her. His hand warm in hers. His step sure on the night path. The evening's warm air gusting his beer musty, deodorant scent back to her. He was real, and here, looking out for her, being considerate. While she was elsewhere. Her thoughts collided with him as he pulled her into the open patch of grass, rippled with darkness and dying light and gently opened his arms to pull her close.

'Is it totally weird that I want to kiss you in a graveyard?'

She could see the smile hovering on his lips as he admitted it.

'All these old graves make me want to hold you close. Is that alright?'

She nodded and let herself be pulled in, trying to focus.

He pushed her hair back from her dipped face, tracing the line of her chin. His fingers, sanded into roughness from his work, coarse against her skin, sending a shiver through her. His arms wrapping her close in response. His dark eyes matched the shadows amongst the trees. His hair curling at his temple as he leant in, paused and asked, 'Can I?'

She nodded, let his face touch hers. His lips fleeting across her cheeks, her forehead. Plump and warm and moist. She had forgotten the feel of skin. Skin close and wanting to know skin.

The touch of a child was different. It asked for a different sort of love. There was need in a child's touch, not this want she felt in Steve. She sank into that memory. Let her arms relax to encircle him. The feel of muscle, the shape of ribs, the ripple of movement in his back as he leant into her. She felt his hands trailing along her spine, pausing in the hollow of her back, rising back up to her shoulders. His lips found their way to hers, the flutters settling on her mouth, pausing, waiting for her. She kissed him back. Felt her tension seeping down into the hard, lingering warmth of the ground beneath her thin sandals. He kissed with deep attention. Patient and devoted. Somewhere between the rushed shyness of James and the consumption of Kit. Isabelle's resistance sagged in his arms and, when he pulled away, she searched his eyes for a reason why it had ended.

'Sorry, you'll think me mercenary, dragging you away and taking advantage.' He stepped back at arm's length, holding onto her hands. 'I've wanted to do that for a long time, hope you'll forgive me.'

'Nothing to forgive,' she smiled at him. 'I think I'd forgotten what it's like to be kissed though.'

'Did you remember if you enjoy it?'

'Yes,' she laughed at him. 'I think I'd forgotten that.'

'So might we try it a bit more?'

She nodded.

'Awesome,' he tucked her hand through his arm and tugged her back to the path. 'But come on, I promised to get you home.'

She let herself be pulled along. Feeling the shape of his arm as they walked past the old Staines house, no longer a crumbling pebbledash facade but a precisely repointed stone frontage with gleaming carriage lights beside the door. It cheered her to see the renovation and pride that shone out from the property she had once owned. It had never felt like hers, she had sold it within months of inheriting the estate, to help James and Asha realise their dream of owning their own farm.

'Shame what they did with this place,' Steve said as they walked past the two new houses that occupied the land which had once been lost garden to the original house. 'Always someone making money out of selling land.'

'I rather like them,' Isabelle protested. 'I thought the planners were pretty fierce on what they allowed.'

'I guess,' Steve looked at the two oak-panelled houses peeping over the high stone wall, 'though I can't help wish they'd leave well enough alone.'

'I know the lady who used to live there,' Isabelle added. 'House was falling down round her ears. She lives in a great bungalow now, which is good because she's not so steady on her feet these days.'

They walked up the hill toward the curve of the road. In the quietness of the hour Steve strayed onto the road and let her stay on the narrow pavement. Where the road took under the boughs of the trees that lined the castle slope he slowed again.

'Mind if we try that kissing thing again?'

She was still stinging from his comments about the Staines house. Wanting to resist and then telling herself to relax. Moving into his embrace, she remembered her own mouth, her lips, her tongue, by how they moved against his. Stunned by the warmth and touch that had become absent in her life. Irritation forgotten. His hands on her back more reluctant to leave, his frame a coiled tension as the kiss ended this time. His breath a slow fierce release as he stepped back and ran his hands through his hair.

'Agh,' he complained, taking her hand again. 'Come on, nearly home.'

They walked on, past the playing fields lying flat and expansive in the darkness. The river a dark edge at their border.

'I hate the fact they shut the boats down,' Steve complained. 'Private deck only now. When I first moved here, I loved going out on those boats.'

'Health and Safety, probably.'

'I go swimming there at night sometimes,' he told her. 'If it's been a long day and I'm sick of the customers. You ever go swimming in the river? Like, really swimming, letting yourself get swept into the current?'

She remembered it vividly as his words drifted into the dark. Moth, lying in the river with his arms supporting her. The overwhelming conviction that they were moving along, and the river was still.

'Yes, I have.'

'Let's do that together one night?'

She squeezed his arm in mute agreement, trying to imagine the river with Steve. Without Moth. Silent the rest of the way back to the arched gates of home. His feet crunching with vigour across the gravel.

He kissed her again on the porch. Gentler this time, retreating out to the flutters that followed the curves of her face, the falling line of her neck. Finishing where her skin gave way to jersey, stepping back off the porch and holding her hand.

'I gotta go while I can,' he told her, taking another step back, letting go of her.

She was shivering. His absence a chill that crept across her, the house a rising bulk calling her in.

'I'll call you, tomorrow?'

She nodded.

'Goodnight, Isabelle.'

She watched him turn and stride out of the courtyard, lingering in the soft puddle of light upon the porch. As he vanished beyond the high wall, she turned toward the doors. Moths were flitting against the old glass cover of the light, she could hear the ping of their bruised bodies reeling away into the darkness, drawn involuntarily back.

Rob had dozed off in the deep armchair in the bay window of the drawing room, a paper strewn across his lap. She put a gentle hand on his shoulder to wake him, laughed when he startled and told him to go to bed. He yawned, shaking his head when she told him she'd had to leave the others behind, they had out partied her.

'We're falling into middle age, Isabelle,' he told her as he left the room. 'Really must show more resistance.'

She left him getting a glass of water and fleeted upstairs to Indigo's room. It was empty, she had snuck out of bed and crept into hers. Isabelle sat on the side of her own bed and looked at her daughter, lost in the expanse of mattress, the duvet dragged round her like a twiggy nest. Imagining pulling Steve to this door and having to negotiate the fact that her bed was already full. She straightened out the duvet, encouraged Indigo to the other side, stroked her hair to settle her and went back downstairs. Rob had retreated to his room. The house sat quiet with her as she paused on the bottom step, her hand curling round the sweeping volute. The expanse of the hall had returned, Gosia's patience stretched too thin. Boxes carted to the charity shop on a wave of irritated Polish. The flower design on the old rug highlighted in silver from the window behind her, warming as they reached

toward the warm lights of the porch. She should go to bed
too. Kate would not be back for hours, it was pointless to wait
up. She walked across the hall and locked the door, switched
the lights off and made for the stairs. To her left a light shone
down the east corridor. Her study door stood open, light
pooling out onto the hallway.

She walked toward it, weary and full of lingering kisses,
thinking of bed and reaching round the doorframe for the
light switch. On the desktop sat her laptop, open. Her hand
paused over the switch. She moved into the light, perched on
the stool at her desk and saw the names in her inbox. Her
hand moved to ping it open, the words pulling her back into
the stream of Moth's life.

Please send money.

Her tiredness and the lingering sense of Steve's lips on
hers crumpling like fine wings against the words. She sat and
stared at them, until they blurred into shapes that held no
sense. Send money. How could she send money and not ask
for more details? The truncated request a stinging wound.
The lack of information about where he was, what he was
doing, why he needed help. The searing wakefulness that
surged through her, chasing the evening out. She glanced
across the tabletop, her eyes resting on the diaries piled upon
the low table. She shut the laptop and went to settle into the
sofa.

What sense was there in emails or kisses? At least the past
was solid in her diaries.

'RIGHT, come on, let's do this.' Kit called order and moved to
the whiteboards. The team were downing coffee with bagels,
croissants and expectant faces.

They had never let him move on from these Monday morning meetings. Ever since Elsa's conversion in Swansea had kick started the tradition. He had grown through boredom, back into delight, out the other side into boredom again. He wondered if that was what a long-term relationship meant. Growing repeatedly through the end of boredom. Kit repressed a shudder. Adele had called last night to suggest they spend Christmas and New Year in London.

'Pipe down at the back!' Kit told Fred who was always the last to shush, talking to Jamie.

He waited an extra minute before beginning. Noticing that Vee had chosen to sit next to Jamie. Away from both Lou and Henri.

The conversation with Adele had not gone great. It would have been better in person, where they could have diffused the difficulties with touch and pleasure. They'd been together over two years and Kit had struggled to not yawn through the argument. It hadn't helped that he started by saying he was already decorating the house, he'd set his mind on having Christmas at home. Adele had made it worse by pointing out he wasn't being fair, he'd already decided about Christmas once without him.

'Right, Lou you go first.' Kit dispelled the unpleasant memory.

Lou first, then Henri, a precise stab at ego management. Henri needed to know he was displeased. He passed the baton on to Vee. Who hadn't yet adjusted to the idea that she was supposed to contribute to these events. Actively contribute. Which is why he made her go third. Even if she was looking to Lou and Jamie for affirmation on each point. Kit listened idly as the team brought each other up to speed on their jobs.

Kit was regretting his choices. He felt impatience with Vee sidling into his impatience with Adele. An impatience which let him know indifference was only a step away. Kit didn't want to be indifferent. Adele had kept him focused and, if Kit ended up bored or indifferent, it wasn't getting any easier to find someone capable of distracting him. He sucked in his lips to control a frown as Vee stared at her hands.

Vee was not confident enough to make a success of this job. He could see that. The conversation with Henri had seeded a sour truth. Not that Lou couldn't be strident, or that it had taken a bit of adjusting to, but Vee was overwhelmed from the start.

Staff. They were the biggest challenge of his life. Finding the good ones, keeping them, inspiring and challenging them to stay fresh. Kit hated it when he saw parents preaching their own importance. One of the irritating quirks of Instagram, putting up with the self-satisfying bollocks of parents who acted like they had the most important job in the world, raising the next generation of little humans. As though he didn't spend each day worrying over and investing in the current generation of not so little humans sat round his kitchen table. Looking at Vee, with her tidy hair and precise eyeliner, he wasn't convinced he wanted to invest in her personal existence.

Give him Lou with her hair up and her head shaved beneath, holding fake conversations with him about Japanese craftspeople to cover his absence from the business. Give him Fred with his suspension damaging weight that needed to be carefully swapped from passenger to driver seat over all the vans, without letting him know this was what the rota was doing because Fred was suffering from fraternal heartbreak. Give him Hester with her gossamer confidence and ability to select a colour palette that made Kit gut-punched with jealousy. Give him Ed and his ability to know exactly which team member needed which piece of support or encouragement, while pointing out to Kit the tens of thousands they weren't making by ignoring the garden of each client they worked for. As Vee finished, he caught Henri glancing at her with an encouraging smile, before tapping his pen against his own notepad, underlining whatever he'd written there.

'Hester, your turn,' Kit moved on, trying to focus.

He watched as Hester moved from her chair to stand at the front, a little away from him. Hester had added the visual element to these team meetings, connecting his media system up to their phones and downloading her photos for the Monday team meetings. Hester had realised she worked behind Kit and slightly alongside Henri in the schedule and was privy to advance information she could give the team for when they arrived on site. Hester had started using the photos to arm her colleagues. Henri had followed suit and used them to control the team. Where they should park, which access to use, which rooms they needed to work on. Kit had watched it happen. Aware of what they were both doing long before Lou came to him and asked if Henri was being a condescending twerp, or was she being oversensitive?

Kit watched Lou hanging onto Hester's words and making notes with a slight frown between her eyes, her top lip tugged between her teeth in concentration. Yes, she was oversensitive. That was exactly what worried him. Lou opening a new chapter in her sex life left her open to heartbreak and the inevitable repercussions it would bring to them all. But Henri was a condescending twerp too. Kit leant against the worksurface and twisted the watch on his wrist. Henri hadn't always been a condescending twerp. He'd been committed and trustworthy when he came. He'd practically held the company together when Elsa had sprung the surprise of the decade on them all.

But Hester had a way of spotting details no one else, bar him of course, could see. She picked up on nuances that Henri missed. Opportunities that only her artistic eyes noticed. He'd seen it first in Swansea and, after that was finished, he'd asked her along to advise on some other jobs. His clients warmed to her, she provided a crisp, nuanced accent and subtle diplomacy that spoke of old money. Advice had turned to participation. The staff always happy to have her along. Hester was not the Hester who'd stormed out of the study at Riverdell, who'd left her brother's wedding early, who'd erupted at Isabelle and been thrown out of her own childhood home. She no longer wore her hair in a subdued plait over the shoulder but tousled on top of her head. She'd dropped the long cardigans and cotton trousers she'd favoured, replacing them with linen slacks and cute little blouses. She'd both softened and pulled herself together. Her work with them ran alongside her painting, her devotion to Nat, a cautious social life encouraged by her unlikely friendship with Lou. They'd even gone to Amsterdam for a long weekend. One day soon, Kit even thought she might forgive Rob enough to date again. Perhaps she'd even given up on the hope of children at last.

Staring at Hester, thinking about what might come next in her life, he became aware she was staring back. He straightened up, saying, 'Great stuff, yes.'

'Are you even listening to me?' she asked.

'At least partly.' Kit moved to take her place. 'The point is, are you all listening to her?'

Because, Kit thought, that really was the point. If he and

Henri were going to have a bust-up, there was a fair chance Hester would take his place. Henri's trouble was he took the job for granted. The rises and Christmas bonuses. Kit smirked to himself. Well, things could change. He was the boss after all and the bonuses were supposed to be just that, a bonus.

'Anyone else got anything to add?' He looked directly at Vee when he said it, saw her glance at Henri, blinking in discomfort. Henri's face showed nothing, his pen tapping against the cover of his notebook. 'No bugbears we want to air? Great, that's it then. You have two weeks off. Hester, Ed, Henri, take it in turns to be on call. Lou, Jamie, Vee, you're on back up. Fred, you're on boot camp. Don't call me unless a house literally falls down.'

'EVERYTHING GOOD?' Jay asked from the sofa as the front door upstairs closed on the cheerful banter of the team departing.

'Yeah, why?' Kit looked up from his phone. He had been dragged into Instagram again without even noticing it. He refocused, saw the mess of the table and began to move toward it.

'Just seemed a bit tense,' Jay said.

'About average.' Kit loaded plates on top of each other. 'The team is getting bigger, it gets harder to keep it together. I can't be everywhere at once.'

'You outgrew yourself, huh?'

Kit, tidying away the breakfast remnants, glanced from the kitchen to the sofa where Jay was half-listening to him, half-reading and felt the odd statement worm into his thoughts.

'You ever wish you could?' Kit asked.

Jay glanced at him, caught on the wistfulness in Kit's voice. Kit finished loading the dishwasher, went over and sat on the sofa opposite Jay. It was uncomfortable, seeing his mother's handwriting on the open pages. Her thoughts laid out before them.

'I mean, do you ever wish you could sort of shed a skin, like a snake? Grow into an updated version of yourself?' Kit asked him.

Jay closed the diary and put it to one side. 'Surely the snake is still a snake, but in a bigger skin?'

'I think it would feel different,' Kit argued. 'You feel different to yourself if you change your hair or your style, right?'

'Can't say I've ever done those things.' Jay laced his fingers together in front of his scrotum. 'Even if I did, reckon I'd feel the same on the inside.'

'But imagine it, actually shedding your own skin?' Kit looked out the window. 'You'd leave all the ugliness and scars behind and be reborn.'

'Scars are more than skin deep,' Jay argued.

'Oh alright, forget it. What were we talking about?' Kit settled into the sofa and put his sock-clad feet up on the low table between them.

'Your business problems.'

'Oh, yes. They're boring and tedious. Let's talk about something more interesting.'

'You get bored too easily,' Jay told him.

'No, the rest of the world gets bored too slowly, and when they wake up to how tedious their life is, they feel robbed. Do you ever wonder how it feels to be permanently told you're the problem, not everyone else?'

'Boring?' Jay asked with a grin.

'As hell.'

'How about we talk about your mother's childhood?'

'Why the hell would we want to do that?'

'Well, it's certainly not boring.'

'I did warn you.' Kit soothed the line of his trousers down against his thigh. 'How far have you read?'

'Not far. I've about got them in chronological order, I think.' Jay crossed his legs and sat upright on the sofa. It was a movement of flexibility that Kit could only marvel at. He was built for strength, for endurance, bending was getting harder. 'They start when she's about eleven. Most of the early ones focus on her complete disgust with being sent to boarding school.'

'I can relate to that,' Kit told him. 'I remember being pretty pissed about it myself. Gave my mother merry hell. Not that it made a lot of difference.'

'I'd say your mother did the same with your grandmother, sorry, great-grandmother.'

'Can't say I blame her.' Kit crossed his feet on the table. 'Passed from parent to parent to grandparent like a hot potato then tossed off to board.'

'Did you ever trace back through your family tree?' Jay asked, cocking his head to the side in curiosity. Kit felt like a worm, being inspected by a bird. 'Find out who her mother was? See what relatives you might have? Looks like you're rather well descended.'

'I've seen enough of that crap at Riverdell over the years,' Kit told him. 'Family are nothing but a curse, mostly. I had all I ever needed in my mother and Granny. Besides, well descended or not I was only ever going to be the bastard of a bastard.'

Kit let the words drop onto the smooth polished walnut of

the table between them and ripple across the surface.

'Never bothered your mother,' Jay said. 'I see a lot of you in her younger self.'

Kit didn't respond. It was weird, sitting here in the house he'd renovated, Jay dragging the relics of the past into the morning light. He wondered what Granny would say about what he'd done to her house. What his mother would say about what he'd done with his life.

'Did you tell your mother about Lydia?' he asked Jay.

Jay stared back at him with terse lips. Kit found it perversely pleasing, how the mention of the bitch's name produced this shuttering effect.

'I guess not, huh?' he concluded. 'When did you last see them?'

'Christmas, briefly,' Jay said. 'Stop changing the subject, we were talking about your mother.'

'Oh, sorry, I thought we were talking about family.'

'What about your father?' Jay asked. 'Did you ever find out who he was?'

'For all I know he could be dead too. What use is a father anyway, bar to straitjacket you emotionally?' Kit stretched back against the plush cushions. It was too easy to provoke Jay when he was this subdued. It was remarkably close to having a conversation with the old Hester. 'Unless you're going to suggest that having a conversation with my father would be more emotionally fulfilling than you ever found it?'

'My father's dead,' Jay told him in a flat tone. 'You came to the funeral, remember?'

'Uhm, probably for the best that he was dead when we finally met. I might have told him what an arse he was.'

'He was not an arse, he was a product of his own culture and upbringing.'

'You still telling yourself that?' Kit asked in disbelief. 'Did you get any therapy yet?'

'Did you?' Jay snapped back.

'Yes, a few years ago.'

'And how did that work out?' Jay asked him.

'It was boring,' Kit admitted. 'As is all this talk about fathers. Look, yours was a wanker who ignored you the moment you refused to follow his carefully laid out path for you, and mine was what Mother always called a technical necessity. Surely there must be more interesting stuff in those diaries to talk about?'

Jay glared over the table, pulling back from the brink of an argument. It would be easy to nudge him over that precipice. Jay should have been a doctor or a lawyer. Only those two professions could have justified the challenges Jay's father had gone through getting himself and his parents to England from Bangladesh. Losing his own parent's respect by marrying a white doctor's daughter. Determined to earn it back by raising kids to follow the golden highway of medicine. Only it hadn't worked with Jay. Who had refused the course set him and got his first job in a pub, causing a chasm between himself and his father that had never healed. Fathers. The best one he'd ever met had been Richard and look at how David had turned out. Kit was glad he was mother raised.

'What if the diaries tell me who your father was?' Jay asked him.

Kit thought about it. What if his father was another loaded aristocrat? That could be useful. But, knowing his mother, it had probably been some hopeless jerk she'd taken pity on. And that could prove awkward.

'My mother saw fit to go to her grave without telling

anyone,' Kit said. 'I think, if you do find out, perhaps keep that to yourself. I could do without ending up in therapy again.'

They stared at each other across the table, Kit behind his arms, Jay behind his crossed legs.

'How about who your mother's first lover was?' Jay asked.

'I thought you'd only got as far as her school days?' Kit protested.

'She started early.'

Kit paused. He wasn't sure he could face finding out the ugly secrets of his mother's life. It had been hard enough discovering Moth's, but he'd rationalised it. Moth was doing his own thing, growing beyond it. Secrets. They had always been a lightly held thing, until Moth. Then secrets had assumed a power he couldn't take back and broken him and Kate. Jay was offering him a Pandora's box insight into his mother's life. What might he not be able to put back in that box once they opened it?

'Was it good or bad?'

'Pretty cool,' Jay said.

'Ok, who?'

Jay looked at him, hoarding the knowledge he had.

'Stop teasing,' Kit told him in irritation.

'It was Isabelle's mother, Beth.'

Kit felt it bubbling through him. Thoughts he'd had percolating for years, trickling through. Uncomfortable hints from Elsa, determined avoidance from Kate. He could feel it shifting him sideways. The uncomfortable depths of igno-rance picking at his shield of confidence. Yep, secrets. He should have known better than to start this. Kate had taught him that lesson already. Why couldn't he have left it all safely wrapped up in that untouchable box?

9

H ow time moves when you make a decision. The last few years have dragged their feet like corpses and now I can barely keep up with the months.

It is my birthday. I'm getting ready to go out and do not know myself in the mirror. What hope and optimism I felt as the last year died. Did I think I would be reborn from its ashes?

It has not been the great adventure I imagined.

The steps toward gender change are arduous and isolated. I have told no one what I am doing. Not been back to Riverdell since Christmas. Hidden the changes from my work colleagues beneath my clothes and style. But I cannot do it any longer. I must step out of the shadows. Yet, standing naked before the mirror, I feel lost.

What I am moving toward is not me either.

Kit knew it in an instant. The moment he came home from school. Our long summer together starting with a frown on his face. He was silent, seeing all I have been at pains to hide from him and others. Gave me a great hug that nearly broke me. How strong he is becoming. A child has a weight that you can lift, move, articulate. The shape of the adult comes in the weight of him. The solidity of his form a recrimination that I have let his childhood go. He returns home to find his mother gone. Here I stand instead.

It was a relief to leave London for the summer recess and come home. The discomfort increased as the weather improved. My breasts do not cope with binding. It is painful and leaves me sore for days afterward. But as I switch to masculine clothing it is necessary. There is a restraint in men's shirts that irritates me. My breasts have not shrunk. They sit, refusing to conform to the other changes the drugs are wreaking on my body. The shape of my arms has changed, as have the muscles across my shoulders, they look bigger. I am growing hairier. My nipples sprouting hairs like alfalfa. It looks hideous and I pluck them. Taking the drugs to achieve the changes and rushing to cancel out the effect. Tonight, I must bind again. The doctor says it will take top surgery to make a difference. I have had a suit tailored and promised myself I would wear it. That I would dress as I shall be and go out for my birthday as a man. Yet here I stand, in love with the freedom of my breasts and the softness of my underwear. Stuck between a promise to my future self and a longing for who I have been.

Looking at my own portrait and not wanting to give up the woman in that image.

My hormonally confused genitals are swollen to a point of making me feel permanently aroused. It is a constant distraction, and my desire has broken through an invisible wall to heights I had no idea existed. Is this what men feel or is this just me? This tautness that pulls my eye to any point of humanity with a scanning attention. Is this what I am moving toward? The doctors say I must take the drugs for at least eighteen months before surgery. I am five months in and not sure I want to go any further. I started this process with a clear idea that I was moving away from myself, and in moving away I had to move toward a clear alternative. But this emerging manliness is a discomfort that feels no truer than my feminine self. In fact, no, it feels less true. I feel squashed, swinging like Newton's ball between the pressure of two opposites, squashed in the way my breasts are crushed, squashed by desire I cannot fulfil and distaste for the body that is changing. I am more miserable, not less.

Why do I even want to go out tonight?

Kit would love me to stay in and play cards with him and Granny. We could curl up in bed afterward and spend the night talking. Why do I push myself to do this thing?

Because I long to know that moment. I carry it within me as a promise. The barrier I know I must pass to find certainty. That I shall know my desires are true, and lie with a man, as a man, pegging him, before I commit to take the surgery.

This is the task I have set myself.

Ten more minutes and I shall dress.

I promised myself I would write you. To thank you for my birthday gift. The sash is beautiful. The fineness of the silk reminds me of the shirt I wore at your wedding. I still have the top hat and cane, they sit beside my wardrobe, a memory to keep you close.

Do you know it was that night which started me down this path?

I remember my jealousy, imagining you with Ted. How I hated the thought of him taking your body for his own pleasure when I could only mimic him. I decided I would expunge the jealousy on your wedding guests. It was the first night I let a man penetrate me. But all I could think of was you with Ted. One wasn't enough, I took another, and another, and how fucking useless they all were. Pleasure for a man begins and ends with himself. I was nothing more than a receptacle to them.

I shall not be that sort of man. I took no pleasure from them bar wondering if I could give more pleasure if I had the same tools.

I cannot write this to you.

I never yet told you about that night. Or Kit, about his origins.

What will you make of all these ramblings? While you sit in your gilded mountain cage and pretend you are free. Is it pride, that keeps you there when your marriage is a failure? I see through the positivity, the chatter about your work and purpose. You are stuck. Between a promise you made and a desire you don't feel. You should take a lover. I bet Ted has. And you will not come home, will you? To admit to Elsa your marriage is a sham, her brother a failure to you.

Or is it me? Will you not come home and face me?

And why do I not come to see you? Oh, I know the early years with Kit were a barrier to so much, but that excuse has faded now. And though Ted asked me to leave, for your sake, his presumption no longer worries me. I know you are unhappy, he had his chance and failed. Yet I do not come. Why do we both keep from the other? Is it fear that there will be nothing left between us? Is the bitter twist of life to be this lingering fear that the flame we found together might be alive only in our memory, not in reality? What would I be if I had to face that truth?

There is so much I want to write, but here, have what few lines I can send.

. . .

DEAR BETH,

Thank you for the lovely gift, I shall wear the sash tonight when I go out to celebrate. Kit is eleven and steaming full on into puberty. His body strong from rugby and his eye a roving one too, he knows his own desires less than I do mine. I predict he will be either gay or bisexual. And either an artist or stylist perhaps, though poverty will never suit him. He has developed Granny's taste for caviar and champagne and is a snob about his shoes, which his damn feet outgrow every other month. You will know that Elsa had another boy, James, and he is as sunny as David is stormy. Massive baby, 11 lbs, she nearly broke in the delivery. Kate is writing a book and Elsa is editing it as she nurses. Richard is delighted and they are all as happy as much-reduced, lower-rung aristocracy can be in their privileged little world. Granny is getting slower and her tongue sharper, and Kit is learning it all and practicing his contempt on me. You say you have moved to Kashmir and taken my advice. You and Kish have set up a school in town and are training local women to teach. I am proud of you. You were getting awfully colonial and saviourish before. Parliament is its usual vipers' nest of self-serving, lying bastards. If you're not prepared to shag them, you're touted as lesbians or animal activists. We're stuck between choices, a woman at the top or a labour man. It's a hard choice and all the talk, but is there a real chance that Maggie will make the cut? It's one thing to have a woman as Shadow Leader, another altogether to think the country might vote her in. And to be honest, if they did, I'm not sure I could cope with a woman whose dress sense is worse than Elsa's telling me what to do. I am sad that the child thing can't happen for you. It's a terrible thing to want and be denied, I hope you have not become sour from it. Even though Ted refused to adopt, does it prevent you from considering it? And I? I am fine. Changing, in lots of ways, hopefully for the better. I will write you all about it when I know myself.

Love, Rose.

THERE, a more insincere set of platitudes never left Elsa's lips, how proud she would be. How relaxing it must be to write about babies and houses and work and lovers without having to bite back this incessant, tormented dialogue that is banned from polite conversation. What would Elsa and Kate say if I sat down to breakfast in the kitchen at Riverdell and asked over my eggs, between talk of baby formula and grammar, whether I should have a penis surgically created or, is using a strap-on dildo on a man going to be good enough for my satisfaction and, how exactly do you go about meeting a man who wants you to peg him? Surely, if he did, he'd just get a man to do the job properly in the first place?

Enough. I am going out. This bollocks is intolerable. I need sex. I shall dress as I did for your wedding. I can't bear to bind tonight, I shall wear my new suit with a woman's blouse and tuck my desire in my purse.

Perhaps I shall get Kit to cut my hair off this summer. That would be a huge step. What do I look like, stuck in this hinterland between opposites? Lingering over the curves of my body, the fall of my hair. Longing for the hardness of a man's equipment. What unnatural freak am I? Who could love someone neither one thing or the other? Will I become just a challenge to the troubled, to see what they can make of me? Yet, vented now, and thinking of you, I feel more myself in this unknown place than I think I shall if I make the full trajectory.

The world always needs to label itself, to assign a category, an identity. What if the identity I seek is not in the world? How do I become what doesn't exist?

Here he comes in his self-conscious shoes, clacking down the hall, I shall ask him what he thinks of my hair...

10

Moth blamed Inci. Up until their conversation he hadn't been looking for the others, as she called them. Thoughts of Luca had pulled him inward. It had been private. This thing he was trying to work out. This promise he was keeping.

Avoiding.

Thinking about.

A three year's promise is avoidance on the highest scale.

After his conversation with Inci he started looking outward. That was when he found the camp.

His trips between Suruc and Urfa narrowed down to a four-day routine. One where he was present enough to not worry Dilru and get his head crushed, distant enough to stop her worries about Inci. Regular enough to be of use and earn a hot meal, not too often to get under foot or cause irritation. Given time enough to email Isabelle. Busy enough to stop Dilru nagging him about Bonn. Because, as he pointed out, it was nine weeks since Bonn had left, and no news had come.

Yeah, but you didn't point out you gave him the wrong email address.

It hadn't been an intentional act. Only one number wrong. A moment of irritation with Bonn.

That look when you gave him Luca's name.

Moth folded himself into the tent and tried to forget that moment. Bonn had been subtle. A hitch in his speech, a second of delay to his response. But it had stung. Causing a gut reaction, scribbling down his email wrong. He'd figured it gave him three more days before he got back and gave him the right address. And, after a week of coping on his own, when he'd started to wonder if he would regret that reaction, he'd figured Bonn could track him down if he was determined enough.

And he hasn't.

Which told Moth all he needed to know about Bonn's efforts to get him a place at the table.

Outside he could hear the makeshift, illegal camp quietening down. Turkey had a different sound to Europe. Here, sound travelled high and wide at night. Damped down by heat in the day, rising with its release toward the stars. He lay on top of the sleeping bag, the open zip not even stirring in the absence of a breeze. The end of August topping out at a brutal ninety-six degrees. At least it was cooler than the end of July had been.

It will be cool enough before you know it.

He gave the makeshift frame a gentle test. It shook but held. Three crooked, rusting metal tubes with their ends crushed and jammed into one another supported the thinning canvas of his tent where the bike should be. Compared to the others, it was a palace. A complete pod not a propped sheet of cardboard and a scrap of plastic held in place with a batten. Held up with precision tensioning between tent pegs.

It won't stay upright in the first dew.

Moth could hear the boys finishing the remnants of food he'd brought back with him. He'd walked into the camp, food box in his arms, relieved that his tent was standing in the place he'd left it. Sagging where the lines needing tightening. He'd found the camp because of Atabey and Kadri. And he'd found them by following the eyes Inci seemed to have put in his head. Atabey and Kadri were cousins...

... no, they're not...

... claimed they were cousins. Atabey was tall, thin, a frown permanently etched on the soft olive skin puckered above his brows. Kadri was stocky, a huge grin stretching his deep brown face as he tackled everything with determination. If they were cousins, it was from a large and diverse family. All of whom they'd managed to lose on the trip out of Syria. Not a single parent, sibling, aunt or uncle had accompanied them north. While the others all had a relative they could, would, claim; parents or siblings in the official camp that lay behind hills less than five kilometres away in Onbirnisan, an uncle in Gaziantep, a married sister in Erzurum, third cousins in Ankara, mothers left behind in Raqqah, sisters taken and brothers conscripted into Isis, these two cousins had no family. Spoke about no parents waiting for them or siblings gone ahead.

Moth had found them on the streets of Suruc, pleading for food from one of the aid agencies Fehran delivered to. Watching as they got turned away. Two young men who could fend for themselves, too many children and pregnant women who couldn't. He'd followed them, watching as they tried to steal food from the market, picking up discarded herbs from the floor, sharing a rotting, raw eggplant down a side street stinking of summer rubbish. He'd seen Atabey folding into a hunched crush of despair, trying not to retch. Kadri sitting on his haunches next to him, arms pulling him close in comfort. Eyes darting down the street and, finding Moth, jumping up away from his "cousin" with the whites of his eyes showing in fear.

Lying in the tent, trying to relax in the thick air, longing for a whisper of cool air, Moth remembered that look. That fear. Atabey curling into his terror while Kadri kicked him to get up. It was a look he couldn't forget.

He reached into his backpack and pulled out the printed sheet of Isabelle's email. She wanted to know what he was doing. How were the bike repairs? When would it be road ready? Where was he thinking of going? Where was he staying? Curiosity hidden between sentences about home, family. Leaving Moth feeling picked apart. She wanted knowledge for her money. Answers for her help.

He stared up at the canvas ceiling. Wishing the light might dim long enough to give him two or three hours of deep sleep. He'd spent four years in this tent. Calling it home. Yet now it felt too small. Tight on his limbs, close on his chest, overwhelming his eyes. But better than looking over the pitiful state of the camp outside.

That first day he'd met the cousins, he'd shared his own food. Pittas and stuffed vines from his precious backpack supplies. Told them to meet him in three days' time, back in the market. Sign language and basic words. Left them, wondering if he'd ever see them again.

Three days later, waiting on the edge of the market with an old plastic bag of food, he'd seen Kadri. Four days later the same. Three weeks later Kadri had taken him back to the camp. A hidden dust bowl on the scraped-out sides of an old stone quarry, pockmarked with withered shrubs and abandoned rubbish. An hour and half's walk from Suruc town, bare hills away from the official camp. A motley assortment of scared older kids and wary young adults, kicked out from tents too small to home them.

And now home to your homeless arse.

He came every fourth day, carrying two bags of food the near three kilometres from where Fehran dropped him. Stopped a night and left. Praying the tent would be respected in his absence. Moth looked down at the printout. No, she couldn't make him a new tent without having either the original or the bike to work from. How about he bought a new bike? With a new tent? Come home and pick one. They could plot which way he went next, get visas sorted, give him the chance to work.

Moth grimaced. She was doing exactly what he'd asked for. Helping. Only helping seemed tied up in unspoken provisos and conditions.

She sent you the money no questions asked.

Yes, she had, £1000 emailed to his empty account. Enough to enable him to half wheel, half carry the bike through Urfa to the only bike repair shop in town. Where he'd missed Luca negotiating in swift Italian for repairs, translating explanations in the smart shop on the mainland opposite Venice.

Luca doesn't speak Turkish.

And Husnu hadn't cared enough about the bike or him to put even a fraction of energy into the exchange. Sullen and impatient that Inci had insisted he go.

He'd been back three times since. The bike hadn't moved from where it had been propped against the wall. It wasn't what they were used to. He wasn't what they were used to. Perhaps if he'd taken Inci it might have been different. God only knows what Husnu had told them.

Moth scanned the emails again. An awful lot about furniture. The house. The magnolia tree. Then...

... the real teaser...

... what did he think about going to India?

That was the point he kept coming back to. India.

Why would you want to go to India?

Outside, he heard an argument start. Raised voices, curses he couldn't understand, the sound of tussling. A scrap of food or waste material being fought over. Moth tensed, holding his breath with the silent others, waiting to see if it would grow or ebb. Relating the distance of the scuffle to the nearness of his tent and the boys immediately close to him. Wondering how Atabey was coping. It had been their thin belongings stolen before. He tensed, resisting the urge to push his way out of the tent and see. It would be an hour or more before the scuffles stopped. Before the heat ebbed enough to lessen the misery. He would do no good going to help. He was barely tolerated as it was.

Every time he came back the faces changed. It was dangerous, the fluctuation. For all of them. Not knowing who brought what danger. The camp had been there over a year, and news spread. When the streets got cleaned by the military, or the aid agencies had to shut their doors, or there was a spate of violence by the residents, new stragglers would arrive. If too many came at once the camp broke out into violence. Atabey had been attacked twice in the last year while Kadri was away, trying to find work in the local towns. But that was as much as Moth had found out. The English-speaking lad he'd met when he first arrived had not been there when Moth returned the third week.

He'd tried to get Dilru to help. Even asked Inci to intercede. But Dilru would only work through the aid agencies. She wouldn't take a risk beyond sending him out with as big a pack of nearly over food as she thought he could carry.

Outside, the shouting dulled into thuds, fists hitting flesh. He shut his eyes and counted through it. Silence was good. It would end sooner.

In his own silence he could sense the others, huddling into their corners. He looked down the length of his legs, stretching into the low point of the tent. All this mass of his ought to be worth more. Give him the confidence to throw himself between one young man's frustration with life and another. He'd taken a thrashing in the nightly patrol of Bonn's camp and gone back out for more. But at Bonn's there had been a medic tent, backup. The thuds stopped. In the retreat of wounded parties, frustrations released for the night, he could hear the smothered sobs of Atabey.

All strength was relative. In Bonn's shadow he'd had the weight of authorities to bolster his confidence. Out here he was thrust back into the fear that had ridden with him through Europe. That vulnerability of being utterly alone, with no back up. No way forward. He remembered that.

You used to live for a plan.

He had. Day to day, moving forward, aiming for a destination. When that had been taken away, he'd chosen helping others as a replacement. When that had been taken away, he'd set his head on stubborn refusal to be told what to do.

Now here you are again, stuck without a plan.

With India dangled in front of him.

Or living like a gutter rat with the rest of the rubbish.

Strength was relative. Moth wanted to manage his own life, find his own solutions. Give help, not need it.

Unlike Atabey, who was crumbling under the combined pressures on him. Moth listened to Kadri trying to hush him and stared at the tent fabric.

If it was Luca, how would Luca cope. Luca with his future laid out before him, a yellow shimmering brick road waiting for him to skip down. Where would all that skinny charm and well-groomed hair get Luca in these circumstances?

Outside the thin tent, Atabey's breathless panic became the only noise competing with the insects and birds enjoying the rising heat waves. Moth wished him strength.

The strength to shut the hell up before he gets a kicking.

Atabey stood out in the camp. Against a rough group of young men made hard and desperate, he had the look of a boy who had dreamed of books, education, a bed with soft pillows and a loving family. Moth found it hard to like Atabey. He was always flinching or moaning. At best he sat in a stupor of depression and ignored the world. The impact of displacement a bruise that had stained his inner and outer being. But, if Moth found it hard to see the appeal, the other boys outright despised him. Atabey's misery reflected their own desperation, coupled with an unseemly emotional range that they were all trying to ignore in themselves. Moth tried to like him. Tried to think about his perspective.

You're thinking about Luca.

Luca. Not in Geneva. Not with a future. All those hopes reduced to a crumbling, dirty, smelly mess beneath a cardboard hovel. Hunger taking the shine out of his fine frame. Moth struggled against the fact that he couldn't find the compassion for Atabey that he wanted to feel. He focused instead on Kadri. Kadri he could relate to. A grim determination not to give up. A screaming defiance in the face of impossible odds. If Luca were here, Moth would move the damn stone quarry to get them out.

Yet you won't go back to Geneva and face that truth.

Moth listened to Atabey's noise lessening as his panic subsided. There was no way they would survive this hell much longer. There had to be a plan he could make, a way of getting them into a camp or a shared place in one of the towns. Or even further away from here, on the road to anything other than this lingering kiss of death.

Play the knight protector rather than face your own battles. Kit warned you about that.

He couldn't go to Geneva. He wouldn't fit in there. He wouldn't know how to live that life.

You're too scared to try.

It was overwhelming. Even thinking about the name, the place, the city. The normality. He'd been away from it for too long. He couldn't go back to that.

You liked Venice.

Venice was a sodding holiday. He needed to stop thinking life would be a Venetian dream revival. That was the problem. It was a great memory. But life wouldn't be Venice. Life would be people looking at him and Luca. It would be Luca wanting to do normal things and dragging him into it. Friends, parties, careers, shopping.

Shopping?

Moth grimaced and pushed the ridiculous thoughts away. There was as much a gulf between him and Luca as there was between Atabey and hope. He looked back at the emails, the words swimming their way in desperation toward a single clarity. One word.

India.

Why not? It's been a while since you had a good plan.

That was what he needed. He recognised the desperation gripping his muscles. He needed to make a plan and stick to it.

Bonn wasn't going to get in touch. Moth had grown dull, waiting to be told what to do, where to go. He'd been over-whelmed by the need of other people. First in the camp, now here. Bonn had told him to try and save one more person from disappearing if he could.

You thought you could save them all.

He would focus on the bike. Get himself out of Turkey. Decide if he was going to India. But first...

... no, just don't...

... he would get Atabey and Kadri out of this shit hole...

... that's setting an impossible task...

... he couldn't leave them here...

... and what if you have no choice?

Moth stared up at the ceiling of the tent. The fibres stretched and thin. It wouldn't keep a winter out.

Yet you think you can get them out.

He would give it his all. For Luca's sake.

You're doing this for Luca?

Moth couldn't go to Geneva. He could see that as clear as the ragged spaces between the fibres of the tent. Whatever they had shared in Venice, whatever he'd been keeping this promise for, he couldn't go to Geneva. Their experiences were too far apart. He thought about Kadri, wrapping his short, muscled arms round Atabey to soothe him. Trying to hold the broken pieces of their life together.

You're thinking about Luca.

Maybe he would always think about Luca. Maybe he'd made a promise he couldn't keep or break. Maybe he was waiting for Luca to break it himself. But he would not think about going back to Europe again.

And India is definitely not Europe.

ISABELLE SAT AT THE MACHINE, hand guiding the curved hem through the foot. Outside she could see Kate's class going through their yoga session. Bending in rhythm to the folding of the fabric. The river a slow green sludge beyond them. The grass a sun-worn late August tiredness beneath their jarring array of mats.

Finishing the hem, she rose. On the table were two piles. Cut pinnies with their sewn ties waiting to be attached slipped between the piles. Finished pinnies interleaved with their order sheet. In the middle an iron fizzed at her, unhappy with having been left on all day. She pressed the creases out, the contrast of the ties delighting her as she tucked them into the folds and smoothed it ready for packing.

A lack of concentration one day, a glazed tiredness and a drifting mind lost on the river, and she had attached the wrong ties to a plain Dinham apron before she realised it. Stared down at the product in confusion and reached for the snips to unpick it. Knowing the stitch line would look inter-rupted and heavy where she had to replace them. The ties had looked jaunty with their difference, confident in their mistake, uplifting the plain design. She had sent it to the customer along with a second, made correctly to the original design, and asked for their opinion on her new line.

Such a simple change and life had expanded. Well, her orders at least. It was annoying that she hadn't thought of it before. She had shared this with Kate who had replied, in one encapsulating word, 'Motherhood' as though that explained all her mental blips. It wasn't enough for Isabelle. Yes, motherhood was exhausting, overwhelming, belittling. But it couldn't kill the entire creative spirit, surely?

'I've worked on movie sets, I mean that's intense! And it's always about the details. Details are about the only thing I do see clearly for God's sake. How can I have missed a creative detail as simple as changing the colour of the ties on a pinny?'

Kate had looked at her with suspicion, a single precision-etched eyebrow rising from her perfectly made face. 'What's this really about?'

'What?'

'Don't "what" me, Isabelle.' Kate had planted her feet solidly on the kitchen floor. A fact which had made Isabelle pause. Rarely did Kate have both feet on the ground at once, let alone for the duration of time it took to call them planted. 'Are you going to drag those damn fabric jugs out of the attic again?'

Isabelle had blinked in the intensity of Kate's focus.

'No. I'm only saying it's pretty obvious, you'd think I could have thought of it before.'

'And why do you think you didn't?'

Isabelle, sat at the kitchen table, had pulled her knee up to her chest. Thinking into her cup to avoid the long look.

'I suppose I haven't, you know, maybe… it's that maybe I need to, you know…'

'Stop evading the point, what is the point?'

What had been the point? Over a month ago now and she hadn't managed to work it out herself, let alone solidify it enough for Kate. Isabelle picked up the next order and returned to the sewing machine.

She glanced out to see the women in wobbling tree poses.

It felt wrong, looking out at them. Watching their self-conscious efforts in front of the yoga teacher. She would get a drink and have a ten-minute break, the class would soon be over.

She walked down the corridor into the empty hall, revelling in the bliss of her Thursday. The early hours of the morning had been productive, a comforting pile stacked on her table. Asha had not arrived with Deryn, Kate would soon be up for lunch, the afternoon stretched ahead, the evening a happy conclusion. In the kitchen she was comforted by the small clinks of solitude, the tap of a spoon against china, the click of the dishwasher door, the rustle of a biscuit packet that felt furtive and precious.

She walked down the corridor to her office, the smell of coffee wafting back over her, the bliss of her full and peaceful day settling onto her shoulders. The corridor was darkened by the impact of light at both ends. The colourful prisms dancing through the hallway behind her and the sharp angles of light crisscrossing in the doorways of both study and workroom, trading strength and shadow as they merged. She paused, captivated by the play of the lines as the sun danced along the carpet, her eyes pulled to the great sweep of the India map on her right. It had become a thing she walked past innumerable times a day, this map that had once dominated her workroom, this country that had once pulled her to it. A thing precious to Mummy that Must Not Be Touched. Dire implications communicated to both the girls were a Sharpie pen ever to make it across the painted silk as it had once made it across the back of the sofa in the drawing room. Were ANY pen ever to come near the silk. Isabelle had removed all permanent markers from the house, wondering if she should move the map somewhere safer, higher. But it was huge, there was no other wall large enough to take it. Here it fitted, and the domination of the wall made sense. Elsewhere it would overpower the other aspects of a room and look "hideously colonialist" as Kit had complained when she'd rung him to share her worries. Isabelle raised a hand and touched the surface. Waiting for the impact of the fibre, pulling warmth from her palm toward itself. Silk. Even buried under the centuries and the paint, she could feel its potency. She caught memories, drowned out by parenting, by the repetition of her days, the slim line of orders she moved through. From one uncut cloth to each finished pinny, Ludford to Whitcliffe to Dinham, and back to the start. Stood there, lost in the shadows, Isabelle found her point.

Life should be so much bigger. Creativity got lost in the details, not found in it.

She was stuck in a rut again. She removed her hand, walked on to the study and broke through the angled prisms of light on the floor. She sat down on her stool and felt overwhelmed by the longing that wanted to take her far away, to something fresh and daring. Wondering what Kate would say to that.

Outside the windows of the study, she could see Martin making his way round the borders, pulling out the overblown plants. August heat curling the stalks brown and weary, hiding the green below. Behind him, at the edges of what was clear, the empty branches of the magnolia clawed the space between the house and the rearing bank of the castle, recriminating her indecision.

She pulled the latest diary to her. 1918. She had skimmed through the years before Ted's birth. Post war years of her grandfather, William's life as a young man. Learning to cope with the estate, his passion for the army and his posting to the East India Regiment. His first marriage to Alice. There was such a strong optimism in the tone, sitting against the cold references of the older man's life. Turning the pages ever swifter, expecting to close the diary and move backwards to the next, she missed the change. The pages converted to a new hand, softer, more angled, with lilting slopes to the descenders. A woman's hand. Isabelle went back more carefully. August 3rd, 1918. Mother is frail from losing Father. She fears the same misfortune awaits all officers. August 2nd, 1918. William comes of age tomorrow and Riverdell is his. My time is done. I beg God nightly this war will be over before he is sent to the front. I could not bear to lose him too.

Isabelle slipped into the life of William's mother, Margaret. War news conveyed in short, fearful sentences. The pages moving through two years of a woman's hand before William had inherited. The ballroom converted to a retreat for injured officers during the final years of the First World War. Reading in stunned amazement that her great-grandfather, Arthur, had died in the Battle of the Somme. The anger felt by his wife when he had signed up aged forty-one in the first days of Kitchener's campaign, before he passed the age hurdle he was on the doorstep of. The clipped fear of his absence, the hollow disbelief in his death.

The diaries had become a source of fascination. A link to her unknown ancestors. She had felt nothing for them, these people whose faces lurked in the depths of an unused bedroom, staring sullenly at one another in the dimness of curtains drawn to protect them, but the diaries brought the house to life as she read. The romance that lay between the two handwritings which filled those years before the Somme. News from the farm, issues with the servants, horses lost, and new ones trained. The barn across the road restored to stables she could visualise and wanted to keep forever out of the hands of Kit's eco-friendly builders. She imagined them, Margaret and Arthur, sat here in her study, discussing the momentous and the tedious. Perhaps she had stitched by the fireside while he sat at the desk to write. Or she had taken up the task while he was out with business. Two hands at the tiller, guiding the home and family on. An exuberant joy in challenging each other in their different entries. Their pain as children failed to arrive or arrived and all too swiftly were buried. An unspoken fear that lingered in the page, breath held for nine precious months before William was safely delivered, destined to become their first and only child to live to adulthood. The happy-go-lucky child she had read as a life-cooled man. Isabelle sifted through the pages, pulling this marriage toward her, wondering what it would have been like. To be that in love, that optimistic, that unaware of what grief was to come.

She glanced out of the window and into the courtyard. She couldn't even decide about a dead tree and her great-grandparents had faced a hideous war together.

In the blare of horn that cut across her thoughts, barely softened by passing through the leaded glass, she saw Martin jump back onto the path cursing. The old glass rippled as the gleaming black outline of a low-slung car swept onto the gravel at aggravating speed and crunched to a sliding stop. Her heart, still thumping from the noise and Martin's shock, sank into a booming realisation. Her day was sabotaged.

Kit.

Kit, as in-your-face and dramatic as his new car.

She closed the diary with a sigh of despair. It was such a simple change. One minute her day was her own. The next, Kit had assumed all their days. She thought about Kate and grimaced as she left the room. Kate would not be sweet for a week after another of Kit's unannounced visits. Her hand lifted to touch the map as she passed down the corridor, breaking through the beams of light and trying to catch hold of the realisation it had left in her. That there was a grander design beyond the boycotting details of her daily life. That there was a world out there, beyond the lights of Riverdell. A world that Moth lived in. That she had once lived in. She tried to cling onto that thought as she opened the door and watched Kit get out of the sleek BMW and hold his arms open to her.

'Eh, mia familia,' he cried, pulling the shades from his eyes. 'I'm back!'

'Martin, are you alright?' Isabelle asked, walking across the gravel. 'Do you have gravel rash from the speed of his bloody entry?'

Martin grinned at her as she walked into Kit's embrace and got wrapped in a cuddle that felt so familiar, firm and grounding she never wanted to leave. She sighed in happiness and settled onto his chest. He even smelled like bliss. As though spring had held onto him and kept him cool and fresh while they festered with the dying magnolia.

'It's my workday you know,' she told him.

'Every day is a workday, Isabelle.' He held her away and looked over her with an appraising eye and a grin. 'Doesn't mean you get to ignore your family. Besides, I hear there's fresh meat on the board, I came to check him out.'

'How do you know about that?'

'I have my spies.'

'Polish bitch,' Isabelle muttered.

And anyway, where's my favourite baby girl? I have gifts to receive adoration for.' He turned to go back to the car and saw the magnolia tree. 'What the fuck happened to the tree?'

'It's dying.' Martin had joined them and leant on his spade to observe the grim twisted branches.

'Dying?' Kit jumped up on the low wall and tested a branch, it came away with a dusty snap. 'Dying suggests there's a process left to go through, this thing's already dead. Why on earth haven't you ripped it out. It looks hideous, oh and I had such plans for it at Christmas.'

He turned to look at them both. Beside her, Martin must have given a glance her way for Kit looked toward her.

'We don't know if it's dead for sure, it might come back next spring.' Isabelle shuffled her feet under his gaze. 'And we're still talking about Christmas.'

Kit sent an exaggerated query Martin's way. Whatever look he got back it obviously wasn't convincing.

'Really Isabelle, are you in charge here or what?' Kit jumped down from the wall and stood back to look at the tree with huge disappointment. 'This won't do at all. I have lights I specifically wanted to go there. Right, come on, let's get it out.'

'What?' Isabelle couldn't keep up. 'But surely we should wait until...'

'... call the new meat, tell him we need muscle. I hear he has plenty of it...'

'... or at least prune it back and hope for...'

'... Christmas waits for no man, Isabelle. I couldn't hang a dead mouse from that tree let alone fairy lights. Do you have a spare set of boots?' Kit asked Martin. 'I didn't plan on labouring?'

'In the truck, I'll go get them.' Martin headed for the barn car park without looking at her.

'But Martin, surely we...?' Isabelle tried one more time.

'Are you calling him, or am I?' Kit asked her. 'Steve, isn't it?'

'He has a job, a shop to run. I can't just call him and demand he comes to help me.'

'Can't or don't want to?' Kit opened the boot of the car and pulled bags out. 'Here, take this lot inside for me. And I'd love a coffee.'

'Kit, can you ever, you know, maybe call, give me notice, a chance to prepare for you?' Isabelle complained.

'You're evading the point, and anyway, I love surprising Indie. Where is she?'

'At nursery. What point?'

'Are you calling him, or am I?' Kit undid the top few buttons of his shirt, pulled it from the waist of his trousers and stripped it over his head in one swift motion, piling it onto the bags in her hands. Breathing out in delight as the sun rippled across his tanned skin, flickering in the curling hairs on his chest. Martin dropped a pair of rough boots at his feet and Kit kicked off his smart shoes. 'And where's the other half of my welcome party?'

She watched him peer around her toward the house. Looking him over she shuddered at the thought of Steve turning up. Kit could still send her flesh into goosebumps, no man who had just made inroads into her life was going to enjoy finding her semi-naked ex in her garden. What would Kate and her class think of it?

'In the garden doing yoga with her class. I'm not calling him. We need to talk about Christmas.'

'Oh, well, I've time to get a sweat on to impress her. Right, I'll call him.'

'You don't know his number.' She knew she sounded petulant. 'I haven't told Indigo yet.'

'About Christmas or the new muscle in your life?' He flipped out his phone, scrolled, tapped it and held it up to his ear. 'Whorled Reclamation, right?' he whispered at her. 'Hate the name. Oh, hello, yes, could I speak to Stephen please?' Kit switched to his most exaggerated polite voice.

She scowled at him and walked back to the house.

'Americano, no cream,' he called to her retreating back. 'Hi, is that Steve? Marvellous, what are you doing right now? Isabelle told me to call and ask for your help. I think it's time you met the best of the family.'

She walked into the house with a frown on her face and rigid back turned to his taunting. What would Kate say to it all?

'DO YOU MIND!' Kate retorted to Kit's strained swearing at the "tenacious old bitch" of a tree. 'That was both ageist and sexist.'

'Isabelle, I hope you're recording this momentous event,' Kit asked with a sweaty smirk at having provoked Kate.

'It's indelibly etched in my mind.' Isabelle was perched on the stone step of the porch with Indigo pinioned between her knees. An enormous velvet teddy bear was the only thing keeping Indigo from climbing onto Kit's back and clinging to his hair as he tried to finish the job. Isabelle found her eyes returning to the stitching with admiration. It was beautiful, dimpled, plump and soft. The fabric exercising a hypnotic power over Indigo's fingers. She was jealous of the idea, a business she could relate to on a fibrous level, wondering if she was missing a trick by not using more daring fabrics herself.

'Resistant bitch,' Kit griped as he deepened into the strain.

'Oi!' the general response greeted him.

'Stop encouraging him,' Kate complained to her ladies.

She was struggling not to grin at the chaos on the driveway and, though Isabelle could practically see a tail flicking under the swishing hems of her trousers, there was an air of joy in her too. Like she had been at the Brewery Company, or on the days when she strode into the kitchen with a new idea having woken her up. Kit's disruption of their day had taken Kate back to the constant challenge that running her bistro had been, and Isabelle realised that it suited her. That perhaps life became a rut for others too, maybe even for Kate. When today was over, she would ask her about it. Whenever today was finally over. Isabelle moved her chin from side to side over Indigo's curls. It was a rare moment, to have her this quiet and cuddly outside of bedtime and she savoured the moment, thinking about her lost day.

Her courtyard had quickly become a carnival. Kit's car, parked now against the borders beneath the study window, doors open with music playing, had two of Kate's women sat in the seats. Glasses of wine in their hands as they watched the proceedings. The other five women from the course were perched in a gaggle on the kitchen chairs dragged out via the boot room and arrayed in front of the garage. Asha was sat on the porch bench behind her, Deryn curled up with her head in her lap, an equally preposterous teddy clutched to her chest with both arms. Kate was supplying drinks via the back door to all, flitting between the house and the courtyard, the drinks and the people, irritation and joy like a summer dragonfly. Beautiful and scary in equal measure. Isabelle was surprised she hadn't bolted the door on her class of women and refused to engage. She had entertained the thought herself. But as much as she knew Kit was loving the attention, it was impossible to resist the carnage and the sheer amount of muscled sweating flesh on show.

Steve had come. Of course he had, who could resist a challenge like that? The day had grown hot, the stone sides of the courtyard holding onto the heat. Soon she had three underdressed men, dripping with sweat, grunting and cursing, covered in soil and taking her stone wall down a slab at a time. The roots had gone deep, and the magnolia was no push over. It had been like this when Gosia arrived home with Indigo, when Asha, no doubt informed by Gosia, unexpectedly turned up with Deryn, and when James finally arrived to see where his family had disappeared to. James had taken one look, given a contemptuous sigh, backed the Landy up to the magnolia and attached a long strap. The courtyard had held its breath to see if Kit's thunder was about to be stolen. But of course, no. Not even James could steal power from the God of Thunder today. James had frowned, detached the strap and set to with another shovel. Ten minutes later he had removed his own shirt. To appreciative cheers from the crowd of women and a smirk from Asha. This was when Rob had arrived after work, hoping for his usual Thursday evening delights. The nose of the Evoque had edged into the courtyard, taken one look and reversed across to the car park. Rob, walking into the scene in his solicitor's crumpled summer suit, had been greeted with cheers and demands to strip.

'Not a chance,' he said, hands rising to defend himself. 'I'm a paper pusher, nothing more. I'll do food. For, let's see, four, seven, ten, thirteen, sixteen and myself. Right, food for seventeen coming up.'

'Rob, look, look, look,' Indigo was squirming on the top of the pile of earth that had spread across the gravel. She and Deryn sliding down its sides and pushing the soil even further into the gravel.

'I can see,' Rob told her filthy face. 'You need a bath.'

'No bath.'

'No bath, no presents,' Kit, sweat and dirt streaking his face, had corrected her. Pausing for a moment to lean on his spade. 'Rob, you're a man of more sense than action. I admire that about you. I mean it Indigo. Bath or no presents. And get down from there before Rob does a Health and Safety assessment and sues me.'

Rob peeled Indigo from the earth pile and dragged her inside, Deryn trailing behind. Isabelle had smiled at him as he passed, put a hand onto his arm in apology. Turned back to see Steve watching her, Kit watching Steve, Kate watching Kit and smiled awkwardly in the vague direction of them all. Asha had pulled her down onto the porch bench with a glass of wine and made her sit for a moment.

'You know, I can think of worse ways to spend a summer evening.' Asha smirked over her wine glass as the men returned to the digging. 'Half-naked men doing the work while we sit drinking.'

'It's not as much work as the clearing up will be, you do know that?'

'You are correct, but at least we get to enjoy the moment.'

'You told Kit about Steve,' Isabelle poked her shoulder.

'Of course I did,' she admitted. 'Kit gets everything out of me, you should know that by now. Anyway, now you two are officially an item, why not?'

'An item?' Isabelle had gagged on her wine. 'What does that mean?'

'Well, you are, aren't you?' Asha had looked at her over the rim of her glass, eyes twinkling, elbow nudging her side. 'You know…'

Isabelle, uncomfortable with the wine in her voice reaching other ears than hers, had stood up, moving toward the door. 'I'm going to help with dinner.'

'How terribly domesticated of you.'

'Drink your wine and shut up.'

She had retreated to find Kate fretting in the kitchen. Defrosting meat in the microwave, stirring onions in a huge pot on the Aga. 'It'll have to be pasta and sauce. What bread do we have?'

Now, sat back out on the step of the porch, a clean Indigo between her knees, watching the men tiring and the sweat chilling on their bodies, the scent of slow cooked tomato, fennel, onion and basil wafting across them from the open door, Isabelle wondered if she was going to end up with a bigger mess in her driveway than she had started with. At least there had been a structural beauty to the dying tree. A pin holding in place the memories of this courtyard, all the comings and goings of her life and many others. She wondered who had planted it there, dreaming of its future. She wondered what Moth would say when he came back.

'What am I going to replace it with?' Isabelle asked Kate as she came back to the doorway.

'They haven't got it out yet,' she said. 'Don't count your chickens.'

'She's coming, don't fret,' Kit called across.

'Good, because dinner is almost ready. You've got another twenty minutes. We're eating out on the patio.'

'How romantic,' he tossed back.

'I'd hardly call pasta and sauce for seventeen "romantic",' she retorted. 'And you boys will clean up first.'

'I'll eat this damn tree if it doesn't come out soon,' James complained. He and Steve were straining on the strap, pulling the trunk toward the castle while Kit and Martin dug out the roots. 'Whose bloody idea was this? You know we could just leave it and I'll bring the tractor over tomorrow.'

'But this is so much more fun,' one of the class women called, her phone filming the details.

'You can't get the tractor through the arch,' Asha corrected him. 'Stop showing off.'

'Mini-digger?' Steve grunted through gritted teeth.

'How terribly practical of you both,' Kit stood up straight and stretched his back. 'This is my gym workout for a week you know. Some of us like a challenge that can't be solved with anything other than manpower.'

'Fifteen minutes.' Kate warned them and turned to walk back into the house.

'Do you need any help?' one of the women by the garage asked, getting up from her chair.

'That would be lovely, thank you. It's going to turn chilly, could you grab some blankets up from the ballroom?'

'Chilly?' Steve asked, adjusting his sweaty hold on the strap. 'Chance would be a fine thing.'

Isabelle had an uninterrupted view of his body, the low slippage of his jeans down his hips, the straining thighs beneath the denim. Steve had a stockiness to his torso. Solidity and strength without the laser edge definition of Kit's workout abs and chest. A compactness that stood out against James' engrained muscle that sat lean on a body used to constant work and serious machinery. Beside them Martin was the quiet beauty. A lithe cast, his legs strong from permanent squatting. It was disquieting, all this flesh on show. She was glad for the distance of her vision, keeping them all at a comfortable retreat. Her daughter's warm skin snuggled up in her arms, tired breath on her upper arm where her head rested, the wings of Riverdell surrounding and sheltering them both in the nook of the porch.

'Can't you plant another magnolia?' Asha asked, her voice heavy with tiredness and wine.

'You'll need to leave the soil to cleanse,' Martin said. 'It might only be old age, but there's a chance of disease. Wouldn't be wise to plant another magnolia straight in. Perhaps a different variety altogether and anyway, there's the wall to rebuild first and...'

'Could we do the design consultation after the tree comes out?' Steve complained.

'He does have a point,' James added.

The strap they were leaning on shuddered and threw them both backward. Their faces lit up with hope as they scrabbled to regain their footing.

'She's coming!' Kit crowed. 'Come on, one more push baby.'

He and Martin disappeared back down into the hole, spades chipping, old roots snapping. Steve and James took another step and leant into the strap.

'Ooh, come on girls, let's help!'

Kate appeared back at the door, tea towel in hand and watched her class jump to take the load of the long strap in front of James. Gathering up the slack and leaning into it with mirth, their bodies still clad in yoga Lycra.

'That's a sight you didn't expect to see today,' Steve quipped from behind him as James tried to look anywhere but in front of him.

Kate sighed on the doorstep and glanced across at her, 'This is all your fault, I hold you responsible if they end up with twisted backs.'

'Me too,' Asha agreed. 'What were you thinking, Isabelle?'

'I was thinking what a lot of work I was going to get done this afternoon,' Isabelle said. 'That's about the last thought I remember having in peace today.'

'HEAVE,' Kit called out.

The two men and six women pulled, and Kit and Martin pushed against the far side of the trunk. Rob appeared at the doorway behind Kate.

'Are we making progress?' he asked.

'Yes, toward hospitalisation...' Kate began to say.

With a deep tear, a rip of timber and suck of earth the magnolia slipped, stumbled and toppled its way out of the pit dug about its roots. Soil and loose stones crashed upwards and pattered into the open doors of Kit's car and onto the porch as it crashed toward the far wall of the courtyard where the women ran screaming from its path and Steve and James jumped out of the way with a scrabble.

Isabelle grabbed Indigo, jumping backwards into the porch. The branches snapped and crumbled as the weight of the trunk pushed them down. With a soft rebound and a creak, the tree lay its soul out on the gravel and the courtyard reverberated with cheers.

'That was bloody close to the house!' Isabelle told Kit.

'It was bloody closer to my car!'

'No you don't.' Isabelle grabbed hold of Indigo as she tried to go to the tree. Even Deryn was climbing down from the bench.

'Well done,' Rob called out of the doorway. 'Impressive.'

'Dinner is served,' Kate added.

'Oh, give us our moment of glory,' Kit told her. He jumped up onto the wobbly trunk of the poor magnolia and bounced on it. 'I need a victory pose!'

'Kit, get down,' Isabelle told him as Indigo squirmed out of her arms. But she was too slow and ended up holding a velvet teddy bear. 'I give up. Bring her with you. Kate, what can I do to help?'

She glanced backwards as she went through the door. Indigo was in Kit's arms bouncing on the thick base of the trunk where it had a soily skirt of roots. Perhaps it was moving to a different viewpoint, or the fact that the tree was now upended and vanquished on the disturbed gravel. The courtyard looked stark, empty of memories and familiarity. The wall and gates a hard outline to the empty space. The men dirty and smug as they stood over the dead tree. She shivered and went indoors.

'I told you it would suddenly go chilly,' Kate said, following her and seeing the shiver.

'It wasn't that.' Isabelle glanced her way as they walked through to the kitchen. 'I felt someone walk over my bones.'

'You need to stop reading those diaries, you're getting sentimental on us. All I see is a bloody great mess he's made that we're going to have to clean up again.'

'Kit will always clean his own mess up,' Isabelle defended him.

'Marvellous, delighted to hear it.' Kate took over in the kitchen. 'Isabelle, take that stack of plates out. Rob, dish that pasta into those warmed pots. We'll have to do a self-serve, or it will be cold by the time they sit down.'

With sneaky glances out of the windows and doors she passed, Isabelle did as she was told and moved the food out to the patio. Full of the images in the courtyard, she exited the lower floor stairwell to the top of the patio and found her scattered thoughts pulled up sharp. Kate had taken the time to set it up for a special occasion, candles were lit, tables pulled together and set with soft vintage cloths, cutlery, glasses, flowers.

'Wow,' Isabelle said. 'This reminds me of your house-warming.'

Kate turned from putting a dish down to look at her with a pained twist to her lips, making Isabelle wish she had kept the thoughts to herself. That had been a night best left in the past.

'That feels a long time ago,' Kate returned her attention to the table.

'It has rather slipped by,' Isabelle agreed.

They looked up to hear the crowd coming through the house. Emerging at the top of the steps, Kit framed in the doorway with Indigo on his shoulders clutching a snapped branch in her hand. Isabelle turned away first and saw Kate watching Kit lead the descent, turning to see Isabelle watching her and grimaced.

'How about you get them sat down, I'll go help Rob with the last of it.'

Time slipped again that evening and she was aware of memories merging with the noise and fun. How different it felt to that evening when they had first sat on the patio, freshly unearthed from its years of shrubbery by Kate. Asha thick with child, Rob heavy with the grief of divorce and herself swaying in shock at the vast responsibility Elsa had thrust on her shoulders, while Moth had vanished from their lives. Now she felt resonant with the stone of the patio, the rise of the house, the last kiss of the summer sun on the lawns, the light reluctant to leave Kate's beautiful garden. Her eyes were constantly drawn to the weir and a restless wish to leave the group, go down to the river and pull her shoes off. Remember Moth as she felt the chill of the water run across her feet. She thought he would have enjoyed the challenge of the afternoon, the company of the men. Moth would have drifted away to the river as the quiet night fell across them all.

Martin was the first to leave, kicking off the recognition of tiredness in others. Kate's women taking the emptying bottles and blankets up to bed with them, giggling as they slipped up the stone steps. James and Steve offering steadying hands and guiding them into the house and up the twisting stairs to the top floor of the house and their bedrooms.

'They're going to have hangovers tomorrow,' Kate complained as she watched them go. She had settled, after the tables had been cleared, into a lounging chair away from the tables, her toes tucked beneath her folded legs, her favourite blue cashmere wrap around her shoulders to chase away the evening chill. Isabelle remembered borrowing it from her when she went to Italy but had thought it lost in the commotion of finding Moth. She had been shocked to see it on her and wondered if perhaps it had been purchased as a replacement, but the shade was so exact, that exquisite crystalline blue of a deep lake on a summer day. She would remember to ask Kate about it tomorrow. 'So much for focusing on their big task. You've sabotaged my schedule.'

Kit glanced at her over Deryn and Indigo's heads. They were cuddled up in an arm apiece, their new teddies clutched beneath their star-struck eyes, thumbs in mouths as they tried to stay awake. 'You're welcome.'

'And they're going to be impossible tomorrow too.' Asha nodded at the girls. 'You can face the consequences in the morning.'

'I won't be here,' Kit told them. 'I've got to head back tonight.'

'It's gone ten, Kit.' Asha told him. 'Surely you'll stop the night?'

'You've been drinking,' Kate reminded him.

'Alcohol-free,' Kit held up his beer glass at her and then asked Isabelle, 'So, how's the new love life?'

They all turned to look at her. She blinked at the outright question and prayed Steve wouldn't come back.

'Eh, yeah, weird, good, I think.'

'What do you think of him?' Asha asked Kit. 'I think he's perfect.'

'I second that,' Kate added. 'He is rather adorable, don't you think, Kit?'

'Well, when Isabelle dumps him at least he can get consolation from one of you two,' Kit retorted.

'She can't keep dumping good men,' Asha complained. 'It's not fair.'

'I'll say.' Kate took a swig of her wine and looked out over the garden. 'It does rather smack of arrogance.'

'What?' Isabelle asked, her contentment scattered like blossom in a sudden wind across the space between them. 'Why am I getting all the grief here?'

'Because he's adorable and you're ungrateful?' Kate mused.

'Because you've had every man here bar Rob?' Asha added. 'I mean you do realise that, right?'

Everyone looked at Asha in various stages of surprise and consternation. Isabelle dipped her eyes in distress.

'I might take that personally,' Rob dropped into the abyss with a quirk of his eyebrows at her. Isabelle didn't dare look at Kate. Didn't dare respond to Asha.

'How do they all compare?' Asha asked. 'Which is the one who, you know...' Asha winked and wriggled her hips at her, looking over at Indigo.

'Someone give this girl another glass of wine,' Kit said approvingly, pulling the girls into tighter cuddles, where they snuffled like woodland animals and burrowed into him, averse to the remotest suggestion of removal. 'Honestly, I was born to be an honorary uncle, these cuddles are beyond compare.'

'You buy them with the most extortionate gifts,' Kate told him, pushing them on from Asha's drunken indelicacy.

'In my experience, the most expensive gifts make no difference to a woman's affections,' Kit countered, staring at her as she pulled the blue wrap tighter to her throat and drank her wine. Isabelle, more sober than the rest, and trying to look anywhere other than at Asha, saw her pointed refusal to look at Kit.

'What about a man's?' Asha asked.

'A man knows exactly how to appreciate a gift,' Kit looked away from Kate to Asha. 'We receive them so infrequently. You should try buying yours one. So, Isabelle, how do we all compare?'

'Leave her alone,' Kate told him. 'Stop being provoking because you're jealous. Anyway, she's not going to dump him, are you?'

'I've barely started dating him,' Isabelle complained.

'I'm not jealous,' Kit told Kate. 'I've got a relationship. And we'll see if he's still here for Christmas. What's the sex like?'

'Yes, what is the sex like?' Asha needled her.

'We're taking it slowly.'

'That sounds tediously reserved,' Kit told her.

'Not everyone is as swift in their pace as you,' Isabelle retorted.

'You never minded my pace before.'

'You're the sort of man who sets his own pace, Kit,' Isabelle complained. 'And I'm not complaining.'

'Sounds like it to me,' Kate said. 'What's this about Christmas?'

'I just want to take this at my pace,' Isabelle explained. 'I'm not as, as…'

'Appreciative?' Kit offered.

'Horny?' Asha suggested.

'Confident?' Kate added.

'Needy?' Rob ended and they all looked at him in surprise. 'Not all of us need a full-on relationship. In fact, speaking personally, I rather agree with Isabelle. It's always easier to get into something than it is to get out of it. A lot bloody cheaper too.'

'That's bitterness speaking, old chap,' Kit told him. 'Nasty bust-up like yours would leave a wound an asteroid crater wide.'

'I'll say,' Asha agreed.

'… as certain it's what I want. Thank you, Rob.' Isabelle smiled across at him. 'That's exactly it. I'm happy, and I don't want to upset that with a new relationship. I like Steve, but I want to take my time.'

'Hmmm.' Kit looked at her, his chin resting on Deryn's head. 'Honestly, if he were floating your boat, I don't think we'd be hearing this. You'd be dragging him upstairs rather than kicking your heels down here waiting for him to leave.'

'Floating your boat?' Asha asked. 'What does that mean?'

'Reaching the sweet spot,' Kate told her. 'Let's get back to Christmas.'

'Raising the love juices,' Kit explained. 'Is he hands on or has he got that same hideous English priggishness as James?'

'Excuse me,' Asha complained. 'How do you know what James is like?'

'I have a keen imagination.'

'I'm really not sure it's tactful to interrogate a man's previous girlfriend in front of his wife,' Rob mooted in the air generally.

'I'll say,' Kate agreed. 'Perhaps those girls should be put to bed.'

'I dare you to take them from me,' Kit said. 'Does he linger in the foreplay or move straight to the main event, Isabelle?'

'Right, I'm off to bed.' Rob rose from the chair and went to pick Indigo up.

'You're staying the night?' Kit asked in surprise.

'I'm on childcare duty Friday mornings,' he told Kit. 'I'll be the one dealing with their tiredness, thank you very much.'

'Gosh, they've got you right where they need you, haven't they, the sly pusses.' He gave Indigo up with a scowl and pulled Deryn into a closer cuddle. Indigo put her head on Rob's shoulder and promptly closed her eyes.

'I prefer to think I'm right where I want to be,' Rob countered and walked toward the stone steps.

'I better find James and head home,' Asha sighed and struggled out of her chair. 'Damn this extra weight. Do you think if I had another child, I'd lose the baby weight from the first?'

'If you do, that's a recipe you can sell,' Kit said.

'Right, come on, don't you dare,' she warned Deryn's attempt at a moan. 'I'll see you all in the morning for hangover support before work.'

Isabelle decided in that moment to sleep late, watching as Asha humped Deryn higher on her hip and wobbled up the stairs. James and Steve appeared above her, framed by the doorway. Isabelle could see Steve looking in her direction, trying to entice her away, before turning to shake James' hand in farewell.

'He has spent all afternoon digging your garden up,' Kit whispered at her. 'Least you could do is offer him a blowjob.'

'Do you mind?' she asked, pulling herself up from the chair. 'I'll go and say goodbye.'

'Doesn't he stop the night?' Kit asked. 'Or has he not offered childcare duties in return for the privilege of a bed at Riverdell?'

Isabelle went over and kissed him goodnight, saying close to his head, 'I don't need your advice on my love life. Stick with the house.'

Climbing the steps to the top patio she heard Kit say to Kate, 'What about you, do you need my advice on your love life?'

'No, I bloody don't. Tell me about Christmas.'

Isabelle grimaced. She would definitely lie in tomorrow. Asha on a hangover and Kate having found out about Christmas. Both to be avoided. She looked up at Steve waiting for her and steeled her heart to his easy grin. She needed her own bed tonight and no more guests for the morning. How could such a huge house feel so full?

'No, don't do it that way.'

'Jesus Christ, you are doing my head in.'

'Look, if you're going to help, at least help. Otherwise sit down and let me do it.'

'Is this what it's like working for you?' Jay stood back and put the strand of fairy lights in Kit's hand. 'How do your staff put up with you?'

'Because I look after them,' Kit took the lights and looked at the tree reaching toward the ceiling of the basement kitchen. 'High standards build higher standards.'

'They're fairy lights, Kit.'

'Do you know how much I charge to personally dress a Christmas tree?' Kit looked at Jay with amusement.

'I don't want to.' Jay went and sat down on the sofa again. 'I work hard at thinking good of you, I don't want to discover you're a complete rip-off merchant.'

'You can't throw them at the branches.' Kit felt the branches of the concolor fir. 'You need to see the shape you're reaching for, and you do not *wrap* the lights.'

'You told me to do the tree!' Jay complained. 'I didn't realise I was getting judged on the result.'

Kit circled the tree. He'd left it late and his supplier had laughed at him when he requested a Canaan fir. Isabelle had a lot to answer for in messing up his plans. Still, it was beautiful, and not the tree he could ever risk recommending for a client. Because when you were paying enough for your tree to purchase a car, you wanted it to look beyond picture perfect. You wanted it to be Insta Divine. Not this contrary, dishevelled array of blue-tinged green that was going to make his lights lollop.

'We're always judged on the end results,' Kit told Jay. He picked up the first set of lights and climbed the ladders to reach for the top branches.

'You don't start at the top.' Jay complained.

'Do not tell *me* how to dress the tree,' Kit told him.

Kit felt the length and weight of the uppermost branches.

Spiralled the first lights along their lengths out to the tip and began to carefully weave in a triangular section downwards. He got two-thirds of the way before the lights ran out. He tucked the wire toward the trunk and reached for the next box, switching them on and unwinding the end. Playing with the weave, the depth inwards, the wrapping of each third branch. It was soothing, watching the depth of the tree come to life, feeling the bounce of each branch. It shouldn't really be called "dressing" for by the time he'd finished a tree Kit always felt more intimate with it, not less.

'Do you always use that many lights?' Jay asked in disbelief.

Kit stepped back from his fourth set and looked at the tree with a critical eye. It was taking shape. 'Uh-huh, 150 lights per foot.' He would keep adding the segments downwards before weaving the lower third of the tree in straddled rhombus shapes. It had taken him weeks of practise to discover the perfect method by which a living imperfect tree must end up looking impeccable. The basement living room, the sitting and dining rooms filled with every variation of fir tree he could find in September, thousands of lights strewn across the house in a fire hazard that had Lou tripping out with panic.

'Wow, and here's us wondering why there's an environmental crisis,' Jay quipped.

Kit picked up the next set of lights and remounted the ladders. His basement living room looked exciting from up the top. The glowing bulbs strung along the walls, tucked behind foliage swags, nestled in wreaths. Draping along the three-tiered sprawl of the table centrepiece. It was homely, fresh, fragrant and excessive. He'd spent hours on it, while Jay sat and watched him, turning the pages of yet another diary.

Though he wanted to adore it, Kit couldn't help comparing it all to the plans he'd had for Riverdell.

'Every Grinch at Christmas raises that,' Kit told Jay. 'Get over your own misery and engage.'

'Engage?' Jay asked. 'In what? My sisters haven't invited me and where's your family this Christmas, huh? What are we supposed to be engaging in?'

'Christmas itself. Why should we only do stuff if we have people to share it with?'

'So, you'd be doing this all for yourself if Adele and I weren't here?'

'Of course,' Kit lied to the tree, thinking of all the years he'd packed his car with booze and food and trawled from one house to the next so he could enjoy Christmas without having to do it himself. 'Why would I not?'

'Oh, please,' Jay muttered to the ceiling.

Kit began threading lights again, the plastic bulbs pinging against each other as he moved them through the branches, the leaves of Jay's diary turning. It was unnaturally quiet.

'Siri,' Kit called out, 'play...'

'Siri, don't you bloody dare,' Jay said louder.

'I'm sorry I didn't hear that,' Siri said.

'Good, shut the hell up,' Jay told the device.

'You can't even listen to music now?' Kit came down the ladders and nudged them a foot clockwise. 'She wrecked your life that much? Not just dancing but music too?'

'Did you know that your mother gave away her best friend and lover in marriage?' Jay ignored him and countered. 'Probably on the same night you were conceived?'

'Stop right there.'

'Oh, I'm sorry, are there some things you don't want to talk about?' Jay asked.

They both returned to silence and concentration.

'Kit?'

'Uh-huh?'

'You ever worry about being on your own?'

'Nope.'

'Not even a little bit?'

'I think the real question is, do you?' Kit left the line of lights trailing out from the tree and went to sit down. He poured another glass of red wine and kicked back in the sofa. Wednesday night. Adele would be back tomorrow, for two days and the end of a debate that had not been neatly wrapped up to put under the tree. Where they, as in he and Adele, not including Jay, should be spending Christmas.

'Your mother never married, did she?' Jay didn't look at him. 'Gave away the first love of her life. Did she ever find another?'

'She was never short for company.' Kit took a slug of wine. 'And we had each other, and Granny. She never seemed miserable.'

'Do you ever wonder if she was... maybe, lonely?'

Kit could see the length and shape of that word as clear as the illuminated tree. There had been times. Brief interludes in his life when he had seen the depth of loneliness. It had felt quiet, as the house felt quiet. Too quiet. Noticeably quiet. After his mother had left, he'd drowned the loneliness in a bout of annoyance so gargantuan as to get himself expelled from school. And two years ago, when he and Kate had parted, right before he ended up in Japan... well, he'd drowned that out too.

'I think,' he nodded over the top of his glass at the diary, 'if you're reading between the lines looking for lonely, you ought to ask why you're looking for it.'

Jay shut the book and put it aside on the flecked grey tweed surface of the sofa. Kit was getting bored with it, as he did with all things that offended him with their dullness in winter. It was time for a recover.

'How old was she?' he asked. 'Your mother? When she died?'

'Forty.'

'You think maybe she didn't grow old enough to feel it?'

'To feel what?' Kit asked. Perhaps he might consider one of the bright linens that Colefax had brought out this last year. Perhaps a turquoise or cobalt, to really impact the space. Adele would love it. He looked at Jay to see him frowning at him, wanting more reaction. Kit refused to help him out. If Jay needed to explore the grim end of his thoughts, he would have to drag it out there himself.

'I mean, I'm hitting forty-two next year, what about you?' Jay asked.

'I could tell you but then I'd have to kill you,' Kit retorted. 'What's your point here?'

'I didn't think I'd end up on my own, did you?' Jay looked down at the journal. 'I'm not sure I've got the sort of courage your mother had.'

'I'm not alone and you're between partners.'

'But what if I never meet anyone else, like your mother didn't?' Jay stroked a hand across the cover of the diary by his side. 'What if she was the one, Kit, and that's me done? And I know you've got Adele, but well, have you ever felt this way?' Jay held up the diary.

Kit decided he would go back to therapy in the new year. At least the therapist had no problems of his own he had to pussyfoot around.

'In a way, perhaps I did, about my mother,' he told Jay. 'I

remember being crushed when she left, feeling it was my fault.'

'You can't compare your relationship with your mother to an adult one with a partner,' Jay complained.

'Can't I?' Kit asked. 'Why not? Because it's too cliched or you don't want to think it might be true?'

'No, because you didn't fuck her!' Jay complained. 'I'm talking about full relationships here, Kit. The ones that didn't work out like you hoped. Didn't you ever feel crushed, about anyone?'

'Yes, I've felt it. But I'm capable of remembering when I first felt it, and that was with my mother leaving. You really think this breakdown over Lydia dumping you has nothing to do with your father dismissing you?'

'I did not have sex with my bloody father!'

'And you think sex and love are different?' Kit asked. 'Not connected at all?'

'Yes!'

'Why?'

'Because every woman I've ever dated tells me they are,' Jay defended.

'What?'

Jay crossed his arms over his chest. It was good to see that the workouts with Fred had successfully reduced the stomach bulge that had protruded only a week ago.

'Your abs are coming back,' Kit told Jay, pointing at his gut with his wine glass. 'You'll be back on the dancefloor in no time.'

'Screw you.'

'No thanks, I'm taken. So love is different to sex?'

'Yes.'

'All of the women said that? Or just Lydia?'

'I don't remember a lot about the women before Lydia, but that's the basic feedback, yes.'

'What feedback?' Kit leant forward to pull the boxes of tissue wrapped baubles toward him. He had a glut of choices with the enormous selection he had put aside for Isabelle. It was going to be a struggle not to drown the tree. He should have bought some more trees. Holding up a translucent glass bauble with etched trees on it, he turned it to catch the light. He glanced at Jay through the bauble. 'Sorry, you were talking about feedback.'

'Never mind.'

'Don't be petulant.' Kit put the bauble down and focused again. 'You do realise that whatever feedback you get is only fifty percent about you, tops. It's like unwrapping a Fortnum's hamper. By the time you get past the name, and the ribbons, and the packaging, and the protective wrap, there's negligible actual meat inside.'

'I guess that's a handy way of avoiding your own responsibility,' Jay told him. 'You should surely finish those lights and start putting your balls up?'

'They're baubles, I am not putting my bollocks on the tree,' Kit told him. 'What frigging feedback did Lydia give you? Don't make me throw glass baubles at you until you tell me. They cost a sodding fortune to use to break your thick skull.'

Jay stared at him in irritation.

Kit lifted a glass bauble and bounced it thoughtfully in his hand. It would be a shame to break it, it was one of a perfect dozen. Jay quirked an eyebrow at him. Kit threw the bauble high toward the ceiling and caught it with a fleshy thunk in his hand.

'Oh, enough.' Jay said. 'She told me I couldn't separate

between love and sex. That she wanted sex to be sex. She said I made it feel like she was shagging her brother sometimes.'

'Wow,' Kit held the bauble lightly in his hand and tried to take the weight of Jay's words. 'That was harsh.'

'Yeah, then she dumped me for a black guy and said she needed her man to make her feel like a woman, to be more...'

'... more?'

'... manly in the bedroom. Less loving.'

'Ouch.'

'Yes, thank you. Are you happy now?'

'How did it feel to you?' Kit asked him, kicking back in the sofa and stretching his legs back onto the table. 'The sex?'

'It felt like making love to the woman I adored.' Jay picked the diary up and put it across his lap. 'I never thought about it as sex.'

'How do you mean. Didn't you think about sex with Lydia?'

Jay stayed silent. Kit, watching him try to disappear back into the diaries, tried another tack.

'My mother told me, growing up, that love and sex are interconnected. That sometimes, sexual desire arises out of love, and other times love arises out of sexual desire. For most of us they are interconnected. Not always, she was wary of generalisations, but mostly they are interconnected.'

'You had this conversation with your mother?' Jay asked in disbelief.

'Every conversation I had about intimacy started with my mother.'

'That would explain a lot.'

'We're talking about you, not me.' Kit pulled another box of baubles toward him. 'Were you looking too hard for love?

Did you really feel sexual attraction to Lydia in the first place? Is that what you need to address?'

'I need to address getting the hell out of your Christmas meltdown,' Jay told him. 'You're so bored you'll end up twisting me into a tangled mess.'

'Avoidance.'

'Look who's talking,' Jay tossed back.

'Double avoidance.'

'Why is it wrong that I want to be in love?' Jay asked in exasperation. 'That I think love is more important than sex, not less?'

'So, you'd have a relationship without sex?' Kit asked him. 'That would be enough for you?'

Jay growled and threw his head back against the sofa. 'It's not that I don't like sex...'

'I never said that, are you saying that?'

'... what? No, I didn't say that!'

'So, you do like sex?' Kit insisted.

'Of course I like sex, it's just...'

'... just?'

Silence stretched out between them, a crystal thread attached to a glass bauble, Jay's attention held one end and Kit trying not to pull too hard and snap the line.

'I don't enjoy it as much as I should,' Jay admitted.

'Should?' Kit asked, his voice suspicious. 'Should according to Lydia, or according to yourself?'

Jay put the diary down, stood up and walked to the wide windows.

'I don't know,' Jay told the indifferent glass. 'At first, when I found out she was cheating on me, I thought it was because I didn't want it enough.'

Kit struggled to hear him speaking to the window, stood

up and filled his glass, moving to stand at the far end of the
window, keeping a wary distance. The lights of Bristol were
glittering through the bare branches of the trees at the end of
the garden.

'I thought it was my fault. She'd always said it was wrong
she had to initiate sex, that I never made her feel wanted. But
I've always hated how it's supposed to be men who made the
moves. Like, how can you be sure you aren't pushing yourself
on a woman?'

'So, she always initiated sex?'

Jay nodded.

'But you enjoyed it?'

'Mostly.'

Kit could have bit his own tongue to ask more. Trying to
keep space for Jay was as slippery as trying to provoke Moth
to talk about himself, and he'd failed spectacularly there.
Moth had taught him to try harder.

'What bits didn't you like?' he asked.

Jay stayed as silent as a bird at the window, looking down
the long garden toward the distant view. Kit tried not to move.
Itching to dig deeper.

'It always felt a bit...'

Kit could feel his back muscle threatening to spasm with
the frustration.

'... brutal.' Jay put his head against the cool glass. 'All that
pumping in and out, you know. It felt more like aggression
than loving someone.'

'It doesn't have to be aggressive.' Kit thought about the
number of times he'd walked away from a session feeling like
he'd left the gym and frowned. 'Maybe you had the wrong
partner. Maybe what Lydia needed to feel turned on wasn't
the same as you.'

'That's the thing,' Jay turned his head to look at him, his skin still against the glass. 'That's what I tried to tell myself after she left. That whole, "it's about her not you" crap. But the longer she was gone, the more I realised I didn't miss it. The sex.' Jay turned away and looked down the garden again, his voice reducing further. 'I missed our life together. I missed waking up together, making breakfast, going shopping. But I didn't miss dancing with her, I didn't miss the sex. It had become this performance I had to do.'

'Ten months on, you haven't missed it at all?' Kit asked. 'You haven't wanted a shag, knocked one off, brought a sleeve?'

'You always have to go a step too far, don't you?'

'I'm trying to understand, that's all. Because if you've gone ten months and never thought about sex, maybe it's clinical depression, maybe your hormones are out of sync.'

'That's what I'm trying to tell you, I don't feel depressed about not having sex.'

'Finding you curled up in isolation in your spare bedroom makes it hard for me to believe that.'

'It wasn't Lydia going that put me in that place.' Jay pulled back from the window and put his hands in his pockets. 'I mean, yeah, it hurt. Especially how she did it. But it didn't break me. There was almost some relief, on not having to perform any more. I was dealing with it, right until... Uggs died.'

Kit wouldn't have believed him if it wasn't the first time he'd heard Jay say the dog's name and his voice thickened with the difficulty of saying it.

'You got this depressed because the house was empty?'

'That's the whole point, Kit. What if it *is* me, and I just don't want sex? I'm going to end up alone or with a load of bloody chihuahuas, because what woman is going to want me when I don't want her? Can you imagine having a relationship without sex?'

Kit went to speak and tried to visualise it at the same time, and realised he had his mouth gaping open. He couldn't imagine it, not feeling desire. Nothing at all. An emptiness inside deep enough to drown in. Sex was how he loved. Any relationship without it was little more than a friendship. Even his relationship with Isabelle had changed, lessened, into more of a sibling situation. And as for Kate. He recalled the visit in late summer, half-naked and uprooting the dead tree in the courtyard, desperate for Kate to stay and watch him. Everyone going to bed and leaving them alone on the terrace. He didn't know how to have a relationship with Kate that didn't include sex. He'd left as he always did, feeling waspish and dissatisfied.

'Exactly.' Jay put his head against the window. 'I'm a failure.'

'Not wanting what someone else wants does not make you a failure,' Kit protested. 'And you can't know yet, not for sure. Maybe this is you, but maybe it isn't. You've had a shit year, mate, don't be surprised your libido is missing in action.'

Jay replied to the far distance outside the window. 'Lydia said I needed therapy, to understand my sexuality.'

Finally, Kit understood Jay's touchiness around his own flexible sexuality. Doubt in yourself needed certainty in others.

'For a start, sod Lydia's opinion. Maybe she didn't love you mate, and her banging on about the sex not being enough was her way of denying that was all she wanted.' Kit moved back to the table and put his glass down. 'And sod all her labels too, she'd rather label you than herself. All the years people have been trying to pin labels on me, none of them ever fitted. Drives me nuts. I mean, if it helps, great, choose one for yourself, but stop trying to stick them on others.' He picked up a box of baubles, white china painted with ice blue and lilac polka dots. 'I prefer to see life as a moving scale we're permanently sliding along. We're not static, we're constantly responding to our circumstances. You don't know who you'll be with someone else.'

'I don't want to be sliding along a scale, I want to know who I am. What I am. I want to be clear with someone else about it.'

'You need to stop analysing it. Shag someone else. Or don't. Go dancing again. Join a club, meet new people. You won't find the answer sitting in a darkened room. Come on, you need to come hang some baubles.'

'You'll tell me off for doing it wrong.'

Kit looked at Jay and realised why he had been so touchy about the lights. Felt a glimmer of guilt before righteously offloading it onto Lydia.

'No, I won't. It's virtually impossible to hang baubles incorrectly. You choose the ones you're going to use and space them out. Lights, yes, harder. Not baubles.'

Jay walked back toward the table in resignation.

'I'm glad it's you reading those diaries.' Kit handed him a box. 'I think you'll get more out of it than me. I was lucky enough to have her growing up.'

Jay followed him to the tree and plucked out a bauble with no enthusiasm, began to hang it on the end of the branch.

'No, you need to put it further in than that...' Kit began to tell him.

Jay looked at him, the bauble hanging in the air, swinging from his hand. Kit struggled to keep his lips from quirking.

'... you know what, you're doing great. I'm going to let you get on with it.'

Kit took a new string of lights and got down on his knees to begin dressing the final part of the tree. He could see Jay hanging baubles in all the wrong places. He would have to come and adjust it later, after Jay had gone to bed. Santa would never forgive him, not to mention the team would take all shades of piss out of it. The ice blue and lilac polka dots swayed against the blue tinge of the tree as Jay hung them up. Twirling into violet as they swung. They were soothing and fresh. Perhaps he would recover the sofas in a deep shade of violet.

11

My father has died. Of a heart attack on New Year's Eve.

I read of it in The Times. He was at a party two streets away from the one I attended. Not the best way to ring in the new year. All this time I spend trawling through the papers for work and I find my life unwritten in the obits.

Sir Alfred Hoare, Viscount Templewode. Dies childless and his baronetcy dies with him.

Stunning. Thanks, dear Father, your parting gift that you'd rather lose the peerage than admit you had me. Loyal enough to your wife to reject your bastard, not devout enough to be faithful to her.

There's a full write-up about you, all about your notable efforts as Ambassador to Spain during the war, working to keep Franco from joining the Axis powers, how they gave you the peerage for it. It doesn't mention the child you came home with in December that year and passed quietly on to your mother. That wouldn't do at all, would it? I shall keep it for Kit, it will amuse him no end to one day know his grandfather was a Lord and a Liar. Childless. Damn you too.

You are to be buried in Norfolk and leave your grieving wife behind. Daughter of an Earl no less, how thick the blood runs. Granny says she was a cold-hearted bitch with a withered cunt. I guess Granny might not have been the easiest mother-in-law, not least when she told her own husband to go suck. Lady Templewode was a youngest daughter, whereas Granny was the eldest daughter of her own Earlish father. Here's a whole host of ugly old history creeping out of the seams. Granny never mentions her untitled husband, who turned out to be as much a disappointment to her as he was to her own father. She says little more about her own son, except that she will not attend the funeral of a man who denied the birth of his own child. I love her for that.

I never realised how much I loved her, until I sit here reading this, trying to feel any connection to a dead peer. I wonder if my mother is still alive, reading this? Or ever wondered what happened to the child she sent away, ill consequence of a war romance. Granny says she doesn't know who she was, father only ever told her it was a mutual mistake of married parties. It. I. I was a mutual mistake of married parties. All my life I haven't given a damn. Until now.

It hurts. This denial. Enough to let a peerage die out. I wonder if Kit will ever feel this sense of inadequacy. Of not being good enough to acknowledge.

I bloody hope not. I hope he knows how much I adore him, how much he means to me. How little I needed or wanted anyone else in having him and Granny. They have been my family. My whole family, and you. I have needed no one else.

Well, father least dear, rest in eternal unpeace. I'll come

dance on your cold grave one day. Or perhaps make love on it. To remind you I live. You cold-hearted bastard.

While he was gasping his last, having the life squeezed out by an iron fist round his chest I was happier than I have known in a long time. I hope my orgasm timed with his deathly climax.

I have a new lover. His name is Ben, and he trusts me.

Yes, I finally found someone who gave me the same answer as you.

He trusts me absolutely. There are no barriers between us. We explore our bodies with the same reverence you and I once did. We met late last year at a party in London, and he is asleep here with me now. I should have been in Bristol for Christmas but confess I couldn't bear to leave him. Kit spent the holiday between Granny and Riverdell. I lied to him, saying it was work. Even though he knows I have never allowed work to disturb our holidays before. Perhaps he understood, for he didn't seem bothered, and if there is one thing for certain in life, it is that the displeasure of my son will be made abundantly clear.

I am glad for his tolerance anyway. While my son feasted at Riverdell and my father gasped his last down the road, I made extraordinary, sweet love to my new beau.

He is the first man I have ever loved.

Ten years younger than me, with coltish limbs, long, curly hair and collarbones like china cradles. He is barely a man, is twenty-five a man? Uncertain what manliness means to him, in love with women and yet, yet, oh, it is so intense... he takes me within him, as you once did, as other women have since. Gasping at the pleasure it causes him. Sweet Aphrodite, you have sent me the perfect love. I cannot catch the glory of this. There is agony in the anticipation. How he looks at me, a moment of apprehension, passing behind his fluttering eyelids as he surrenders to my claiming of him. It is as I always thought, when he gives himself up to me, there is a grace, an elegance, a glory, which captures me as I love him. This is not healthy. Or is it? Is this the healthiest I have ever been? Finally, what I am meant to be, a top, tupping the men beneath me.

When we are together, I can think of nothing but my joy. Now, afterwards, when he sleeps, the thoughts tumble over me. An ocean of doubt and confusion. I wonder if this is a fad, a latest, newest addiction, and this thrill, this glory of happiness will ebb, and in months my current conviction to have the surgery will disappear. As did my belief that I must make the full transition.

I remember the night Kit came to me in my bedroom, it was my birthday, and I could barely write to you. I asked him to cut my hair and he refused. He dressed me to go out that night, picking the clothes. Trousers, jacket, a green silk blouse that sits low and gaping. He thought it a great dressing up game and played with me. Trying on a dress, my heels, my jewellery. There is such faith in his good opinion of the world. Kit believes labels are for idiots and we are all on a journey to understand our unique place in life. I asked him if he thought he might be gay, and he said he can't decide yet. He's not convinced he ever will make a choice, but he's already tired of people thinking they must. For one moment I wondered if I have damaged him, messed up his own certainty in life. I asked him, had I confused him? No, he told me he had no confusion at all. Then, what he said, I shall never forget it.

He thinks we should desire a person, not a gender, or an

age, or a colour, or a shape. We shouldn't put labels on what we're capable of loving.

These children of ours are fearless, he filled me with pride and hope and tears. Kit refused to cut my hair, he thinks I'm rushing it, trying to convince myself. Since then, I haven't felt the need to label my body or my wardrobe, masculine, feminine. And I don't hate my body. The doctors are all looking for hate as proof of love for the other. If I hate my body, it is a step closer to my conviction for surgery and their approval. But I don't. I love this body. I remember your hands first stirring it and I could not give up this body that holds my memory of you. In Kit's smile I find the right level of identity. In his frown I know I have pushed too hard, striving to be someone else. He is my mirror and my rule. I have lowered the dose of medication and feel much happier. I wear what I please and the world thinks I am the height of fashion. And, if I have the final surgery, I shall still refuse to comply to a label.

The night I met Ben I wore the dress that I am wearing in my portrait back home. A full-length purple velvet dress, open to the thigh and slashed down to the ribs. I removed the diamante brooch that used to adorn it, dressed it instead with a cravat and accompanied with the cane and hat. The other women in their bell bottoms and bum length skirts were laughing at me, I know.

I don't care. I don't care anymore.

Clothes aren't a cultural statement of where I fit, they express how I feel. I must wear such carefully curated suitability for work. The old bastards of parliament want a woman to look pretty when they're being petitioned. Maggie knows she can't wear trousers, even when she's angling to carry the balls of Britain. She'll get in, I predict. The men in

Downing Street think they can use her as a puppet, and she plays the game with all her demure bloody skirts and 50s hair.

But I dress to turn myself on, not others. The feel of that dress caressing my thighs makes me feel wanton and alive. How the hell can anyone possibly want wool against their skin? But, Hera, I'm losing track. Kit, my hair, Ben. He knew I was naked under the dress, went down on me in the garden, behind a wisteria. The scent of it was intoxicating as I came. And, afterward, do you know what he wanted? He wanted me to use the cane on him. He said the cane turned him on. But I told him I had a better idea. And then I asked him. Our question. And I shiver now remembering the response.

Am I imagining this bliss? Or superimposing our memory on it? The doubts creep in with the streetlights while I strain to hear his breathing. Light as snow fall. I can imagine the world being wiped clean outside the window when he sleeps. It will be an empty sheet I can rewrite.

Is it wrong? This thrill in taking a man. Is it the same deep joy I have in being with women or is there an air of taint or revenge in it? Am I loving this man or taking delight in the domination?

In a gay relationship, male bottoms are seen as effeminate. They are allocated the same role as women in straight relationships. Submissive, lesser, under. Is that what my desire is about? Do I seek to masculinise myself to prove my worth? I wonder, if I had been a boy, would my father have denied my existence? Was it my bastardry or my gender? Does all of life narrow down to the relationship we are avenging with our parents? Elsa has no idea how blessed she is. The first daughter to inherit in a line of lesser sons of lesser sons. How I wish she'd had only daughters and bred a grand matriarchy. That would have had old Clive turning in his bloodied, trophied grave.

My pen is not swift enough for my thoughts. Where on earth did all this start? Think, think...

What is right or wrong in my desire? Where do I go from this point?

I can crystallise it in only one way, a mantra I can hold onto. When all the labels confuse me, the decisions, the options, the drugs, the surgery, the destination. I know only this, I desire to penetrate. To penetrate with my own body, not a strapped-on fake. I desire it when I wake. At night when I cannot sleep. In the dreary hours of life and work. When I close my eyes with heat, it is this desire that rises in my mind. The thought was with me always, from long before I fully became this woman the world decided I am. It was with me in the whispering sheets of our dormitory when Elsa and Kate went home for the weekends. It was with me when I knew I had to part with you and couldn't let Ted have you first. It crushed me when I gave you away. It has always been part of me, buried beneath the veneer of what my body should want: to be submissive, to be penetrated, to be receptive. And when Ben lies before me, fondling my breasts and asking me to straddle him, it unleashes a voluptuousness I cannot deny. I orgasm as I take him. He does not need to do anything to me, I am more aroused than I have ever known. A pleasure that begins in the mind and ends in the body.

I have realised there is a part-way house, this unnamed place that feels my best self. I shall wait the year to be sure, before I go for the surgery, but whether I can convince the doctors that this part-way house is real, I don't yet know. I must at least have my own conviction buried deep before I begin the persuasion.

Though I can see a way of finally belonging to myself, I do not know where I can ever belong afterward. For all the liberal optimism of progression, I know without any self-fooling doubt, there will be no place for a half-gendered, ill-begotten bastard of a dead baron in this life I now live.

In the halls of Westminster? Or the drawing room at Riverdell? And you, even you, would you want me?

12

'Mr Moth, we have finished the bike for you. Haven't we been swift?'

Moth tried not to blink.

You're staring, blink.

It had been in the shop for two months.

To be fair, that is swift for Urfa.

He looked at the bike as it was wheeled out of the dimly lit depths of the workshop. Leaning into the proud hand of the mechanic in the patch of light spilling through the tatty metal doors.

Perhaps he had been expecting too much. Maybe a bike that was now over twenty years old and had been built to spec for a giant was more than a bike shop on the outskirts of Urfa could handle.

It's a bloody bike. There are literally no engine parts. This is personal.

Everything was becoming personal.

He watched as the mechanic...

... don't flatter him...

... explained, via Inci's interpretation, that they had fixed the kink in the frame by cutting out the old frame and welding in a new one.

Moth took the bike out of his hands, looking at the welds. The inserted metal was twice as thick as the old frame and the welds were ugly enough to look embarrassed about themselves. He threw a leg over the frame and put his foot to the pedal. His knee almost hit the handlebar as he rotated the pedal backwards to a comfortable place. He pushed off and tried to do a circle around the space. His knees aching on the down thrust because of the angle of his leg. He pulled up in front of the mechanic and got off.

'But how did you measure the length of the frame?'

The man looked at Inci while she translated, looked back at Moth, looked at the bike.

'We measured from the original.'

'Which original?' Moth asked.

The guy looked at the bike and scratched his head in bemusement.

How the hell are you going to fit on that thing?

There were a whole three inches less space between the saddle and the handlebars.

Inci began to suspect there was an issue and a crease appeared between her eyes. All Moth could focus on was resisting the intense urge to sit down and put his head in his hands.

The mechanic yelled over his shoulder at another one, who set about calling for another, until most of the shop had downed tools to gather round the bike.

Round Inci, you mean. You should have brought Husnu.

Husnu had refused to come and, in the rare absence of

her mother, Inci had wrapped her headscarf snugger, tucked away her hair and decided to come with him.

Inci away from the curry kitchen was a glimpse into the world he didn't know. She had reduced herself, following close at his side. Even now, in the depths of this confusion, she was a lesser shade of her confident self. He stood, a head height over all of them, watching the bike disappear as they tried to work out what the question was. Inci retreating from the surge of argument and excitement.

Perhaps you could cut three inches off your legs?

He'd grown since the years he was cycling through Europe. Perhaps he'd outstand James in a room now, let alone a group of fine-boned Turks.

Grown and put a stone on.

He looked at the fleeting glimpses of those welds. They might stand up to the demands of smooth roads, but...

... you're a long way from smooth roads...

... and would they hold his weight.

'They all say each other measured the frame.' Inci was talking to him. Behind her the mechanics were getting louder.

'Does that mean none of them did?'

'It's a common way of denying responsibility.' She shrugged her shoulders.

'It looks like they cut two bikes into pieces and patched them together.'

'At least they managed to make a whole bike.'

'It's a bike. A bloody bike. How could anyone make such a mess?'

'I'm sorry, Moth. I know this was important to you.'

Important? That's an understatement. How the hell are you getting out of here now?

'I can't ride that,' Moth told her, pointing at the bike. 'It's too short for me.'

'Can they make it longer?'

He looked at her. Sweet brown eyes, dimpled chins, creased forehead. No, not forehead. There must be a name for it, that space between the eyebrows.

If you'd stopped long enough at school you'd probably know.

'Longer?'

'Add another bit back in?'

Does she know anything about welding?

'No.' Moth felt his shoulders sag. Behind them the shop full of mechanics...

... don't flatter any of them...

... were waiting for his response.

You could ask them to have another go.

Moth looked at his bike. James' bike. The bike that had taken him away from England and been his ticket to freedom. It looked bruised. He wouldn't leave it here to go through more. Even if it was now useless to him. He wouldn't leave it to rust with the other carcasses littering the walls, to be pulled apart and welded to other lesser bikes.

'Can you ask them for the bill?' he asked Inci. 'Tell them I'll bring the money tomorrow and fetch it.'

He turned to walk outside, and she caught his arm.

'Moth, don't leave me alone with them. It is not...' she trailed away, flustered.

Moth looked over the assorted men, five or six of them, with more edging away from the scene. She shouldn't be here, her mother would have an epic fit if she found out. He nodded and stayed a pace away. As soon as she finished, he put an arm out for her to lead the way out of the shop. The weight of her light hand on his forearm connecting him to the role of protector. Discomfort rippling across his back.

All you've bloody done in Turkey is protect people. What's the difference?

What was the difference? This strong independent woman scurrying to hide by his side. Discomfort for Urfa increased. If this was how a woman felt, where did a gay bloke like Atabey fit in?

Atabey?

'I'm sorry,' he said to Inci as they walked away. 'I didn't mean to make you feel uncomfortable.'

'You don't know our ways, Moth,' she smiled from under her scarf. 'If Anne had found out I was alone in that place, she would have thrashed me.'

'You're kidding?'

She looked away, and didn't answer, removing her hand from his arm. Leaving him feeling both inadequate and relieved. 'I should have made Husnu come, I was foolish to offer to come with you.'

'Can't you even walk through the streets of your own town?' He looked about the shops and apartments. Urfa seemed a modern town. It had high rise offices, men wore Western clothes, women had high heels. 'It looks modern enough to me?'

'We want to believe we are modern, but a woman's honour is lost with one false move.' She nodded subtly at the people moving past them. 'Even being out here with you, I take a risk. For both of us.'

'Both of us?'

'I draw attention to you, Moth.'

'Perhaps you just draw attention?'

She continued walking, quiet, hiding within the curve of her scarf.

'Inci, are you happy?' he asked. 'With your life?'

'What sort of question is that?'

'Don't you wonder... what your life could be if you moved away?'

'Urfa is my home, Moth.' Inci tugged the side of her scarf straighter. 'My family are here. Who would I be without them?'

'Who might you be without them?' He reduced his stride, aware he was always moving away from her in pace. The only woman who had ever kept up with his long legs was Isabelle. Though that walk to the train station was a distant memory. 'I became who I am because I left my family, not because of them.'

'And who are you?' she asked with warmth. 'A man with no visa, no job, no home. Is this what you would have me become?'

'No, of course not.'

'You think it is this easy.' She snapped her fingers together, her pace increasing. 'You jump on a bike and away you go. You think I can do that? That any woman can do that? That we wouldn't end up dragged from the road and raped? Beaten. Forced into slavery. This is my life, Moth. Don't make it small and pathetic because you have choices I don't.'

Well, now she mentions it.

Moth stopped where he was, watching Inci storm down the road. He had been. Dragged from the road. Raped. Beaten. And he'd recovered.

Really? Have you?

He hadn't lost his courage. He'd got back on the bike and kept moving.

Kept moving or run away?

Because it had been easier, to get on the bike and keep moving, rather than stay and face reality. His age. His education. His choices. His beating. His feelings. So much easier to get on the bike and keep moving.

Except now the bike is wrecked.

Inci pulled up, refusing to look back, waiting for him. He caught up with her, reaching for her elbow to hold her back.

'I'm sorry,' he said. She snatched her arm away from him. 'I'm sorry, I was angry about my bike. I took it out on you.'

She stood at arm's length, face averted, body rigid with anger.

'You're right, I was being arrogant. I am sorry and thank you for coming with me. Husnu's an arse for letting you come, he knew better than me. Let's get back before your mother does.'

'It's not Husnu's fault. He gets tired of being responsible for me.' Inci pushed her scarf further back and looked at him.

'Rahim Katili,' Moth smiled as she grimaced at her nickname. 'Please tell me, what do you hope for?'

'Why?'

'Because I want to understand, not pretend I know already.'

She smiled at him. Stood a little prouder and relaxed.

'That's the most intelligent thing you spoke today.' She looked at the people moving past them, thinking before replying. 'I want to marry someone I love. A clever man who doesn't expect me to be his servant. Who understands that I want to work, to run the agency better than my mother does. Raise my children better than my mother did.' Inci flashed him an evil grin. 'My mother always lights a candle in the window at night, did you know this? To make sure we know the way home, to let her dead children know she waits for them still. I want to be like that, a light to my family, as she has been to us. Is that not enough, Moth? Why would I want to run away? Ignore the difficulties of my life? They are *my* challenges, and I will stay to fight them. Where else will I be Rahim Katili? Anywhere else, I will be nobody.'

'Is that what you think I am?'

'What does it matter what I think?' She nudged his arm and began to move along the street, encouraging them on past the watching eyes of the passers-by. 'Who do you think you are? Who are you to your family? Who are you in the eyes of God? Who are you compared to yesterday?'

'What about the man you want to love?' Moth asked. 'Doesn't it matter who you are for him?'

'If I am myself that will be enough,' she said. 'Allah forbid I be like Husnu and dance to any woman's tune. He will make a terrible husband. Or be like you and run from all the women.'

'I'm not running from the women.'

'No?' she teased him. 'The women say you are too scared to look. Moth will not be tied down they say. He is too addicted to the wind. Floating along on it. None of them would have you, you would make a worse husband than Husnu.'

'You make me sound like a piece of rubbish.'

'A lonely piece of rubbish.'

'I'm not lonely.'

'How can you not be lonely?' she asked. 'I would go mad with loneliness living this way.'

'Now who's judging who?' he laughed.

'Yes, Moth, you are a sad and lonely piece of rubbish,

stuck on the wind.' She jabbed his arm with her elbow. 'All the women worry about you, and you don't even know it.'

And now you have a broken bike to boot.

They were close to the aid agency, he could see Fehran's truck parked up the road.

'Dikkat. Buraya gel!'

Moth felt Inci stiffen at his side. The words were called out behind them at a distance.

'Moth, keep walking.'

'What...' he began to turn.

'Don't!' Inci snapped. 'Go, get to Fehran's truck, send him to me, then run. It's the police.'

'But...'

'Moth, get to the truck and run, you English idiot. If they find you with us with no visa we will be shut down.'

She turned and walked away behind him. Talking in a bright tone as she left. Moth kept walking forward. Heart pounding. He was no more than ten steps away from the truck. Thoughts swirling too fast to catch. He should go with her. He shouldn't leave her alone. He would get them all in trouble. His stuff was in their lockers, his rucksack was in Fehran's truck. Ahead he saw Fehran's face appear at the back of the truck, looking down the road past him. Heard the big man call into the gaping maw of the roller door for Husnu and Dilru. Five steps.

'Dikkat!'

Two steps.

Ahead of him Dilru came running out of the shop, her face red with anger. Behind her Husnu appeared, a bright red mark flowering on his cheek. They ran toward Inci, not even looking at him. Dilru crying out as she went. Fehran grabbed

him, pulled him behind the truck and threw his rucksack into
his hands.

'Pazartesi, Onbirnisan'da.' Then he pushed Moth away,
pointed up the hill and pushed him again. 'Git!'

Moth stood and watched him run past the side of the
truck. Downhill he could hear Dilru getting into full rant,
shouting at Husnu, Inci placating her. Whatever racket they
were pulling, they needed him to be gone before the police
arrived. He turned and ran up the hill away from the truck.
Turning a corner he pelted along a side street, the noise
retreating as he went. Breathless with the suddenness of
danger, heart pounding, legs quivering, he threw a look
behind him and ran harder.

MOTH WAITED until the castle closed. Watching from the
garden paths as the walkways up the hillsides were checked
by the staff. Lingering under trees and avoiding the looks
thrown his way.

You might as well walk around with a sign on your head.

Anxiety sat on his skin with the day's sweat, itching his
neckline. He'd spent the last six hours dodging his way
nervously through the streets, trying to figure out what to do.
His height a curse. He missed his beanie hat. The urge to pull
it over his head, to cover his foreign, apricot hair, overwhelming. He hadn't had that hat for over two years, since it unravelled on the northern border of Turkey when he tried to cross
over into Georgia. Missing it reminded him of European
roads and old problems. Where to eat that day, where to sleep
safely. He had grown adept at what now seemed impossible.
He moved along the paths, picked another tree, sat down
behind it cross-legged. Waiting.

Waiting for what?

Behind the castle the setting sun was sending shadows down into the trees and pathways. A golden rim spreading across the lower part of the sky while above, intense blue bloomed as the harsh summer sun lost its power. As the air breathed out in relief the ground heat began to radiate back up. It would be a warm night with clear skies. He saw the final people leave the castle pathway. The low-level barrier being closed.

Behind him the patter of feet on the pathways quickened, anticipating the adhan before it was released. The chant echoing out into the sky. Pulling crowds to the Magarasi Mosque. He had been here with Inci and Husnu not long after he first arrived. Inci loved the Magarasi, the pools of Balikligol. He'd wanted to climb the castle hill, they had been less keen and, when he insisted, traipsed reluctantly behind him up the winding paths.

He'd understood their indifference when he got to the top. From the lower levels the castle promised rich rewards. And it did give a worthwhile view down over the pools and across the north and eastern city. But there were no grand ruins to find on the top. Two tall sentries of stone, a roughened patch of dry earth and foundations, and a grim view across the poorer south and west. Tightly packed houses with their flat roofs strung with washing. A wire fence and a narrow road close beside it. The indifferent backs of billboards hanging over the hills.

It's no Ludlow Castle.

He'd climbed to the top of Ludlow Castle tower with Isabelle, preening over the fantastic Inner Bailey, Riverdell huddled at its base. The glory of Urfa was all below the castle line and the locals ignored its disappointment politely.

Which was exactly why he planned to spend the night against its warm stone walls.

It would be a while before dark yet, but he needed to get onto the lower levels. Moth moved out from the pathways of the Balik gardens and onto the first paved walkways that snaked their way up the hill. There were pockets of cypress trees, benches, gathering areas. People lingered, those who were not going to prayer. Eyes followed him. He stayed confident, struck his way further in. Sat down and looked out over the city. Just another tourist, admiring the view.

By wandering in this way from pocket to pocket, he made his way up to the tall stone cliffs of the foundations. Sitting at last with his back to the warm stone, protected by a clutch of low trees defying gravity. Watching as the city skyline was cast into shadows, the domes of the mosques curving above the flattened roofs. Listening as the traffic slackened on the roads. Scooters stinging their way with increased speed as the cars began to dawdle. The contented emptying of the Magarasi when prayers ceased released his watchfulness. He clutched his backpack to his chest and relaxed into it. He'd forgotten the energy it took to find a place for the night. Tomorrow he would get the bike and get out of town. Urfa was no longer a haven.

Your options are running out.

He'd spent worse nights. Sitting on his bleeding heels beside a wastebin in Italy. A cat watching him with disgust. Moth hunkered down into his body, his legs crossed, supporting his tiredness and the backpack.

Doesn't mean it won't get worse yet.

He faded into the shadows of the walls as night leeched away the colours of the sky, watching until the final adhan was called. The mosque shimmering into life again for its last worship. He didn't want the day to end. Beyond the next sunrise he had nothing solid in front of him.

If you could call a four-day round trip from one meal to the next solid.

A piece of tattered plastic brushed across the short thin grass beneath his tucked in feet. Spiralling on the warm rising air and drifting along the hems of the castle until it got caught on a low prickly bush. Watching it struggle and twist in the soft breeze and sag into resistance, Moth felt a chill reach into his toes and tucked them tighter. He was no better than that piece of rubbish. Inci was right. He was drifting on the wind, unable to move forward. Too nervous to go back.

It's not enough anymore.

He leant his head back and looked up at the sky. Far in the eastern distance, he could see stars peering over the edge of the deep rim of night. They'd witnessed more of his life than any other person or entity. Checking in on him to see what mess he was in now. Twinkling in amusement. Was it such a terrible thing to sleep beneath the stars? Stuck at school and home he'd longed for the freedom he had now. The freedom to sleep where he wanted, go where he pleased.

You're not a school kid anymore.

No, he wasn't. His aching legs told him he was too tall and solid to be tucked up beside a bin or on a rocky castle butt. He wanted...

... yes ...

... more than this. More than a tent stuck in a camp of homeless refugees. Moth shuddered at his reality. Every refugee he'd ever met wanted a home, whether it was the home they'd left or a home they'd build again. They wanted to belong.

He didn't belong here. Hunched against the walls of Urfa

Castle. Watching the lights sparkle over a city that didn't want his unemployed, visa-less arse cluttering up its streets. And he couldn't get to where he'd been planning on going.

Maybe it's time to try some of the options. At least give them a chance.

Those options were either go home, to Riverdell, perhaps to then go to India with Isabelle, or to make good that promise he'd given Luca. But it was more than that. It wasn't just about where he could go. It was...

...where do you belong?

He let the question linger as the stars poured over the rim and came to watch him figure it out.

THE PROBLEM with a pep talk given at night, Moth decided, was it rarely lived up to the light of next day. He let go of the mouse in disgust and sat back in his chair.

So much for giving them a chance.

The Urfa cafe reeked of Turkish coffee with an intensity that was setting his brain ringing. This was not a modern, European internet cafe. This was a small, hot, dark shop that had two old desktops with keyboards that looked capable of giving you a lethal infection, coffee the Turkish way and not much else. Moth had asked for a bottle of water with his drink and not touched the black treacle sitting by his elbow. It had taken him long minutes of being watched by every other person in the room to find an internet connection that could attach him to Gmail.

Dilru's old kitchen pc doesn't look so bad now.

At least there he had been granted privacy, the use of a printer if he needed it. Here, he had the collective weight of Turkish masculinity peering over his shoulder. He'd opened

Isabelle's email with a glimmer of hope that had not bloomed, that had wilted as he realised why she was thinking of going to India. Garbled issues about Riverdell, Asha, some bloke named Steve. Interspersed with confident sentences about how Indigo would enjoy India. How she wanted her daughter to see more of life than Riverdell. Ludlow. England. A list of details about visas and vaccinations that was overwhelming. Ideas about where to meet. Where they could go when they got there. Maybe he could base himself in Mumbai with them. Aware of the quietness and curiosity at his back, Moth tried to make sense of the rush of words. But it all boiled down to the same thing...

... it's not about you.

She was running away again. Whatever was happening at Riverdell, Isabelle was freaking out and running off to India. He'd end up as her babysitter while she tried to piece herself back together.

He sent a short reply. He had stuff to sort here first. Wasn't sure when he'd be free. He'd get back to her.

Hope was hard boiled when he'd clicked on Luca's email.

So, that's that.

Luca rambled even more than Isabelle did. Beginning each sentence with a firm warning that he had to ask Moth an important question, drifting into anxious queries about his health, his loneliness, his feelings, his plans. Ending with an admission buttered up in guilt. He'd been asked out on a date. It had been three years. He was trying to build his life. He was lonely. How long must he wait? Was Moth ever coming home? What should he do?

Moth stared at that question for the longest time. Moth had never wondered about Luca keeping that promise. He'd assumed it was his to hold. All this time, he'd tumbled the thoughts over in his head, pretending to figure himself out, waiting for this moment, this request, to realise...

... you were waiting for him to prove himself.

And here was the proof. Luca didn't want him. He wanted a life. Cosy and settled and normal. A career, a flat, a partner to share it. Luca knew exactly where he belonged.

What did you expect? That he would give up his own dreams and come running after you.

Moth closed his eyes and swallowed the disappointment. Yes, he had been waiting. He'd wanted life to be as it had in Venice. Sharing his life, his freedom, with someone who could live the same way. Quiet rooms and slow mornings. The sea moving through a city and warping any sense of solidity. Moving on the next day. All this time, he'd been waiting, not realising what he was waiting for.

Brown eyes that were sun-glinted. Hair too optimistic for its own good. Collarbones you could pool water in. Hips too slim to hold up trousers. Behind his eyes, Moth could see all of it.

Thinking about that request, permission asked for a date, Moth crushed his hands into bitter fists. He wanted to write no. No. No. No. You can't. The thought of someone else touching Luca, laughing with him, waking up with him, ran along his spine with the same savagery as the knife that had opened his face up. Moth put his clenched fists to his cheeks, feeling the tightness of the skin still healing. He tried to visualise himself, in Geneva, trying to find work while Luca built his golden career. Himself, uneducated, broke, cleaning hotels or working in a supermarket. He could never belong there. Moth opened his eyes to clear away the grim image of that life.

What should he do?

Moth typed his response. Bitter and scared, rebuffing the pain and loss that swamped him, the overwhelming testosterone of the café's clients crushing him inwards.

Do what you need to. Geneva's not home to me.

He sent the message, watching the blue swirl of indecision on the screen and when it showed him the message sent icon, felt a gaping hollow in his flattened chest. The space where he'd hidden an impossible thought. Beneath the idea of finding courage in his own choices, of Bonn getting him a real job, of getting his life on track. The thought that Luca might have given up his life to come and find him. That courage and choice were things he was waiting for someone else to prove.

Well. That was bloody stupid.

Moth cleared the cache. Closed the screen down.

It's time to go.

It was time to go. Time to leave Turkey. He had nothing left to stay for. Luca had found his home in Geneva, same as Mila had found hers in France with Beau, same as Bonn belonged with the camps, same as Isabelle belonged at Riverdell, even if she hadn't yet found the courage to stand up for it. Moth didn't belong there with any of them, and he didn't belong here.

Moth hitched his bag onto his shoulder and walked out into the streets.

ISABELLE SAT ON THE PORCH, surrounded by tree catalogues. Indigo and Deryn curled up like sleepy kittens in the open back of the campervan in the drive, wrapped together in a blanket against the teasing September chill. Sucking the juice from apple slices to ward off the hour before dinner.

'There are so many to choose from,' she told Martin. The brochures were glossy and stunning, showing the trees in all their youthful grace. Like teenagers, upright and slender, their first year's flowers shining in the photographer's lights. An image of Moth standing beside the willow tree in the garden floated across the pages. How much would he have changed now? Luca's life would fit one of these catalogues, snapped on all his social media channels. Vigorous, unashamed, humming with energy. Moth was invisible by comparison. A fading memory of a boy-man caught in the wavering light of an Italian lake. Sharpening into focus in all too brief moments, crisp as the catalogue pages. Fading away as she looked up at Martin. 'I have no idea where to start. Surely this is Kate's province?'

Martin shrugged and considered his work. Selecting another stone from the pallet of new beside him, hefting it in his wide hand, turning it round, applying lime mortar and letting the weight sucker into the mix as he added it to the rising wall. Isabelle knew that diplomatic shrug. Kate had refused to help her choose what to replace the magnolia with. She returned to the books and flipped the pages. Malus Rudolph, Cercis Canadensis Texensis, abeliophyllum distichum, laburnocystisus… she couldn't even pronounce the last one, and it sounded distinctly like a health issue. The photos were alluring but the attached information froze her mind. Height, position, spread, soil. It was impossible.

'How does Kate know how to plant all the right stuff?'

'She has a gift for it.' Martin selected another stone, this time from the pallet of old. 'Plus, she reads herself to sleep with those things.'

This also bemused Isabelle. How a wall could fall, and then not have enough stone left to rebuild it. The patchwork colours of the old and new melded together as the layers rose. Soaked hessian trailing over the section that had been done before, keeping the lime moist through the warm September days. Martin peeling the filthy stocking back each time he returned to continue. Kit had come and gone in an afternoon. The reconstruction process was taking weeks.

Isabelle glanced up at the high windows of the second floor flat, the windows stood open, and she could hear Gosia stripping the empty beds. Elsa had always loved Sundays at Riverdell, the one day when the guests left, and the house was theirs. For Isabelle this was Friday afternoon. The course guests checking out, Kate putting her feet up on a chair in the kitchen and opening a bottle of wine. Waiting for Rob to return from work and casually stay the weekend. She frowned down at the catalogues. No, Friday had been her favourite. It seemed to have altered in the last month. An unspoken expectation of where she would be, who she should be with, creeping in to stilt her joy.

'Maybe try not to think too hard,' Martin suggested.

She looked up, the frown stuck on her face, 'Huh?'

'It's only a tree, Isabelle.' He paused in his work and stepped back, checking the feel of the work he had done. 'No need to frown that much.'

'Oh, it wasn't the tree.'

The campervan rocked in the driveway, unmerged language coming from inside. Isabelle's frown converted to a smile. Martin had had to bring it to work for the last two weeks while his work truck was in the garage trying to pass its MOT.

'What is it about that van? I reckon I could leave them in there all day, and they wouldn't move.'

'It's basically a house on wheels to them.' He smiled back at her. 'Though to be honest, it's about the same to me.'

'Any news on the truck?'

'Umm, she's as dead as that magnolia was. I'm looking for a replacement.'

'Don't look too hard, we like you coming to work in the camper.'

'Well, I might not have a choice.' Martin selected another piece of stone. 'If I can't find the right truck at the right price, she'll have to go. They've gone up so much.'

'Oh, you can't sell it. Her. Why are vehicles always female?' Isabelle looked again at the VW. It was a poorer relative to Kit's gleaming vans. Snub nosed by comparison. Wheels thin and the body high. Her paintwork a frosted almond blue, topped with an ugly white canopy. But it was tenderly cared for. The paintwork patched but polished, hubcaps shining, neat curtains at the window. Careful worry in Martin's face as he hauled his work tools out the side door. Maybe that was why men always thought their cars were female, not because of how they looked but because of the care they lavished on them. 'How long have you had it?'

'Since '98.' Martin glanced at the VW with pride. 'Been labouring over her ever since.'

'Have you done much travelling with it?' Her Skoda gave her no such pride. It was a car, functional, begrudgingly needed, happily ignored. Moth would relate to Martin's feelings about the camper, he was the same about James' old bike.

'Yep, every winter. Europe, Asia, South America. Never done Africa, would have loved to do that.'

'How did you get to South America?'

'A long boat trip. That was a while ago, it's harder these days.'

Martin stretched out his back and pondered between the two pallets. Isabelle tried to guess which he would choose. She had given up thinking she would ever work out the process and this was the addictive part of the patchwork effect. The part which pulled her out onto the porch each Friday evening as he began the rebuilding work that Kate had banned him from doing during the week. The mess and noise of the mixer disturbing her business vibe in the week. She glanced beyond him to the open gates, the late afternoon chill seeping into the stone beneath her cheeks. The conversation with Kate that morning fresh in her mind as she remembered Asha would soon be here to collect Deryn. She thought about the work she had not got done that week. Isabelle frowned at the catalogues, remembering Kit's instruction to replace the tree with something mature enough to hang lights on, even if the price tag was prohibitive.

'You're thinking too hard again,' Martin told her.

'You're right. I have no idea what to pick. It's impossible. Kate will have to decide.'

'Pretty sure she already refused to do that.'

Kate had plonked a pile of catalogues down in front of her the morning after Kit left, saying, 'Here, you can decide this for yourself while you make your fine plans for Christmas too.'

'Well, that's not fair, she's the damn gardening guru here.'

'It is your house.'

'You think?' Isabelle laid the catalogue on her knees and rested her chin on the blossom of an Amelanchier. 'Sometimes I wonder.'

'I thought you enjoyed it, this cooperative style of management?'

He coerced a thick slab of old stone into the sharper angles of new, the lime squidging out with the pressure, scooped up and platted back down on the board.

'I do, of course. I love how involved we all are,' Isabelle said.

'But?' he asked the wall.

Isabelle let the question hover behind his turned back. It was a short word for a host of issues as unclear as the edges of his tools. Martin didn't press her. Hands caressing the edges of each stone piece, tucking them in, rejecting them, selecting fresh. She hugged her knees and tried to get a handle on that but.

It was the sharpness of Kate's frown as she'd warned Isabelle that morning she had to stand up for her own time or ruin her business. It was the shape of Asha due to arrive, tired and grumpy on a Friday evening, exhausted from a huge commission job and with James working 24/7 on the planting. It was the size of Steve, rolling in a little later with the puppy dog eyes of a man who now assumed he would spend Friday evening at Riverdell. It was the hitch of Rob's left shoulder when Steve turned up. It was the length of her job list, unsewn, unpressed and unpackaged. It was the sound of Indigo and Deryn playing together after a full week spent together. It was the distance between her and Moth and the density of that aching ball that sat in her stomach whenever she thought about him. It was the regularity of the emails coming from Luca, the drip, drip, drip of his desperation to see Moth. It was the length and texture of the India map warming beneath her hand when she passed from one end of the eastern corridor to the other. It wasn't even remotely the look of the trees beneath her chin. She sat up, shut the cata-logues with a sigh and put them down.

'But maybe I don't want a tree at all?'

Martin looked over at her, a curious eyebrow riding up at the edges of her sight.

'Well, that's an interesting thought.' He glanced at the empty stone well growing before him. 'I hadn't thought about that. Lot of options that route.'

Isabelle blinked in the dimming light of the sun going down behind Riverdell, the roof sending shadows to creep across the courtyard toward them.

'That's possible?' she asked.

'Of course. Anything's possible, isn't it?' Martin scraped the last bit of muck up and, with a quick flash of a trowel, edged the new pieces with a fine line. 'Nothing to say you have to follow what's been done before. A rose garden, or an evergreen, or even a sculpture could fit the space.'

A car slowed outside the gates and Isabelle looked across to see Asha nosing her way in. A hunched figure over the steering wheel. Her stomach did a lurch. The conversation between them now painfully close.

'I'll have a think for you,' Martin cleaned the trowel against the edge of the hessian and draped it over the new work. 'Only thing you'll need to decide is if you infill with fresh soil or need a solid base for a sculpture.'

'Thanks, Martin.' Isabelle put the catalogues aside and moved over to the campervan. It would help if she took the brunt of the girls' moaning to be separated. 'Deryn, Mummy's here, let's go make her a nice drink together.' She gathered a child apiece to a hip and turned an encouraging smile to Asha. 'How was your day?'

'Bloody long, I hope you've got the coffee on?'

'Of course, come on in, tell me all about it.'

ASHA WAS STRUGGLING to digest what Isabelle had said.
Which, combined with the way Kate had uncrossed and
recrossed her ankles on the kitchen chair, a scratching of
linen and rustling of lining the only sound to accompany the
grinding of mental gears as Asha tried to put the words into
place, must mean she hadn't said it clearly enough.

'So that means what?' Asha asked with a crease between
her eyes and the chink of a cup on china as she put her cup
firmly down.

'I can't help you next week, I have a lot of orders to catch
up on.'

'Not at all next week?'

'I really need the days back, Asha. It's been two weeks
now of having Deryn every day, Indigo has missed nursery
for two weeks.'

'That's because you said it's easier to have them both
together.'

'Which it is, they've loved it.' Isabelle resisted the urge to
bring her knee up to her chest. 'But I'm really behind and I
have to catch up. I can't even manage to keep up with my
current orders, let alone think about how I want to grow the
business. Or create more designs or, I don't know, source
some new fabrics from somewhere, maybe a buying trip. I
just, I... I need a few weeks back now and for us to think
about making some changes going forward.'

Kate poured another glass of wine for herself, reaching
forward to pick the bottle up, putting it back down. Settling
back into her chair with a hitched eyebrow watching the
storm cloud of Asha's face gather in silence.

'But I can't find an alternative that quickly,' Asha spoke slowly as her mind tried to process. 'James is useless while he's planting, and I can't afford to lose this commission.'

'I know it's tough but...'

'No, you don't.'

The whole room froze. Asha's voice was a brittle snap of annoyance. Kate's wine glass hung in mid-air, light catching the sourness of the wine.

'Sorry?'

'Let's face it Isabelle, you have no bloody idea what tough is. We've had an awful year on the farm, I'm paying the entire mortgage from my wages while you sit here playing Lady Muck and telling me you understand how hard it is.' Asha pushed back her chair and stood up. 'And you expect me to magic childcare out of thin air so you can make your stupid pinafores for other rich mothers like yourself with more money and time than sense.'

'Whoa, now wait a minute,' Kate interjected.

'Shut up,' Asha threw at Kate. 'Do you think I don't know you've put her up to this.'

'Hang on,' Isabelle protested, glancing through the open doorway to the hall where the girls had snuck away, hoping to avoid a parting. Their heads had snapped up at the change of tone in the kitchen. 'There's no need to get upset, we can find a way that works for all of us. I love having Deryn, you must know that. We all adore her being here. But I want to work, same as you.'

'I don't WANT to work.' Asha put her hands on the table, reminding Isabelle of Hester and sending a shudder across her shoulders. 'I wanted to work before, now I HAVE to work. While my husband does nothing to help me, and I miss my daughter every day. But at least here I know she is with family, not stuck with an indifferent childminder. But that's fine, you prioritise your precious pocket money business while you sit back and let all your rents roll in, smug in your great big secret about your daughter's father, who you don't even need, you're that rich.' Asha's voice had reached a crescendo that made Isabelle curl into herself in shock. 'Because of course you WANT to work.'

Asha stormed out of the kitchen and snatched Deryn up from the hallway rug. Isabelle followed her out, picking up Indigo whose face was pinching into outrage. Kate came up behind her and took Indigo, retreating to the drawing room with the deepening cries of fury. Isabelle followed Asha outside, where she was trying to strap a rigid Deryn into the car seat, tears streaming down both faces.

'Asha, please, don't leave like this.'

'Leave me alone.' Asha slammed the door on Deryn's screams and walked away from Isabelle, ignoring Martin who was mighty busy putting away his tools, and opened her driver's side door. 'You have no bloody idea.'

Isabelle stood back to watch Asha drive out of the court-yard. Trying not to let tears well in her own eyes. If that was the success she had at resolution, perhaps she should give up right now. As Asha's car disappeared down the road toward the bridge, Steve walked in the gates from the town side.

'Did I miss Asha?' he asked cheerfully.

She stared at him, trying to adjust her mind.

'You missed a nasty little squall,' Martin muttered as Steve waved hello.

'Oh.' Steve looked from one to the other, trying to take in the atmosphere. 'She does have a mighty capacity for irritation. Pressures of motherhood and all, I guess.'

He walked over to Isabelle and took in her crossed arms,

tight lips and blinking eyes. Weighing up the outlines of her mood and shape. Why was it she felt like a piece of furniture being assessed for stripping or painting. He laid a hand on her crossed arms and a light kiss on her cheek.

'Well, I'm glad to see you,' he told her in a soft tone. 'Though you look punched in. How about a drink?' He moved past her to the wall and lifted the hessian to admire the latest extension. 'Coming on a treat, Martin. You'll be replanting it by the end of the month.'

'That's optimistic,' Martin countered. 'The lime will take a good while to dry before we can infill.'

'You've done some nice pointing there. Do you have to rework it again or is that it?'

Isabelle walked past them into the house, forcing her distress into a smile as she headed into the drawing room. Kate was stood at the far end, jiggling Indigo on her hip, looking out through the bay window over the river and gardens. Crooning to the child, wiping away her hair where it clung with tears to her cheeks, finding a tissue for the snotty nose of misery. Kate looked up to see her walking through the room.

'That went about as well as expected,' she said.

Isabelle took Indigo without a word, her daughter nestling into her shoulder with an exhausted wail and giving her determination not to cry a run for its money. Kate reached up and wiped the escaping tear from Isabelle's cheek.

'You did good,' Kate added with a comforting smile. 'It was a hard conversation, and you stood your ground. She'll come around, give her time.'

'Steve is here,' Isabelle told her, her throat swollen and thick.

Kate nodded, stroking Indigo's hair back, a hand on Isabelle's arm where it supported the weight of her daughter's bottom. 'You two go do bedtime. You're both wrung out, an early night will do her good. I'll look after Steve for an hour. We can cook dinner together.'

ISABELLE LAY BACK on her pillows, staring up at the ceiling, willing her body to respond. Aware of the shape and feel of his tongue and mouth. Parting her, toying with her, seeking a response. She closed her eyes to the distant paintwork and focused. Any time now, she would respond. She felt Steve shift in the bed, getting comfortable. His one hand stroking her belly. His hair cradled against the skin of her inner leg, his shoulder nudging her thighs apart. His other hand cupping itself over the top of her thigh, running up and down the skin. She tried to ignore the odd irritation it kindled, the overwhelming way it drew her mind to that point and away from the fire she was trying to kindle in her belly.

Sex with Steve was as great a difference as it had been between Kit and James. She shuddered at the thought popping into her mind and felt Steve tighten his grip on her thigh in expectation. She should not be comparing notes in the moment. Kit had been demanding, swift, endless, unpredictable but he had known exactly how to arouse her, and she had never had time to think during their lovemaking. Try as she might she could not move her mind back from the awareness that Steve was caressing her thigh as he had once felt the turning on the dining room table legs. Her tension reached him and he paused, lifting his head as he considered the lack of response. He moved up her body, kissing trails over her skin. Lingering around her navel, where she felt aware of the stretched skin and kept her eyes firmly closed. He continued along her ribs, beneath the breasts that had shrunk even more with failed nursing. Isabelle reached out for his torso and wrapped her legs round him, waiting for the pressure of his penis on her. Moving her hips to pull him in, feeling his lips along her collarbone. She felt him pause, the resistance of the condom on flesh too dry. She opened her eyes. His face was close beside her, kind eyes and easy smile. She smiled back in encouragement, gripping him with her legs.

Steve pulled away and lay down next to her. Pulling her into a close embrace, wrapping his leg over her, his erection pinned between them. Kissing her cheekbone and stroking a line from her clavicle down between her breasts to her navel. Pulling the duvet up over her naked legs and unresponsive body.

'Long day, baby?' he pillow-hushed in her ear. 'Don't fret, it'll be better tomorrow.'

He pulled away and slipped the condom off. She could hear it twang against the fullness of his arousal. She tried to reach for him, guilty and distressed. He caught her hand and lifted it up to his chest, pulling her toward him and slipping them both in a spooned position. His arms clamping her. The stiffness of his erection resting against her buttocks. The duvet pulled up round her shoulders. The light of the hallway a thin line beneath the door.

'Get some sleep,' he murmured in her ear and kissed the back of her head.

Isabelle stared at the crack of light and tried not to move. She felt the pressure of his dick slowly retreat, the breath on her neck increase to an uncomfortable warm eddy akin to a bedtime version of water torture.

She lay there for over an hour, reliving Asha's words and

trying to piece together the ways in which she could have handled it better. Tormented into an uneasy lull that pitched her in and out of recrimination, shallow sleep and confused wakefulness. Startled by the sound of crashing china in her dreams and lurched from the nightmare of Asha throwing the rest of the majolica at her in rage, Indigo sat in a circle of green shards and crying, freshly made pinnies crumpled into balls in the corners of the room. At one point she woke to rhythm of the bed moving beside her, Steve masturbating quietly. Reaching for tissues from the nightstand, curving away from her and settling into a solid back and a contented sigh on the far side of the bed. Light toying with the edge of the white cotton that softened his outline. Herself pulled down into a tearful exhaustion.

She woke again. Confused by sound and movement. The thin line beneath the door extended into a light-filled shape. An unhappy complaint pulling her out of sleep.

Steve stirring beside her, moving from the bed faster than she could rouse herself. Pulling on a pair of shorts and heading for the door.

'It's alright, go back to sleep. I'll put her back to bed.'

The shape of him moving toward the rhombus of light and concealing the little figure clutching a velvet teddy bear seared itself on her mind. Isabelle stumbled from the bed in gut-wrenching reaction.

'No.'

Her eyes trying to open and see properly as she moved toward them and blocked Indigo from him, pulling a nightgown from the chair and covering her nakedness.

'You're exhausted, get some sleep.' Steve protested. 'I can manage.'

'No.' Isabelle tried to push away the roiling thoughts.

Tried to calm her voice. Hearing the caw of its desperation, seeing the surprise reflected in Indigo's night huge pupils. 'No, it's alright. I'll do it.'

She closed the door between them and pulled her daughter onto her hip. Shuddering at the chill in the dim corridor. Seeing Moth's face peering out from the shadows in her mind. Shaking away the memories of his words. Slapped into wakefulness by the awful surge of terror Steve's shape between her and Indigo had caused. Her sense of guilt over Moth as sudden as the cold in the hallway as she took Indigo back to her own room.

She curled up with Indigo in the teddy and cushion filled space of her queen-size bed, stroking her hair until sleep closed her eyes again. Mouth open, head stuck on Isabelle's shoulder, forming a warm sweating ball in her armpit. Isabelle pulled the unresistant form into her arms and buried her head in the curls of her daughter's head. Knowing she should go back to Steve, lingering in the trust wrapped up in her arms. Remembering the nights in Italy. Moth hunched in a ball of unwrought misery, wasted from tears and anger and spent with the effort of telling her. Images of his father in the study she had never seen. The light of a Sunday afternoon she had never known indelibly etched into her mind with all the capacity of her artistic visualisation, hurtling through time and across countries to arrive reformed in the shape of a man between her and Indigo in the depths of her own home. She eased Indigo onto the mattress, tucked the covers in and left the room. Stood outside her closed door with cold sucking on her toes and teasing up her bare legs, avoiding returning to her own room. Clinging to the comfort of her home and wishing she could go downstairs to Rob's bedroom and share her concerns with him. Voice the hideous doubt chewing at her and chase it away with his reason.

She turned the handle to her own room and saw Steve, propped up on the pillows, a night light switched on behind him. Waiting for her to come back. He smiled, pulled back the covers and beckoned her back to the bed.

'She settle alright?'

She nodded, pulling the dressing gown off and slipping beneath the duvet. Steve pulled her toward his warmth. She shivered against him.

'You got cold, nights are getting chillier.'

Isabelle could feel her cold skin recoiling from him. She placed a hand on the rising cave of his chest and focused on that, trying to push memory away and focus on the present.

'You should have let me put her to bed,' he said. 'I would have managed.'

'I know.'

They lay there in silence, his chest rising and falling beneath her hand.

'You're not comfortable with me doing it?' he asked, soothing the top of her hand.

She felt the bulk of resistance in her chest. A tautness to his that told her he was holding disappointment in with a tight breath.

'She doesn't know you well yet,' Isabelle said.

Steve kept his hand moving over hers. Not replying. The silence getting tauter between them.

'I sense it's more than that,' he finally replied.

Isabelle removed her hand and pulled away from his body. Retreating to her own space in the overfilled bed, pulling herself up against the pillows and trying to take the duvet with her. Overwhelmed by the absence of a nightshirt on her skin.

'I haven't had to consider this before, someone else being involved with my daughter,' she looked toward the thickly drawn curtains. Like the bed and the drawers, the mirrors and chairs that now filled this room, the curtains had moved with her from her old bedroom. Refitted to match the new window, keeping continuity with her life. Looking at the padded folds, understanding crept in slowly as the peeping rays of morning light would through the thick layers. She had changed while the furnishings stayed true. She was not the woman who had lain with James or Kit in the old room. She had known both all her life, would have trusted them with any part of her or Indigo. She did not have the same trust in others. Moth had changed that when she exorcised his truths. What had once been unknown had been made part of her world. 'I can't entrust her to people that easily.'

Steve eased onto his side, propped up on an elbow. The duvet a twisted diagonal line that left him exposed while pulling up to cover her. She resisted the urge to get up, dress, sit in a chair. The bed did not feel her own and she resented it.

'But you trust Rob?' Steve toyed with the floppy Oxford edging of the pillow.

'I've known Rob for many years. He's part of my family.'

'But we're sleeping together, Isabelle.' He clamped his hand into a fist and flicked it out flat on the mattress. 'That's a whole other level of trust altogether.'

'And I should trust you with my daughter? Because I trust you with my own body?' Isabelle asked him.

'Surely, yes?' Steve pulled himself up in the bed. 'I mean

what greater form of trust is there? I couldn't sleep with you if I didn't trust and respect you.'

The bulky knot in her chest distorted, pulling in memories of conversations with Moth. His incredulity that she thought he should trust his family, just because they were his family. She had been pulled through the wall, to the other side where Moth had been forced to live.

'It's not as simple as that,' she said.

'Isn't it?'

His incredulous dismissal made her shrink, wanting to deny it, appease him. Isabelle closed her eyes and thought about Moth, looking at her, wondering if she would deny his experience to avoid the conflict beside her. Isabelle opened her eyes and looked at Steve.

'No, it isn't.'

Silence built itself into a stonewall between them. Things she couldn't share with him. Secrets he could sense. Knowledge she could not unknow. Resentment he could not unfeel.

Steve sat up in the bed, putting his feet to the floor. 'I struggle with that.' He seemed to pause there, on the edge of the bed, waiting for her response. Recrimination in the silent set of his shoulders.

She would not apologise. Pull him back to bed and make up. She could never forget what had happened to Moth, what he had trusted her to hear.

In her silence, he rose naked and moved toward his clothes, dressing with his back to her. Isabelle pulled more of the duvet to her and sat higher against the headboard.

He moved toward the bed, sat on the side next to her. 'I need some time to think this through. I know you had a rough time with Asha. You're tired. Get some sleep.' He belittled her doubt, leant forward and kissed her cheek. 'We'll talk about it, at a better time, I know we can work this through. I'll let myself out the back door. You'll be safe, yes?'

She nodded, watching him walk toward the door, open it and pause, waiting for more from her. She had never imagined it would feel this real and tangible and close, the threat someone could pose to her daughter, until she woke and saw him close to being out the door and herself fast asleep. That the image of his shape moving toward Indigo's had pulled horror out of memory and into the home she loved. Steve registered her silence, she heard the door click closed behind him, pulled the duvet to her chin with relief and sat watching the immovable curtains and their darkness.

FROM HER STUDY window she could see sunlight reaching across the roofs of the town and over the courtyard wall to caress the windows of the second floor flat. Even now, she couldn't help but think of it as Moth's flat. That it was waiting for him to return, to settle in their life here, to be part of the family. She turned from the window and went back to her desk. Lingering over the old diary that had been keeping her sleepless company since Steve left. Dousing her confusion that she was glad to see him go, wondering if he would return, upset with herself for not wanting him, anxious that she was an ungrateful fool of even greater proportions than Asha believed.

It had been comforting to fall into the late years of the nineteenth century and the courtship of her great-grandfather Arthur and his wife Margaret. It was only when Margaret's sloping script first appeared in the diaries that she realised how overwhelmingly masculine the records of her house were. Margaret had been there, a shy young wife in

Arthur's first absence after their marriage. Arthur is away for four days to London. He leaves me to care for Riverdell. How empty it feels without him. Though Aunt Martha does insist on visiting daily to check I can manage. She claims the long walk from Home Farm is an excellent constitutional. I fear for the poor road.

Isabelle had smiled at the quiet wit and turned the pages further back in time as the house ticked quietly toward Saturday morning above her. Eyes drooping with weariness. Heart pounding with disquiet and resisting the urge to sleep.

She read of the younger Arthur's grief when his grandfather Edward died, the emptiness of the house as he cared for it alone. Arthur's hand had come early to the diaries, for his mother Constance remarried in 1887 and moved to Shrewsbury. Arthur elected to remain behind with his grandfather and was soon drawn into the management of the estate, his young but confident hand filling in for the increasingly shaky older one. Their scripts merging as Arthur and Margaret's would later. Isabelle picked her way in confusion through the evaded distress of the two years preceding this. Reading in Edward's near illegible script of the arduous process by which he had enabled his daughter-in-law to divorce his own son. Constance's distress at having to prove her own false infidelity. She read further back to the distress of the old man when gossip arrived of his distant and estranged son. Disgust turning to cold anger. Alfred refuses my summons to return to England, his wife and son. He insists on remaining in Bombay. I have warned him of the consequences. It is an evil I cannot endure, I could never leave Riverdell to a sodomist, Rowena would turn in her grave. I pray Arthur shall never know the truth.

Isabelle kept turning the pages. Arthur growing up at

Riverdell with his mother, grandfather and aunt Martha. His father Albert absent in India. That had given her heart a lurch. To realise she shared with Arthur the long days of childhood at Riverdell. That Arthur too had been born in India and returned to England in 1875 as a toddler with his mother whose health did not manage the foreign climate. Isabelle's discomfort at the paternal abandonment bolstered with pity for Alfred at how his family had treated him.

Isabelle glanced out of the window, the absence of the tree's withering branches a forlorn loss. It was strange to read backwards, to see the impact of the decisions and actions made before she came to the choices themselves. She wished it were possible to know her own life forward. To see what would become of them all from the decisions she made now. The empty pit of the growing wall outside demanding a choice. The distress of Asha's anger an unknown impact on her future options. The bleak weariness of the argument with Steve a crease of doubt in the newness of their relationship.

She returned to the diaries. Coming up against 1874 and pausing with Edward's retirement from London to Riverdell. The company is done. Undone, I should say. Rowena would dance for joy on the lawn if she were here to see it. She despised our dependence upon it. Well, now I have Riverdell to tend without its support. How empty the house feels without her now I do not have that distraction to ease her loss. How will I fill my time and life?

She had come upon the difference in the diaries. The motif that Rob had noticed on those frontispieces noticeable by its absence against the plain red paper of the following years. In his first entry for 1874 Edward had written; This is the last diary of its kind. No more will carry this mark and all the tarnished grandness it conveys.

Sitting at the desk as she heard the house begin to pop and stir with warming pipes and moving boards, Isabelle put 1874 on top of the pile of finished books. The remaining pile was much smaller now, reaching back to 1846. She moved the finished diaries back to their shelf, where they toppled sideways in absence of their companions. She thought of Arthur, returning from India so young it had never been a memory. Of her own memories of that place, forged in both childhood and as a young, independent woman. She thought of Indigo, growing up only knowing Riverdell. Time ticked across her exhausted mind as she tried to reconcile the crush of emotions and thoughts. Asha was right, how could she reasonably summon childcare from thin air? Steve was right, why would she not naturally trust him with Indigo? The desire to run away from it all, to pack a bag as she had once done and leave on a morning train with her fabric bag thrown over her shoulder, was enough to put her head in her hands and tears set to flowing. How had life become this weighed down with consequence and duty? How had she lost the lightness of the life she had loved before?

Isabelle reached for the laptop and brought up her email. Kate was right, she had spent too long in the past with the diaries. She found Moth's last email and wrote a rambling reply where she tried to piece together the future she wanted.

'You're the most devoted friend,' Adele told him.

Kit closed the oven door on the crisping pastry of the beef. How pastry was supposed to crisp on the bottom shelf of the oven was ridiculous, but when you were trying to cook three main courses for five people, alongside the numerous vegetables to accompany those three dietary options, the most critical factor was that the meat option had to be on the bottom shelf so it couldn't infect either the vegetarian or vegan options.

How did cooking a meal get this complicated?

'Do you like it?' Kit asked, turning to see him leaning against the counter, glass of wine swirling in hand. Adele drank with caution. Another poison to be aware of. He'd been on the same glass for over an hour. 'I'd thought you'd have approved of my humanity?'

'Perhaps I'm a little jealous,' Adele gave a small smile. 'Or wondering if you needed an excuse.'

Kit went to put napkins out. Aware that their private conversation was dangerously close to listening ears. Jay was sat in the corner of one sofa, opposite Hester and Lou on the other sofa. Five was such an awkward number, he was annoyed he hadn't been able to get any of the others to join them. But the rest of the team had claimed other commitments and Jay wasn't yet up to strangers. Five had to be easier than three, right?

'An excuse?' Kit returned to the counter, laying the plates out for the starters. Pulled the dressed, ambient salad leaves from the bowl with tongues and divided it between the five plates. 'An excuse for what?' He shaved sheer slivers of parmesan from a block, adding it to the leaves. 'Could you get the bread out?'

'You never did want us to spend Christmas in London, did you?' Adele murmured, putting his wine glass down right in Kit's working area as he went to pull the bread out of the upper oven.

Kit waited for him to come back, aware of the others in the room and the fact that Adele was manipulating their presence to have a go at him.

'All my plans for Christmas got sabotaged by Isabelle and it isn't as though I made Jay have a total breakdown.' Kit moved Adele's abandoned glass out of his way. 'What do you want me to do, ask him to put his collapse on hold while we go partying?'

'Really, the most wanted Christmas decorator of the country can't organise his own Christmas. Who'd have thought it?' Adele picked up his glass and took the rolls over to the table without waiting for his reply, going to sit down on the far edge of the sofa occupied by Jay.

Kit resisted growling, closed his eyes and reopened them to focus on cutting the sun-dried tomatoes into fine slivers. They had been chilled, to firm them up and to take the edge off their tang. It was a fine balance, between warm and cold, sharp and comforting. He rinsed the oil from his fingers. Reminded himself there was only one more night. Adele was leaving in the morning. Then told himself he shouldn't be counting the hours until his lover left.

Adele was jealous, that was the problem. He was sulking that Kit wouldn't push Jay aside for just two days and join him in London for Christmas. He was upset not so much that Isabelle had cancelled their plans, but that Kit wouldn't concede control of their choices to Adele as a way of making up for their being dumped by the family. Honest to God, if it weren't so lucrative, Kit would ban the word Christmas along with the event from his entire life. Adele seemed to have forgotten that he'd been trying to organise a Christmas for the very purpose of including them both in the family inner circle. How much more devotion could he show?

He pulled the Castelvetrano olives out of their pot. Fresh that morning from the deli. Behind him, Hester laughed at Adele and Kit paused, an olive in the fine tongues, hovering over the salad. It retained the power to surprise him, the sound of Hester laughing. He wondered what she would have done, had they all made it to Riverdell for Christmas after all. He'd been so busy thinking about himself and all the decorating plans, he'd not fully thought about Hester's presence there, with Isabelle as Queen Bee. Would she have even gone? When he'd first suggested it to her, in front of Elsa and Nat, she had raised her eyebrows and refused to comment. Later she'd claimed she had other intentions and, when he pushed her to know what they were, refused to elaborate. He'd called her bluff and jokingly threatened to sack her. "Think about Nat," he'd said. Perhaps he had been a little bullish. He put the olive down on Hester's plate.

He glanced over at the sofas. Adele was being charming. Which was at least one of his superpowers. Kit looked back at the olives. Gave Adele's plate an extra one. Kit wouldn't leave Jay for Christmas, wouldn't even ask Jay about joining them, and Adele felt bottom of the list and needed to reclaim his pride. Which all added up to a domestic chasm between them. With Kit knowing Adele would punish him right up until he left in the morning. Which meant even the sex would be a guilt trip. Kit took the olive back and put it on his own plate.

'Come and eat,' he called to the sofas, taking plates to the table.

'Who's sitting where?' Adele called as he stood up, tossing out the obvious challenge to stir the evening pot; Kit's organised this jamboree, now let's see who he's going to prioritise with seating arrangements.

'Sit where you want,' he told them as he went back for the other plates. 'It's supper not a royal banquet.'

He cracked the oven open a centimetre, checking the

mains. Avoiding watching the four of them decide who would sit where and who would take the head of the table position. He took the final two plates over.

'We put Jay in charge,' Adele said with a grin.

'Well done, you all made a decision without me.'

'Yes, though normally we'd risk being sacked for that,' Lou quipped.

He put the last plates down in front of himself and Jay.

'Apart from you, Hester.' Adele flapped out a napkin, laying it out on his lap. 'You're freelance anyway, right?'

'I'm not sure that makes me less sackable,' Hester contended.

Kit sat down in the leather bucket chair next to Adele, opposite Lou and as far away from Jay at the head of the table as Adele could have manufactured it. Adele wasn't the only one being adorable. Hester was being the perfect daughter of manners and breeding. Encouraging Lou to be the sociable, not working-day Lou. Kit took a large sip of wine and watched Lou trying to work out who she was in this uncertain situation of supper at the boss's house. He took another sip. Not chilled enough, he preferred it steaming from the fridge.

Adele reached across and selected a roll. Kit wasn't sure why, because he would eat one chunk of it and abandon the wheaten poison of the rest. He could feel the mean streak in his thoughts and, annoyed with himself, reached across and put a hand on Adele's shoulder.

'How about you, Jay?' Adele asked. 'How's your work going?'

Kit removed the hand from his shoulder and picked up a bread roll. Adele knew well enough Jay hadn't worked for months.

'I've got a few options to consider,' Jay said. 'Nothing too exciting.'

'It must be nice to pick and choose.' Hester picked up the breadbasket and offered it to Jay sat at her left hand. 'That's the mark of a successful business, being able to turn work down if it doesn't inspire you.'

'Surely you do it anyway but charge more money?' Lou asked, as Hester gave her next choice.

Kit noticed how she left herself until last and wanted to tell her to stop it. It made him feel bad. He pierced a forkful of salad and looked at it. The careful nuance of content, preparation, execution. He put it in his mouth, hoping for the tang of Mediterranean earthiness and salt. The crisp bite of the succulent salad. The tingling drizzle of the dressing.

'This is crap.' Everyone looked at him in surprise. He hadn't thought the words would come out. 'Salad, in December, what was I thinking?'

'It's food someone else prepared, tastes great to me,' Lou countered.

'It's perfect,' Adele added.

Kit ate another mouthful. No. It tasted bland and flat after all that expectation. He stared at the salad with irritation. It had absorbed his mood.

'Do you ever wish you had a job that didn't involve you relocating so much?' Lou asked Jay.

'I've always enjoyed the variety.' Kit watched Jay forking his salad with a dutiful indifference. 'I get to see new parts of the country.'

'A pub's a pub, surely?' Adele asked. 'Does it make much difference where it is?'

'You'd be surprised,' Jay answered.

Kit put his fork down and sat back. He wasn't hungry.

That was the problem. Cooking three different main courses had been tedious and taken the edge of enjoyment. He felt trapped by the bucket chair. The tedious conversation. The tedium of the last week. His crossed feet began to jiggle below the table.

'Have you ever worked in another country?' Lou asked. She was making a sandwich with her roll.

'This is not Pret,' Kit told her.

'Tastes better this way.' Lou tucked into her roll, squishing it down with her fingers.

Kit watched Hester, who was breaking the roll into small pieces, raise the first piece to her lips with a conspiratorial smile at Lou. He watched from the far side of the table, wondering what it meant. Hester had styled her hair with gentle waves to fall in a long bob, moved from the central parting to a side one. A long fringe sweeping across her forehead to tuck behind her ear. She had swapped her habit of pulling the plait end over her shoulder to tucking the fringe back behind her ear. As Lou grinned back around her sandwich, Hester reached a hand to tuck her hair back before glancing up to see him watching them, blinking and turning her attention to Jay, deepening her smile for him and asking with grace and charm enough to draw the entire table's attention, 'You've never told me how you and Kit met.'

'We met at the local pub, just round the corner,' Jay said. 'I was there trying to work out whether to take it on or not, and Kit came in and got me drunk.'

Kit felt a shiver rattle from his neck down the length of his back. He drank another sip of wine, his glass draining. There were odd moments, like this, when he didn't entirely trust this Hester. It was too different to what he'd known before. No, it even worried him.

'After he'd told me exactly what the manager was up to and why I shouldn't bother taking the job, I took him dancing.' Jay grinned at Adele, who hadn't heard this story either. 'It was the first time he'd been to a salsa club.'

'Imagine that,' Adele said with a tight smile.

'Of course, he loved it, and I couldn't drag him away.' Jay turned his attention to Lou. 'You know Kit, he pestered me every night for the next month to go dancing until he could do it.'

Kit wondered if this new, shiny, syrupy version of Hester would have stayed the same under the searchlight of Riverdell, if they'd made it home for Christmas. Or hardened and snapped like brittle sugar. To reveal something bitter and sour still lurking underneath.

Home. For Christmas. Kit shook his head. Had he said that.

When had Riverdell become home to him.

This was home. Right here.

He shuddered again, this time enough to make him quake visibly.

'Are you cold?' Adele asked.

'What?'

'You shivered. Are you warm enough?' He put his hand out to place over Kit's thigh. Warmth in his eyes. Concern.

Kit felt a swirl of guilt. Glanced up to catch all their eyes on him.

'Yes, no, I'm fine. I'll go check the mains.'

Kit pushed his chair back and walked to the kitchen area. Not cold, no. Shocked.

He pulled open the oven, let the warm air blast over him. Saw the beautiful golden glow of the pastry and felt relieved. What was Riverdell after all, but a childhood haunt. Maybe

Isabelle had messed up his chance to demonstrate how happy he and Adele were, he would find another. It didn't need to be Riverdell, the whole family. He didn't need to prove anything in fact, to anyone. His disappointment over Christmas was no more than a lost photo opportunity to market next year's season. He needed to focus. On Adele. On dinner. On fixing Jay up and getting back to work in the new year. He pulled the trays out of the oven and lay them alongside each other on the surface. Beef wellington, salmon en-croute and the vegan nut roast for Adele. None of them tempted him.

'They smell divine,' Adele said, walking up behind him and peering over his shoulder. 'What's up?'

Kit turned around in the tight space between the steaming pastry and the bulk of Adele, snuck his arms about Adele's ribs and pulled him in close. His hands caressing the thick muscles that rippled down his back under the fine jersey cotton of his top.

'I'm starving.' Kit kissed him, closing his eyes and letting the warmth of Adele's lips warm his own. Felt in that blind moment the softness and weight of lips kissing him back. 'Salad, honestly. Who was I kidding? It's meat I need.' He opened his eyes and looked into the twinkling amusement in Adele's surprised eyes.

'I'm never going to turn you vegan, am I?' Adele asked, kissing him again.

'Not a chance. Come on, let's serve this, I'm in need of dessert.'

Locked in the tight space of each other they smiled, bodies leaning closer.

'Oi, boss,' Lou called from the table. 'Dessert comes *after* the main course. Put him down.'

They heard laughter from the table. Kit shivered in delight and pulled away. Distracted back into a good mood.

KIT FILLED his hunger with determination. He kept Adele on the edge of orgasm, built it, released it, took him back to the edge. His mouth teasing, lingering, demanding. The taut stomach rippling beneath his one hand, the thigh flexing and relaxing beneath his head. He lay, halfway down the rumpled bed, hours past midnight, the guests long gone and Jay reading down in the basement, his head warm on Adele's sweat slicked thigh. One knuckle taunting the rim of his butt, Adele's other leg a taut triangle over his shoulder, his naked heel pressing into the hollow beneath his shoulder blade. Kit had forgotten any irritation about what roles they might assume tonight. Guilt hadn't made it past the bedroom door in the race with need.

They'd barely made it to the top floor dressed. Mumbling desire and consent as they crawled onto the bedroom floor, a bottle of icily chilled wine in Kit's hand abandoned on the drawers, leaving a puddled mess to drip into the open drawer where he'd grabbed a condom. Adele hung over the end of the bed, burying his head in the duvets as Kit penetrated him, handing him to a mutual climax. It had been swift, guttural. A messy and unprepared slaking of tension and frustration that made them both laugh, washing each other in the shower afterwards before heading back to the bed and lingering for pleasure.

'Enough,' Adele called out. 'You're killing me. End it.'

'How?' Kit mumbled. He felt Adele lift his leg over his shoulder. Pull out of his mouth. The rearrangement of muscle effortless. The thigh beneath him rose gently, pushing his head up.

'Lay back,' Adele suggested, pushing his shoulders back toward the foot of the bed.

Kit wriggled back and forth, letting Adele pull him into place. He rested his head on the far end of the bed, felt his hips moved upwards. Adele loved the arch, either way. It was a playful position, where tiredness could be passed back and forth. It was his favoured end of sex position. Kit lifted his hips and watched as Adele rose onto his knees. Pulling off the condom Kit had sucked most of the way off, rolling on a fresh one, smoothing lube up and down his hard on.

'You good?' Adele murmured.

'Ummm,' Kit responded.

He closed his eyes as Adele rimmed him, pushed him open, teased his way inside him, making Kit arch higher with the pleasure of it. The ripple of his muscles tautening, relaxing, allowing. Adele's hands gripping his hips, pulling him closer and deeper. Kit felt his back twinge and pulled in his abdomen to support it. The arch was not his favourite position, but it showed off Adele's fitness to a peak and, if he could stop worrying about his back, the pleasure was always worth it.

'I'm tired,' Kit muttered, closing his eyes and grasping Adele's thighs to help hold himself. Feeling the stretch in the back of his neck. Like yoga really, but with an orgasm. He felt his dick harden and pulse. Adele's hand releasing his buttock to take it, tilting them off kilter and making Kit strengthen his back muscles to counteract.

Adele was close already. The pace built, Kit's head moving stroke by stroke further toward the end of the bed, Adele's grip tightening. Kit felt both their muscles contorting with effort and counted the rise to orgasm in their pulsing. They finished together. Adele gasping over him, his hand slickening with the final strokes as he made Kit come. Kit reached a hand up to feel his chest. Hard. Every inch of this lover was hard. Muscled. Strong. It thrilled him, making the orgasm linger, surge and pulse through him.

Adele gurgled to an exhausted repletion, sinking down onto his knees. Kit prayed for his back the next day as Adele slipped out from under his hips. He watched an upside-down Adele walk to the end of the bed, lean down and kiss him, their tongues toying in tired delight. Watched him walk away to the bathroom, lying, exhausted, replete as he heard the shower switch on.

When Adele came back in, he was propped up against the pillows, his phone in his hand, swiping.

'What's up, looking for my replacement?' Adele quipped, sliding into the sheets as Kit closed the app and put his phone down on the side table.

'You know I'm not on that,' Kit retorted, putting the phone down. He needed a shower too. 'I'll be ten minutes, don't fall asleep without me.'

'You better make it five, I am whacked.'

Kit watched him snuggle into the thick pillows. He'd always had white cotton sheets before Adele came into his life and would never have believed he would change. For the first few months of their relationship, it had been a dick kick of attraction to see him naked against those white sheets. Another fact he would never admit. To anyone. Adele muttering about the sea of white had persuaded him to casually have a decor change. He'd moved to dark grey linen. With grey silk pillows. Kit missed the white. The sense that he went to bed righteous and replete from his day's work. He turned onto his elbow, pushed up and looked at Adele closing his eyes. Saw him flicker them open and smile at him.

'What you gawping at?' he murmured, his voice low and tired.

'You, lying there looking all sated and adorable.'

'Stop staring and go wash. I need to sleep.'

Kit leant forward and kissed him on the cheek. There was no way he'd be awake in two minutes, let alone five.

'Adele?'

'Hmm?'

'You enjoyed it?'

Adele pulled him down onto his chest.

'Enjoyed it?' He rumbled over Kit's head. 'You kidding me? We're matched, man. Sex with you is off the chart.'

Kit lay on the softly rising and falling rib cage and felt comfort and guilt try to mix.

'I'm sorry about Christmas,' he told Adele's grey linen ensconced chest.

'It's cool. We'll make it up another time.'

He was falling asleep, Kit could tell. He sat up, watched the chest deepen its breathing, the head relax, the lips slightly part in sleep. He never tired of watching a lover sleep. Apart from Dee, who had driven him mad. Because when he'd watched her sleep it was while trying not to stab her for snoring loud enough to wake him. Other than Dee, he never tired of watching a lover sleep. And Adele was better to watch than most. Kit moved quietly farther away, resting on his elbow. They should have spent Christmas together. He'd avoided the domesticity of it. Adele expecting him to make it perfect. Bullshit. Himself needing to make it perfect. He slipped from between the sheets, went to the bathroom, closing the door to silence the noise of the shower.

He did want it to be perfect. And he'd never minded being the one to make home life perfect. For his clients, for Riverdell, for his own home. It was only in a gay relationship that it began to rub wrong. He slipped beneath the stream of water and let it wash over him, on the outer edge of too hot to bear. Same as gay sex. It wasn't that he set out wanting to be a top. It was that being the guy that did the domestic stuff, because there was no way he was ever going to be in a relationship where he wasn't the one in charge of living arrangements, ended up shoehorning him into the bottom position. That was the problem. The fact that he began to anticipate what would happen in the bedroom and begin resenting it in the kitchen.

Kit closed his eyes and ducked his head beneath the heavy overhead shower. He let the water pummel against his sore neck. Easing out the kinks from his back. Watching the water swirl past his toes.

Adele was right, they were matched. In the bedroom. It was only him who got uptight, expecting problems that never occurred. And, if it weren't for Isabelle, and Moth, and Jay, they would have had a glorious Christmas together.

He got out, drying slowly. Weariness running through him with the rough passes of the towel across sore muscles, trying to block out the insistence of his thoughts.

Back in the bedroom Adele had curled into the middle of the bed, pulling his pillows down and wrapping his arms round them. Kit sat on the edge of the bed and looked at him. He needed to make it up to him. On the bedside table he saw his phone, resisted picking it up. Lay down in bed and tried to think about a Christmas consolation prize. His mind fighting his body. Trying to relax. Puffs of sleep emitting from Adele at a speed he could set a clock by. Kit picked up his phone to calm his mind. Fingers taking him straight to the guilty page. Her feed. Down and down until he found it. That one post he could never resist.

Kate's feet, bare, the toes polished a deep lacquered indigo, the water on the weir flickering over them, creating a kaleidoscope of blue and flesh tones. In her hands, with nails to match, a handmade earthen cup of herbal tea. An aesthetic shot only, Kate would never drink herbal tea. Her feet, chilled by the water, were that shade of blush that he could never resist. The terracotta inner of the cup was echoed in the plump thenar of her hands supporting it. He couldn't save it, that would be disloyalty. Neither could he quite resist it. Kit stared at those toes for a long time. Looking at the patterns in the waters. Listening to the patterns in Adele's breathing. Waiting for his mind to settle.

13

The great and the good die and we are summoned like faithful sheep to mourn.

Lord Mountbatten is laid in his grave and many a person no doubt wishes to piss on it.

I went. Granny insisted on it, though I argued the air blue with her. The bloody logic defeats me. She never attended her own son's funeral but the second cousin, once removed of the Queen, that we cannot ignore.

It was all such upper-class snobbery as to make me sick, and mostly at myself for being there. The great Lord Mountbatten, with more ribbons and trinkets than a royal whore, blown to bloody garters by the IRA. They have owned it, sweet Goddesses have they owned it. "The execution of Lord Louis Mountbatten is but one way we can bring to the attention of the English people the continuing occupation of our country." Execution. They pulled no punches, even if they didn't mention the two children killed, the old dowager. Better they had made sure he was on his own, the sympathy is more for the other dead than Mountbatten. And they are right, this will bring the troubles to the fore, they have struck at the heart of British government and monarchy in one blow.

I'm quite the liberal, as I walk through London behind the coffin of a bloody prince.

But Granny insisted. Mountbatten's mother was her own family and, in the face of national affront, the family must stand together. And she knows her health makes me weak. I would do anything for her, and she asked sweet as a child, knowing full well I can't resist her... wily old bitch. Oh, to be old and have the world dangle at your bidding.

But, let's be honest, it wasn't Granny who persuaded me.

It was you, and all the mess of that night comes down to the lies I'm telling myself, the lies I try to cover with my bright life that's as thin as a British ray of sunshine.

Ted rang Elsa the day after the bombing to say you were coming. Mountbatten was his godfather. And, of course, Elsa rang me all in a fluster and asked me to help. She knows nothing about London, her hands full of war between David and James, Ted too busy making arrangements to fly out to book hotels. 'At last, a chance for us all to be together, Rose.' How easily I caved. How little it took to blow the veneer from my own life. I abandoned Ben to book hotels. Full of the importance of my special friends coming to town.

All of it, all of it, all of it, born on the longing to see you. Which he must have seen through clear as day.

Except you didn't come. Again.

And not because Ted didn't give you the chance. Oh, how he tried to find his wife in the cupboard and dust her out for the occasion. How furious he was that you refused. How humble he was asking Kate if she would stand by his side instead. I could scream and weep and cheer. I am so sick of

Elsa and Kate laying out their lives for this wayward brother who turns up, sweating horse in hand and leads the way into the halls of greatness. Elsa should have spoken at her own father's funeral, not ceded the place to Ted. Kate should have told him to face the ranks of his brethren with the shame of his absent wife. I should have told them all to sort their own arrangements, lied to Granny and spent the funeral giving Ben a blowjob. Now look at the fallout, as bloody as that boat splintered on the water.

I am proud of you.

This pride, entwined with loneliness, is the same pride I feel for Kit, but older. I am proud of you for telling Ted you would not come. That it did not suit you this time. I am glad for you standing up for yourself when he has kept you like an embarrassment on a purse string. I am glad for your school that matters more than the death of a man who half-destroyed the country you have come to love. I asked Ted, in front of Elsa and Kate, if he could not have brought his mistress in your stead. You should have seen their faces, I hope you would have been proud of me. Do you know what he said in response, the bastard, he told me not to judge others by my own standards. Elsa barely spoke to me for the rest of the day. You know how sentimental she is about death. Full of the labours of the buried, their virtues and graces, the stolidity of decorum in counting their passing. And Kate, poor Kate, playing peacekeeper in the middle. Knowing I was stung by the magnitude of your absence, knowing Elsa was remembering her own dead, knowing Ted was full of wounded pride. And what did I do to help her?

Nothing. I did nothing.

The shame of this squeezes me tighter than any other part of the mess that damned day and night have caused. One day, the clock ticking away and all my life tumbling like a stack of cards in a sea breeze. All the raging and pride I feel for you, the irritation with Elsa and Ted, are nothing compared to the shame that I let Kate down. That she has been given the least of all of us and returns the most. One day I will have to admit this to you, and you will be ashamed of me. Better that I face it here and get used to it.

I will write to you, later, and tell you the moment I realised my lies and false life, the moment that it all crumbled away. I will tell you that I failed to protect you, to protect Kate, to protect myself. I will tell you that I have hidden my pain under anger, under desire, under anything than admit the truth. That I have been unkind to you because you never came back instead of facing that I abandoned you to your own heartbreaks as revenge for mine. A truth which made itself palpably clear to me as I sat in Westminster, among the noble grievers of the realm, representative of a family I have never met. Sitting beneath the vaulted ceiling and lead lights, all because I hoped to see you.

I am, and have never been anything more than, a moth to your flame.

All my life, loves and morals abandoned, on the barest whisper of you winging your way back to me.

A truth so overwhelming I tried to drown it.

And maybe we all had a few burnt hopes to drown that night. I wish I could remember the whole of it. From Ben's letter I suspect that my not remembering the details will make all the difference. His absence in the morning, the emptiness of the room I found myself in, the scene I returned to in our flat, all these useless, useless details do not help in restructuring that lost night.

How much do I tell you when I write?

Should I even try to remember?

Or is it better left here, never shown the light of day, along with all my greatest failures and hopes?

The weather was typically British, fleeting darts of sunshine interspersed with grey skies about as leaden as the damned coffin. I remember joining Elsa, Kate and Ted at the hotel and none of us much talking from the day before. How bleak a bunch we looked taking tea in the foyer and how I longed for a cup of decent bloody coffee. Ted frowning at my trouser suit and watching me put on a bright purple lipstick with something akin to disgust. Watching me as he might a cockroach. Elsa looking anywhere but at me, ashamed of me in front of her godly brother.

I remember the awful music in the abbey and how hard the chairs were and the sickening stench of too much perfume. Were they sent a Royal missive that the stench of the dead might rise strong that day and to wear their best florals? I wanted to retch. I remember missing Richard and wishing he could have been with us, not babysitting the bloody kids. I remember thinking Elsa had reached a level of dress perfectly aligned to the Queen's and how depressing it looked. I remember thinking I wanted to feel moved by the music but felt more sympathy for the poor bastards bearing the coffin than anything else. I remember thinking all the while that I needed a drink. Afterward, when we lesser mortals dispersed and they sent the coffin off in a Land Rover to the station, and the Queen and all her Lords and Ladies had departed, the lesser of us mortals looked at one another with a little discomfort. The sham of our rush and hurry to attend revealed in the ease with which we were discarded. I should say the pubs in Westminster were filled swiftly with bitterness. It was lunchtime after all, and nothing feeds hunger like a funeral.

They all looked to me, and I thought, typical, now I'm of use! I know the lie of the land and can provide refreshments.

Elsa left us after one drink. Claiming weariness and the desire to catch up with Richard and hear news of the children. Ted put her in a taxi back to the hotel and he and Kate decided they wanted to walk in the park. The sun had strengthened and maybe it chased some of our bitterness away. I wish now I had shoved him in the taxi with Elsa and gone to make my amends to Ben. But I didn't.

I recall sitting on the grass in Hyde Park and listening to Ted and Kate talk business. She has become a minor celebrity and I hope he took great umbrage in knowing she ignored all his bloody advice and built her business her own way. She asked him about you, and how often you return to Bombay. Ted was all about how your work keeps you in Kashmir and his is spread further afield, the home in Bombay is often without you both. This is how I hear, second hand and littered amongst what is left unspoken, what your letters do not say. You two are estranged. His refusal to adopt was the last wedge. I hope he is miserable, and you are happy. I was left in wretched awareness that all our happiness has been compromised by the poor choices we made so many years before and, though I mock Elsa, she has had the greatest share of joy of us all. I plucked the grass, watched clouds straggle across the sky and did not realise my worst choices were all conspiring against me. Before making an ever stupider one.

I took us out. Desperate for a slice of happiness to counteract the gloom, inspired by the false sunshine, Kate's peacemaking, who knows. I took us out and got us good and proper drunk. I remember Ben appearing. I remember him not being alone. That he arrived with a young man and drove me mad kissing him. I remember leaving Kate and Ted, despite her concerns. I gave her the keys to the flat. I remember that, but not why. She was staying at the hotel and had no need of my keys. I remember more pubs, more drink, dancing and then a room. Making love with Ben, but it is lost in all my other memories of making love with Ben. And I remember the naked skin of the other boy. His muscles, his arousal, his laughter.

And that is all. Until the morning. When I woke to find them gone and myself in a strange hotel room at dawn. Nothing but my funeral clothes laid on the chair, and the blouse missing. Sick with hangover. Then the scene at the flat. How I wish I could forget that.

I left London and came home. I couldn't bear being with them another day. Three days they have left to play the caring womenfolk to Ted before he leaves for India. I want to catch a plane first and come find you.

There, I've said it. The gospel truth I found in Westminster and faced, hungover, in the mirror of that empty hotel room.

The only place I have ever belonged is with you. And I have failed everyone in denying that.

All the pleasures and dalliances of the world cannot drown my aching need to hold you. I have lost myself in desire, all in the hope to find the love I once knew.

The only thing I have left to do is find my way back to you and beg you to forgive me.

And I would leave now, while Ted kicks his heels in London, but for this letter from Ben.

This letter. These photographs. This betrayal.

All of it paling beside the realisation that I don't care except in that it delays me from coming to you. Whatever joys I have found with him have been a salve to forget the bliss we knew. And I made that clear to him before I knew it for myself. I made it clear by tossing him aside on the merest whisper of your return for five days.

I will sort this first. Make peace with the demons I have bred here. I will make arrangements for Kit and then I will come and find you. Whoever I am, whatever I become, it is only going to be truthful if I face that self with you.

I know this because it takes the shape of fear. This fluttering rawness inside that you may turn me away, as you did Ted. That what I need to find peace for myself may not be what you need any longer.

Here I sit, writing a diary, when all along I've been writing to you without the courage to send it.

14

M oth sat, cross-legged, bag tucked into his body, waiting for Fehran on the outskirts of Onbir-nisan. A sprig of dried lavender twirling between his fingers.

This is the last time.

'Pazartesi, Onbirnisan'da.' Monday, at Onbirnisan.

It had been three weeks since Fehran sent him running from Dilru's warehouse with those words. He'd waited three hours on the first Monday. Trying to convince himself that the route must have changed and Fehran would show up. The second week, he'd waited until a farmer had turned up after lunch. Today he'd been there since first light and would wait until dark.

Then that's it, not again.

He would accept Dilru had given up on him and make the decisions pressing in on him. He'd picked a spot close enough that Fehran would spot him and discreet enough to loiter. Five hours he'd been sat here, looking first one way then the other. Praying the squat flat-roofed tin building he was wedged into the lee of would stay empty. Ahead of him dark green fields stretched out in neat rows. He could see up the road to the junction where Fehran had always dropped him off. A wide space where five lanes collided and drivers had to work out for themselves who had right of way. On his side of the junction lay the unofficial rubbish tip of the local town, the "building yard" for their makeshift camp.

A crossroads should look tidier. A clear-cut bisection of choices with neat signposts and obvious choices. Leaving England had been a choice between a life he didn't want and a single shot at crafting a life for himself. The only challenge finding a safe home for Nat, dealing with his guilt at leaving her.

Maybe there's a bit of guilt you're still carrying.

He looked down the road to the camp. It had been a rough three weeks. Fehran not turning up the first Monday had pushed him back on his own resources. Eking out the money from Isabelle to keep finding enough food that he could still walk into camp and not be beaten up for his tent and thrown out. He hadn't dared to take the bike back there. He'd found an old track, unused and overgrown that ran alongside the road he took out of Onbirnisan to the camp and hid the bike there. Tied to a tree with the chain and covered with branches. Every night he lay awake, wondering if it would be there when he went back.

Moth looked back at the junction. The rubbish dump grew relentlessly. Locals justifying the ease of dumping it there as a charitable donation for the illegal camp while complaining to the district about the very same camp. He'd picked a distance far enough away to avoid the worst of the smell. Kadri would often turn up with a timber strut or piece of plastic, proud of his rescue, victorious without a rat bite. Atabey wouldn't go anywhere near it.

Can't blame him. It bloody stinks.

The junction remained empty. The second week, after Fehran failed to show up again, he'd made the long trip to Akcakale to blag food from Aidan. But Aidan had gone. Jonah had gone. Jose had gone. It had been four months since Bonn left. When he found Eba out in the camp, she'd given him a smile and a grimace but not stopped moving between tents as she visited her women. The teams were being split up and sent on elsewhere. The residents were expected to start self-governing and building a sustainable future.

'How is this a sustainable future?' Moth asked.

'There's nowhere for them to go, Moth.' Eba was deft, persistent in her presence in the family arena, soft with her voice and hands. She had a way of fitting in, not causing aggravation between families. Moth could sense the men watching him, tightening up at his presence. 'It's what happens. Camps start out temporary and become permanent.'

'What about the ones not in the official camps?'

She straightened up from her position, checking the health of a tiny, crinkled baby lost in a huge nappy. A hand patting the mother's arm. Inside the tent doorway Moth could see four more children peeping out at the strangers. How did you raise five children in a tent in the middle of a football pitch of other tents? Eba finished her consultation, picked up her bag and began walking down the pathway.

'They either have to get to a camp that will register them or try to find work in the nearby towns.'

'And if they can get to the borders?' Moth asked, not looking at her.

'Greece is doubling down on registration. They're doing anything they can to send them back to Turkey or funnelling them onto islands to stop their movement. The conditions there are far worse than here. Overcrowding, underfunding, lack of medical access. If you know anyone trying to get to Europe, tell them not to bother. Chances are they'll end up with the traffickers or in a Greek island camp.'

Moth didn't reply.

'What about you?' Eba asked. 'I thought you were heading home to retrain.'

'Yeah, still waiting for the call.'

'You got some place to stay?'

'Uh-huh. Friend of Bonn's in Urfa.'

'Are your visas current?'

'Uh-huh.'

Eba pulled up in her stride and looked at him, dropping her bag between her feet.

'I hope so because the military are getting hard on illegals. Any excuse to deport anyone they can, and they'll be all over it.'

He didn't respond. She was too sharp by far.

'Bonn been in touch yet?'

'Not yet,' he admitted.

Unlikely to either, with the wrong email address.

'He will, they messed him about big time. Sent him on a fact-finding mission for months between camps. He had to go to New York to deliver his report. I'm not sure he's even made it to UNGO yet. Or if he's going to get there at all before he has to go to Zaatari.'

'Where did Aidan go?'

'Not sure.' She stretched out her back and picked up the

bag again. 'He fell out with Yves by the end of the first week and decided he needed to find work elsewhere.'

That means you're getting no food from here.

'I'll let Bonn know you called in, remind him to sort that training.'

'Nah, don't worry, I got other plans now.'

'Really?'

'Yeah?'

'You going home or got work elsewhere?'

'Yeah. I better let you get on. Good to see you, Eba, take care.'

He started to walk away, she was getting too curious.

'Moth, wait,' she called out. 'You sure you don't need anything?'

'I'm good, yeah.'

He'd kept walking before she asked too many questions. Walked back out the mile to where he'd left the bike. Looked at it and remembered all over again how hard it had been to keep going through Europe, get back on the bike each day. Keep pedalling. Back when bad memories had been strong enough to push him on.

And that was when the bike fitted you.

Because it had been a long, uncomfortable trip from Suruc to Akcakale. The bike truncated and cramping his leg rhythm. His hips rigid with discomfort when he got off. Looking at the bike, he'd had to fight the urge to throw it at the roadside and walk away.

But that guilt thing kicked in again, didn't it?

Moth leant back against the shed, staring at the junction, counting the details again. The soft verges, the turning space carved out from the dried, compacted soil, the ragged spokes of the five lanes that met, the lumps of looser earth that sat in the middle.

He looked down the road in the direction of the camp. He would go that way, at the end of the day when he knew Fehran wasn't coming any more. He would go back to the camp and tell Kadri his plan.

Plan? That's a stretch.

It was a loose plan.

And a stupid one at that.

But Kadri would snatch a fart from a drunken sailor if it blew his way. Moth had returned from Akcakale in the late morning to a camp ripped apart. His absence for two days spanning the dawn arrival of two army transport trucks and a squad of baton wielding soldiers. The camp had scattered, disappearing into the expanse of the old quarry, running for cover into the surrounding fields like mice before the cats.

More like rats.

It was an image Moth didn't want to focus on. The wriggling plastic mass of the dump too close for comfort.

The army had trashed the camp. Flattening the hovels it had taken all their energy to salvage and create. Leaving a churned dusty bowl of rubbish and a bitter battle for what was left. The older lads beating up on the younger children to claim bits of wood and plastic. Anger and fear a wall of scent Moth walked into and choked on. Eyes searching for the faded blue of the bike tent, his heart sinking at its absence. Berating himself for leaving it there because he didn't want to scare Kadri and Atabey that he was going.

Berating yourself for looking for the tent first.

Moth crunched himself round his bag with discomfort. He had panicked, looking for the tent before he'd looked for them. It had been humiliating. The combination of despair, loss, desperation, hatred. When he'd managed to push away the surge of panic, he'd looked up and taken in the reality. No more than half of those who'd been here when he'd left two days ago remained. Many of the youngest ones had gone. Too slow or too scared to run fast enough. Perhaps it was better that way, they would stand a chance of being registered. He began to look for the boys. Searching through the scuffles and knots of desperation.

He'd found them in the end. Kadri fighting away efforts to snatch what little they'd salvaged. His backpack slapping against his back. Atabey curled up in a foetal position, clutching a soft blue shape that Moth had to prise out of his fingers. They had snatched his tent before they ran. His tent, the battered metal cooking pot with a broken handle and the old blankets they slept on. Everything else was lost. Their spare clothes, their wash stuff, the precious stores of food they'd salvaged.

That first night had been grim. Camping in huddles, taking it in turns to stay awake, startled out of sleep by the sound of violence at every hour. Moth had gotten up twice to go and see what was going on. To try and help those he could hear shouting or crying. In the face of this new violence from the outside those on the inside had turned against each other. Each time Kadri had stopped him. While Atabey fell even deeper into a catatonic stupor of terror, rocking himself into a tighter ball.

He'd left the next day focused on getting food, rolling the tent into his backpack. He couldn't risk leaving it there again. He'd gone to Suruc, hoping to build connections with the aid agencies. Hoping to come back with clear news about where they might all move to.

Moth looked back to the junction. The sun was creeping

south. It must be getting near midday. His bit of shade at the
western side of the tin shed was leaning away from him. The
days were still warm but shortening, soon the nights would
begin to close in with a chill.

He'd returned to Suruc every day for a week, badgering a
local mechanic to help him alter the bike, counting the last of
his money from Isabelle, wondering how long it would last
split three ways. The aid agencies had tightened their doors,
fearful of the military. There was nothing for him or the
others here. When his money ran out, he'd be reduced to
begging or stealing, same as the rest of them. He bought a
tired bunch of lavender flowers from the fruit seller and set
out back to the camp with the finished bike. The scent rising
from the too small plastic bag of supplies. Teasing at him
with memory. Riding through the late harvest fields of Octo-
ber, watching as the farmers pulled their final crops from the
ground. Wondering what Leon or James were up to. The
memory of their hectic life as stable as the road beneath him,
while he floated across the top of it.

That's what really stings.

Not the violence he had to listen to at night. Or the beatings the next day. Not even the worry about another raid,
which would surely come. Not even the overwhelming sense
of relief that he got back to camp and Kadri and Atabey were
still there. He'd given Atabey the lavender and had a hug in
gratitude. A hug he had needed too. Even though his back
rippled with fear at who might see it. A memory of Italy
rising in a strange mix of crushed petals and sweaty, long-
limbed closeness.

Even that didn't hurt the most.

Moth pulled his warming toes out of the sun, shuffling
backwards another half foot. He should give up already.

Fehran was not going to come. Dilru wanted nothing more to do with him. He should head back, pack up and find a way to communicate with Kadri what he wanted to do.

It was a logistics point. He knew what he needed to do. But how to do it? Moth pulled the rucksack open and pulled out the map. He'd looked at it often enough to know it by heart. But the image of it, the shape of landscape, roads, boundaries, gave him a focus that thinking about the plan didn't achieve.

You're out of practice.

He'd lost the knack, the ability to push aside doubt, set a point and steer toward it.

You only ever had to get yourself there before.

He put a finger down and traced the roads snaking north.

If Eba was right, the borders through Istanbul into Greece would be harder than ever to pass. It was such a narrow focus of land. Not enough scope to get through. He couldn't go back through Istanbul, and neither could Kadri and Atabey.

South and east are out.

Which left only one way. They had to go north. They had to find a way through Georgia or across the Black Sea and come into Europe from the east. It was not going to be easy but...

... but you don't belong here.

Moth looked up from the map and felt the pressure of that thought as relentless as the sun. He couldn't stay here. He was going to run out of money, out of food and out of luck. But he couldn't leave them behind. Even if he hadn't worked out yet where he was going, he knew he couldn't walk away from Kadri and Atabey, leave them to this hopelessness. It would wake him in the night for the rest of his life.

A horn blared at the junction. He looked up, the sun

glaring off the side of a white truck. Fehran's white truck. An arm stuck out the window and waved at him. He scrambled to put the map away, tucked the backpack into the bushes at the side of the tin shed and loped down the road.

'Hey, I thought you'd given up on me,' he greeted Fehran as the guy climbed out. The guy's big arm grasping his, pulling him in for a back-slapping Turkish embrace.

'Mothy, thank Allah, you are well.'

Thank yourself. God had no part in this.

'How's Inci? Has Dilru forgiven me?'

'Big argument!' Fehran shook his head with a grin. 'Dilru angry for weeks! She shout your name to Allah and thrash Husnu.'

That's not good.

'Inci shout right back at her Anne.' Fehran leant back against the closed door of his cab and lit a strong cigarette, taking a deep pull on it.

'So, I'm in trouble?'

'Moth.' Fehran shook his head. 'Police come to warehouse all days to check for illegals.'

Moth hung his head. He'd never meant to bring difficulty to them. And now he'd lost his last friend in Turkey. Bonn was gone, Aidan, now Dilru.

'I can't come back, can I?'

Fehran sucked his mouth into a pucker with a deep pull on the cigarette and shook his head, unwilling to express the news he had to impart.

'Tell them I'm sorry.' Moth looked up at Fehran. 'I never meant to hurt them.'

'Ah, you know Dilru, too much hand and mouth. She is scared for her children, talks big and hits first to protect them.' Fehran pulled open the door to his truck and reached into it. Taking a step up and lunging across the seats to grasp something. Moth looked away from his big backside leering over the top of his pants.

Yeah, he's no Luca.

'Inci send you this.' Fehran dropped a box of food at his feet, reached back in and pulled out his panniers. 'And these.'

Moth looked at them sat on the dusty road and thought how pathetic they looked. Had he really left England with no more than those tired looking pannier bags?

'Inci say I must ask you where you will be?' Fehran crossed his arms and looked down his long nose at him. 'Will you stay in Suruc?'

'No, I'm going north.' It was as close as he'd got with the route. Even though he knew it might change. 'Tell Inci I'm thinking about home.'

The man nodded in approval, beaming with happiness.

Moth knew his language was not sharp enough to catch the nuances. And it wasn't an outright lie, he was thinking about home.

Just not your own.

'I must go, Mothy, it is time to say our farewell.' Fehran held out both arms and grasped Moth's, looking hard into his face. 'May Allah keep you safe and help you.'

'May Dilru not bust your arse on a daily basis,' Moth returned. 'Thank you, I'm glad to have met you, Fehran.'

'And may Allah bring you back to us again when life is good once more.'

Moth stepped back as the truck rocked toward Fehran climbing back in, the door slamming closed behind him. He reached through the window as he started up the truck and waved farewell. Moth watched as he veered round the dust-bowl in the middle of the junction and pulled away from him.

The noisy truck clunking through gears and speeding up. Wondering if he would ever hear Dilru's voice berating him again or see Inci's dimples as she mocked him.

Moth swung the panniers across his shoulders and wrestled the heavy box of supplies into his arms. It was going to be a logistics exercise to get it all back to the camp.

Well, logistics is the game you're in now.

Moth went back to the tin shed and dragged all his loot behind it. It was past midday. He had the rest of the day to think through his plan and get back to base. He sat down, the tin popping behind his back as he leant against it. Looking out across the fields toward the north. The end of yet more friendships sharpening his longing.

It wasn't enough to have a plan that took him from one day to the next anymore. Bonn had given him a taste of more. A sense of what he wanted.

He gave you a sense of belonging.

The same thing that took James and Leon into the fields each day, knowing what they were about. The same thing that took Bonn onto the next shifting field of his life. That kept Inci working toward a vision of her life only she knew. It was what had taken Luca to Geneva.

A sense of purpose and worth.

Travelling through Europe he'd belonged to himself, running from a life that wanted to tell him otherwise. He'd belonged nowhere, to nobody, and it had been perfect. In Bonn's camp, he'd known belonging for the first time in his life. And he missed it.

Moth missed Bonn giving him grief, he missed Aidan, the team meetings, the sense of exhausted achievement he'd gone to sleep with. He missed Dilru and Inci. All of them telling him to go home.

Home.

It was nothing he'd ever known. Whatever memories from his childhood he held, his father had poisoned them all. Riverdell had only been home for five brief months, no matter how important those months had been to him. He'd found a real home here, where he thought he belonged. And it had felt great.

Sitting in the filthy illegal camp waiting for the next raid was not purpose. Begging money from Isabelle to survive was not independence. Travelling alone was not belonging, it was an escape. And whatever he had shared with Luca had not meant enough for Luca to do something about it.

Perhaps he didn't have a home to return to, but maybe he could at least try to get Kadri and Atabey to a safer place. He could give them a means to get there. The bike that had worked for him could work for them. While he figured out what to do next.

He couldn't go home like this. He couldn't face Nat, or Beau, or Mila, or Kit, let alone Luca. Perhaps Isabelle was the only one who could help him, like she had before. And in return, perhaps he would go to India with her. And see if it might be the next place he could belong.

India. He tried to visualise belonging there, in such a huge place. He couldn't get a grip on that idea. It was vast and empty in his mind.

He pulled out the map again, unfolding it on his lap. A map helped make the future real. He traced his finger north to Samsun. A bold name on the edge of the Black Sea with dotted lines running away from it across the blue water. Moth put his finger to the spot. All three of them had to get there.

No, first, you need to get all this tack back to the camp.

No, first he had to hide this tack, not take it back to the camp.

Moth hitched his backpack, tussled the panniers and the box up and into his arms and walked back to the road. There was a lot to do.

HE WALKED into the camp weighed down with doubt and came hard up against the atmosphere. Taking in the strange silence and averted eyes as he wove between the huddled groups. Arriving on the trampled ground that had been their reclaimed spot.

The plastic sheet caught on the splinters of a broken pallet had gone. The pallet was upended and busted. The fire had been kicked across the open space, the cooking pot was gone. In the dusty mess left by the skirmish, Atabey was a hunched figure, clutching Kadri's ripped bag to his chest. Lying next to him, a burnt blanket was covering a shaking, foetal-curled mass. Strewn across the trampled space, the lavender flowers were crushed and driven into dullness by dust and the simmering darkness.

Moth wanted to feel anger. He wanted to find the person responsible and drain the sickening mass of feelings that rose with the scent of crushed lavender into that person one fist at a time. Anger would have been easier to deal with than the trembling mix of fear, memory and guilt that was gripping his innards. It was his fault. He should not have left them here alone.

Atabey flinched when Moth crouched down next to him. Moth put a hand on his shoulder, feeling the tremors ripping through the thin frame. Atabey lifted his face to show eyes puffy with crying, a lip swollen from a punch. That Atabey had taken punches of his own showed how bad Kadri must be. Moth prayed it had only been a beating.

'Come,' he said to Atabey. 'We go now.'

Whatever state Kadri was in, it was better to get him away than risk another night in the camp.

Atabey stared at him through dust-riddled eyelashes, tears and dirt clumped into dried, ugly mascara. Making his eyes even larger, his distress more exaggerated. Moth gritted his jaw against the anger and fear it touched in him.

It was too much to face. The thought of walking all that last, long hour back. With both damaged boys. Even in the worst nights in Bonn's camp, he hadn't felt this hopeless. He'd had back-up, the ability to bring those in trouble to someone who would help. The strength of a good day's sleep to keep him strong, regular meals to keep him healthy.

Perhaps you should leave them.

How would he get these two boys all the way across Turkey and out of the country? He'd have to practically carry them. He'd underestimated the scope of it.

You've overestimated yourself.

He couldn't possibly ask them to try this. To leave, to trust him, to take a chance.

Moth sat back on his haunches and looked at Atabey as he hunched over the bag. He placed a hand on Kadri's leg beneath the crisped edge of the blanket, felt it flinch and wrap tighter up. The terror strengthened him.

He'd done it himself. Left England alone, travelled across Europe.

You weren't alone. You had help, resources, months of planning and preparation.

Yes, he had. But he'd still done it. And there was a time he'd thought it equally impossible.

'Hey.' He squeezed Kadri's leg. 'It's me, you need to get up.'

They need hope. That was what the bike had been to him. Hope. A chance. An idea that grew and fed his determination. From the moment Isabelle had told him about it.

He nudged Atabey again. Dusk was threatening. If they didn't leave soon, it would be too late to see by. He had to get them away, get them back to the bike, get Kadri into the tent. They couldn't risk another night here.

'Atabey.' Moth gripped his shoulder again, made him look up. 'You must get up. We go now.'

Moth took the backpack from his back, opened it and prised the bag out of Atabey's hands. It was ripped and torn, and lighter than it had ever looked. Everything the boys had gathered had been stolen. How they had managed to hang onto the bag was a miracle.

It probably made the beating worse, they should have given it up.

Moth tucked it into his backpack. He turned his attention to Kadri, peeling back the edges of the blanket. Kadri assumed the tightest knot of a protective curl he could. Arms over face, elbows protecting stomach, knees curled up. It was a position that made Moth want to kick someone. He knelt, prised the hands away from his face. Held the shaking fingers out and ran his hands over Kadri's arms.

Have you got any breakages to deal with?

He'd watched Eba enough to know. Arms, shins and ribs took the brunt.

A broken leg is going to make this a whole lot harder.

He ran light hands along the outer extremities of Kadri's protective curl. Teasing him out of the knot, talking in a steady murmur, giving him encouragement. If there had been a leg breakage he would have flinched by now.

In Akcakale it had been a case of picking his battles. He'd guard one toilet block knowing he'd be leaving another vulnerable. Part way through the night, he'd move on, give another area of the camp a chance to use the facilities with safety. Often arrive too late and pick up the bruised or bleeding. Get them into the medic tent with strong hands and whispered courage.

It wasn't the pain you had to talk your way through.

It was the shame. It always came down to facing the shame. Not being able to turn to those you counted as family. Too scared to seek their help, dreading their disgust.

You know all about that.

Isabelle and Kit had finally pulled him through that curtain of shame, in Italy. Making him face up to his roadside rape, to his father's abuse. The memory of those days still made him warm with discomfort, but he had locked it away behind the gates of that villa. Safe in Isabelle's hands, put down at last. But he would never forget the shame that he'd carried for all the years before then.

'Kadri, get up,' he told him. Kadri opened swollen eyes and blinked at him. The level of dirt and blood caked onto his face had none of the ridiculous appeal it added to Atabey. He looked the victim of the attack he was. Moth peeled his arms away from his body and began to check his shoulders, running probing hands down his chest and onto his ribs. When he reached the lower rungs Kadri grunted and sucked in a shallow, agonised breath.

Ah, ribs it is.

Ribs he could cope with. He eased an arm beneath Kadri's shoulders and lifted him gently up. Gasping sounds of resistance and pain trying to stop him when the strength to resist was gone.

'We have to go,' Moth told him, firm but kind. Atabey lifted his head from his knees and began to cry at Kadri's shallow gasps.

'Atabey,' Moth called. He pulled his backpack closer and, one arm supporting Kadri, pulled a long-sleeved T-shirt out of the bag.

Moth began to wrap the T-shirt round Kadri's ribs. Padding out the loose, spongy section with the body and stretching the arms to tie it in place. It would be ruined, but it might help them get through the long next few hours. Kadri's resistance at least brought Atabey to help. Moth let him support Kadri's back, focusing on the difficulty of tying the short, bulky ends of the sleeves.

That's what you looked like the night they found you up that mountain.

Moth pushed the images away. Shame and hatred accompanied those memories.

He replaced them, with gratitude. The couple who had found him, Luca arriving, Kit and Isabelle in Lovere. It was good to be on the other end, being the one who helped. He crouched down and put a hand under Kadri's shoulders. Thankful for all the inches and ounces of his massive frame.

You're going to have to practically carry him out of Turkey.

'Get up,' he told Kadri. 'Rabe, heval. Em dicin.'

Bit by bit, groan by groan, with encouragement from Atabey, he moved Kadri. First to standing, then to leaning against Atabey. He was grateful for Atabey's height, balancing his own and giving Kadri a chance at staying upright. Moth rolled the blanket up and tucked it into his bag. He glanced up, evening was settling fast. He took Kadri's arm across his shoulder and began to move them forward. Staring down the scathing eyes that followed them. The time for planning was gone.

It's time to go.

He felt it creep into his bones with a conviction he had been missing since the days cycling through Europe.

It *was* time to go.

IT TOOK four excruciating hours to get Kadri the three miles it had taken him an hour to walk. Every wincing step down the lane Moth had wished for a white campervan to show up and rescue them while dreading the sound of vehicles approaching. His ears straining to hear over Kadri's ragged breathing and the shuffling of his feet. It was a shifting night of patchy cloud chasing over a searing moon. Though the road stayed empty Moth felt spooked. It was bright, too bright. They would be visible from a good distance and unable to hide. When they'd reached the back path that followed the dried-up brook, he'd felt safer, but their pace had slowed. Kadri stopping repeatedly to catch his breath. Moth sat apart and watched them huddle up in a knot of pain and desperation. Excluded. Needed but not yet trusted. Pushing them on before they were ready.

It was well gone midnight by the time they reached the dense tangle of scrappy bushes and fallen branches that covered the bike and his belongings. Kadri buckling on the weed covered ground and curling into exhaustion, his head on Atabey's knees, the blanket thrown over him. Their shapes a huddled, single mass in the near dark. Moth was exhausted, his body twisted from supporting Kadri, but he didn't sit

down. Focusing his pain on getting the bike out. Lightening
the load in the panniers. Putting all he could into the backpack and strapping it tight. Checking the tyres. He watched,
between his tasks and the passing clouds, the vivid shine of
Atabey's hand as it soothed across the dark curls of Kadri's
head. Creating ripples as it passed, settling like disturbed
water, returning to start again.

Moth finally sat down, hands empty of distraction.
Listening to the sounds of the night. Pulling a handful of
fatigued weeds into his hands and picking them apart.

This is too close for comfort.

He hadn't got them far enough away from the camp. They
needed to be further away, before Kadri found the strength to
think, to complain, to stall the momentum.

Anyone could have followed you.

He let the minutes tick away, watching Atabey's head
droop and snap back as he curled over the lump in his lap.
Another hour's rest and he would move them on. North. Over
the other side of the main road that ran to Urfa.

He felt his own head droop.

Don't!

Moth's head snapped up. If they fell asleep here it could
be the end of it all. He stood up, slapping his arms to wake
himself. Atabey lifted his head, blinking at him. Moth
checked the bike one last time and nodded at Atabey. He
shook his head in resistance. Moth rolled the bike over,
scooped down and pulled the blanket off them. They had to
get moving. To use the quiet hours of night to get away from
the camp, away from Onbirnisan. They could sleep when
morning came. Pushing, prodding, needling, he made them
move. Rousing Kadri back to pain, pulling him up from the
ground. Strapping the backpack onto Atabey and pulling it

tight. Stumbling along the dark track until they came back to the road. Moth let Kadri slump to the ground one last time and stood upright, stretching with relief. It was agonising, supporting the shorter weight of Kadri on one side, trying to control the heavy bike with his right hand. The exhausted mess of Atabey on the far side dragging them all down. He moved toward the road, wondering how he would ever get them through the next day, let alone through Turkey.

It's a toss-up which is the greater burden, Kadri with broken ribs or Atabey with a backpack.

Moth hovered in the cover of the final trees to peer down the road, the old tin shed glinting back at him. The clouds had receded, turning the road into a leaden thread chasing through the fields. He peered up the road toward the camp, turned to look back toward the junction. There were about three hours left before dawn. He wanted to be on the other side of town, in the fields on the back roads north before he let them stop and rest. His back was a mesh of pain and rigidity. He crouched down to relieve its pain, curling in on himself to stretch the pain outwards, heard the whine of brakes at the junction and glanced up. Lights flashed across the tin shed as they turned right to head down the lane toward him. Moth shuffled backwards on his feet into the cover of the trees, glancing at the bike. It was leaning against a tree, the boys huddled up together in front of it. He looked out at the road from his low position. Watched as the lights came closer, as one, two, three, four military trucks glided by in low, muffled gear. Moth's heart lurched sideways. His ability to act cut into slivers like the road between the passing brightness of lights. He stayed immobile as they passed. Seeing the badges on the caps of the guards up front.

They're heading for the camp.

There was only one reason military trucks would be using this road. It ran to nowhere.

Getting into position for another pre-dawn raid.

Moth looked up at the skies as the dust they raised resettled, scowling at the stars and listening hard. The road was now ten times more dangerous. Would any more trucks come this way? Straight north was the swiftest route, but it took them close to the main road, the route the army was likely using. Did he wait the night out in the trees?

No. Move. As fast as you can.

He had no more than two precious hours before the roads were crawling with military searching out the scattered camp refugees. If they were coming back this soon, they weren't going to be lenient. He went back to the bike. Kadri was sitting cross-legged on the ground, huddled over his ribs, Atabey was looking at him with eyes wide with fright. He'd seen the trucks too. He knew exactly where they were going. And that, with them leaving the same night, they could never go back. The suspicion would fall on them. His breath was short and fast, panic kicking into him.

'Lesker,' Moth said. Soldiers. 'Dive em bicin.'

Atabey began to mutter back at him, language overpowered by fear, sputtering and rising on a note of fear. Moth tried to shush him, but the night had taken its toll. Kadri reached a hand up and gripped his leg, pulling at his knee to calm him, talking to him.

'We must go,' Moth told Kadri.

Kadri nodded and held a hand out to be pulled up. Moth wheeled the bike the last few yards and out onto the solidity of the lane. Listening hard for any sound of traffic. Hearing the softness of wind in the leaves.

Let's hope this works.

James wouldn't recognise the bike. It had been butchered beyond any plans he had once had for it. Moth had added to the ugly welding and reshaping that had begun in Urfa. He'd had the mechanics in Suruc fit a triangular back seat that folded down over the panniers and added foot pegs onto the back wheel axle. The slim road wheels he'd cycled through Europe on had been replaced with sturdier, thicker versions.

The problem was, he'd been counting on Kadri's energy and determination for the pedal power. The plan couldn't work until Kadri had recovered.

But it doesn't need to work yet. It only needs to get you out of town.

One chance is all you need.

In the darkness Moth couldn't help but grin. It had been a long while since that quote tormented him. He wondered what Luca would have to say about his plan. One chance indeed. That was about all they had, and he'd catch it by the tail if he had to.

He made Atabey hold the bike upright and pushed Kadri onto the back seat and put his feet up on the pegs, tapping his feet to emphasise the importance of keeping them there. Before either boy could complain Moth straddled the bar of the bike and began to walk it forward. Action would overcome what language was incapable of. If he could move them forward for the next few days, they would see what he was trying to achieve. Atabey walked alongside, muttering and stumbling under the weight of the backpack. Moth didn't wait, he slipped a foot to the pedal, pushed himself back onto the seat and let his foot catch the other pedal as it rose. They were away. Moving down the road. Kadri gripping to his shirt. Atabey trying to keep up. The extra weight on the bike a shock on his leg muscles. Within ten heavy rotations Atabey had fallen behind and was calling out. Moth kept going. If another truck came now, it was all over. Behind him he heard Atabey's feet gather into a slapping run. Kadri called out to him, coughing with pain. Moth looked forward and focused on the pull at his muscles. He'd been too long out of practice. It was going to test him. The tin shed crept up on them, rippling as he passed it, fell behind. He approached the shapeless mass of the scrap pile, passed round the dusty middle of the junction, the first houses creeping closer. If he went any slower, they would tumble. It took momentum gained and sustained to keep the weight moving. As soon as they reached the buildings he stopped, put a foot down and took the weight of the bike. Behind him he could see Atabey stumbling along the road.

'Barkirin!' he called back. More anxious of soldiers in trucks than residents in houses.

Atabey tripped and fell in the road, the rucksack taking him down hard. Moth swore.

Be patient. He's been through more than you.

Moth manoeuvred the bike into the shadows of an alleyway opening. Tilting it to lean against the wall, struggling to keep Kadri on, get himself off and keep the bike upright. He grabbed Kadri's hand and made him prop himself upright, turned and belted back down the road to Atabey. He was sitting up as he got there, pulling off the backpack and kicking it in frustration.

Moth grabbed it, threw it over his shoulder and hauled Atabey up with a merciless grasp on his upper arm, grabbing him round the chest and turning in one hard movement to drag him back to the buildings. As he straightened, he could see all the way to the main road, to a line of lights in close formation moving his way. Silent in the distance.

He had less than a minute before they made the junction.

Shit. Move your arse.

'Come on, bloody run.'

Moth dragged Atabey along, the bag heavy and slapping on his back. The line of lights turning down the road that led to them, a distant hum the building pressure of their imminent arrival. Atabey crying out in fear as he saw them.

'Shut up! Run.'

The noise of the trucks building, gathering speed and force even as they slowed down, coming closer. The lights disappearing behind buildings. Moth looked ahead, he was the wrong side of the junction they would come to, beyond it he could see the darkness of the houses, the alleyway where Kadri and the bike hid.

You're not going to make it.

Atabey was losing speed, not gaining it. Overwhelmed and terrified. His legs stumbling into each other as they ran, knocking his feet off course. The lights of the trucks appeared again, flashed back out of sight. They were only a few bends away from the junction.

You're not going to make it. Turn back. Hide.

Panic flooded through his muscles, weighing them down, slowing his speed. He couldn't turn back. There was nowhere to hide.

Moth pulled the bag from his shoulder and threw it into the dark edges of the road. He tightened his grip and dragged Atabey's feet from the ground as they hurtled forward. They came level with the stinking junk pile.

You're not going to...

The lights swung into a laser point, focusing on the central scrap of dirt in the junction, darkening the road as they lit up the funnelled point. Engines reverberating into the still night, brakes squealing as they prepared to turn.

... make it.

Visions of a Turkish jail loomed in Moth's mind.

A small cell with no light and too many bodies.

The stench as real as the junk pile.

Desperation stirred him. Moth shoved with all his might. Pushing his weight and frame onto Atabey and taking them both into the stinking pile of plastic and wood. Closing his eyes and putting a hand up to cover the gasp of air taken to fund Atabey's scream.

He twisted in mid fall, wrapping his arms and legs round the thin, struggling frame of the boy. Letting his weight take them into the nest of splinters, nails, reeking refuse and rats.

Feeling the bite of metal and wood in his back, the flurry of small bodies and the closeness of skin as the plastic swallowed them. The swinging light of the trucks illuminated the sky briefly before it all disappeared. The plastic shutting out the truck lights, the moonlight, the stars and air. Filling his lungs with a deathly, suffocating stench and sucking them both downward.

'FOR THE SAKE of the rose you must water the thorns.'

'That's a terrible thing to say about anyone,' Isabelle protested.

'The truth normally is,' Kate said.

'She's worn out and mad at me, you can't blame her.'

'She's mad at everyone rather than face being mad at herself and find a solution.' Kate was making lunch with Indigo on her hip. 'This is no good for spine alignment, we're going to end up crippled.'

Isabelle watched them move about the kitchen gathering a meal from the safety of the kitchen table, avoiding the remotest flicker of guilt that she should take her daughter back. Indigo had developed a ten-minute window of calm before she became restless and miserable. Roving through the house looking for Deryn and clinging to anyone she could find before becoming restless again.

It had been two weeks since she'd asked Asha to find alternative childcare. Which was impossible. There was no way the exhaustion of that time could be compressed into two weeks. Well, sixteen days, to be precise. Working in snippets of disturbance, making more mistakes than normal as she clawed her way up through her orders. Asha, having left in a storm, had maintained a total radio silence.

'Don't you get bullied into going back on it either.' Kate pointed a soupy spoon at her, moving it rapidly out of Indigo's reaching fingers. 'Too hot. Hot, hot, hot.'

'I can't go back on what I never meant to happen in the first place.' Isabelle's eyes roved beyond them, to watch the clouds whipping across the pigeon sky through the large window behind the sink. 'I never meant her to stop bringing Deryn altogether.'

'Maybe you didn't explain yourself clearly.'

'Duh, you think?'

'Sarcasm will not help the matter,' Kate retorted.

'You seem to use it often enough to suggest otherwise.'

'Isabelle!'

'Ok, sorry,' Isabelle puffed a stale, exhausted breath out.

There hadn't been a night when Indigo hadn't slept with her since Asha stopped coming. Creeping into her bed in the small hours and kicking all night long. On those nights when Steve stopped over, Isabelle had taken her back to bed and fallen asleep there, rising both Saturday mornings to find him gone to work. A note left on her pillow or by the kettle. Against the grudge that Asha was holding, he seemed to be compensating with an impossible level of consideration. The two presenting themselves at the same time was making her teeth ache. Or maybe that was the sheer level of caffeine needed to keep the show going.

'You should go and see her, make it clear you're sorry and work out how to fix it. In a way that works for both of you.'

'You know, you have this knack to make the impossible not only sound reasonable but almost enjoyable.' Isabelle put her head on the table.

'Head off the table, woman,' Kate told her. 'You won't get anywhere talking to the wood.'

'I won't get anywhere talking to Asha,' Isabelle told the table.

'Not while you've got your head on the table, you won't.'

Isabelle lifted her head and propped it on her folded arms on the table. Looking sideways at Kate made her appear somehow more capable, not less.

'You need to be clearer about what you want, what you need.' Kate swapped Indigo to the other hip and teased her with the dripping spoon. The scent of parsnip and paprika wafted across to Isabelle. She was even tired enough to be hungry.

'Isabelle?'

'Hmm?'

'Do you know what you want from this?'

'More time to work?' She watched them from the odd angle of her turned head.

'Specifically. More time on what days? For what exchange of care in return for having Deryn?'

'Deryn?' Indigo said and they both winced and waited.

'No, parsnip soup,' Kate countered. She scraped a finger's worth of cooling soup from the wooden spoon, blew on it and put her finger to Indigo's mouth.

'Is there a way you can arrange more childcare support here at the house, which you both pay for?'

'She can't pay for it, they're struggling as it is.'

'They're struggling because they wanted it.' Kate waved away her concerns with the spoon. 'You don't see James bemoaning the pressure, he's working his bollocks off. It's exactly what she came here and asked you for, remember? The chance to own their own home.'

'So why does she hate me?'

'She doesn't, stop dramatising it.' Kate walked round the table and passed Indigo to her.

Isabelle sat back in her chair and put her daughter on the edge of the table, cradled between her arms, her feet furling over the edge and into her lap.

'She's a hard-working mother with a farmer for a husband. One day she'll look back and be proud of what she's done and grateful she can call it her own. She might even have the decency to blush at some of her finer tempers, but we'll not be the ones reminding her of it. She's got a bigger heart than to stay mad at you forever. Besides, Hester holds that spot already. If you go and give her solid dates and long-term solutions, she'll forgive you the argument and move on. Maybe smooth it along with a good dose of humility.'

Isabelle felt Indigo's chubby legs swinging across her lap as Kate got out bowls and began cutting bread. Solid dates. Long-term solutions. She tried to visualise that. The weeks creeping toward Christmas, the rise in her orders, the increase in phone calls from Kit. She looked at the growing pile of tree brochures and felt more overwhelmed.

Kate put a platter of bread on the table, swapped Indigo for a bowl of soup and put her on the chair between them.

'So, can you have a solid think about which days you want to work? I know you're tired, but we can't go on as we have these last two weeks. You girls have the same problem, you should be able to solve it together.'

Isabelle thought about those two weeks. It had been hard enough in the week. Indigo clingy and disturbed. Kate squeezing in the last of her groups for the year and trying to do more. Rob taking both Fridays off work and being there when Steve turned up. Rob going home only to return the next morning and spend the weekend giving her the chance to work. The weekends had been even harder. Because she had felt both redundant, able to work freely, able to think near enough to the edge of reason and visualise how she and Indigo might take some time away and go to India, go and find Moth, go and get a break from the relentless routine of work and child, work and house. Only to face a call from Kit with a question about the tree, or a request to measure the banister for a garland. To watch Rob curled up with Indigo in his lap and a book between them and the world. To find Steve had brought fresh steak from the butchers with him and was there in the evening helping Kate to cook a family meal. Pouring her a glass of wine as she walked into the kitchen, talking to Rob about work while Indigo played with a small spindle he'd carved for her.

The elements of her life did not fit into a tidy whole she could arrange into the neat solution that Kate could visualise.

'I'll try.'

'What's making it hard?'

Isabelle picked up her spoon and looked at the soup. It was artistically finished with a combination of toasted bread-crumbs, bacon and a flutter of parsley. It was perfect. All she had to do was eat it. Stirring the crunchy top into the depths, she remembered the stinging comment Asha had hurled at her about Indigo's father. A bitterness that tainted every day since. It turned her stomach when she had a moment alone to gather her thoughts, or sat down to eat, or soothed Indigo to sleep. Isabelle slid the spoon along the edge of the hot soup, the delicious smell sticking in her nostrils as she faced the thought of Asha raising that subject.

'I have no idea.'

Kate stirred milk into Indigo's soup to cool it and switched between her own lunch and attempting to control the spread of spicy parsnip gloop from gluing together the covers of her gardening brochures.

'What are you afraid of?'

Isabelle looked up. Kate was focusing on Indigo. Only the super cool tone of her query, the nonchalance, the absence of any look in her direction made Isabelle realise she was worried.

'Afraid?' Isabelle asked.

'I know you don't like confrontation,' Kate said. 'Asha can be fierce, but she's not Hester. You two have a great friend-ship, it can weather some storms.'

'I know.' Isabelle began to eat. 'This is lovely, thank you.'

Kate finally looked at her, spoon raised and held out to the side in disbelief. The kitchen seemed to focus its sparkle on the raised spoon. Isabelle looked beyond Kate's raised eyebrows, to the raised covers of the Aga like eyes looking at the disturbance, the dinner plates on the dresser leaning closer, the slight drip of a tap hinting at pressure behind it.

She blinked under the scrutiny and wished herself outside, on the other side of the wide glass, beyond the garden, the river.

'What?' Isabelle said. 'It's delicious.'

'You're complimenting my cooking?'

'Don't I always?'

'No, Isabelle, you don't.' Kate sat back in her chair and frowned at Isabelle, then looked at Indigo between them. She sucked her lips in and asked, 'Is it this?'

Isabelle watched Kate side-eyeing Indigo. 'Huh?'

'Is it Asha always asking questions that are none of her business that you're scared of?'

Isabelle looked out of the window again. In the distance she could vaguely see the curve of the trees on the opposite bank of the river as they bent away to the west. Opening the vista for the perfect sunset displays that lingered on Riverdell's western walls and graced the gardens. She resisted the urge to put her spoon down, pick up Indigo and go for a long walk.

'Some things are easier to avoid than sort,' Kate said. 'Is that what you're thinking?'

Isabelle stared into the depths of her soup bowl and wondered if she had the courage to admit it. Kate let the silence build to a cake-cooking pressure level. Even Indigo seemed to be watching her. The house leant into the moment, the sense of its weight and scale above them cracking Isabelle.

'I just, well, I was thinking of going to see Moth,' she admitted, looking at Kate.

'In Europe? Is he still in Europe? Turkey, wasn't it?'

'We were thinking about taking a trip to India.'

'India.'

The word sat between them, quiet, worried, spoiling in the light. Kate put her spoon down on the table and gave up trying to control the spread of Indigo's soup.

'But, what about Christmas?' Kate asked. 'I thought you were hoping to get him home for Christmas. At least, that's what you said Kit doing Christmas was all about.'

Isabelle didn't answer.

'Or are you planning to go away for Christmas and leave Kit in charge of the rest of us?' Kate demanded.

'No.' Isabelle protested. 'I don't know. I'm trying to focus on work, and I don't know how to sort Asha, and I want a break from it all. I haven't been away for over four years, Kate. I feel, sort of...well...'

'Stagnant?'

'Kind of, yes.'

'Stuck?'

'Sort of wedged.'

'Trapped?'

'No, not trapped.' Isabelle sat back in her chair and looked up at the high ceiling to gather her thoughts. 'I love our life together, all of it. But I miss the ability to travel, I miss India. I can feel the shape of my life being pulled into a place that fits those around me but not necessarily me. And I'm worried that Moth is a bit lost too. And I don't want Indigo growing up thinking Riverdell is the centre of the universe. It's a rather warped perspective on life.'

'You took far too much of what Asha said in the heat of the moment to heart.'

'Perhaps.' Isabelle looked back at her soup, stirring the soggy croutons into the cooling mush.

'And mounting a rescue mission for Moth is the excuse you need to leave and avoid facing Asha?'

'It's not a rescue mission. I don't want to leave. But maybe take a holiday.'

'How long a holiday?' Kate asked. 'Most people think a holiday is a few weeks, you used to go away for half a year or more.'

Isabelle thought about the email she had sent Moth, suggesting they use Mumbai as a base. The query she had made of her tenant's intentions out there. She looked at Indigo and tried to imagine her daughter in India.

'What about Rob?' Kate asked softly.

Isabelle stopped stirring and put the spoon down. This was closer to the questions they didn't ask than she wanted to go.

'What about Steve?'

Isabelle let out a long breath of irritation.

'What about me, you selfish rat?' Kate lightened her tone. 'I'd miss you both horribly for anything more than a few weeks.

'You wouldn't have time to miss us, you'd enjoy the break and probably start a new business or take a lover in our absence.'

'Well, it looks like Steve might be free sooner than he realises.'

Isabelle laughed at that, and the room seemed to pull back and release her. It had been so hard to broach this thought to Kate. She had been holding it in, brooding over how to tell her but as Kate's blue eyes twinkled back at her around a smile, Isabelle felt the first real hope that it might be more than a wish she dare not utter.

'Indigo, no,' Kate admonished as the child reached for a brochure with hands dripping in parsnip slime. Using a tea towel to wipe the drips from the cover.

'Hmmm,' Kate mused. 'Well, I can see why you aren't rushing to resolve things with Asha. That's a thorny subject she keeps picking at and it's hard to break a silence once you've started it.'

'Yes, oh wise one.'

'Darling, I can't tell you what to do.' Kate rolled her eyes at Isabelle's look of incredulity. 'Don't mock me, you have no idea the level of restraint I'm practicing. All I ask is that you don't run away to India to escape the problems you want to avoid here. I know how much you miss Moth...'

'It's not just that I miss him...'

'You miss how he made you feel?' Kate gave her a small, sad smile. 'I understand, really. You don't talk about it, but I can see it. It's hard to find someone who understands you, and when, if, it happens, it rarely comes in a neatly tied package. You and Moth have a close bond, I get that you want to help him but are you sure you're the right person? Does Moth need you, or is it you that needs him? And are you hiding behind helping Moth to avoid battles that are easier ignored than fought?'

'That really wasn't...'

'I haven't finished.' Kate held her hand up to stop her, the tea towel turned to a baton of tension-screwed fabric. 'If you want to go away, take Indigo travelling, refresh and inspire yourself, that's a really sound thing to build into your life. To plan toward. If Steve doesn't fit that picture, face up to it, don't run away from it. You have a business you've worked hard to get going, family and friends who need and want you here. Not to mention Christmas that you've leased out to Kit and if you leave me here with that to manage, I shall be spiteful for an entire year. Be careful you don't tip the baby out with the bathwater, Isabelle, by throwing away everything that you do love to escape the things you struggle with.'

'You don't think Asha might be right?' Isabelle asked the table. 'That I should tell her.'

'Should?' Kate loaded the word with distaste. 'You don't owe anyone an explanation, Isabelle, other than her, eventually.' Kate quirked her eyebrows at Indigo, who was too busy with writing soup shapes on the table to notice. 'And I understand your doubt, really, I do. There's never a good time to tell the things we've chosen to keep to ourselves but, if, and when, you're ready to talk about these things, that's your choice. If people choose to take upset about it, that's on them. You can't be bullied into sharing before you're ready.'

'What if I'm never ready?' Isabelle asked, looking up at Kate sat at the back of her chair, an encouraging smile crooking her lips into a kindness that helped ease the memory of Asha's spite, making it easier to say what really worried her. Sat in the great aching quietness of the kitchen she had known her whole life, realising she no longer walked into it dreading who would be present, as she so often had when Hester was there. What hurt the most about Asha's accusations were that she had finally come to feel safe and protected in the home she had always loved. Asha had sent her spinning back to the days when she had walked on eggshells and Moth had been the only person she could confide in. 'What if I hurt everyone else in the meantime, never being ready?'

'If I were you, I would worry about the circumstances conspiring against you when you are ready,' Kate told her with a precise tone and a direct look. 'Life can be spiteful like that.'

Isabelle tried to gather all those loose threads of advice into a useful shape.

Kate stood, picked Indigo up and said, 'Come on rascal, you've used my soup as make up.' She went and got a dish-cloth, warmed it through and wiped the surface layers from Indigo's face.

'You tidy up lunch and go focus on work.' Kate hitched Indigo onto a hip again. 'I'll have Lil' Miss with me for the afternoon. She can help us cultivate the ground.'

'I thought your "cultivating the ground" session specifically meant ditching children and responsibilities to others to cultivate the ground of self?'

'Don't quote my own marketing back at me. Indigo can be the distraction we need to avoid.'

'Rather than life-size pictures of Jason Momoa?'

'Well, we might use those too.' Kate grinned. 'They're mostly for me after all.'

Kate danced her way to the door, distracting Indigo from the separation. 'Oh, and pick a bloody tree will you, or they'll all be sold out. Start with that one choice.'

A FEW HOURS LATER, Isabelle stared at the image on her laptop and tried to find words.

'Don't you love it?' Kit demanded from the phone as she tried to take in the email he had sent her.

Isabelle adjusted her jaw to close her mouth.

'No, I don't love it. Tell me you didn't order it?'

'I bought six and five are already accounted for. This one has some slight damage and I've negotiated a massive discount on it. We just need to get it up to you.'

She looked at the life-sized, ice-blue wicker sleigh and tried to picture Kate's face when it arrived.

'Where the hell are you going to put that?' she asked. 'And tell me you're not arranging for live reindeer?'

'Don't be ridiculous,' he frowned into the phone. 'You do realise Christmas is supposed to be fun, right?'

She watched him peer at his image in the small screen, flick his hair back, lift his chin, adjust the angle of the phone to give her a better image. She didn't need to worry about him looking at her appalled face.

'I thought we could park it out on the drive after the girls are asleep and pretend Santa left it there in the morning.

'Have you spoken with Elsa yet?' Isabelle asked.

'Of course I have. Not all of us leave Christmas to the last minute, Isabelle.'

'I get the feeling you never stop thinking about Christmas.'

'I've told Elsa, threatened to sack Hester if she doesn't turn up...'

'... I hope you're advertising her post, she won't come...'

'... and told Asha to get over her spat and we're celebrating Polish Christmas Eve the night before and they're stopping over. Did you get the rooms tidy yet? Do I need to send Lou and the boys up for a week? We should plan that, how about the last week of November?'

'Kit, slow down. You don't need to send them. I have Gosia here, remember.'

'Then we'll be ready to put the decorations up at the beginning of December. Is Kate excited?'

'Overwhelmed with anticipation.'

'You're being sarcastic.

'You wouldn't be the first to mention it today.' Isabelle

glanced at the study door, she should be working. The afternoon was all but over, Indigo would be back upstairs and grouchy before long.

'And what about Moth, have you sorted him yet? Nat is hopelessly excited about seeing him.'

'Jesus, Kit, did you tell Nat already?' Isabelle felt sick at the thought. 'What if it doesn't happen, she'll be gutted. I haven't even heard from Moth for weeks. It's not as easy as snapping my fingers and magicking him back.'

'Why not?' Kit looked at her with genuine confusion. Isabelle had to remind herself that the snapping of fingers was exactly what Kit charged an extortionate amount for and had made himself brilliant at. 'Honestly, Isabelle, do I have to do everything?'

'I'm trying to sort Moth, I promise. And I don't think Asha is ready to forgive me yet.'

'She can't hold a grudge much longer.'

Isabelle stared at him with an incredulity that outweighed even what the sleigh had put on her face.

'Did I say that?' Kit asked.

'Yes.'

'Okay, scrap that. Even if she can hold a grudge with Hester for three years...'

'... and counting...'

'... she adores you. You need to sort out this childcare issue. Come on, you've got this. Look I must go. I'm glad you love it. I'll get it shipped up to the farm. James can put it in store until Christmas and help us get it across to Riverdell. Love you.'

She hadn't managed to draw a breath before he rang off. Leaving her staring at the sleigh on her laptop screen. It was preposterous. How could he not see that? It was as though Kit only saw what he wanted to see. She closed the tab. What on earth would Moth make of it? She opened her email up. Nothing from him. Between the gushing enthusiasm of Kit and the radio silence of Moth, she felt the hope inspired by her conversation with Kate that morning melting like early snow.

How was she going to persuade Moth to leave Turkey to go to India, only to demand he come home for a Christmas that looked set to shame the Kardashians?

She put her head in her hands and groaned.

How was she supposed to make sense of anything when she was this tired?

She lifted her head and looked for inspiration.

The room had found its new layout one alteration at a time, rather than having it imposed with one of Kit's grand visions. Less a study, more a snug. Her desk set at a rakish angle that drove Kit mad, between the window wall and the door, half inclined toward those who entered, overlooking the fire. She had moved it that way after Indigo was born, when she left her wriggling on her back on the sofa, piled inside a nest of cushions and watching the fire flicker. It had never moved back. Isabelle preferred an angle less rigid than Elsa had previously used, all furniture neatly aligned with walls and bookcases. She enjoyed that the cushions arrayed along the back of the low sofa were all different. That the walls were no longer dominated by maps and oil paintings, but mostly bare, showing as soothing pale spaces between the bookcases. Indigo and Deryn's dirty handprints scrubbed from the lower wall by Gosia but leaving a shadow. She tried hard to keep the house less formal, less grand than it had been when Moth left. Four years and climbing.

Could she ever persuade him to think of Riverdell as home?

She looked through the window to the second floor flat. It wasn't available for him anymore. She really would have to get those other bedrooms cleared out. Moth could have Elsa's bedroom. It would give him the same view of the river he had enjoyed from his bedroom on the floor above.

She pulled a sheet of paper toward her and made a list of names down the side. Indigo. Moth. Kate. Asha. Rob. Kit. She paused and at the bottom wrote Steve. Her email pinged on the computer. She glanced at it. Another order. Christmas was kicking in already. She left it unopened and returned to her list, trying to find calm in the process she used for managing work. It always made her feel better, to see the enormity of it written down, pinned up over her machine where she could cross it off and make progress. Above Steve she squeezed in Nat and Elsa. Below Steve she hesitantly wrote Hester. Another email pinged on her computer. She glanced quickly, work again, rejecting its pull on her attention.

Outside the window she heard steps across the gravel, saw Martin heading for the gate. The lists were helping, giving her back control, vision. She needed to focus on it. Time was running out and Kate would soon be back with Indigo.

Down the right side of the page, she drew two columns. A line across the top to create two boxes. India written in one. Christmas in the other. She stepped out of her own confused mind and slipped into the thoughts of those names she had written. Focusing without thinking, she placed a tick in the box she felt they would vote for. Moth's name she paused too long on and had to move over, leaving his choices uncrossed. She moved down the page. Indigo, Kate, Rob, Kit, Nat, Elsa. All Christmas. Easily, without a question. Hester, she put a tick in India, for it was clear as a crystal bell that Hester would turn into the Ice Queen herself before returning to Riverdell to play happy families round a bedecked fir tree. Besides Steve's name she put a tick for Christmas and felt herself focus on that tick as she did his hand rubbing her skin. A pleasure that morphed into an irritant.

At the bottom of the page, she put her own name. Tried to slip back into her own mind. Her hand moved up the page toward Moth, reluctantly put a tick in the India column. She was fooling herself to think that there was anything but a slim chance he would want to come home for Christmas. She had been seeing only what Kit knew she wanted to see, Moth back at Riverdell. Her hand retreated to the bottom of the page and placed a tick for herself. Surprised at where it ended up. Moving upwards she hovered over a tick in the Christmas column and watched as her hand, moving as though without her input, converted a tick into a cross. Putting down the pen, Isabelle sat back and looked at the neat array of logic in front of her, trying to let the reality of those choices settle into place in her mind.

She heard a vehicle pull up on the drive and looked up, dazed.

Martin, packing his tools away for the night. The side door of his campervan sliding open.

Heard another ping on the computer and looked down at the screen, expecting another order.

Luca. She opened the email without thinking. It filled the screen. Misery running through the paragraphs. His sense of desperation from Moth's email. His confusion over what to do. Emotions run amok. Not the confident Luca who kept in touch with her as Moth's relative. This was a man in agony. Desperate for support.

Isabelle looked at the list in front of her, at the van being loaded outside her window, at the email on her screen. The house seemed to breath with her, as though it too had been holding its breath. The silver thread in the weave of the curtains shimmered to catch her eye, the fireguard twinkled back at her, the embossed spines of the diaries glinted as she looked around. The house supported her, sustained her. She felt it in the warmth with which the pen sat between her fingers, the comfort of the stool beneath her legs, the whispers of life that resonated down the corridor and through the open doorway.

Courage, Kate had said. It took courage to craft the life she wanted. She glanced back at the page. Added Luca's name to the lists, let her hand place a tick in the appropriate column. The words told her what to do. There was a soothing calmness about their truth that overrode the exhausted buzz in her head. She just needed to do it.

She responded to Luca first, a few light lines, promised to write more later that evening. Her mind sharpened to a fine point by the grating edge of his distress. She glanced out the window again. Lingered with the courtyard's hazy images as they solidified her thoughts. She pulled the tree brochures toward her. Picked them up and moved to the fire to put them in the bin for burning. She would not make all the decisions. Looking back out the window from the cold hearth. Only the fire in the drawing room had yet been lit. Soon the cold of winter would begin to set in properly, but not yet. Autumn was mild and wistful. The willows cascading amber confetti across the lawn. The leaves not yet turning to mush and ruining Kate's aesthetic. Isabelle moved over to the window and opened it.

'Martin?'

He looked up from the van, 'Uh-huh?'

'Could you spare me a moment? I need some advice.'

'Eh, yeah, in there?'

'Please.'

He nodded at her and slid the van door closed. As he moved toward the front door, she slipped back to her table, shuffled the lists and hid them under her pile of orders.

'HAPPY CHRISTMAS EVE,' Kit said as Adele descended the stairs into the kitchen the next morning. He was stood at the stove, frying mushrooms and peppers together in a large sauté pan. Cherry tomatoes splitting their skins at the side of the pan, a combination of beans simmering in their releasing juices.

'What time did you get up?' Adele asked, coming over to see what he was cooking. 'Smells divine.'

'I can't remember.' Kit hadn't slept. He'd been on the computer trying to pin down the exact shade of Kate's painted toes since Adele's deep sleep beside him had turned irritating.

As Adele checked the food, Kit moved to close the computer down. The software he'd needed to create the paint range had cost a fortune. The corruption software to protect the paint range master copy had cost even more. He was so close to completing the full range, that elusive shade of blue that haunted him almost captured in the night's long hours. He updated his password and shut the software down, moving back to the stove. 'Did you see Jay on your way down?'

'Heard the bathroom, didn't see him.'

'I've made a decision.' Kit went to pull the baking bread out of the oven. He bought the rolls par-cooked from a local baker, froze them and finished baking them himself. As close to bread fresh from the oven as you could get. They were even vegan, making him feel truly smug.

'Should I be worried?' Adele asked, going to the fridge to find green sludge.

'We're going to have a New Year's Eve party. Here.'

Adele shut the fridge door, bottle of kale and celery smoothie in hand, stunned expression on face.

'What the actual fuck?'

'I know, it's short notice. But to hell with it. You're right.'

'I am?' Adele unscrewed the bottle top. 'About what?'

'Christmas. First Isabelle, then Jay. I've put us last. I'm sorry.'

'Okay, get out of my boyfriend's body, whoever you are.' Adele leant against the fridge door and grinned a sleepy amused smile. 'You shag me to within an inch of my life then drop a party on me?'

'I'm making up,' Kit admitted. He put the bread out on the table, moved to the bottom of the stairs and hollered up them, 'Jay! Breakfast!' turned back to Adele and added, 'Let's have a party to end all parties.'

'With one week's notice?' Adele asked. 'Most people are booked up already.'

'Most people are about to realise they don't want to follow through with the stupid plans they made two months ago. Everyone changes their mind last minute about New Year.'

'I'm glad I'm not the other hosts who made all those

plans,' Adele quipped. He came toward Kit at the stove, snuggled in behind him, one arm wrapping round his chest. 'You could ask anything of me today, I am mush. Thank God I'm not in the studio for a few days.'

Adele kissed the back of his neck and Kit curved into the intimacy. It felt divine. Adele close behind him, fresh food rising from the pan in front.

'Is that a vegan breakfast I see before me?' Adele asked in disbelief.

'Fetch me an avocado, would you?' Kit asked.

As Adele moved away to the fridge, Jay's feet appeared at the top of the stairs. Barefoot and padding downward. Jeans topped by a brown T-shirt that made him look nude. Damp hair flopping sideways over his eyes. Kit had cut it himself, Jay refusing to go to a salon. It was a wretched job, but a step forward.

'Tell me Fred's not coming this morning?' he asked as he reached the floor.

'Fred's not coming tomorrow morning.'

Jay groaned.

'Oh, that's nothing,' Adele told him, coming back from the fridge with a ripe avocado. 'Wait 'til you hear the rest.'

'Yes, I've made a decision,' Kit agreed.

'You cancelled Christmas, forever?' Jay asked hopefully, moving toward the table, stretching.

'No, we're having a New Year's Eve party.' Kit tapped the spatula against the rim of the pan. 'Breakfast is ready.'

Jay stopped flat in the middle of the space, arm crooked behind his back in part stretch. 'Say what now?'

'Yup.' Adele confirmed with a grin, peering over Kit's shoulder. He could feel Adele's smile in his chin where it sat against his bone.

'Yes, we are.' Kit agreed.

'I'm going home.' Jay headed for the stairs.

'No, you are not.' Kit pointed the spatula at him. 'You, my friend, are going to help me decorate the house.'

'What?' Jay asked, pulling up. 'We already decorated the house!'

'Oh, please.' Kit distributed food between plates. 'Not even close.'

'Let's make it fancy dress,' Adele suggested.

Kit thought about it, looked at Jay's mutinous face, at Adele's glowing sparkle. 'Yes, let's do that. Adele, pick a theme.'

'You have got to be kidding me,' Jay complained.

'A night at the ballet.' Adele did a pirouette and took a leap from the floor to end with a thud in front of the table where he grabbed a chair for a barre.

Jay stared in disbelief at Kit. He was damned if he did. Damned if he didn't.

'Works for me,' he said. 'Adele, you have to bring costumes back.'

'This is going to be epic.' Adele began going through positions. 'Who are we going to invite?'

'I am not wearing a fucking tutu to a New Year's Eve party.' Jay crossed his arms in the middle of the room and looked as immovable as the floor.

'You, and only you, are excused fancy dress.' Kit took the plates to the table. 'Come and eat, Adele has to leave this morning and Fred will be here in an hour. Let's make the most of what time we have together on Christmas Eve.'

Which was as close as he could say to "We'll talk later." Between Adele's twirling and Jay's dragging feet, Kit felt a shimmer of sympathy for Isabelle. It was as bad as being a parent. He went to the large cupboards that backed the one wall. Seamless touch-opening storage essential to the minimalist look of the kitchen.

'We have presents,' he called, pulling the gifts from the back of the shelves and turning to them. At least he could manage things better than Isabelle. 'I officially declare Christmas open!'

THE NEXT MORNING, he woke to an empty bed and a quiet house. The alarm clock telling him he was awake before most five-year-old kids. Kit stretched out in the empty bed and pulled his fuzzy head into shape.

Christmas morning. He had that strange moment that always came.

A sense of delight that built before flatlining in disappointment.

What after all was Christmas to anyone other than a child? A gross splurge of money and effort for the gratification of your year-long working misery. The attempt to bring together a family better left apart. The hope to see innocence and magic shining in your child's eyes to cover the weary disillusionment in your own.

Sitting up in bed, pushing disappointment aside he felt the ugly waft of that next emotion Christmas always brought drifting closer. Loneliness.

Christmas had never been the same since his mother left. Leaving a void that he filled by gate-crashing other families. Playing Santa. Dropping presents and food treats and moving on to the next household before he was asked to wash up or reconcile a family argument lubricated by too much Christmas spirit.

He wasn't sure it would be any better if Adele were here in the bed with him. It wasn't sex he craved. It was the happy sense of belonging. The thought of going into his mother's bedroom and jumping into her bed for cuddles. Doing the same with Granny. Dragging them both downstairs to begin the day.

It was the reason he had ended up refurbishing the entire house. Bereft of their presence, the swirl of house gowns round ankles, the tangle of unmade hair, the freshness of undressed skin, the squabble of disagreement wrapped up in love, the house he'd inherited had become an echoing tomb of memory. He'd hated the emptiness of the rooms with their closed doors. Taking down doors, moving walls, recreating the house had made it his own.

And it worked, each day bar Christmas. When he woke, longing to be that child again.

Kit reached over and picked up his phone. Pulled himself up against the pillows. He opened the app and let the Christmas smugness scroll upwards. Knowing these apparently spontaneous photos had been taken weeks, if not months, ago. Flicking without seeing. Tapping the centre of those posts he had a financial incentive to engage with. There should be a Grinch option on Christmas Day. Tap twice for a heart, thrice for a Grinch. Except he'd be too tempted to Grinch all his clients for the hell of it. Having made himself rich from their excess. There were too many photos to find the one he wanted. He'd have to search through his following to find it. Which went against the rules. But Adele wasn't there, so did the rules count? He'd found it before he could finish the argument in his head.

Then wished he hadn't. Really wished he hadn't.

Because why would she choose to post that? Except to taunt him.

A blushed glass bauble with a white frosted heart resting beside a sprig of mistletoe on the ruched blue silk of a scarf, a crumpled bed out of focus in the background.

He knew that blue scarf. Missed it. Wished he hadn't given it back to her.

He would have grinched that post.

Wondered if she was lying in bed too, thinking about the emptiness of the day ahead.

Tapped the centre twice before he could stop himself.

Wondered about untapping it. Wondered about calling.

Kit threw the phone to the end of the bed and rolled over to bury his head in the pillow.

It was an unsolved riddle he couldn't let go of. A messy, bitter ending that hadn't been a proper farewell. Kit would arrive at Riverdell determined to fix it. To talk through what had happened, to get an answer out of her. But when he saw her, happy, successful, part of the family Isabelle was building, he'd feel as inept as he had all those years ago on the beach in Swansea, hiding an engagement ring in his pocket. Remember the way she'd refused to tell him why she hadn't gone to Italy. And the doubt would build in him again, acid and burning. So that he left, showing only how full his own life was, how little he cared about the past. Come home and throw himself into busy until the riddle was pulled to the surface again.

Kit punched the mattress beside him. When would it go away?

What if it never did?

He stopped the punching with that thought. Pulled himself upright and blinked.

What if it never did?

What if he was always looking sideways at her life through an Instagram lens when he should be looking squarely at what his life held. At the people who wanted to be part of it.

The empty room stared back at him. Slick ochre walls, sharp mirrored edges, hard wooden lines, crumpled slate sheets. Structurally neutral to let him change the paint colour and bedding and have a total refresh. That's all it took, a lick of paint and the rise and fall of linen and he could recraft the most intimate room of his house.

Kit hated the ochre. Looking at it with the sickening thought that he might be chasing the perfect shade of blue everywhere he looked for the rest of his life. He left the bed, heading for the shower. Because he wasn't on his own after all. He had Jay to celebrate with.

The Christmas Grinch himself.

'RISE AND SHINE!' Kit pushed the door open balancing the tray on his arm and tried to see into the darkness of the room. Jay was a lump beneath bedclothes. Unable to see Kit falter on the threshold.

It smelled like his mother. Even now, with Jay in the bed and the room refreshed weekly by cleaners. He could smell her. The combination of paper, ink, perfume, intimacy. A memory strong enough to freeze his stride. Her diaries stacked on the desk as his eyes adjusted to the curtain-dimmed light.

'What time is it?' Jay rumbled from the covers.

'Breakfast time.' Kit moved forward, glancing at the wardrobe, expecting to see the outfit she had chosen the night before. It had been a habit of hers. To pick out the next day's clothes before she went to bed, after writing in her diary. He had forgotten it, the way he would see who she would be the night before anyone else.

'That could mean anything with you.' Jay stirred further and rose from the mess of covers.

'Did you fall asleep with Mother's diaries?' Kit approached the bed, put the tray down on the chest of drawers and picked up a stray diary lying on the cover. Her handwriting an urgent, sloped scrawl against the page. It was unguarded and personal, bringing her even closer.

'Ugh, yes, about three in the morning.' Jay twisted his wrist to see the time. 'Oh, come on, you are kidding. I've only been asleep four hours.'

'Well, you shouldn't have stayed up reading so late. Move over.'

'What?'

'Move over, we're having breakfast in bed.' Kit lifted the covers and inhaled the musty smell of night man that emanated. He pushed a grumbling Jay across the huge mattress. 'Stop fretting, this bed is big enough to give even your homophobic arse space.'

'Why are we having breakfast in bed?'

'Read to me.' Kit handed him a cup of coffee. 'You smell delicious in the morning, by the way.'

'What?'

'I bet a woman can't leave you alone first thing.'

'Shut up.' Jay took his cup and scowled at him.

'Which diary are you on?' Kit pushed the pillows into a comfortable position, their warmed scent rising as he moved them. It gave him a happy buzz, this sense of climbing into his mother's bed, warm from her body, sharing secrets and intimate time. 'Surely there can't be many left?'

'I've been skipping a bit. Did you know that you're related to the actual royal family?'

'Umm, distant earls and stuff I think.' Kit handed Jay a plate of warmed croissants. 'Load of wankers probably.' Kit picked up his own croissants. 'Are you hungry? I'm not cooking a turkey by the way.'

'What? You mean you kidnapped me for Christmas and now you're refusing to cook?' Jay bit into his croissants and scattered crumbs all over the bed.

'Oh my God, I could not live with you. The crumbs! That's why I gave you a plate.'

Kit swiped at the annoying crumbs. He pulled another diary onto his lap and opened the pages with a delicate finger, aware of grease.

'How can you be so prissy about crumbs and not give a shit about your heritage?' Jay grumbled.

'I care deeply about my heritage. I live in my great-grand-mother's home, I let you sleep in my mother's bed. Even with your monstrous crumb issues.'

'What about the rest?' Jay looked over at him, plate held up to his chin as he took another bite. 'Really not curious about the relatives?'

'Just read to me.' Kit handed him the diary.

Jay frowned at it and put it down, picking up another. He began to read slowly, pausing over the illegible words. Kit listened to his voice, his eyes resting on the portrait of his mother at the end of the bed. Her face surrounded by curls, peering down on him, curious about what he might do next. That lurking smile that had always seemed more dare than caution.

'... Or perhaps make love on it. To remind you I live. You cold-hearted bastard. While he was gasping his last, having the life squeezed out by an iron fist round his chest I was happier than I have known in a long time. I hope my orgasm timed with his deathly climax. I have a new lover. His name is Ben, and he trusts me.'

'Yeah, let's stop there,' Kit shook himself out of a reverie.

'But what about the bit before?' Jay asked. 'She adored you Kit. Isn't it good to hear that?'

Kit looked back at his mother's portrait. He'd never questioned being loved as a child. Not until the therapist had started asking him about Kate.

'I think it gives you the thrills,' Kit told him. 'You're going to need therapy at the end of reading all this. Let's go to the seaside.'

'What? Today?'

'Yeah, why not. I want to go to Weston and take a picture of our feet in the surf. We'll have fish and chips for Christmas lunch.'

15

I am home from Riverdell and can breathe. The place suffocates me. I can't believe how much I used to love it, but perhaps that was the happiness of our time there which covered over the upper-class hypocrisy of it all. Kate says it is my own fault, I have become too angry and can no longer find happiness in the smaller details of life.

Angry?

I'm not angry. I'm savage. I'm sickened. I'm furious. The sort of fury that could topple kingdoms, wreck countries, destroy a people. I have never known such hatred for the world I am part of as I do now. "Angry" doesn't even begin to touch it.

Kate doesn't see it. How she is suckered in and compromised by it. She would not listen to a word of sense and has banned me from speaking to Elsa, whose pregnancy must take precedent. The damn golden-haired, silver-spooned child and her needs come first.

Ugh, I'm being vile. Perhaps Kate is right.

Elsa is distraught with terrible morning sickness. This

pregnancy is entirely different to her others. She has lost weight, forces herself to eat for the baby and then endures the retching afterwards. In the mornings, it was all we could do to hold her hair back over the toilet and wipe her face. Poor love, she doesn't deserve this. Richard is pale with worry and coping with James. David is her devoted shadow. I had never seen before how utterly he adores her. All his difficulties faded to anxiety in the light of her struggles. I wonder what will happen when yet another baby arrives to take more of her time from him? If it arrives. I wouldn't be surprised if she lost it. The physical stress was all too stressful, coming on a wave with all my troubles.

But Kate is wrong too. She is determined to continue with her plans and leaves for her "culinary tour" in less than a fortnight. Elsa is trying to be strong for her, insisting she go. Bleating about how it's the first trimester, it will soon improve, and this is a once in a lifetime opportunity for Kate's career. I had to bite my lips to keep my mouth shut, Kate staring daggers at me the whole time. Richard knows something is up, you couldn't hide a pint in a brewery under his nose. But he is focused on Elsa and Kate has me stitched up good and proper to keep my mouth shut. My secret for hers.

If I stand a chance of keeping this case private, I will fight to do so. I don't want Elsa to know about this, not now, she will torture herself with anxiety while already enduring enough. She'll find out eventually, once I've won, and all the grief the Threlfalls and Mountbatten have brought down on me will be pointless for her and Granny to worry about. If the anxiety would harm Elsa, I think it might well kill Granny. The trial will go public, but if I can keep it from her for a bit longer, I'd rather. From her and from Kit, who doesn't deserve to be in the middle of a public laundry-washing about his mother.

And so, who am I to chide Kate for her secrets and how she keeps them. I admire her courage. She was always the toughest of us. Perhaps I was the loudest, the one always leading the affray, but she has always been the backbone. I swore once I would never listen to her again, that her advice all those years ago blighted my life. But now?

I always thought people who kept secrets were liars and cowards. If you had the courage to live your life for yourself, you didn't need secrets.

But I guess there are some secrets we all want to manage ourselves. I keep mine close enough here, in these pages. It's not about if, or when, they come out. But about how. Who will be harmed? Who will we lose in the reveal?

Granny would be heartbroken to know her insistence I attend that funeral caused all this. And it is not her fault. It is not even Ben's fault. He sees my hypocrisy. My great rants of naked socialism in the night lying alongside my glossily attired life. I holiday with my wealthy friends at their precious home. I represent my grandmother, Lady de Lavelle, at the state funeral of a dead Prince. I choose the lovers I take and how I take them. No, it is not their fault. I no longer enjoy Riverdell because it shows me the truth that Ben saw.

My anger is all at myself, for risking the ones I love who will be most damaged by this.

My anger is at the shine in the eyes of those who see the promise of damages being rewarded to keep truths silenced.

My anger is at the great heft of social veneer which will not change, which pushes to one side or the other those who must be judged.

And it judges me for my sexuality far, far above how else it might measure me.

If I were a man, well... if I were a man, now, women such as myself would be baying for blood. Pounding the halls of Westminster in my shiny high heels demanding his head. For men are protected by the veneer. They close ranks tight as a Roman army and push their dicks to the front like spears. Claiming, as I do, they were drunk, they cannot remember, it is all lies fabricated to attack them? And they are excused, for after all they are men.

But a woman, wearing a strap on, indulging in a ménage à trois, taking younger men under the influence, unable to remember a thing, photographs taken. That is more than inexcusable, it is an obscenity.

If I reversed the genders, I would be sickened. I would not stop to consider, as no one will for me, how come the photographs exist with the victims? How come the accused had a consensual relationship with the victim for months before her family wealth became known? How come the partner never told her about his other lover? Lovers? How much have I not known about as I shared my deepest self with Ben? When he said he trusted me absolutely he didn't mention I shouldn't trust him.

In 1967, I was so busy working for the Abortion Bill that I took only fleeting interest in the Sex Offence Bill. Perhaps my interest was less focused on the rights of men as I worked for the fundamental lifesaving rights of women and because, after all, I was not as close to the gender line as I am now. I was not attuned to the nuances of danger, so that only now do I see the precision with which that night was set up. That there were three of us present and in a public hotel, that the third member was twenty years old. Old enough between women and men, but not between men, and I performed that night as a man. That they two claim consent was not given, and I led them to the venue, paid for the room. None of which I recall.

I have watched from afar and pursued my own interests with the great privilege of class behind me. Perhaps I am only the abandoned bastard of a dead baron, but I am also the great-granddaughter of an earl, and the men I was with will be portrayed as innocent peasants to my gilded aristocracy. I should have paid more attention to the world I was gliding closer to, how stupid and arrogant I have been. It is not a line that exists between the genders, it is a crack, leading to an abyss of legal nonexistence. Will I be tried as a man or as a woman? It doesn't matter. I will be tried for sexual indecency at best, rape and sodomy at worst. And, rankest of all, is that my being in the right or wrong is nothing to my accusers. They keep it private for now out of hope that I will settle out of court. This is not a fair fight. It is not about honour or right or social advancement. All the big cases I have read with idle interest in the papers for the last few decades have been fought not for themselves, but the bigger hope of a repressed segment of society. My accusers assume I must have inherited wealth and will pay to protect the honour of my family and friends.

The only way I can pay the damages they demand is to beg it from Granny or extortion the widow of my father.

No, I shall force them into the open.

If it is a battle they want, I will take it as public as I need to. They dance a fine line of danger for themselves. To hell with them. I will not lower myself to beg for assistance, they cannot make me sink that low. What have I got to lose? I won't belong in any acceptable place when I am done, and all this keeps me from pursuing the course I have promised myself.

But, no... on the cusp of hope I see it leak through the cracks.

Though I will fight this tooth and nail for myself, I battle a greater and deepening doubt that I am in the right. For I cannot remember, I was the elder party, I am more than capable of doing the acts they accuse me of and, if I could remember, I would probably cherish the great pleasure I took in them.

I must own all the parts of who I am. The do-gooder determined to save her career. The granddaughter, mother, friend trying to protect those she loves. The woman who finds her greatest pleasure in penetration. The partygoer who loves her clothes and image. The fool who thought she was above the dictates of society.

If I lose the case, I could be facing a prison term.

The thought of dragging Kit through that is more than I can endure.

Oh, hell and plunder. I talk myself in circles and come back to doubt.

Perhaps Kate is right. Perhaps her way is the best after all. While I charge into battle she sits back and surveys the war, choosing the path of least casualty. I could not do as she does, swallow bitter truths and digest shattered hopes. I yearn to disembowel my enemy and dance a gig on their bloody entrails and shattered bones. But she does not, she sees far ahead and takes the long shot. I wonder if she will look back in regret.

I sit in a pregnant limbo, waiting to see what will happen, what will come, what may be lost. I cannot control myself or my choices, same as when I carried Kit. I must wait, wait,

wait, and see what the next month brings. It is dark outside, the lights catch the thin branches of the trees. Blossom buds are beginning to form.

I will never forget Mountbatten's funeral. I have been stuck on a gasping, poisoned breath since. It will linger in my memory as the day I realised who I truly was, and the night I threw it all away for a drunken shag.

16

A tabey did not forgive him.

Apparently, saving his butt does not count for drowning him in rat piss.

Moth had grown used to being ignored or flinched at.

Keep trying to convince yourself.

He walked down the streets of Adiyaman in the cool of an early November morning. Enjoying the solitude of the three miles into town from where he'd left their camp. They had cycled until the night sky began to lighten and he was tired and tense with anticipation. It had been a long six weeks since he'd last checked his emails in Urfa. Weeks of waiting for Fehran to turn up, of converting the bike, of escaping the illegal camp by a limping, moonlit whisper. Moth felt strung out like the washing on the lines he passed on the outskirts of town, pulled tight with hope and worry about what he might or might not find when he logged in.

He stretched out his pace, enjoying the lightness of his nearly empty rucksack on his back. Covering ground with ease. Resisting the idea that he could keep on walking. Leave them the tent, the bike, the plan. Let them figure it all out themselves. It had taken them weeks to cover the few grid boxes between Suruc and here. Weeks of travelling during the evenings and into the nights, resting during the day. Waiting for Kadri to recover, binding his ribs tight, encouraging him back onto the bike. Taking another item out of the backpack each day to lighten the load for Atabey, dropping Kadri off, cycling back and picking up the other. Repeatedly going back for the backpack that had been thrown on the ground in disgust.

Trying not to smack the idiot for ingratitude.

Grinding his teeth with frustration that the plan was clumsy, exhausting and covering ground at a snail's pace. Every day wondering if this was the day they would be stopped, hauled off the bike, arrested.

Moth glanced down the side streets. Adiyaman was a smaller city than Urfa, less gregarious in its makeup. A persistent Kurdish presence in the languages over the shops. He felt all too visible as he searched the streets. The distrust on the faces of those shopkeepers he passed as clear as Atabey's.

Moth had ignored it during their journey as best he could. It wasn't as though he'd planned on throwing them bodily into that stinking pile. He'd responded in visceral terror to the idea of being caught, locked up.

At least you took the brunt of the damage.

He washed the bite marks on his legs and the scrapes and cuts on his back and thighs in boiled, salted water every night. And every night he woke, gasping for release from the suffocating plastic, wrestling with his sleeping bag as he had Atabey to keep him quiet, rats running over their bodies and faces in the disturbance. It was enough to give anyone nightmares, no wonder Atabey mistrusted him. Moth would count

himself forcibly back into sleep. The journey was too
demanding to deal with sleep deprivation as well.

There had been hills, from there to here. Hills he'd pretty
much hauled the three of them, the bike and the backpack
over, one numbing mile at a time. There had been the wide
lakes glistening at the bottom to call him on. The moment
they crossed the Euphrates, passing out of Urfa province,
he'd taken them away from the main road. Pushing them
through tiredness all the way to the heights of the Ataturk
Dam. That was the advantage of being the map man. He
knew where they were. Where they were going. What called
them on for the day.

It had been a good moment. Watching Atabey before the
mass of the huge dam, tracing the sweeping lines of the
immaculate concrete edges with his hand, gasping with
delight and pointing out the details to Kadri, Moth had seen a
glimpse of the person life had once promised Atabey to be. A
man capable of grasping the immensity of a building project
that scaled the horizon, incapable of allowing the necessity of
being dragged into a rat-filled pit. And it had been impressive.
After the rough nights in the camp and the grimness of life
hiding in the borderlands, the dam had stunned them all.
This, it had said, this is what you should aspire to be. Magnif-
icent, majestic, purposeful.

Kadri had sat down hard on the empty ground of the
darkening parking lot, watching Atabey jumping about with
the happiness of a kid on a school trip and buried his head,
silent and shuddering, on his arms. Moth had watched them,
watched the sun dipping down into the hills they'd ridden
through, throwing a warm light to catch the sneering top lip
of the dam, and felt the same pressure as that towering wall
of determination. He'd sat down beside Kadri, overwhelmed

by his own insignificance and the impossible task ahead. Crushed by the immensity of the dam. Both waiting until Atabey's enthusiasm ran out. Leaving in a subdued silence that had stayed with them for days.

They had followed the lesser roads round the lake, weaving closer and away, toward the water and back, as they took a general route northwest toward Adiyaman. They had needed the water. All of them. The nights when they camped close to its edges and bathed, a washing away of more than the day's travel. Moth felt the small distance they kept from him as they bathed together. They might be three, but the space held between them marked him out in solitude. Their hands reaching, supporting on the pebbly surface of the lake floor. Laughter directed from one to the other but never at him. Moth would leave the water first. It was easier to be alone on dry land with his clothes on.

Later, round the campfire, when Atabey would cook for them, Moth worked at releasing the hundred points of irritation the day had built up.

Face it, you're never going to like him.

Moth would settle for not disliking him. It seemed important, to get over the irritation he had developed for Atabey. But try as he might, Atabey seemed determined to irk him. The brief respite from his complaints about the day's demands morphing into fussing and tutting to himself over the few ingredients Moth brought back from his incursions into the small villages they passed through.

He's like an old woman.

No, old women he could cope with. Elsa, Kate, Beau, Dilru. Old women in his experience had been hard as concrete and scary as a dancing cobra. Atabey was neither. He seemed to be a composite of all that he thought a woman should be without the self-assurance of any of the women he'd ever met.

Is that what ...

Moth focused on the streets again. Internet cafe time.

Great. What joy awaits this time?

Moth struggled with the surging confusion that rose, thinking about those waiting emails. Over the previous few years, they had become a source of pleasure. A lifeline if he needed it. Six weeks ago, he'd been curt to Isabelle, dismissive to Luca. Would there even be emails waiting for him?

Now that you need them.

Moth pulled his thoughts back into line. Being in the streets unsettled him. Others eyeing him up as a wild man of the hills, sneaking in for a night raid. He shrugged the backpack into a more comfortable position, scanning carefully, looking for the right shop. This was why he'd left the boys behind.

You don't want to see how others watch him.

There was a part of Moth that blamed Atabey for the attack on Kadri. Even though he knew the thought was unfair, Moth couldn't dislodge it. He disliked the end-of-day, fussing Atabey. It irritated him, and he understood how that irritation had riled others. Moth passed the high covered windows of a small supermarket and saw himself in the reflection. It caught at him, pulling him to a stop.

Who would you be?

Forced into close company with the boys, Moth was most comfortable with Kadri. His easy strength and confidence. Wounded, weak, but coming back to himself. Looking forward, attending to the plan. But Kadri encouraged Atabey to be different. To care and fuss over him at night. It was as though there were only two roles available. The strong and the weak, the leader and the follower.

And you can't stand it.

He didn't want that. For other people to look at him and assign him a role, to look at his partner and assign them the role Moth could see Atabey playing out. It made his skin crawl until he turned away from them and rolled into his sleeping bag. Shutting his eyes and trying to close his ears to their banter.

This isn't about Atabey.

Moth stared at the supermarket version of himself, his face hazy behind the words. He reached up to feel for the scar lost beneath his scraggly chin.

This is about Luca.

Moth looked away from the window reflection of his hulking frame and wide shoulders. A street full of men and women. It was that obvious. The women reducing themselves, the men loud and visible. Clothes and voices identifying roles. He looked and judged them, as others would judge him. From the outside in.

You've been too long in Turkey. It's not like this everywhere.

And outside of Turkey, in a country where gay people didn't have to hide themselves, what then? He'd been dragged to a gay club by Kit in England, he hadn't fitted in there at all. What if that was the life Luca wanted?

You're assuming Luca wants anything after the last email you sent him.

Moth felt his momentum seeping from his knees, leaving them weary. What would an email from Luca tell him? That Luca had got his last message loud and clear. That Luca had moved on and he need not worry at all about what Luca might want in a...

... go on, say it...

Moth couldn't get past that final hurdle.

... in a...

A word as overwhelming as the dam.

... relationship.

Moth looked down at his stuck feet and battled the wave of heat that he could feel rising through him. Unable to look up at the passing strangers. Trying to face his cringing thoughts.

That watching Kadri and Atabey at night as they relaxed into each other's company made him ache. Made Turkey seem an impossible stretch of space he had to move through to get back to Luca. The boys an unbearable, discomforting weight he had to drag with him. The bike an anchor pulling him down with its inadequacy. Three years an impudent amount of time to ask someone to wait for him.

Moth lurched forward. Sweat reaching his forehead. Scanning the shops, hungry, tired, and desperate for a computer. He needed to know if there was any help waiting for him. If Isabelle or Bonn had sent him a lifeline that could get him back to Luca and tell him what a stupid mistake he'd made. Moth wiped his brow. The day was slow to warm up. People would see his nerves.

The weather was changing, the nights getting sharper, cooler. Something else he had to find soon, proper sleeping bags for the boys. Their burnt edge blanket wasn't going to keep them warm for long. Neither was his sleeping bag going to stave off the damp mornings when they came. The two boys squeezing inside the narrow confines of a tent made for one man. Even if it was the hulking scale of James.

Yourself.

Moth looked down at his legs, the tired trainers pacing out in front of him. What would Luca say about that. Would he still find him attractive? Would Luca be the same or would Luca have changed too?

It's not what you need to focus on.

Money. It always came back to money. He had nothing but change left. He had to email Isabelle and ask for more. And the only way she would agree was if he agreed to go home, leaving Turkey. Which he was. But not alone. And he wasn't coming home. But closer. Close enough to meet up. Close enough to go to India with her, if that was what it took to get them all out of Turkey. But first, he had to go see Luca. He had to know at last, what it was, or wasn't.

No, first, money.

Yes, money. Money. Sleeping bags, preferably another tent. And another bike.

She's not going to send you enough money for all that.

No, she wouldn't. But he needed those things. He needed a second bike to get them as far as the coast. And a tent he could throw up at night and sleep in. Or at least a plastic cover he could pull over himself. It had taken them too long to get this far. At this rate it would take them until next year to reach the coast. Where he had to somehow get them across the waters to Europe.

You might have set yourself an impossible task.

True, he might. But he would get them that far, one way or another.

There is the other way.

He hadn't done that in a long while. There had been the money from Mrs Staines that Kit had given him. And when that ran out, there had been the camp, Bonn. He'd worked for his living. He hadn't had to steal anything for a long time.

If you get caught now, you're no longer a minor.

An adult and an illegal traveller in a strict country.

But even if he emailed Isabelle today it would take time for her to respond, to send money, to withdraw it.

You don't have many choices.

He glanced down the road. There were hundreds of bikes, thrown against walls, loaded with baskets. They looked cheap, flimsy and two a penny. Would anyone really miss them?

Moth spotted an internet café on the other side of the road. He crossed over, the smell of coffee and food reaching him and turning all thoughts to queasiness. Moth hitched his bag, walked into the dark interior and found himself the subject of every pair of eyes in there.

Well, at least don't steal a bike from right outside. They're going to remember an outlandish freak like you.

He put as confident a smile on his face as he could find, shrugged the bag from his back and ordered. Found a table with a grimy old pc perched on it.

Be grateful if you can connect further than the next shop.

It was slow to warm but eventually he found web access. Logged in, waiting, gut clenched, scanning the list of his inbox. His body twisting into a deeper tangle of wretchedness as he read them.

THE WRETCHED BIKE HE ACQUIRED...

... stole...

... from Adiyaman was no tourer. Built for city streets and shopping errands it irritated him as much as Atabey loved it.

Especially the basket on the back. And even though he tended to ride it as though he was going to fetch food from the market, increasing their progress at an incremental level, it did improve their odds. Moth tried to let go of the silent suggestion Atabey conveyed that it was the bare minimum he could have done. That he hadn't returned from Adiyaman with a cartload of groceries, decent food, herbs and a doctor to heal Kadri, but nevertheless the second bike was an acceptable scrap. That he'd found a tatty piece of tarp was irrelevant, boring even.

Kadri was improving. That was the main thing.

He had gone from silent and hunched over in pain, to looking at the maps with Moth, checking the bikes at night with him. Learning how to fix punctures, clean brakes, check for fine thorns or splinters that might exacerbate the next day into a time-consuming flat tyre. By mid-November, two weeks after leaving Adiyaman, with his morals about stealing food now overcome by a constant sense of hunger, Moth convinced Kadri to take turn on riding the bike daily. He began with ten minutes. Ten minutes in which he made him cycle away from them and back with all the bags piled high for a weight test. Moth and Atabey watching him retreat to a speck before growing again on the way back in a deepening silence neither of them bothered to break. Aware that Kadri getting to grips with the bike was the only way they were getting away from each other. The next day Moth increased it to fifteen minutes.

At night, trying to ignore the sounds coming from the other tent, pitching himself always a little further away, Moth could feel the cold biting down at the edges of the tarp. Looking into the hugeness of space he let his mind pull him from star to star. His mind flitting from one person to the next. Atabey to Luca to Isabelle to Bonn. Rereading in his head the emails he'd received in Adiyaman, trying to keep the words clear in his memory to stave off the exhaustion, loneliness, hunger, doubt. The oddity of the name Jacques Bonnier creating a sense of civility that had not been backed up by the contents.

Moth, you lying little fucker. When I find you, I will kick your gargantuan arse from one side of Turkey to the other. Do you have any idea how much extra work you made for me? Like I've not been hauled from one sodding meeting to another for the last four months and you answering none of my emails. It better have been a bloody spelling mistake and not you giving me the wrong email address. I should leave you there to rot. Where the fuck are you, you little cunt?

At least you made an impression.

... I don't have time for your "I can save the world on my own" bullshit. If I have to come back to Turkey to find you, I will make sure you regret it for the next twenty years. I'll have you cleaning toilets for the damn peacekeepers in Angola. WHERE THE FUCK ARE YOU? You write back and tell me. You have one month, or I swear I will come looking and make you pay. And you can thank Inci for having more sense in her little finger than you do in your entire dick and letting me know you are still there. Heading north? Heading north to fucking where? Answer the damn email. Bonn.

The email had been a week old in Adiyaman. Inci must have got in touch after she heard the camp had been raided again. He'd replied. Hey Bonn, great to hear from you too. Yes, heading north, to the coast of the Black Sea. Help whoever I could, those were your words. Found two lads who needed help. So, can you? Help? Tickets out of Turkey would be a start. For three. Then you can send me to clean toilets wherever you want. Moth.

Isabelle's emails had been less brutal, more anxious. Where was he? What was he doing? Did he need money? Was he coming home? Did she need to come meet him? Christmas was coming. Kit was driving her mad about it. Queries gathering momentum to a tauter degree of worry. He'd replied. Apologies, circumstances, yes, he was leaving Turkey, yes, he would meet her. He was heading to the Black Sea, hoping to get a ferry to Europe or Ukraine. More apologies, yes, please, some money would help. Was she still thinking of going to India? He would come with her if he could just go see Luca first. More apologies.

How are you going to go to India and clean toilets for Bonn and see Luca?

He felt crushed between the compromises he'd agreed to get those boys across the border into Europe. To get himself out of Turkey. To get to Luca.

He would lie, looking up at the endless sky, hanging onto stars before lurching across the darkness to the next one, replaying the words he had read, covering the absence of the words he'd been hoping for.

Luca had not sent an email.

The absence of his name had been a glaring void in the space of all those other emails. Moth was now clinging to a wish, a hope, a prayer that...

... you're not too late...

... that he could get to Luca in time to put it right. To make up for ignoring him for three years. To ask him for...

... you don't deserve...

... another chance. Dark hours creeping by as he wondered if the email he'd sent from Adiyaman had been in time, to undo whatever damage he'd let happen in those six weeks after he'd told him to move on.

I'm sorry. I'm an idiot. One more chance is all I need, please.

Clinging to that thought as he curled up against the biting cold, pulling the tarp over his head and blocking out the immensity of it all. Burrowing down into the memory of gelled hair that fell floppy after a shower, brown eyes flecked with amber streaks, hands that reached out to flutter across his skin. His sleep broken and wretched.

HE PUSHED THEM ON. The hope of an email waiting for him at the next big town luring him on. Each mile covered a step away from despair, closer to chance.

The roads north of Adiyaman held a further challenge. They lacked the expanse of lakes and regular washing that had marked the start of their journey. By the time they arrived on the outskirts of Darende they had passed only one lake. Otherwise, it had been scooped handfuls of water from streams that ran down the high hills. Meagre amounts of boiled water to wash hands and face in. The rank smell of dirty sweating men a cloud they couldn't escape.

Moth was even gladder to walk away from them on the outskirts of Darende than he had been eighteen days ago in Adiyaman. He'd lain sleepless through the final early hours of the night and set out just as dawn bit into the sky, the boys deep asleep in the tent.

His first sight of himself in the shop windows nearly sent him running back to the tent. His outgrown stubble making ragged waves and clumps across his jaw and up his cheeks. His hair caked into sweat streaked lumps. His clothes stained and sagging. Moth turned away and went to look for deodorant in the nearest supermarket. Keeping his eyes down when the cashier wrinkled his nose at him. He found the grimmest looking internet cafe he could and took a seat as far away from anyone else as possible. The overwhelming scent from the can battling the smell underneath and sticking in his throat as he sat down into its truth.

He was homeless, without money, without work, with only distant family. His next meal, his next wash, his next bed at the mercy of their charity. Moth looked at the dirt engrained under his fingernails as the internet dragged out his torture, longing for Venice, with its endless water and its sky full of sparkle. It would be good to go back to feeling as inadequate as he had in Venice. Not here, stinking, filthy, clinging to the hope of a single email.

He left with his heart blistered numb.

She had sent money. Less than she normally sent. Short messages that he had to come home, to get the right visas, to travel further. She was working out how to get him back. She had received an email from a man called Bonnier, who was helping her. Who was he travelling with? Moth had to get to Samsun, a port on the north coast of Turkey, and let her know when he arrived. She would support him going wherever he wanted to, but he must come home first.

How Bonn had got in touch with Isabelle defeated him, but the added weight of their conspiring to get him back to England, alongside the absence of any other options, greeted him in the vivid daylight of the street outside the internet café and crushed him.

He withdrew the money, found a cheap and filthy hotel. Stood in the shower and let the ragged emotions run out of him as the dirt puddled round his feet and refused to go down the hair clogged drain. Looking in the mirror he held a pitiful disposable razor in his hand, staring at the blue eyes that peered back at him. Between the tousled damp hair and the scraggly, itchy jawline, Moth couldn't see any light left in them, they blinked in curious flat detachment. The sharp line of his nose, which reminded him of his father, sat with a vague skew. His eyebrows were too pale and wide. His lips, his smile, his scar, lost beneath the beard. What difference did being clean make? It couldn't change who he was. Moth decided against shaving, he didn't want to see what he looked like underneath.

He thought about lying down, sleeping until all the thoughts and feelings had emptied out of him. Waking up with no emotions left to torment him. He closed his eyes, wishing for that emptiness, opened them to see the small, crumpled bed reflected behind his back and felt his skin itch. He dressed in his spare set of clothes, barely any cleaner than the ones he forced stiffly back into the bag and left. His feet heavy and legs aching as he walked the streets, looking for supplies.

He found a small tent, barely large enough to house him. Bought packets of dried food and gifts to compensate for the fact that he returned cleaner than he had left. He gave them both new sleeping bags. For Atabey, a sauté pan to cook in, a selection of herbs in plastic packages, a notebook and a pen. For Kadri, a new backpack, a penknife, maps of the countries round the Black Sea. Watching Kadri's pleasure as he packed and repacked his own backpack, and Atabey's as he opened the herb packets and breathed in their scent before pulling a sprig out to add to their food. The scent rising in a brief, sharp surge before being swept away on the cooling air of the day, Moth sat apart and straightened out his own backpack, feeling none of their joy. The afternoon was fading, as soon as they had eaten, it would be time to move on. To get on the bikes and keep pedalling. The thought of it drained him even further and the memory of Bonn's email sucked away what was left of his energy.

He was a fucking idiot. What did he think he was going to be able to do with two unregistered refugees trying to sneak into Europe? He should be grateful if they managed to get him out. Did he know he was now on the Turkish unregistered immigrant's database? He was to get to Samsun and wait there. Perhaps, just perhaps they might be able to get them on a boat. He had to get there fast too, Bonn was being moved about again. By next year he mightn't be able to help. If Moth changed the plan, Bonn promised to get in touch with the local police himself and have them all arrested.

Next year? You'll be lucky to make Samsun by next decade at this pace.

Watching while Kadri traced the distance between them and Samsun on his new maps, Moth toyed with his share of a packet of reconstituted quinoa and rice. There had been other messages, from Nat and Kit. The focus on their lives, the delight in Christmas approaching, in his possible return, the demands of work, clients, staff and school friends. The combination of tasteless food and an overblown Christmas made him nauseous. The feeling that he was being dragged back for a scolding turning over and over with the cloying grains of food. Moth put his bowl down, ignoring the looks they threw his way. He had no positivity left for them. Bonn thought he was an idiot. He'd just wanted to give them a chance.

You wanted one yourself.

Moth went to check the bikes. Crouching down to feel

their tyres, turning his back to the boys. Placing his forehead against the cold, clammy metal of the frame and closing his eyes, Moth faced the emptiness down.

Luca hadn't replied.

Nothing.

Among the flurry of emails, orders and demands from Nat, Kit, Isabelle and Bonn, there was a glaring absence of chances.

Moth gripped the metal frame of the bike and clenched hard. Life narrowing down to that aching point. Knowing he had to get up and lead the boys out into the evening, down the long hard road to Samsun and whatever hope Bonn could conjure for their future.

What chance was there left for him to hope for?

You blew it.

IN THE DEEPENING chill of an early November evening, Isabelle sat in the drawing room with Kate on the opposite sofa and Indigo curled up asleep in her lap, listening to the fire popping and her daughter's steady breathing, reading about her great-great-grandfather, Albert.

She would never know the truth of Albert, or his life in India. All she had were glimpses of what he left behind, a wife abandoned, a child raised by a grandfather. She read of the child Arthur's birth, in India in 1873, able to picture Arthur all the way from his death at the Somme to his beginning in a country she knew. In Bombay, in the same house she herself had grown up in. This a shock, to realise that too had always been part of Riverdell. She read backward to the marriage between Albert and Constance, recorded by his father, Edward. Back to 1869 when the heir to the great Clive fortune, Lady Harriet Windsor-Clive, died and left it to a distant grandson, the same year Albert had joined the British India Regiment. She felt the schism of this year. The way her great-great-great-grandfather Edward, noted this disconnection by the Windsor-Clives, a forgetting of his own family as the more important one moved on. Pride nevertheless in his son's posting to India. Delight in the hasty marriage to Constance. Sending his son married and secure as an officer to a wealthy beginning. She closed the diary and put it aside, watching Kate stroking Indigo's hair in a reverie and finding her thoughts smooth into focus with the repetition.

Behind them, the sweeping, dove grey, silk curtains she had made were drawn across the wide bay window, blocking out the dark night. Shadows hung in their teasing creases and chased the details of the asymmetric folds and swagged trails of tassel edging. They still gave her pleasure, remembering the hours of piecing them together and stitching the complicated folds and drapes into place, hoping for her ideas to work. Working across enormous drops and the fourteen widths it had taken to cover the window had demanded immense patience and looking at that evidence comforted her.

In the past weeks, her lists had held the fraying edges of time and energy together. Bright and fearless stuck over her sewing machine. Quietly cleaved between the pages of her diary. Sewing in the early hours of morning and into the late hours of night, Isabelle felt herself moving toward completion while holding a wide medley of separate parts at bay, just as she had with the curtains.

When Kate's groups had finished, she and Indigo forged an indomitable bond of domestic chaos that put Gosia in a bad mood, but which Isabelle did nothing to curb. The drawing room filled with the unhindered flow of Indigo's collecting instinct. Often, she would walk in to find them comparing finds from distant corners of the house and see a joint expression of mutiny daring her to complain. A look that stretched from Kate's raised eyebrow to Indigo's clenched fist and made them an inseparable force of obstinate indifference. Kate's expression saying "just mention Christmas, I dare you" while her daughter looked at her with the total confidence she was protected by Kate from all interference. Isabelle would take her coffee out into the hallway and look at the carnage that stretched, as unmovable as the rebellion on their faces, as far as her eyes could see. Peering at her through the open door of the kitchen, trailing down the stairs, lolling over the hall sofa and piano stool, trotting down the east corridor to the growing nest in her workroom window. She would look at it, seeing beyond to the ignored bedrooms upstairs, outside to the empty courtyard that awaited a tree, and feel a shiver of fear run through her at the thought of Kit arriving unannounced to check her progress on Christmas.

Her longer reply to Luca's distressed email had initiated a daily barrage of emotional anxiety that she had to switch to WhatsApp to manage, for if she waited to check her email, she would sit down to find he had answered his own concerns three times over and twisted himself into a knot that unpicked all her work and took an hour to unravel.

Martin was her constant in this chaos. Sitting in the study while Kate was busy with Indigo and trawling through sites with her to find the best options. Size, shape, age, cost. It was a rabbit hole of choices she often felt drowned by.

Avoiding Kit's demands became easier as he only ever rang with a swift and curt question as his own work pressure mounted. Her answers developing a murmured sidestep of responsibility or agreement. He was too busy to even notice, used to giving orders and moving onto the next with the confidence that all he said would be followed.

The disagreement between her and Steve about Indigo had been swept under the carpet of his winter social life that she had neither the time or energy for. Her erratic work hours and his demanding social life reduced his overnight stops, their conversations and intimacy dwindling to a polite sharing of bodies and silent post-coital cuddle where she waited for him to fall asleep before shuffling across to her own side of the bed. She knew he was waiting for a better time to talk. And she knew she was trying to make sense of everything before she found that better time, ticking off options, marshalling her lists, steadying her decisions.

Kate glanced up to see her watching them. 'Penny for your thoughts?'

'Not worth it.'

'Liar.'

'Nothing as adorable as a sleeping child,' Isabelle offered.

'Better,' Kate agreed. Glancing at the diary Isabelle had pushed to one side, she asked, 'What are you hoping to find in there?'

'Understanding.'

'About the past?'

'No.' Isabelle traced the line of gold that marked the year. 1865. She was getting closer to the start of Riverdell's story. 'About the future.'

'You're trying to see it backwards?'

'In a way.' Isabelle stretched on the sofa. It was gone 11 pm, they should all be in bed. 'It's scary, reading the consequences before you see the decision. Makes me aware of how awry our plans can go.'

'I wouldn't have thought you needed any more encouragement to avoid making decisions.' Kate smiled at her, eyes twinkling with kindness.

'I'm seeing caution and patience as strengths.'

'Oh, is that what it is?'

'Umm.'

Kate teased the edges of tangled curls apart with garden-scarred fingers. 'What is it you're trying to work toward?'

'I'll tell you when I know.' Isabelle sat up and pulled the diary to her. 'I'll go lock up, it's way past time we all went to bed.'

'You're avoiding the question.'

She paused on the edge of the sofa, pondering.

'Actually, you're avoiding rather a lot of things.' Kate looked at her with pursed lips and a raised chin. Lifting her hand to count on her fingers. 'Choosing a tree for Kit to hang lights on. Resolving your spat with Asha...'

'... her spat with me...'

'... planning a trip away, sorting childcare options, tidying the house up for Christmas, putting those damn diaries back on the shelf. Why do I get the feeling you're hiding?'

'You have a suspicious mind?'

'I have a fine nose for evasion, and a sharp enough mind to know you're hiding it under a heavy workload.'

Isabelle clutched the diary to her chest and looked at Indigo. She wondered if Constance had sat here, a young Arthur on her lap, waiting for Albert to come home. Wondered at what point she had realised he never would.

She stood up and went to bank the fire. Kneeling on the hearth and putting the diary to her side, reaching to put the guard in place. 'I'm not being evasive, I don't want to tell you one thing and then have it not happen.'

'Well, are we at least doing Christmas?' Kate asked. 'Or can I take the total disarray of the house as evidence you're planning to break Kit's heart?'

'Would you care if I did?' Isabelle asked the embers.

A deep pause before her slow answer, 'I wouldn't want to be there when you broke the news.'

'I'll bear that in mind.' Isabelle rose and turned toward the door. 'Go on, head to bed, I'll come get Missy when I'm done.'

'No, I'll take her with me.' Kate heaved herself and Indigo to the front of the sofa and picked her up. 'She'll only wake up at some godforsaken hour and bother you. We can have breakfast together upstairs. Give you a good head start to the day.'

Isabelle stood as they passed and put a gentle kiss on Indigo's oblivious head. 'She'll never want to come back to me by the time I'm done with Christmas orders.'

As they left the room, Isabelle bent to finish the fire. Prodding the embers, which rose, sparked and resettled, enchanted by their glowing form, Isabelle worried if Kate was right. Was this patience or avoidance? And when would the future show her the answer?

IN THE MIDDLE OF NOVEMBER, a piece she hadn't known was missing, slipped unexpectedly into the making and pulled all her tacked together thoughts taut.

It began at dinnertime, as she was sat at the kitchen table listening to Kate and Steve talk. Indigo was on her lap, playing with a small hand-held mirror that he had found in the bottom of a drawer and given to her. The mirror itself was aged and spotty, like the one in Isabelle's bathroom, the handle worn and smooth, the back an etched, dulled silver. Steve had brought a fresh side of salmon for Kate to cook, and they were stood by the Aga, watching it poach in wine and garlic, talking about the virtues of oysters and mussels while the aromas reached for the far corners of the room, when her phone pinged. She reached for it on the table and by the time she picked it up it had pinged again. As she opened the screen a third ping brought their conversation to a halt and their eyes to her. Indigo reached for her phone and, as Isabelle moved her hand away, she saw and strained to catch the abandoned mirror heading for the tabletop. There was a scramble of child, hands, phone and mirror. The phone dropped to the floor and pinged again. The mirror landed on the table glass side down and they all heard a soft crunch as it connected with the wood.

'Shit,' Isabelle said as Indigo scrambled down from her lap and reached for the phone. She picked the mirror up and saw shards of glass fall out onto the table. 'Oh no.'

Kate moved to get Indigo while Isabelle looked at the damage.

'Hey, it's no problem.' Steve reached over and scraped the shards back from the table edge. 'Let's get it cleared up before someone gets hurt.'

'Careful, you'll get a splinter,' Kate warned.

'Probably deserve it, stupid thing to give a young child.' He moved to get the bin. Lifting the top off and holding it to the table edge to scrape the bits into.

Indigo gave the phone to Kate reluctantly and turned to see the damage at the table. She watched Steve knocking the remnants of glass out of the mirror and held her hand out.

'Sorry, kiddo,' Steve told her. 'Busted.'

Indigo took this in and began to simmer on the irritation. Isabelle's phone pinged again.

Kate handed it to her with a frown and tightened her hold on a wriggling Indigo. 'Perhaps you better answer that. It seems important.'

Isabelle took the phone and pushed back from the table. 'I'll be two minutes.'

She left the room as Indigo gave full vent to her frustration. Walking through the hallway she flicked the screen open on her phone. A barrage of notifications from Whats-App, Facetime, Gmail. She retreated to her desk, opening the WhatsApp messages from Luca first. A breathless emotional assault she had to sift through to find sense. A microscopically detailed list from Kit of things he needed doing, arranging, finding, and a date he wanted for fitting Christmas. Amongst the emails, a name she didn't recognise.

Jacques de Bonnier.

She put her chin on her fist and read it. She reread, pondered and thought some more and pulled her lists out from between the pages of her diary, turning them sideways, adrift from the solid edge of the table. Unpicking in her thoughts the shape she had been making, Isabelle felt a twist in the cloth of her life. Elsa had once told her she had a quiet strength, and not to lose it. All she'd seen was her own weakness, her inability to be as strong and determined as those around her. Sitting in her study, snipping the stitches that had held her thoughts together and rearranging them, she could see at last what Elsa might have hinted at. Life was non-resistant, like fibre. You could pull it apart and remake it. Even though the world wanted you to believe it was set. If you had the courage to look sideways at what else there was to work with.

A knock on the door made her jump.

'Hey, you get lost in here?'

She looked up to see Steve standing there and blinked. 'Sorry, I was just coming back. It took a bit longer than I thought.'

'A bit longer? You've been in here nearly an hour.'

'You're joking?' She didn't believe him and looked to find the truth glaring at her on her laptop. 'Oh God, I'm sorry.'

'Working on something important?' He nodded at the pages beneath her hands, the pencil held aloft, quivering with disturbance.

She tried to catch that last thought that had been about to knit itself together and watched it whipped away by Steve's presence. She put the pencil down, gathered up the sheets and tidied them back inside the covers of her diary.

'Yes, sorry, I got a bit swept up in it.'

'No need to apologise.' He stepped inside the study, hands lost in his pockets, looking around. 'I don't get to come in here often. Riverdell HQ, huh?'

'Hardly that.' She stood up and moved to the side of her desk. Aware of his intent gaze at the closed diary sat on the desk beside her. 'I should go see to Indigo, put her to bed...'

'Kate's doing it. You're good, relax for a minute.' He moved to the sofa, seemed to consider it, then sat down. His strong thighs wide apart, his arms resting on them as he leant forward to pick up one of the diaries from the low table. 'What are these?'

'Old diaries from former owners.' She moved to the chair opposite him, watching him open the diary and flick an idle thumb through the pages. Trying not to reach forward and snatch it out of his hands.

'Must be weird, knowing you've got all this to live up to.' He closed the diary and put it down, sat back in the sofa and stretched an arm out along the back, looking across at her with his easy smile. 'I've always felt life was entirely my own to make. Can't imagine having to follow in someone else's footsteps.'

'I don't feel I am,' she said slowly, relishing the sound of those words as she voiced them. 'I'm curious about my old family, but not because I want to follow them.'

Steve nodded and pursed his lips, seeming to weigh up her words, glancing again at the room.

'I've never dated a rich person before,' he told the room as much as her.

'I didn't realise you were dating a rich person.' She pulled her legs up to the cushion, tucking them in. 'I thought you were dating me.'

'It's part of the package though, isn't it?'

Package.

Isabelle got stuck on that word. Seeing a suitcase with herself in it, Indigo, Kate, Riverdell, Rob, Kit.

Package.

It had a reluctance attached to it, a tatty label that had seen too many journeys. Stuck on the thought, she failed to respond, and Steve gate-crashed her thoughts.

'I'm wondering where I fit in the mix. Kind of, well... getting the vibe our relationship isn't a priority for you.' He glanced at the papers on her desk. 'I'm trying to understand what it must be like, to not need a relationship, to be all... this.' He waved at the room.

'This?'

'Um, independent, financially and maybe, sort of, emotionally?'

'Emotionally?'

Steve folded a foot up onto his knee. His arm crushing the soft back cushions.

'I guess, Isabelle, the thing is...' he paused, studied the hand resting on his leg, '... I'm wondering, what do you need that I can provide?'

She looked over her knee at him. Aware that they were sitting on the anxious edge of a critical conversation, limbs barricading the discomfort. It stirred up depths of dread in her, remembering other conversations in this room that had been difficult. She gripped the edge of the chair, its paisley swirls pulling those memories close. She felt them eddy and swirl and realised she could drown in them as she always had, in the face of Hester's antagonism, or James' quiet expectations, or Kit's presumption, or Asha's irritation. Or she could speak her own thoughts and rise to the surface. She could be the strength that Elsa had always seen in her.

'I'm not sure a relationship should be founded on need,' she said.

'Aren't they all?' he asked. 'I mean, look at you and Kate, or Indigo, or Rob. Aren't you all bound together by a need that you're fulfilling in each other?'

'I think we choose to be here, rather than it being based on need.'

'Everybody has needs, Isabelle. To build a life together, or for a family, or for sex, or to make a home,' Steve continued as though she hadn't spoken. 'I want to feel needed, and to fulfil those needs in my partner to feel proud of myself.'

'I struggle with that,' she admitted. 'I don't want it to be about need.'

'I'm not surprised, after all, what do you need?' He twitched his hand at her, the room, the house. 'I see what you have, a family, a home, independence. I'm not sure where I fit in, except in the bedroom, and I'm not sure you even want that all the time. I mean, what do you need when you have all this?'

'I struggled with it even before I had all *this*.' She was tired of him pointing at the room. As though Riverdell was the sum of her, rather than simply a part. 'I've always struggled with other people having all these needs that I must fulfil. I suppose I always tried not to be needy in return.'

He was looking at the diaries on the table, listening to her. Rubbing the edges of his thumb against the sandpaper-roughened imprint of his fingers. She could hear the rasping sound in the silence of the room. Feel a chill where the fire sat dying and draughts licked down the hallway and in the door. It was not the most warming environment for a heart to heart. The tall bookcases seemed to be leering over them, counting every word.

'Okay, so if you don't need me, what do you want from our relationship?' Steve asked.

Relationship.

Another word that caught her in a vortex of thoughts. She had so many different relationships. Their names rose in her mind and their faces twisted beneath her fingers tracing the pattern of the chair fabric as she foundered. Steve waited for her on the far side of the smooth table between them. He was patient this man. He was kind and thoughtful. Attractive and attentive. Yet he existed alongside, a part tucked into the whole, not commanding the scenery of her life.

'I think I struggle with the idea that there should be a primary relationship in my life,' Isabelle tried to speak the thoughts into sense. 'I always feel that my life gets squished out of shape by them. My relationships are wide and complex, and I value them all. I don't know what you mean when you ask, "What do you want out of this relationship?"' She paused and thought about it. 'I don't know what I would say if Kate, or Asha or Indigo asked me that question.'

'And you don't see it as different?'

'Different to...?' she struggled to focus on the meaning threading between the outer words and the inner thoughts.

'You don't see our relationship as different to those?'

'Do you?' Isabelle asked.

'Yes.' His hands came together in fists, tapping their knuckles in agitation as he sat forward over his knees. 'At least, that's what I want. Our relationship to be primary in our life. Or rather, any relationship I'm in to be primary to both of us.' He opened his hands and gave a shrug that suggested it was obvious, really.

'Oh.' She uncrossed her legs and reached toes to the floor, sat back and tried to visualise the completeness of his vision. 'So that would mean...'

'Living together. Choosing our home together. Raising a family together. The normal things all people want.'

Isabelle could feel an edge of irritation in his final words. The same edge she was used to getting from other people. She glanced over at the papers on the desk. Swirling in there were elements of the same expectation. She glanced at the diaries, wondering, was it being a mother, or owning Riverdell, that made her realise she had a choice. She had always run away from the weight of expectation before. Now, she had more reason to stay and fight it.

'I don't think I see those things as normal.' Isabelle looked back at Steve. 'I see them as the choices we make. If they're right for us.'

'And they're not right for you?' he asked.

'I'm not sure they are.' She had a vision of Rob sitting on the sofa where Steve had transposed himself and knew that she felt more comfort with Rob there than she did with this man. That the complexity of her relationships might not be explainable but that it did not look like the finished product that Steve spoke of, looking in at her world and trying to shape it to his own vision. 'I think life is fuller than being committed to one person and I see that as a narrowing, not an enriching idea. I couldn't pick a single cloth to cut my life from. I know what fits together and what doesn't, and I let that guide me.'

'So, million-dollar question coming up,' Steve smiled and paused. 'Do I fit in?'

He didn't fit on that sofa. That was for sure. He sprawled across it, taking too much space. His legs wide open and commanding a funnel vision to his dick. His arm draping expectantly across the back, suggesting where she should be.

'I haven't had time to figure it out.'

Steve took a deep breath, nodding his head as though she had given him a much more solid answer than she thought.

'I know that's a crap answer,' she added. 'But it's the truth of where I'm at and I can't give you anything other than that now.'

'How long do you think you'll need to know?'

How long is a piece of string? Isabelle, who could cut the perfect length piece of thread for any job, couldn't see the length of this one.

'I mean, maybe if we saw more of each other?' Steve sat forward into her silence, leaving the sofa squished out of shape. 'Is one night a week enough for you to know anything, really?'

She tried to consider him here more than one night a week. In her bed, herself staring at the ceiling thinking Kit might have spoilt her for any other lover while Steve caressed her body.

'Any answer would do,' Steve teased her.

'I'm sorry, I need time to consider. I can't give you answers for the sake of it.'

'Fair enough.' He tapped his fingers against the surface of the table. 'I wasn't expecting to have this chat tonight, I've been waiting for a good time. Got left alone in your kitchen a bit too long, began to think you'd forgotten me altogether.'

Which was the point, really. Even if she controlled how often he was there, when present he would expect to be prioritised. When the world was asking her to piece together a puzzle that hung upon another person entirely. And she would not apologise for that. For putting the other people in her life first. Apologise for herself, yes. But for caring for Moth, or Luca, or Kit. No. She would not apologise for that. As she held the apology back that he really wanted, they both saw the moment flip into silence, the rest of their expected evening gasping for breath like a fish landed on the shore. Steve nodded again and she was irritated by it. This nod that told her he knew more than she did. He stood up and shoved his hands in his pockets.

'I think I'll head home for the night.'

'Ok.' Isabelle stood up and folded her arms over her waist. Steve looked as though he was about to come and kiss her, nodded again and walked away to the door.

'Come see me, yeah, when you've had time to think?' he said from the door. 'Ball's in your court, Isabelle. I'm not a pushy guy. I want this, even with all the add-ons, but I need you to want me too.'

She watched him walk out of sight, heard his steps down the corridor. Listened as the front door opened and he crunched across the gravel. His footsteps receding fast behind the thick curtains.

Add-ons.

Is that what they were?

IT WAS ONLY as she stepped out of her car and tried to avoid the puddles that she realised it had been too long since she came to the farm. Five years in fact. She had not been to Home Farm since the end of 2011, before she had left for India that last time. Before Moth and Nat had come to Riverdell. In fact, the last time she had been here was when she and James had faced their second pregnancy together. It had passed into her ownership with the inheritance of Riverdell and out of it with the sale to James and Asha without her having been here. Her friendship with Asha had played out almost exclusively at Riverdell, a fact that stung her with guilt as she looked across the wide turning space that encompassed the house on one side, its low windowsills and sagging roofline speaking its age, the old stone barn that ran perpendicular to it, and the rear end of the modern buildings that sat opposite and ran away toward the fields, their slatted wooden sides giving glimpses of the space beyond.

It had changed. It was no longer only James' farm. The gate that ended the lane hung straight, the verges around the parking space were trimmed, and the door was painted a rigorous, intimidating burgundy. Neat rows of wellies were hung upside down on a rack beneath the cover of the porch canopy. Curtains were flapping behind the open windows, and she could hear Asha's voice inside.

She closed the door of the car and walked toward the burgundy door, the small box in her hand feeling woefully inadequate. There had been a time when she would walk into this house without announcement but, though Asha swept in and out of Riverdell with the same energy as the late November wind stirring the curtains, Isabelle was not bold enough to walk uninvited past that vivid paint. It had taken all her courage to get this far.

In the nine long days since Steve had left her to ponder on the nature of their relationship, Isabelle, aware that he had left her a challenge to answer, and that both Kate and Rob were being remarkably silent on his absence, had found herself focusing instead on all those add-ons. Coming to understand, as she tried to find the answer Steve wanted, just how much she would do to hold onto them. She raised her hand and knocked lightly on the door.

Inside, she heard silence spread. Strained for the sound of movement that didn't come. She waited, looked back at her car, knocked again. She hadn't expected this to be easy. Had deliberated for days over whether to bring Indigo or not. Deliberated over flowers, wine, chocolates, cake. Morning coffee, afternoon tea, evening drinks. She heard footsteps on the stone floor behind the door and stepped back from the hard-brushed step to the weed-jerked gravel. Asha pulled the door open. Her hair scraped back in a greasy bun, a too tight cardigan wrapped across her chest, face red from exertion.

'Why are you knocking? I thought we were family?' She turned her back and walked away from Isabelle toward the kitchen, ignoring the box Isabelle held in her hands.

Isabelle longed for Indigo by her side, to push her

daughter forward to take that first oblivious step. She stepped tentatively inside. The interior had been transformed too. It had once been the lair of an exhausted farmer. Now it was the home of a mother. Pictures, ornaments, plants and photos claiming their space. Walls had been painted. Furniture moved. Toys accumulating in piles where once there had been dust. It stung to admit she had never taken the time to come and see how hard Asha had been working to transform her home. Asha's voice echoed from the kitchen, catching her guilt.

'I'm in the middle of housework, you should have let me know you were coming.'

Isabelle didn't point out the disparity between calling ahead and walking in without knocking. She was thinking how natural it had become to have a housekeeper. She didn't even realise she didn't have to do housework. No wonder Steve found her life odd. No wonder Asha thought her spoiled. What else was she growing comfortable with that should not be normalised? Isabelle moved to stand in the kitchen doorway.

'Can I do some dusting or... anything to help?'

Asha glanced at her from the other side of the room, swilling a cloth in the kitchen sink. Even short-sighted, Isabelle could see her disbelief. 'Why would I want you to do housework for me?'

'I don't know, I thought, maybe...'

'Isabelle!' Deryn came streaking into the room from behind her and nearly took her out with a hug to the knees.

Isabelle bent down and picked her up, giving her a squishy cuddle and a tickle, holding the cake box out of reach. Deryn looked over her shoulder and frowned.

'Oh, honey, I'm sorry. Indigo is at home.'

'Why on earth didn't you bring her?' Asha slapped her wet cloth into the bowl. 'They haven't seen each other for months.'

Isabelle put Deryn down and straightened up to look at Asha. Asha ignored her and spoke to Deryn. 'Go and find your books, Deryn.'

Deryn looked from her mother to Isabelle, weighing them up with a look older than a three-year-old had any right to control. Isabelle remembered a long-ago look on Nat's face in the kitchen at Riverdell and smiled down at her.

They stayed silent as Deryn hung her head and walked back out.

'So, what can I do for you?' Asha asked, cleaning the sink with brutal focus.

'I came to see how you are.'

'Fine.'

'I hear Marge is helping you out with Deryn.'

'Yes. So?'

Isabelle paused and took stock. She'd thought of all the starting points for this conversation. Apologies. Explanations. Offers. Stood here looking at Asha's taut back, at the bulges over the top of her skirt where the cardigan sat into her waist, the ripples forming on her back beneath her bra line, the air of neglect in her hair, Isabelle realised what it was to miss someone, to miss the sound and shape of them deeply, and then to see them again. To have the physical presence of them in your life. A vision of loveliness she couldn't help but stare at and feel seeping into her consciousness. She felt the great absence of Moth. Of his having been gone for so much longer than he had been part of her life. The depletion of memory and the emptiness of that visual imprint. She could hold the pressure of wanting to see him in her hand, grasp it, taste it, like the ripe peach she had given him on that long ago afternoon when they first met beside the river in the gardens at Riverdell. The thought took all her castrated imaginings and compressed them into truth.

'We've missed you.'

Asha didn't turn or respond.

'Indigo and I have missed you both horribly. I'm glad you're coping and you're fine, but we're not.'

Asha's back remained rigid, her head ever so slightly turned to listen so that the curve of her cheek showed. Isabelle took a step closer.

'Indigo won't sleep in her own bed anymore. The house is a bombsite and Gosia is about to quit. I'm swamped with orders and need to find someone to work for me, and Kit's preparing to descend next week and turn Riverdell into bloody Santa's grotto but Steve thinks I need to prioritise him more.'

She could see Asha twitch the cloth in her hands. She took another step across the space. Seeing the clothes stretched in front of the old range to dry. The huge casserole dish covered with a tea towel, ready for dinner that evening. Asha's suits lay out on the ironing board, pressed and ready for tomorrow and the start of another week.

'I miss Deryn's voice ringing in the hallway and worrying all day about the state her clothes are going to get into. I have no idea what to do for Indigo's birthday without her.'

She stopped midway between the door and Asha's stout back, scared to go any further, feeling her palms moist beneath the cake box.

'I can't remember the last time I laughed with you or felt better about my life listening to you venting about a useless bloody farmer. I think that I might have lost the only real friend I have.'

Asha turned and looked at her, resistance written in stone on her face. Stretching her lips into a line, squinting her eyes, puckering her cheeks. Isabelle didn't know whether to step back or smile and froze in her indecision.

'You only ever think about yourself,' Asha said, but Isabelle noticed her lips struggled to stay harsh with the words.

Isabelle held the box out toward Asha. 'I brought pastries.'

Asha stared at her, looking her over. Isabelle could feel the same surprise in her eyes. The unexpected impact of seeing one another. The visual reality against the perceived slight.

'And what, that makes everything better?' Asha demanded, smelling the whiff of her own forgiveness creeping in.

'Oh hell, no.' Isabelle grappled to suppress a smile. 'I know it won't be that easy, I've seen how long you can hold a grudge for.'

They both thought about Hester and grinned. Asha stepped forward and took the box off her, reading the label she'd attached.

'You didn't even spell my name right.'

'What?' Isabelle blinked at the complaint.

'Honestly, all this time, it's A S I A, not with an h.'

Isabelle blushed. 'Why didn't you tell me before?'

'I wasn't mad enough at you before.'

Isabelle watched in silence as she opened the box. Waited for Asha, no, Asia, but not Asia, Isabelle battled the image in her mind of the word rewritten, sounding like the continent

Asia, register them. 'I got your favourite. Almond croissants from Matty in the market.'

Asha, ugh, Asia, raised her chin in defiance. The cake box balanced in one hand, the dishcloth still held tightly in the other.

'So, that's just the ice-breaker,' Isabelle said. 'What else is it going to cost?'

'What's what going to cost?'

'Forgiveness? Friendship? Getting back to you pointing out all my flaws.' Isabelle took a step closer. 'Because I miss you so much, and I'll do anything, absolutely anything, to put this right between us, but there's something you need to do for me too.'

'What's that then?' Asia pushed her shoulders back and her chest out.

Isabelle sucked her paltry frame inwards and tried to gather the threads of difficult words together. If it had felt hard in the study with Steve, here she was breathless with the dread of being honest.

'Childcare we can sort and I have some ideas or, rather, Kate does.' Isabelle saw Asia roll her eyes and shrugged her shoulders. 'My need to work being different to but just as valid as yours we can argue about...' Asia went to open her mouth to complain, and Isabelle held her hand up, '... forever if we need to. But the only person I owe an explanation to...' Isabelle heard her voice wobble, '... about my daughter...' she tried to control it and felt her throat constrict, '... is Indigo.'

Asia tilted her head and stared hard at her. Isabelle crossed her arms in front of her waist under that stare but did not look away.

'I know one day that conversation will come, but it's between me and her, and it's nobody else's business. I won't accept you harping on at me about it or bringing it up in company when you get drunk. Being told I'm a wet dishcloth of a spoiled bitch, yes. That. No.'

They looked at each other. Isabelle wondering if she could pull the words back in, retreat, leave, pretend she had never turned up with the audacity that she could put such words into the world. Both listening to Deryn heading back down the hall toward them.

'Fine.' Asia threw the wet dishcloth at her head, making her duck. 'Christmas. It's going to cost you Christmas.'

LATER THAT EVENING, sat in the study, Isabelle closed the diary with a reluctant hand. She glanced up from its aged leather cover. Indigo was playing on a rug in front of the fire guard, rolling the final apostle Easter egg slowly back and forth, pressure and warmth steadily melting it inside the foil wrapper. She was banned from eating it but wouldn't part from it. Kate was curled up at one end of the sofa, dissecting a competitor's vlog with headphones muting the noise and making notes in her pad. Rob was sitting at the other end, his socked feet up on the table, reading a book on community fundraising. Having failed to encourage his chess club to sponsor a youth division, he was intending to set one up himself. She watched them all from the comfort of the paisley chair, invisible in their focus, the leather covers of the diary on her lap warm from her touch.

It was the final one. Or the first. Whichever way you looked at it. The diary that had seen her first relative walk through the door of Riverdell. A late bride, a lesser match. Riverdell the consolation home that had saved her father's pride in his daughter's misfortune. Bought for his daughter, given to her husband as a dowry. Rowena had never owned Riverdell as Isabelle now did.

Isabelle glanced out of the study window at the dark night of the courtyard, the porch light showing the emptiness she had yet to fill. She could picture her great-great-great grandmother, Rowena Threlfall, nee Windsor-Clive, planting the magnolia in her long skirts, determined to do it herself. Her husband, a local glove merchant, fussing over the dirt, reminding her to be a lady. Recording the moment in his diary, and her response.

I'm not a lady anymore. That's in the past. This tree, this house, they're our future, and I want to be the one that plants it.

It had been worth it, this traipse through the old diaries. To find a woman who had set out to carve her own path. Isabelle would have given so much to speak to her. To comfort her through what was to come. That was the impossible thing, you never could. You never knew what was coming your way. How much harder it might get. How much might be lost. How your decisions might stack up for, or against you. How short those years you were planning on might end up being. They were so far apart, her and Rowena. So many male owners between them. Yet she felt right here, beside her. It had started with a woman, and now it lay with her.

'Kate,' Isabelle called to get her attention. Watching as she pressed pause and pulled the headphones off. Isabelle reached forward to put the diary on the low table. 'I've made a decision about the tree.'

'Steady now,' Kate said.

Rob closed his book and looked up with interest.

'You're choosing the new tree,' Isabelle told Kate.

'What?'

'I concur, for what it's worth,' Rob said.

'No, wait, we talked about this and...'

'No, you talked about this,' Isabelle cut Kate off. 'And now I'm talking about it. I know nothing about trees, and a tree is needed. Being in charge gives me the right to delegate. You're picking the tree.'

'But...'

'I'm not asking,' Isabelle said.

'Well, you do keep telling her to make her mind up,' Rob said to Kate, standing up and fumbling into his slippers. 'I'm going to make tea and find biscuits. Anyone who wants biscuits, follow me.'

Indigo bounced up from the rug to follow him out of the room.

'Your conversation this morning seems to have given you strength,' Kate told her primly.

'Yes, I know.' Isabelle thought about her chat with Asia, stood up too, moving across the room to slide the diary into the final tight spot on the bookshelves. 'Oh, one other thing, I want to plant something around it, so please make sure it's not poisonous to other plants.'

'Anything else?'

'Um, hurry up, I want it planted as soon as possible.' She headed for the door. 'I'm going for biscuits.'

THE NEXT DAY she set the final decisions in motion with Martin beside her.

They had spent the last half hour slogging it out over the final three options. Arguing the toss from all angles. It was the last decision. Since coming home from Asia's yesterday she had done all the other tasks, bar this and one phone call.

'Well, I figure there's next to nothing in it,' Martin announced. He sat back on his stool and looked at her. 'Your money, your choice. They'll all do the job.'

She looked at the three on offer and wondered what they'd think of the one she chose.

'Don't think too hard, go with your gut,' Martin suggested. 'You've got a good eye for things. You'll pick right.'

Kate walked into the study and frowned at Martin. 'I thought I heard your voice, I thought you'd packed up for the day.'

'Just offering a bit of assistance. On me way home now.'

'See you tomorrow, thanks again, Martin.' Isabelle closed the page on her laptop while Kate was still out of view.

'Welcome.' Martin stood tall from the side of her desk and moved toward Kate, saying to her, 'See you in the morning.'

Kate waited until he had walked away and looked at Isabelle from the doorway.

'Do I want to know what that was about?'

'Probably not.'

Kate pursed her lips and considered pushing for information. Instead, she said, 'I really do loathe to bang on Kit's drum, but I thought he was coming on the 26th to do the decorations?'

'And?'

'That's as in this Saturday, the 26th?'

'Yes.'

'Are you going to start tidying up the bedrooms?'

'I suppose I should.'

'I hope you aren't expecting a huge team effort on Friday

because Rob and I have discussed it and you can get stuffed. We do childcare, not housework.'

'That's because neither of you want to do Christmas. If it was a class event, you'd do housework in an instant. Have you sorted the tree?

Kate stared at her. Isabelle smiled back. She had faced down Asia, in her own lair, she was invincible.

'Yes, that's what I was coming to tell you.'

'Really?' Isabelle lowered her phone.

'But I can tell you're busy...'

'Oh, no, please, please, please,' Isabelle walked toward her. 'Really, already? Wow, I'm so excited.'

'Yes, come with me.' Kate walked out of the door.

'Couldn't you have brought the brochure with you?' Isabelle moaned as she followed her down the hallway, trailing her fingertips lightly across the India map. Soon, soon, she must remember that. It would happen soon.

Kate moved on through the kitchen, past Gosia and Indigo, who looked up in surprise, ignoring the piles of tree catalogues on the table and carrying on toward the boot room door.

'Where are we going?' Isabelle asked, skipping two steps to keep up.

Indigo dropped a buttery knife with a clatter and jumped off her chair to follow as they swept out through the boot room and headed downstairs.

'You're not planning to dunk me in the river in revenge, are you?' Isabelle asked, Indigo slipping a hand into hers as they hopped down the stairs after Kate.

'Tempting.'

The hasty scramble to keep up with Kate ended on the lowest terrace of the patio, a place Isabelle rarely came, preferring the mid-level above. The sodden, dull November lawns stretched out beyond the stone semicircle. The weir framed like an arrowpoint between the gap in the stone wall. Kate stopped in front of an enormous, damaged terracotta pot that Isabelle distinctly remembered Ed and Fred refusing to move for the umpteenth time, that hazy day of Kate's moving in. A tree rose from the pot.

Kate placed a caressing hand on the slender trunk, turning to look at her with a face as cloudy as the skies. 'Sorbus cashmiriana,' she announced brusquely.

Isabelle looked blankly at the slender branches and the curling fingers of the narrow leaves clinging on despite the cold. White berries perched like bunched pearls against the waxen bark.

'Rowan,' Kate told Isabelle's blank look and her heart leapt to think about her distant relative, Rowena.

'Believed for centuries to ward off evil spirits and to be a light to travellers, returning home,' Kate added, smiling at Indigo as she slipped a hand into hers, the clouds lessening from her face.

'You are kidding me?' Isabelle said, reaching to touch the luminous berries. 'Why did you not suggest this before?'

Kate looked at the tree as though she wanted to answer pithily and got stuck on the options. Her hand caressed the bark as she pondered.

'I grew it from seed,' she said. 'A friend sent me a clutch of them, this was the last one I planted and the only one that thrived. I never knew where I'd end up planting it.' She fussed at the broken pot. 'Poor thing is pot bound, we might kill it moving it, but it deserves a better life than this.'

'It's beautiful.' Isabelle stood back and looked at it. 'Perfect. What's it called again?'

Kate stroked the tree again, paused, then looked back at her. 'Sorbus cashmiriana, or Kashmir Rowan.'

'Kashmir?' Isabelle blinked at memories stirring. 'Isn't that where...?'

'Beth sent me the seeds,' Kate raised her chin a little as she spoke, reminding Isabelle of Asia. 'Martin's been nagging me to get it out of the pot since I got here, but I've always been reluctant to, in case I moved on again. But...' she glanced down at Indigo, '... I can't think that it could end up anywhere better than here, with you two. I know your mother would approve.'

Isabelle blinked. Tears threatening with a rush she couldn't even begin to understand.

'If you cry, I'll cry and then we'll all cry,' Kate warned her, blinking hard. 'So don't, just don't.'

'Are you sure?' Isabelle nodded at the tree, Kate's sweater swimming against the grey-green backdrop of the garden. Indigo looking from one loved, pinched face to the other with sharp eyes.

'No, so don't ask again.' Kate sucked her composure in and picked Indigo up for reinforcement. 'Weren't you getting some toast, missy?' Indigo snuggled against her jumper and snaked arms round Kate's neck, the long blonde curls burrowing into the short flicks of Kate's wind-ruffled hair.

Isabelle chose. Making the final decision she'd left upstairs. Martin leaving her with three colours, Indium, Deep Ocean or Ontario. Not that the images had matched her idea of those colours at all. Perhaps it was being able to see only the deep blue knit draped casually across Kate's one shoulder as her eyes swam. Looking at the tree that lit the way home for travellers.

'Weren't you about to make a phone call?' Kate pushed

the conversation on. 'Now we've sorted the tree, what's happening with bloody Christmas? And what's happening with you and Steve?' Kate tickled Indigo's chin and headed back to the house. 'I know you're busy, but you'll lose him by ignoring him.'

'I'm seeing him tomorrow.' Isabelle looked at her phone as they passed her by, pulling up Kit's number. She didn't want to think about that visit, not just yet. Her courage was fit for one thing at a time. 'I believe you said you didn't want to be present when I broke Kit's heart.'

Kate turned back and stared at her, trying to process the meaning. 'You're joking, right?'

Isabelle let the tone ring on loudspeaker, raising an eyebrow in response. 'It appears I will be elsewhere for Christmas.'

'Oh, that's going to cost you, believe me.' Kate swept past her with Indigo, a smile deepening on her face.

Isabelle listened to the swift clack of her mule heels up the stone steps and looked down at the phone to see Kit's face. Her stomach backflipped, but she put a firm smile on her face as she followed Kate and Indigo slowly back to the warmth of the house.

'WE'RE BACK!' Kit opened the front door with his arms loaded, pushed it back with his knee and let the full box sag against the door. The call echoed through the empty hallway. 'Jay?'

'Downstairs,' his voice floated up the stairway from the kitchen.

'Come give us a hand.'

Adele pushed past him with a box full and headed down the stairs as Jay came up them.

'Where are your shoes?' Kit asked, looking at his bare feet.

'Upstairs, what you got?'

'At least half the dress department from the Royal Ballet, I reckon.'

'Surely the idea of fancy dress is that people bring their own?' Jay moved toward the stairs with a frown at the box by Kit's feet. It had burst its net packed boundaries and was fluffing tutus out the top.

'Yes, but most of them will make a piss poor effort. I want to have spares.' Kit turned back out the door and onto the drive.

The van was backed up onto the tight driveway, its doors open, boxes stacked high with the house lights shining onto them. It had been a fun trip, him and Adele taking the day to go back to London to pick up all the gear he'd managed to blag. Laid across the top of the boxes were an enormous pair of swan wings made from goose feathers. They were ragged and weary when seen up close but would look glorious in the right lighting. He turned to look at the house, scanning the facade. It was looking stunning already, but the moment he'd seen the wings in a Boxing Day online sale, he'd known they would be the crowning glory. And no one had been there to tell him otherwise before he hit the ridiculous price tag. He watched Jay appear in the open doorway, the hall behind him a tempting sight of twinkling lights, garlands on the stairwell and foliage across the doorways. They needed to be right there, over the door, framing the person stood in it, flecked with tiny lights. His mother would have loved that excess. Granny would have had a fit.

'How do you fancy a pair of giant swan wings?' Kit asked.

'I'm not even going to ask.' Jay walked down the steps. 'You had a good day then?'

'Bloody marvellous. I literally felt like a kid at Christmas.'

'This must be costing you a fortune.' Jay rang a finger down the long end feathers.

'Thank you, Grinch.' Kit pulled the first wing gently out from the van, small white down feathers floating free. They had drifted forward in the van as they drove home, fluffy snow that had made him and Adele hysterical. 'I haven't organised a party like this in years. I am buzzed, man.'

'When was the last one?' Jay took the far end of the wing as Kit backed away from the truck. 'Must be before our friendship, I've never been to a party here.'

Kit was walking backwards toward the door, paused at the question, causing Jay to bump the wing into him. 'I've never actually had a party here.'

'Never?'

'No, they've always been at someone else's home.' Kit began walking again.

'Where are we putting these things?' Jay asked as they walked into the hall.

'Put them down here for now, they're going up outside tomorrow.' Kit straightened up from the floor. The wings weighed more than his back wanted to deal with. It would take Fred and Ed to get them up. And Jay. He twisted his neck to loosen the muscles. 'Let's get the other one, then you can empty the van while I do food.'

'I never thought I'd say this, but I can't wait for this party to get here,' Jay stayed crouched down, stroking the feathered wing.

Kit envied him the relaxed crouch. His back had been playing up since Christmas Eve. Adele and his bloody arches.

Plus, four hours of walking along Weston beach on Christmas Day, followed by four days of intense decorating for the party since.

'I knew you'd get into it.'

'No, I can't wait for you to get out of hyperdrive and stop throwing fairy lights at anything that doesn't move.'

'Struggling to keep up?' Kit teased him.

'Yes.'

Kit led the way back to the van, extracting the second wing, waiting for Jay to ease the end out as he began going back to the house. Adele darted past them and began pulling boxes out of the van.

'I thought the team were off work 'til after the new year?' Jay asked.

Kit peered down the wing tip, catching the tone. The asking-not-asking tone.

'Yeah, they are, apart from Fred keeping you on track.'

'Oh.'

Kit scowled at him. 'Oh, what?'

'It's just...' Jay frowned down at the wing tip. 'I went out, earlier, for an hour. Thought I saw Henri driving away as I came back.'

'Couldn't have been, he's been away all week. He'd let me know if he was back. Besides, I'm not expecting anyone until the party, and he's already said he's not coming.'

'That's what I thought.'

'Must have been someone else?' They walked into the hall and laid the second wing down on top of the first.

'I guess.'

Kit could tell he wasn't convinced. It couldn't have been Henri, he didn't even live this side of town. Even though Henri had keys and frequently managed the house for him as part of their work schedule, there was no reason for him to be here. The lock up had all the gear he might need if he was working on something for next year. 'There's nothing here he needs, the only thing kept at the house is...'

'Are we putting all these downstairs?' Adele interrupted him, coming back in with another box.

Kit turned away from Jay. It was a small and singular box. He could easily have carried two more. But that was exactly why Kit had a monthly massage bill and Adele didn't. He didn't risk his back on anything, his livelihood depended on it. Kit decided he would lift one box only from now on. If he didn't change his habits, the next time the car needed updating he would be choosing it for seating position rather than looks.

'Yes, put them all down at the back by the windows. I'll sort through them there.'

'All of them? Adele disappeared down the stairs. 'I'm not moving *all* of them.'

'... is?' Jay prodded his attention back his way.

'Is?' Kit repeated.

'You were saying... the only thing at the house is...'

'Oh, yes. It couldn't have been Henri, I told you, he's away. Where did you go anyway?'

'What?' Jay asked, following him back to the van.

'You went out, that's good. Where'd you go? Anywhere nice?'

'The post office.' Jay put a hand on Kit's arm as he reached for the boxes. 'Kit, I never mistake a face. It was Henri.'

Kit pulled up from reaching into the van. It was late, he was hungry, it had been a long day, he was sweating, the evening was cold, and his back was tightening. He didn't want to think why, if, Henri might have been here. Or the fact that because Jay had been here, he had left the house that day not thinking it might be empty. Kit let out a big sigh.

'Can we get these boxes in and get me a drink?' he asked. 'It's been a long day and I've still got loads to do.'

Jay stared at him, jaw tense. Adele came out of the house, glided across the driveway and grabbed another box, saying, 'This is my last one. I'm not moving these while you two stand there gossiping.'

He turned away from the van with his back to Jay and threw his eyes skyward in exaggeration at Kit's dallying. Kit watched him walk away and held back a retort. Turned to see Jay staring at him with that prissy stubborn look that wouldn't be ignored.

'Ok, maybe it was Henri.'

'You don't think it's odd he was driving away for the one hour that we were both out of the house? When he's not even meant to be here.'

'No, I don't think it's odd, I think it's disturbing.'

'You didn't show me how to set the alarm.' Jay's face dropped its stubborn mask and revealed the real reason he was hassling Kit.

'I'm sure it's cool. Henri knows the alarm code anyway. He probably wanted to vent about his Christmas bonus. I've missed a couple of calls from him recently.' He'd intentionally ignored them, knowing that Henri would be livid about the lack of bonus. 'Don't sweat it, I'll speak to him in the morning.'

Jay looked unconvinced, turned to get a box.

'Hey, seriously mate,' Kit reached out to catch his arm, pulling him up as he went to walk back to the house, piling another box on top of the one he had. 'It's not a problem, don't fret about it.'

'I just, I shouldn't have gone out without knowing how to set the alarm. It could have been anyone.'

'And I should have shown you. No harm done.' Jay shrugged as he moved away. As he got to the doorway, Kit called, 'What got you excited enough to go out, anyway? Get sick of your own company?'

Jay turned back toward him, two bulging boxes in his arms, was about to speak when Adele appeared behind him.

'Aren't you done yet? I'm going to have a quick shower. I'll be five minutes tops. What's for supper?'

He disappeared before Kit could reply. Leaving him with Jay's face, tight-lipped and eyebrow-raised at Adele's comment. How Isabelle lived with this constantly was beyond him. As soon as this party was over, he was going to get Jay home and Adele back to work. He needed the house to himself for a week before he ended up dumping both of them.

'Yes, what's for supper, sweetheart?' Jay quipped as he moved into the house.

Kit stood on the drive and took in a deep breath, felt his back twitch and stared at the empty open doorway. Heat was streaming out of the house into the puddle of light left by the open door. Moths were flitting drunkenly across it. The streetlights were casting his shadow over them in disdain. He hefted two boxes, kneed the van doors shut and locked it. Sod it, the rest could wait until tomorrow. He would get Fred to do it.

Downstairs he dropped the boxes onto the pile which Adele and Jay had scattered in front of the windows. The large room was warm and filled with soft light that should have helped him relax. Instead, he went and flipped on the computer. The only thing kept at the house that Henri might not have wanted him to know he was looking for, was the paint collection master chart. Kit moved to put the oven on, pulled open the double fridge doors with a prayer that they were not entirely empty and scanned the shelves. He added ordering online to the evening's duties. He began to pull packets out, dragged bread from the freezer, opened a bottle of red wine to breath. Returning to the pc, he watched Jay gathering up the evidence of his day's reading scattered across the sofa.

'You were going to tell me what you got up to today?' Kit tried to smooth the ruffled feathers in the room down, resisting the urge to rub them all the wrong way.

Jay stood upright and held a clutch of diaries to his chest. More were on the sofa, nestling against a large brown package. He opened his mouth to talk just as Kit looked at the screen. When he glanced back, Jay was frowning at him.

'We're going to get some food on the table, sit down, have a glass of wine and catch up,' Kit told Jay. 'You should have come with us today, you'd have enjoyed it. London was buzzing.'

'I found something.'

'Something?' Kit asked, staring back at the screen. Loading, loading, why did everything take so frigging long to load? Life always seemed to be demanding he slow down and people, systems, computers, resentful if he asked them to work at his speed. 'Something good?'

The home screen finally appeared. Kit leant over the keyboard, frowning. He could check the password record, he'd soon know if someone had tried to access it. It wasn't that he was worried, he'd changed the password on Boxing Day morning, after working on the new shade of blue. It was whether Henri had been trying to gain access that he needed to know about.

'Well?' Jay asked, nodding at the computer.

Jay was too sharp by far, Kit ignored him, finding his way through the screens. Jay was also being as evasive as Isabelle.

'What's that?' Kit nodded at the parcel on the sofa.

'That...' Jay paused, glanced again at the package.

'Stop being precious, what you been up to?' Kit demanded.

'Don't be mad.'

The only thing he was going to be mad about was if Henri was trying to shaft him.

'Course not.'

'I read the last diary. There were two numbers, written in the back. On the inside of the back cover.'

'What sort of numbers?' Kit accessed the back data of the pc, trying to remember how to check access. Tech was not his strong point, though he'd paid enough to get this security setup. He had it written down somewhere, but that meant more time to dig it out.

'I researched it. The first was a post office box number. To a box here in Bristol. I went out to find it. I'm sorry, I should have asked first. I got excited.'

Kit looked up from the screen. Now he understood Jay's stress level.

'My mother had a post office box?'

'Yes.'

'Here in Bristol?'

'Yes.'

'And you found it?'

'Yes.'

'How the hell did you gain access to it?'

'I never expected to. Just figured I'd check if it was still there.'

'And?' The access screen flickered up. Kit waited for the blue swirl to stop irritating him.

'It was easy, the second number was a combination key. I punched it in and opened it.'

Three failed access attempts. The little French weasel.

'Wanker.' Kit spat out.

'Who's a wanker?' Adele asked, coming downstairs, dressed in shorts, drying his hair with a towel.

Kit glanced across at Jay and glared at him to keep quiet.

'Client, wants to change their plans.' He shut the computer back down. Well, now he knew. And with a bit of luck, Henri didn't know he knew.

'How dare they?' Adele moved toward the kitchen. 'Smells good, I'm starving.' He picked up a boiled egg and tapped it against the marble to crack the shell, turning his back to them.

Jay raised his shoulders to his ears in worry and held his hand out toward the computer. Kit returned the gesture toward the package on the sofa. They both listened to the tapping shell being cracked. Well, yet another thing to add to his already tedious list of evening's jobs. Kit went and grabbed glasses. He needed a drink, and a sit down, and food. Not more mysteries from beyond the grave. And no sodding arches tonight.

17

All that stuff about Rome not being built in a day, they never mention it fell in an hour.

One hour is about all it takes to topple an empire. A city. A life.

Kit is stomping through the house, furious with me. I'm sure he chose his hardest shoes for the maximum impact on my senses. Emotion is to him two things, love or fury. The rest are beneath him. And, of course, his fury is roused by what, and who, he loves most. He refused to pack, made me do it for him and promptly threw it out of the case in disgust. Granny had to intervene and her silent effort to fold his trousers with her shaking hands was even worse than his throwing them about the room like party streamers.

There is no way I can explain all this to them. He rages in denial, and she looks on in silence, trying to understand. It cannot be smoothed over, it is beyond that. Now I must rebuild my life from the very foundations.

I settled out of court.

It cost me everything. The little savings I have managed to

accumulate, my pride, my dignity. I chose to ask Granny for the money while denying her an explanation rather than extorting the stepmother. Shame heaped on shame, but I wouldn't grovel before that woman, and not because I wasn't prepared to in the end, but because I wasn't prepared to have her say no, I was surer that Granny would help me. A ninety-four-year-old lady who deserves better than a granddaughter who extorts her to buy her own privacy.

I cling to the thinnest shred of justification, that by burying my pride I have saved us all from public humiliation. It is a lie I need.

He is slamming doors now. The fury is running out. Thank the burning brimstone depths of hell, I could not bear him making this sort of scene at the station. I know it is selfish of me to ask him to see me off, but I want every last minute of him that I can have. He leaves for Riverdell in three days. I have arranged a van to take him, there is so much going with him, the train was impractical. The empty house will be a step closer to the grave for Granny, though I wonder if she won't sit down with a huge sigh of relief and pour herself a vodka.

How long before we return? Kit will see her sooner than I, he has promised to spend a week with her in August. He says he wanted to stay here, but somewhere beneath his anger is a truth he doesn't want to admit, he is excited at the thought of staying at Riverdell. But he would rather have me with him than leaving him behind. Granny looks so frail that I think it might be genuine rather than an effort to calm Kit and invoke his kindness. I can't think of it now, it will break me. I will give her all my attention when I return. When I have worked out how I can return.

Ben's lover was a sly bastard. Though I settled out of court to keep my privacy, he sent a letter to my employers, sharing enough to make them realise I was a liability to their cause. No matter the work I have done, the victories I helped secure, my potential damage to their image was greater. The news was shared wide and fast through the office. It was one thing to face that tea-drinking cuckold, who wouldn't look me in the eye as he sacked me, but the women... their disgust, their silent loathing... that hurt. I had failed them, failed womankind, tainted the name of all we'd worked for. This is a taste of how the world will treat me, with disgust and rapid disposure. I can imagine the boss washing his hands and wondering who was going to make his bloody tea. I wish I had spat in each damn cup I had to make.

Damn them both. Ben and his leech of a lover. Damn them to eternity.

I hope they give each other the misery they deserve when the money and the party run out. I hate them. I hate the men they are. I am sickened by the thought I wanted to be some part of that. Male, I could never have escaped the social parlance of masculinity, I would have become part of what I loathe. My own desire is a thing that sickens me, that leads me to this, this... ugliness. This taking, this abuse. I don't want any part of it.

I should have told them to go to hell and burnt the evidence on a pyre. But they had me trapped. The moment I read the letter suggesting the prosecuting lawyers would call for my diaries as evidence in the event of a court case, I knew it was over. Releasing a crushing tirade that matches Kit's. Knowing it is defeated, raging against acceptance.

I couldn't do it. To think about having my most personal thoughts and experiences read out in court. The thought makes me retch. I've kept my broken heart and tortured soul

together in the pages of these books, staggered along the
blind path toward self-knowledge, rescued myself from
despair and tormented myself with false, crushed hopes. I
would rather stand naked in the courthouse than have them
read to the public. And burning the diaries would have been
as great an admission of guilt as refusing to give them up.

My fury is now a spent thing to Kit's spectacle. It is burnt
low and desperate. Rage on, my wild son, with your clickety-
clack shoes and your tossing hair. Rage on and on and don't
let anyone tell you who to be but keep it to yourself and never
write it down. You will be damned by your own hand.

Kate's letter came to rescue me. I hope someone will pull
Kit from the depths of his despair as she did me.

She returns today, adamant as ever and she has asked me
to help her. In helping her, I help myself. Trapped between
exposure and financial ruin I have taken the opportunity to
run. She has bought me the tickets and tells me she has
written you and you are on your way back to Bombay,
awaiting my arrival. It is a frightening thing, this sudden
financial crush. Job gone, reputation tarnished with whispers
that will make it improbable to find another, savings gone,
my only home the one belonging to my grandmother or
rented on the back of a wage no longer available. It crashed
down in the lightest puff of wind, this arrogant, presump-
tuous life I built. The only things I have left are a ticket to
you, a hobbled promise to fulfil what I don't agree with doing,
and the hope to save my family from embarrassment.

Kit is fourteen, I hope he will be young enough to forgive
me when I come home. I'm not even sure how long it will be.
I don't believe for one minute that this pay-out will be the end
of it. When the money runs out, they will be back, asking for
more. If I am not here, their interest will wane. I think they

know they will get no support for harassing the elderly grandmother of their target. I hope my absence will give Granny and Kit peace. While I wait for them to move on, I must find a way to live, a place to go. All these years I've been obsessing over my body, to come to this... not knowing how I will live, let alone undergo major surgery.

So, though I still don't agree with Kate, I take what lifeline is thrown me. And though I come bringing what you desire the most, I know it won't necessarily give me shelter from my own storm. Ted might not even let me stop the night, he never could stand me. He'll see me for the serpent I am, offering riches, praying for treasures of my own. I have waited all these years for you to return and at last I have found the courage, or the momentum, or is it the humility, to come and find you. Will I be salve or death stroke to your marriage? The thought of you is a lure I cannot resist. It weaves alongside this trembling agony of a last hope that I am, in destruction, about to be reborn. It calls me on, sure that I am returning to what I should never have left. Perhaps we will all come home together and leave Ted where he belongs, alone in India, ruminating on his own mistakes, not dragging others down with him.

What will I miss as I run to you? Kit growing into a man. Granny growing toward the grave. Pivotal moments in both their lives and I'm running for the hills.

Oh, the time. Enough. I must prepare.

I shall dress for a party. Broke or not, I'll fly out from London in some damn style. I won't face Kate downcast and destroyed, she'll want my courage not my woes. She returns to what she has always had, a place in the shadow of Elsa's life, empty-handed while she watches Elsa grow in love and children. Believing she does what's best for all, not herself.

While I cover my back and aim for the greatest prize, no matter the cost to others.

Do I hate myself for this?

I ask myself so often now. I stare at my portrait and hate it, hate myself, and long for the fierceness I see in that scowl. I wish Granny had never had it painted, it haunts me as Dorian's did him.

At times, yes, I hate myself. At times, I hate the world. But mostly, I love fiercely.

My wild son, my invincible grandmother, my brave friends and you.

My chance to keep going, to rebuild, to try again.

Life is most precious when at its bleakest, it makes me realise how worthy the prizes are. Joy, purpose, love, bliss.

I know I must stop, prepare, leave this final anguish behind. I close this page to close my diaries. The chest goes to Elsa, and I shall leave the key here with Granny, who I trust to keep it from Satan himself. Elsa will keep them safe for me. She would never have the curiosity to read anyone's diaries, or the courage to read mine, even when her current anxiety about her fragile pregnancy is relieved. I am glad to be away for the birth, I shall leave that bitter pill to Kate. My diaries and son to Elsa and Kate, to keep them both safe. And a prayer for Granny, who I have nothing else to give, that I can one day make her proud of all she has done for me.

It is a fierce moment this. The sun is bright on the street outside. The sky looks endless over the thick leaves of the cherry trees. How I wish it were spring and I could see their blossom, that I have so despised, one last time before I go. The house reverberates with a life I am saying goodbye to. Kit's noise. Granny's high voice calming him down. The smell of her cake tempting us all to the kitchen to parley. My favourite summer coat with its striped lining sits on the wardrobe. The bed where I birthed Kit and cuddled him through childhood. This desk before the window, my pens and clutterings. I love this house in my bones, it has been home my whole life, shaped me, protected me, renewed me.

A final prayer, my fickle Goddesses, that one day I may come back and sit, pulling my scattered thoughts together on these pages and hear my boy clacking down the hallway in his shoes.

That I may stand before this image of myself and know peace.

18

The weather had been the reason he wanted to go south.

When he'd left Europe with such determination, he'd felt sure life would be easier if it was warmer. His decisions had been all about the bike, and the life that went with it.

At night, huddled into a ball in the restrictive second tent, Moth sensed Turkey was spiting him with the unusual cold spell. As his determination to leave eroded one exhausting day at a time, the country sent her worse weather to persuade him he wasn't wanted.

Three unwanted immigrants with no paperwork trying to get out of the country before they were caught and put in a detention centre. No real place to head toward other than away from that threat.

He began to understand how hope got crushed.

As November rolled into December, the days turned wet. Bright mornings appearing with cheerful sunrises and cloudless skies of hope that made it hard to sleep late. The hours thickening the sky with clouds until the weight of it began with a dribble and persisted with a downpour. By late evening, as they slogged away at the road, the clouds sailed away. Leaving them with a dancing sunset to briefly warm their sodden skin, before night took over and they rode on, shivering. The desire for lakes to swim in became the desire to find dry wood, even damp wood, any wood.

In the clinging damp and exhaustion of the journey Moth felt Kadri and Atabey withdraw even more from him. Into the huddle of their own warmth at night.

Perhaps it's not them withdrawing.

He focused on the map. Beyond getting all three of them out of Turkey, there was nothing else to focus on.

Sixteen kilometres a day to make Samsun by the end of the month. Brutal basics in between. Wood. Food. Water. Sleep.

He drew lines on the wrinkled pages, slicing the road to Samsun into a ladder. Each rung a hurdle they had to manage before he would let them stop.

Atabey grew to hate him and the journey, dragging his feet on the tarmac as he sat on the bike behind a sweating Kadri, demanding more stops, resisting getting back on the bike.

Moth wondered every time about leaving him sitting in protest at the side of the road, waiting to be rescued, before dragging him up and pushing them on.

He pushed away the uncharitable thoughts. Pushed away all thoughts. Pain, discomfort, exhaustion, emptiness.

Sixteen kilometres a day.

The spiteful days throwing up bigger hurdles.

The second bike hit an invisible crater in the road during a dark evening downpour. It burst a tyre, threw Moth off with a crunch against tarmac, and left the wheel bust. Moth nursing a bruised and twisted shoulder. Reminding him too closely of the tacks that had first thrown him from his bike in Italy. The callous hand scattering them out the window. The high bank as his body had hit it. His thoughts leading on from that fall to what had followed it. He'd lain on the road and refused to move, curling into his own ball of despair.

Kadri dragged him up and gave him a taste of his own medicine.

Bruised shoulder, bust bike or bleeding heart, they had to make sixteen kilometres a day.

While Moth sat beneath a twisted tree and nursed what heat Atabey could draw from burning its fallen branches, Kadri went looking for a replacement to the second bike.

Moth had stared silently into the pathetic flames and shut out all else, nursing the pain inside. When those dancing flames looked too hopeful to bear, he shut his eyes.

Nowhere he wanted to stay, nowhere he wanted to go. Except the one place he wasn't wanted anymore.

And it's all your own fault.

He curled up against the tree roots and let the pain dig in from the outside. Any distraction was useful from his head. The drowning depths that Bonn was right, he was an idiot. Isabelle was right, he had to go home. Luca was right, he wasn't worth it.

Moth sank into that pain and shut down. Remembering it from the days before Luca found him and took him to Lovere. From the days before he found Beau in Guethary. From the days before that, after his parents died and he had Nat to worry about. Leading all the way back to his father and the stench of shame. Rain sank through the bare branches of the tree and down his neck, each drip a memory of pain, crushed hope and pointlessness that he festered over as the night ticked by.

Kadri returned with a bike late the next morning and kicked him out of the despair, shouting and pulling on his clothes to get him moving. All of them dripping wet and exhausted.

'Sixteen kilometres,' Kadri said. 'Mothy, sixteen kilometres.'

No. You lost time.

Moth recalculated, they had to make eighteen kilometres a day.

How could eighteen kilometres a day be so overwhelming?

You were regularly doing seventy-plus through Europe.

Moth came to hate the road as much as Atabey.

The road, that is, not Atabey.

He didn't hate Atabey.

You don't much like him either.

Moving along the road, watching the landscape pass him behind a falling curtain of water, Moth finally faced why he didn't like Atabey. Atabey wanted only one thing.

A life. A real life.

The road, along with the weather, told Moth only what he didn't have.

A life. A real life.

A bike was not a life. Maybe when he was fourteen it had been the best chance he had of a life. Now, whenever he forced himself to get on it, the pressure that had once driven him had gone. Now he was neither running away from the past or heading into a glorious future. Just a stupid man, making the wheels go round, counting the miles off as his life moved from one pointless day to another. Hating the metal

beneath him. Not even looking at the view. Battling the temp-
tation that each set of car lights coming toward him offered
an end to all the stupidity.

When the road got busier and the traffic heavier, and he
began to crush his hands around the handlebars at the
oncoming rush of each artic, Moth took them over the higher,
lesser road, from Cakalli. Punishing them all with the burn in
their legs to overwhelm the crushing weight in his head.
Instead of cars they passed cyclists, out for the exercise kick
of the road in the dry afternoon. Staring at their bizarre duo
of bikes, the ragged trio of cyclists, as they passed. Moth
resisted the urge to stick his foot out and knock their smug
Lycra-clad shapes from their flashy, trim bikes. As the cyclists
and their stares increased, he could feel the town ahead
looming toward them and began to wish he could turn
around and find a dark cave to disappear into.

They arrived.

At a point when his only desire to see the cliffs over the
Black Sea was so he could throw himself off them, they
arrived at Samsun.

On the 29th of December, with clouds rolling across the
water, and the smell of a port thick in the air. Diesel, fish,
coal, salt.

Perhaps it's you who smells.

Moth looked at Atabey and Kadri dancing on the side of
the road as they looked down over the city, along the road
that declined toward the straggling suburbs, across the dull,
threatening surface of the Black Sea, feeling none of their joy
or achievement.

He felt rank. His clothes had been wet and barely dried
so often they were starting to cultivate mould in the creases.
His chin was covered in a two month, untrimmed, insula-

tive layer. His shoulder had knotted into a dull ache that crept up toward his ear and twisted his back into a cruel angle.

The sea stretched away from him, slapping in irritation against the bay. Moth had struggled to visualise it as a sea. On the map it looked like a huge, grounded lake. But stood at last on the heights, looking out over it, unable to see land beyond, he remembered the cliffs over Guethary and the same stinking level of despair and worthlessness. He looked at the glee in the boys and wondered if he would soon be reading an email that told him this was as far as they would ever come. That perhaps there was a way for Moth to cross that sea, but it came at the cost of leaving them behind.

You got them further than they would have without you.

Moth stayed straddling the second bike.

The third bike.

The third bike, that Kadri had found.

He didn't dare dismount to have to make himself get back on. He left them dancing and singing to each other in the rain-weighed dirt. When he climbed down from the bike today, it would be for the last time. Whatever happened in the next few days, he would not get back on. His old bike didn't even belong to him anymore. Kadri had mastered it and assumed command of it in the grind of the final haul to Samsun. If Moth had to get on a ferry alone, he would leave the bike with them.

You showed them the way. It's up to them now.

He stared out across the sea. Now he was here, it seemed endless. The last impossible distance he had to travel, wondering where he was headed or...

... who you're going to.

At least Samsun had been a destination. The reason to

keep going through all the torment. Arrived, all he could see was the end of reason.

HE FOUND A CHEAP HOTEL, in the loud, rough area of the docks. Left the boys to have the first shower and went to find the nearest internet cafe. Unwilling to sit in the double bedroom and listen to them getting clean together.

That the hotel owner hadn't blinked an eye at how many people were sleeping in the double bed, or the fact that there were only double rooms available, spoke highly about the calibre of the place. By nightfall there would be more noise to deal with. The walls were dirty, the corridors stank and even the Christmas tinsel draped above each room's doorway looked grimy. The place made Moth shudder as he walked outside. It was a relief to walk away from them. A relief to walk past the chained bikes and stretch his legs.

He moved slowly through the dying hours of the day. Light disappearing into the cloudy sky and being sucked away with the sun behind the hills. Samsun a town that lay early in the shadows while colour and light glimmered on the distant reaches of the watery view. His clothes felt thin and crisp with dirt, the aching cold reaching past his tired old Puffa jacket and making him tense. Pain and weariness mingled with the relief of walking and the slim weight of his unburdened rucksack on his back.

Everything you need is inside it.

He could keep walking. Not return to the hotel or the boys, or the weight of either getting them to Europe or facing his failure to do so. He could simply walk away and be no more than another disappointment in their lives.

Moth hadn't got the energy to think the idea through. He

walked until he found a cafe, sat and waited for the emails to show him what he had to do next. Twisting his tired, cold hands together and feeling the sweat of failure rise in them as he waited.

Bonn had emailed him daily for the last week. Repeating the command. Email me as soon as you arrive. Hurry up. What the hell are you doing?

Hi, we're here. What next?

What is next?

If someone sent him the next step, he would follow it. He didn't care what it entailed.

How low you have fallen.

He read the other emails with the sense that he might drown in them, catching up on a world that meant nothing. The barrage of Kit's fury with Isabelle about Christmas dimming to a curt query as to where he was. Nat's quiet disappointment even harder to swallow. Christmas. Had Christmas really been and gone while they cycled here? It was unreal to him. As distasteful as the hotel tinsel. He could see through a narrow rear window the beginning of the sunset reaching across the sea. It would be a relief, to go out and drown quietly in its depths, pulled down by filthy clothes and despair, rather than admit he was going home to all that. He checked his bank account, she had sent no more money.

She wants you home.

Moth stared at the near empty bottom line and could find no thought to cling to, no choice to consider. Bonn replied to his email.

He must be sitting on his inbox, the clucking great hen.

I've sent papers, can't guarantee they'll work. Your aunt has arranged tickets. If the others get pulled up by border control, they'll end up in a detention centre. It's their choice if they take the risk. Don't make them just to satisfy your hero complex. You need to collect the papers in person. Tobacco Pier. One hour. Don't be fucking late, you've caused me enough trouble.

One hour. He should go back and clean himself up. He Googled Tobacco Pier, found it less than a ten-minute walk away. Moth hovered his fingers over the keyboard, wanting to do more, to search for more. Information, options, plans. The world at his fingertips and it all seemed empty. He shut down the screen and left, stood outside looking back in the direction of the hotel, then toward the pier. What was the point in cleaning up anyway? He walked away from the hotel.

TOBACCO PIER WAS DESERTED. He'd dragged ten minutes out into half an hour via a slow walk to ease his hunger. When he got there, the last touch of the sun was catching the furthest white tips of the waves. He had missed the sunset, glimpsing it from between the shops as he dragged his feet. Lingering in the shadows between the shops and alleyways, avoiding the pier full of tourists and photo seekers and waiting on the far side of the road until the last of them left.

Moth merged into the darkness as he walked the length of the short pier. Passing the life-size models of Ataturk and the men who had shaped modern Turkey. The faces of the waxwork figures that strode toward the town in purpose catching the streetlights on their upturned features. They were shorter than him, these men moving past him with determination and command as he seemed to slow and freeze. Their dead past taking life in the evening shadows. Above them the rigging of the false pier-ship rose in ladders to fluttering red flags, the star and crescent rippling in proud vindication of the future these men had sought.

He wove between them, to the far end of the pier, up the three steps and strode across the wooden slats to the far side. Beyond the railing, he could see the lights on the huge boats that lay up and down the shore, anchored out in the bay. He was still early. He moved beneath the covered section, unhitched his backpack and slung himself down against the back side of the wooden pillar holding up the roof, hoping he could not be seen from the road. Hoping nobody would come and check to see if it was clear. Moth pulled his knees up and crossed his arms on them, propping his head sideways where it could stare out across the bay. Thoughts drifting across his mind with the slapping sound of water beneath him. Looking into the disappearing void of the distance. Glad for the frigid wind taking away his scent, making him curl into his own warmth.

It reminded him of the lake in Lovere. Sitting on the fountain where Luca had left him, looking out across the lake and watching the boats speed past. Seeing Isabelle. Falling into the water and watching blood and bubbles rise. At least he looked in better shape than that day.

Barely.

Footsteps clipped along the wooden planks of the pier. He listened to them pace out, a confident jump up the steps. He poked his head round the side of the upright, waiting to see if this was the person he was meant to meet. Saw a tall figure in a long, thick coat stride toward the railing, a fur hat clamped over the head. Polished shoes resting against the spotless white foot rail of the pier. Looking like an Arctic ship's captain about to command his vessel out to sea. Before the woollen hem had stilled, the man turned and looked back along the pier.

Moth caught the edge of an impossible cheekbone reflected in the lights from the road. Saw the curve of full lips sucked between anxious teeth. Watched fine hands reaching out from the coat sleeves to grasp the railing, holding himself back even as he leant forward to scan the pier. Fragments of memory knitting themselves together, freezing Moth's fluttering mind and numbed body. Curling his head onto his arms and pushing the stupidity of hope away. The backpack tumbling sideways as he moved.

No.

He heard a stifled gasp, sharp steps that stopped in front of him. A coat hem swishing above the sound of the wind as it crouched down in front of him. Fingers reaching out to touch his arm.

No. No. No.

'Moth.'

The fingers brushed across his hair as the depth of that voice reached for the hole in his chest and clamped it in a vice.

Moth lifted his head, opened his watery eyes and saw amber streaked lights dancing in the eyes that peered back at him.

'No,' he said. 'No, no, no.'

MOTH SAT on the bench against the cabin wall and watched Samsun retreat slowly into the haze of a foggy morning. He would remember it for three things.

The last time he ever got on a pushbike.

Looking up into Luca's eyes and hating himself for the fact he couldn't see straight.

Luca slapping the Ataturk's waxen butt as they left the pier, his other hand pulling Moth toward the shiny blue VW transporter parked on the road.

He watched Luca leaning against the railing of the ferry, tucking his mobile phone into his pocket, and remembered that last with a smile. Less than thirty-eight hours had passed but, as he watched Luca's skinny black jeans drifting down his hips, the line of his thick black Puffa jacket riding above the incapable belt, Moth still smiled at the disrespect of that hand slapping such a famous butt.

The rest of it, Luca, here, taking control, was all a haze. Meeting the boys, Luca talking to them via an interpreter on his phone, getting them all onto the last ferry of the year. Moth kept losing focus in the details of his face. His hair. His hands. The freshness of his clothes. Even after a two-week journey across Europe in a campervan, waiting for ferries in Constanta, waiting for him in Samsun, Luca looked as crisp and fresh as the first day he'd seen him in Male. He watched Turkey dwindle to a shoreline behind Luca and thought how there wasn't even a wrinkle in the skinny jeans he wore.

'Tell me again,' Moth called to him. 'When did Bonn find you?'

Luca turned from the railing and walked across to sit beside him. Sneaking fingers between his, pulling their hands down into the warm space between them, careful of eyes watching.

'He walked into the logistics department seven weeks ago, fell out with the receptionist and yelled my name out, right across the open-plan screens. Of course, we all stood up to see what the commotion was about, and he started swearing in French. Asking which one of us useless jerkies is Luca Moretti.'

'Sounds about right for Bonn.'

Moth couldn't stop staring at his face. Memory had dulled his impact. And what had been there before, an exuberance that radiated, had been improved by the frustration of his time in Geneva. The shine of optimism had worn off the olive skin, there was a rueful glimmer to his brown eyes, a grimace that tweaked his full lips before the smile blossomed, humility added to his determination.

'My boss freaked out. Do you even realise who Jacques Bonnier is?'

'Yeah, he's the arsehole that's been busting my butt all these months.'

'No, Moth,' Luca sighed at him. 'He's one of the top feted camp commanders of the last twenty years. The guy is practically a God at UNHCR.'

'What? You need to get out of that office more, the guy is an insatiable control freak.'

'Well, that's basically what he said too when I fangirled him,' Luca smiled, his eyes chasing across Moth's face with the same hunger Moth could feel in himself. 'Anyway, I was totally down in the dumps because I thought you'd ditched me, and I went on that awful date and realised I couldn't get over you, and I hated my job, and I hated Geneva, and my whole life was a total bloody mess, and then you sent that email about wanting a chance, and I had no idea what to do, and then Jacques Bonnier turns up and says, "I need you to go to Turkey and fetch Moth Lavelle home so I can kick his arse from one side of UNGO to the other."'

'And you put him in touch with Isabelle?'

'Yes, we were keeping in touch about you,' Luca grinned

at him. 'And even though I'd told her you dumped me, she was all "We must get him home before we can do anything else" and "Don't give up on him" and "You must help me find him".'

'You could have ignored them both,' Moth said. He traced his hand up Luca's arm, feeling the bulge of his muscled forearm beneath the coat. 'Did your Popeye forearms get even bigger?'

'I joined the gym. Well, I couldn't, could I? Because you sent that damn one line asking me for a chance and I was mad as hell at you and terrified that if I missed this last chance, I would regret it for the rest of my stupid life stuck in an office.'

'You could have emailed me back,' Moth complained.

'Oh, no, you do not get to bitch about my lack of communication!' Luca said. 'You have been hopeless at keeping in touch or telling me what you were doing. Then, when Bonnier turned up, I put him and Isabelle in touch and they came up with the plan. Isabelle bought the van and said I had to come here and give it to you. Bonnier sorted the papers. And I decided, no, *you* can be the one waiting to know for a change.'

'I can't believe you drove a campervan all the way through Europe to look for me. Did you sleep with that guy you dated?' Moth stilled his hand on Luca's arm, heat rushing through him in shock as the question slipped out.

Luca put a hand on his knee, fingertips fluttering across the surface before he removed it and said, 'I'll take that as a sign you care and leave you to wonder a bit longer. I like the idea of you being jealous. So, yes, it did seem a bit insane, but when my boss refused to give me the time off, I had to decide. Bonnier promised a reference if I'd do it.'

'And you just quit your job? The job you waited five years to get. On the half-soaked chance that you might somehow find me in the entire length of Turkey?'

'And for a reference from Jacques Bonnier. Are you impressed?'

'No, you're a bloody idiot,' Moth told him. 'What are you going to do for a job now?'

'You can't criticise me for being jobless either, at least not until you've had a shave.' Luca stood and pulled him up, toward the door that led to the overnight cabins. 'Come on, let's go, I'm sick of looking at the view. I want to see what you look like under that beard.'

They walked the length of the clinical white corridor, the boat swaying them from side to side as it headed into the stern wind stirring across the deeper waters, passing the doors to the small cabins. It was a twenty-eight-hour ride to Odessa and Luca had pulled out every charm and piece of blue UN paperwork known to man to get them all aboard. Luca slipped the card into the lock mechanism and pushed the door open. Two narrow bunks either side, an even smaller doorway into a tiny ensuite shower room. Down the hallway Atabey was nursing Kadri through the seasickness that had come over him as soon as he saw the gaping stern of the ferry. Luca pushed him into the bathroom with a fresh razor blade and threats not to come out until he could see his whole face.

Moth stayed in the shower, slogging away with the razor, until the blade was clogged, and the drain hole filled with apricot fuzz. Wincing as his shaking hands caught gashes in his skin. He turned the shower off and stood in the cooling steam that filled the tiny room. He wrapped a too small towel round his hips and stared at the oddity of his face in the mirror. The scar was red from the shower and traced a ragged line across his jaw. He brushed his teeth and realised his courage was about to wash away with the fuzz. With one final glance at the mirror, wishing he looked so much more than he was, he opened the door to the cabin before he lost his nerve.

Luca had pulled the blind down over the window, reducing the light to a vivid glow that softened the harsh lines of the sparse moment. He'd taken off his jacket and sat, head back against the wall, eyes closed on one of the beds. Moth rolled with the motion of the boat toward the other and sat down opposite him, wet feet leaving a trail on the cold floor, his chest knotted into a writhing mass.

Luca opened his eyes and looked at him, really looked at him. Moth watching his eyes travel across the scar on his shaved jaw to his over-long, slicked back hair, to his shoulders, naked chest, down to his thighs emerging from the towel, his knees curving over the edge, reaching out toward Luca's. Inches separating the bare skin from the black jeans.

'I can't believe how much you changed,' Luca said, looking back up at his chest. 'I always struggled to grasp your age, it never sat with your size.' He grinned, looking up at Moth's face. 'You got buff, you look like Chris Hemsworth!'

'Does it look any better without the beard?' Moth could hear the gruffness in his own voice. Feeling exposed in his towel beneath Luca's critical gaze.

Luca leant forward onto Moth's knees, the warmth of his hands on Moth's damp skin causing a shiver to furrow all the way up his thighs and under the towel. Moth leant back and sucked in a taut breath. Luca crossed the sliver of light left between them and straddled him, one jean-clad knee either side of his hips, the narrow bones of his butt weighing down

upon Moth's knees. Moth let his hands rest on the coarse
material covering those slim thighs, feeling the muscle
flexing beneath as Luca put his hands either side of Moth's
face and traced the lines of his eyebrows, his scarred jaw, his
nose. Ran a light finger across his lips. He watched Luca
searching his face, looking for memory, replacing the details
erased by time. The quiver of his lashes over the searching
eyes, their length and thickness, the deeper shade of brown
running into black which seemed to frame the amber lights
within. Moth saw his teeth bite his bottom lip, watched a
swallow trace its way down his throat, the bulge of his Adam's
apple, the ripple as it chased down the clavicle and disappeared below the buttons of his shirt. He could see the line of
the leather thong beneath. He could remember the exact
weight of the silver bead against his skin.

'Weirdly, I thought I hated it, now I rather miss it.' Luca
traced his smooth chin again.

Moth lifted his hand to touch the line of the leather
thong, touched the top button of Luca's white shirt, fumbling
with its miniscule slipperiness. Luca brushed his hand aside
and undid the buttons, leaving a trail of skin showing
beneath. Moth pushed the fine cotton open, his hand resting
on the smooth chest, the silver bead trapped beneath. Three
years of wondering, doubting, avoiding, dissolved in the feel
of skin beneath his hand. The solidity of muscle, and movement of breath, and tension of touch. The bead was warmed
through when he caught it between his fingers. Luca had
filled out too, putting on muscle over his slim frame.

'Office work seems to suit you,' Moth told him.

Luca pulled Moth's ear, tugging his head sideways and
scowled, 'No, it bloody doesn't. I worked out six times a week
waiting for you to decide to come home.'

Moth pushed the shirt further aside, seeing lines. There was a trace of new tattoos over the left rib. The strange white ink Luca favoured.

'Wait a minute, is that...'

'... yes.'

'You got a tattoo of Venice on your ribs?' Moth laughed at him, fingers tracing the rise of the Rialto bridge. 'I thought you hated Venice?'

'Well, you gave me better memories.'

They sat there, hands connecting, flesh and cloth pausing against each other, drinking in the truth of each other.

'What now?' Moth asked.

'Right now?' Luca asked with a grin. 'Or "what now" as in what happens next?'

'What are we supposed to do when we get to Odessa?'

'Well, Bonnier wants to kick your arse from one side of Lake Geneva to the other.'

'And Isabelle?' Moth asked.

'I think she wants you to go home to England,' Luca told him with a frown. 'But she didn't say that as such, she just told me to tell you the campervan is yours, and she's sorry she can't come herself now, but she wants to see you very soon.'

Moth leant his head back against the wall and felt his injured shoulder spasm. He winced in pain.

Home. The thought settled like an anchor dragging him down.

'Where's it hurt?' Luca asked.

Moth shrugged his left shoulder. Luca leant forward and kissed it. The heat from his mouth skittering a pattern across the skin. Moth slipped his hands along Luca's thighs, around the shape of his crouched butt and pulled him closer. Burying his head forward against his chest.

'I don't want to go home,' he mumbled against the skin.

Luca pulled his head up and looked down at him with a frown, opening his mouth to speak.

'Please,' Moth interrupted him. 'Don't ask me to go back to England. It's not home.'

'What about Isabelle, your sister?' Luca asked. 'They love you, Moth. What about me? You can't keep living like this.'

Moth stayed quiet, looking into his face. It was filled with hope and light and fire. No wonder Atabey and Kadri had stared punch drunk at him. No wonder the boat guards had let them all board. Moth hadn't remembered it well enough. Three years had faded the gut-churning good looks into a washed-out remnant. What had he ever doubted?

You don't want to let it fade again.

'You left me in Venice saying you needed to find your confidence.' Luca traced his hands across Moth's collarbone, skipping the clavicle, his fingers dragging against the moist surface. 'Did you find it yet?'

Moth nodded, mute with anxiety about the thought of home.

'And you're sure?'

He nodded again.

Luca leant his forehead against Moth's, their noses touching, breath stirring against Moth's lips as he murmured, 'Then say it.'

Moth gathered his courage and pushed away memory, fear, anger, doubt. 'I'm sure. I've faced it often enough every morning when I think of you.'

'You want me?'

'Yes. I want you.' Moth swallowed, dredging for the shape of words he'd turned over in his head but never spoken, wondering if they would ever fit. 'I'm... gay.'

'And you know it's you, not because...'

Luca trailed away, unwilling to repeat what Moth had told him in Venice. Unwilling to even voice what he'd emphatically refused to believe.

'I'm not gay because of my father.' Moth placed a hand at the back of Luca's head and snaked his fingers into his hair, pulling his head forward and letting their lips touch. Desire curling all the way down to his toes and back up to his groin crushed beneath Luca's straddling thighs. He held Luca's face close, filled his vision with it, pushing away everything that had ever haunted him. 'I'm not gay because I want to be or don't want to be. I'm gay because every time you walk away from me, I notice your trousers need pulling up. I'm gay because I remember your mouth every morning when I wake up. I'm gay because when you're here, I want to stay exactly where I am, and only then. I'm gay because whenever I hear your voice, I feel like I'm already home.'

Luca placed his hands against Moth's chest, the fingertips fluttering where Moth could feel them above his pounding heart. He had missed those dancing fingers trying to right the world.

'Then come home to me,' Luca pleaded.

'Geneva?'

'No, just me.' Luca sat away from the closeness and looked at him. A nervous smile twitching his lips. 'Let's be home to each other, wherever we go. We have a campervan, we can move about. I know you don't like staying still.'

'What about your dream job?'

'I'll get another one, we'll work it out.'

Luca leant forward and kissed him again. A deeper, longer, more urgent kiss. Desire pushing against the crumbling dam of Moth's doubts.

'Really?' Moth asked. 'You'd do that?'

'I should have done it before. Come with you, not let you leave.' Luca traced the line of Moth's scar with his lips, murmuring in his ear, 'I'm not letting that happen again. I've been so bloody lonely, tossing off on a promise for three damn years.'

Moth pushed aside the last of the shirt, wrapping his arms round the full breadth of Luca's chest, feeling the sharp ridges of his shoulders. The warmth of each other's chests held tight together.

'Where will we go?'

'Anywhere you want, we'll decide together.'

Speech and breath and kisses pulling them back together, pushing away the space of three years.

Holding onto his slimmer frame, Moth slid sideways down the wall. They filled the narrow shape of the cot together. Luca shimmying out of his shirt, Moth's towel unwinding beneath them.

'So, is that a yes?' Luca asked, kissing Moth's eyes closed, trailing down his body one kiss at a time. Across his chest, his belly. The silver bead a cool tease sliding across skin left chilled by lips.

'Yes,' Moth said, opening his eyes and looking up to the bright ceiling. 'I'll come home to you. Only you.'

'I HOPE you're ready for this?'

'I was born ready.' Kate adjusted the neckline of her dress, fluffed up her hair for the hundredth time and brushed her skirt into place.

'Really? Because you've been mighty jittery all the way

here.' Isabelle cruised along the street, looking for somewhere to park.

'It's these shoes. I've grown too used to my mules. Can't
remember the last time I had to wear proper slingbacks.'

Kit's party had thickened the parking to overflow. She
wasn't the most confident of parkers either. 'There's a lot of
posh cars on this road.'

'It's a posh part of town. Rose always used to say it was
built on stolen blood and dead sweat.'

'That's grim.' Isabelle spotted a space next to someone's
front access, with room to pull in and reverse. 'Can you walk
from here in those shoes?'

'I'm not an invalid, Isabelle.'

'I was being considerate!'

'Oh, do get on and park, your driving is more cautious
than Elsa's.'

'Says the woman who doesn't own a car.' Isabelle killed
the engine. She would be glad to get out of the car, Kate had
been waspish the whole journey. 'Are you sure you're alright?'

'Fine.' Kate opened the door and got out, leaving her with
the taut tone of denial. 'It's good to stretch. God love Elsa but
she could have bought you a more comfortable car.'

Isabelle got out and looked at the Audis, BMWs, Jags and
4x4s parked up on the street. 'I do feel a bit the poor relation.
Though can you imagine what Indigo would do to a car like
that?'

Kate grinned at her over the top of the Skoda. 'Trash it
with Wotsit stains and blackcurrant juice?'

'Exactly.'

Kate looked down the road to Kit's house. Isabelle
followed her gaze. It had more lights than a super tanker

ribbed across the front, and they could hear the music from where they were.

'When I said it was going to cost you,' Kate spoke without looking at her, 'I didn't think it was going to involve me being hauled down to Bristol for a damn fancy dress New Year's Eve party.'

'So that's what's bugging you?' Isabelle asked over the roof.

'You know he's only trying to prove a point?' Kate looked back at her with pursed lips and a frown, flicking the hair out of her eyes to where it perfectly framed her face. She pulled a fur throw from the car and wrapped it round her shoulders. '"Look at me with my perfect lifestyle and gorgeous boyfriend." That's all Christmas was about, he's just moved the goalpost.'

'Why would he want to do that?' Isabelle asked, walking round the car to the pavement and joining her.

Every trick Kate used in her classes to maximise the beauty of older women had been turned to bear. She was dressed in a floor length vintage chiffon dress that made Isabelle feel seven years old again and itching to touch the fabric. The fabric was woven with two threads, a dusk-dark, ocean shade of blue and a pearly, blushed sunrise pink, so that when Kate moved, the dress rippled its shades like a whispered secret. Her skin shone and sparkled, and her face was made up to grace a catwalk. Kate had always been commanding, but Isabelle had rarely seen her really dressed up, and it had stopped her in her tracks when Kate had walked into the kitchen two hours earlier, ready to go. Even Rob had stared, his mouth agape.

'What?' Kate had asked with a self-conscious hand straightening the sweetheart neckline.

'We need to be asking, "Why are you single?"' Rob had replied.

'We need to be asking, "Where did you get that dress," it's amazing,' Isabelle had contradicted.

'An old favourite I had in the closet.' Kate had shrugged away the compliments, twirling her skirt back and forth in delight.

'Are you sour that you haven't got a gorgeous boyfriend to show off too?' Isabelle asked her with a grin as she put the keys into her bag.

'Well,' Kate took Isabelle's arm as they began to walk, 'if you hadn't dumped Steve, I might have borrowed him for the night.'

'Stop it.' Isabelle nudged her with her elbow.

'Oh, let me have at least one more gripe.'

'You haven't stopped griping about it since November.'

'I know, but I miss his charming ways.'

'I don't.' Isabelle didn't want to think about the last time she'd seen Steve.

Her stuttering explanation met by his casual shrug of the shoulders and hands in pockets leaving her feeling a hideous human being for weeks afterward. Even while she slipped into the luxury of her own bed at night with a cup of tea and a pack of biscuits, feeling it was wrong to be so content. Reminding herself that 'just a drink' was never just that and, until she had improved her ability to say no in particular, she would say no in general. To all drinks.

'Well, we shall have to update our manifesto for your next boyfriend. Less charm, less good looking, more capacity to blend into the background, happy to come second to Indigo, third to Riverdell and fourth to everyone else in your life.'

'Sounds perfect.'

'Yes, except he doesn't exist!' Kate complained as they turned into Kit's front driveway. 'Oh. Dear. God.'

They looked at the front of the house. Fairy lights draped on anything solid enough to hold them. Outside the front door, two enormous swan wings had been pinned to the front of the house.

'Look at what Riverdell escaped,' Kate said.

They looked up at the door with its arching wings in mutual shock.

'Umm, but you must admit James' face with that sleigh in his yard was kind of worth it,' Isabelle reminded her.

Christmas had been a relaxed affair in the end. Asia had hosted at the farm, finding two miniature Shetland ponies from a neighbour to harness to the sleigh, sending a photo to Kit. Elsa and Nat had come from Swansea. Kit had continued sulking and then claimed he had a friend staying, and Hester had not been invited. That was Asia's true price, Hester knowing she was not invited.

Rob had been invited but declined, which surprised her. Going on a long Christmas Day ramble with his other single friends and turning up Christmas evening as they got home. Stopping for three days to play with Indigo and her new toys. It had been good to see Nat, to share their disappointment about Moth not coming home for Christmas. Comfort themselves with talk about how they would soon, hopefully, find a way to catch up with him. Isabelle had felt her heart sink as she encouraged Nat's positivity. She had no conviction they would see Moth soon, despite the same hope lurking in her heart that shone in Nat's eyes. Hope, Isabelle realised, was more important to Nat at twelve years old, than reality.

Kit had refused to talk to her for a whole month until he rang on Christmas Eve and told her she and Kate were coming to a party at his. He had a fuck load of fairy lights to use up, it was ballet-themed fancy dress and no, he was not *asking*. Looking at the house, Isabelle realised he had not been joking about the lights. Still, a trip to Bristol was fair return for the chilled-out Christmas they had enjoyed. Isabelle gripped Kate's arm and nudged her forward.

'Well, here we go.' Kate adjusted her dress again, rearranged her throw, pulled her shoulders back and her chin up.

'Relax, will you?' Isabelle pressed the buzzer. 'You look amazing. I, on the other hand, look ridiculous.'

'The whole thing with fancy dress is never to actually do the fancy dress, surely you know that.'

Isabelle looked down at her three-quarter length net tutu and grimaced. It had been such fun to make, and Indigo had sat in the middle of the net skirt for hours. It had felt ridiculous from the moment she saw Kate walk into the kitchen and two hours of wrestling with it to steer the car had not aided her confidence.

'I do now.'

'I can't recall meeting that many of Kit's friends,' Kate turned away from the door, shivering in the cold, pulling her throw tighter. 'He's always come into my... our life. Do you know many of them?'

'A few, but it's been a while. I wonder if Hester will be here?'

'Oh joy.'

'Stop griping.'

'It's cold, ring it again.'

'Smile will you, it's a party.'

'You first!' Kate retorted. 'And don't forget we're driving

home, don't you get plastered and have us spending the night.'

'No worries there.'

Isabelle pressed the buzzer again.

'And don't you abandon me all evening either,' Kate grabbed her elbow and whispered as the door opened.

On the other side stood a far too large man in a pink net tutu over cargo trousers, with a pint mug in his hand and a pair of tights pulled over his head. He had opened his mouth to speak and got stuck staring at Kate. They both stared back, Isabelle thinking that she was being totally overshadowed and...

'... that's not something you see every day.' Kate gave voice to her thoughts.

'Tell me about it. The bastard has a costume department down there, if you turn up without fancy dress, he picks your outfit.'

'He can bloody try,' Kate said.

'I think you're safe.' The guy pulled the door back and let them in. 'I turned up with a pair of ballet shoes tied round my neck and thought it would be good enough. Should have guessed really. Welcome to the Royal Bloody Ballet... know your way about?'

Isabelle and Kate stood in the hall and took in the mass of the house. To their left and right both main rooms had been turned into set performances and were full of people. On the left, the dining room had been laid out for supper, to the right the sitting room had been converted for dancing. They could see people sitting on the stairs looking back at them, standing leaning against the walls of the hallway. Where the stairs curved down to Kit's converted basement, they could see more heads moving slowly upward. A multitude of coloured disco and twinkling fairy lights created a discomforting clash and filtered across the dancing bodies.

'Shit.' Kate took a step backwards.

'Oh no you don't.' Isabelle grabbed her arm and clung on. 'Where's Kit?'

'Downstairs, look for the swans.' Their welcomer swayed backward, letting them in. 'Food in there, dancing in here, drinks downstairs, chill zones out in the garden or upstairs.'

'I can't do this,' Kate told her, resisting her tug on her arm.

'What is wrong with you?' Isabelle asked. 'It's a party, you love parties. I'm the one who should be shaking in their ridiculous shoes. Come on, let's get a drink. You need to relax.'

'I'm too old for this nonsense.'

'I thought ageism was banned?' Isabelle tugged Kate toward the stairs. 'I thought that was your whole business ethos.'

'This is all your fault,' Kate told her. 'If you'd stood up to him in the first place, we wouldn't be here paying the price now.'

'Not all of us are invincible like you.' The noise increased as they descended the crowded stairs, snatching away her words. Isabelle went first, letting go of Kate's arm as they squeezed through the bodies.

'What?' Kate demanded from above her.

They stood on the last few steps and looked out across the huge basement room. It was rammed. The ceiling high windows at the far end were open into the garden where more lights hung, heaters showed their red gas flames, and canopies looped with fairy lights stretched out into the dark.

'Jesus, this must be costing a fortune,' Isabelle said, Kate's hand on her shoulder two steps above her.

'Told you, it's a "Who is the greatest of them all?" event.'

Isabelle turned to look up at Kate but found her attention had been taken. She looked back into the room, following Kate's gaze. Feeling the hand on her shoulder squeezing, flexing, warming. Kate's sharper eyes had caught sight of Kit. He was stood at the far end of the room, and even her hazy eyesight could see him. Next to Adele, both dressed in swan leg outfits, their torsos gleaming and bare. Isabelle moved to the bottom of the steps and turned toward them through the crowd. Instantly losing sight of them.

'You promised me a drink first.' Kate's hand clutched her wrist and pulled her up. 'Come on, drinks are this way.'

'We should say hello while we can.'

'Fine, you say hello, I'll get drinks. Give him his moment of glory, then come find me.' Kate slipped away into the crowds and was gone before Isabelle could complain.

She stood in the fray and sighed. It was beyond her, this rivalry between them. What had started with Instagram seemed to have seeped into their relationship. It was downright exhausting. She moved toward the windows and came out into a space dominated by boxes of overspilling costume props. A space absent of swans.

Isabelle looked around in confusion. Where she was sure Kit had been, she'd arrived looking expectant in the middle of a conversation between unknown people.

'... but surely you must be planning to come back at some point? Nick, tell him, this is insane.'

'Do exactly what you want and ignore her, it's your life, buddy.'

'Nick!' the woman protested.

Isabelle could see a tall gangly man with a bottle curled in the crook of each small finger, and a martini glass leaning at a precarious angle, stood next to a petite, elegant lady dressed in a Chinese outfit and with traditional geisha face paint on. The guy, Nick, was trying to figure out how to drink from the combination of options without spilling one and was dressed in a pair of cycling shorts with a crossover ballet cardigan stretched around his torso. He was scowling at the olive on a stick that was making his drinking harder. The third person present, who they were talking to, had his back to her. She smiled vaguely at the woman who had clocked her, pulled up and tried to retreat to Kate. As she turned away, hoping she had escaped attention, she caught the unseen man turn to see who had interrupted them.

'Isabelle?'

She grimaced and turned back. Saw poised muscle, hair pushed back into a waved sweep. An indifferent face lighting up with a staggering smile. She pulled up, summoning his face from her memory. Kate's housewarming. Under the fairy lights in the garden. A bubbly girlfriend she hadn't warmed to, a dog she had. She dredged his name last, Jay. He had put weight on the same as her, but the strength was still there, along with the grace. He was dressed in plain jeans and a T-shirt. She saw him glance down at her outfit and gusted a sigh out.

'Oh, don't. I look ridiculous, don't I?'

'Completely,' the guy called Nick agreed. 'But I'm stood here in my cycling shorts so you're in good company.'

'You look perfect,' the lady gushed at her, but Isabelle could see her eyes travelling from her feet in their sandals up past her tulle skirt and over her slaughtered white T-shirt cut into a wrap effect. An immaculate manicured eyebrow raised itself in perfect line with the false smile accompanying the words and Isabelle instantly disliked her.

'Jay, it's been ages.' Isabelle ignored the woman and stepped toward Jay. 'Kate's housewarming, right? How did you escape the fancy dress?'

Jay took a step toward her, putting his drink down on the precarious top of a basket, holding out his hands to take hers. She remembered this. The way he took one hand in both of his and held it there, pulling you close and making you stop a moment.

'I helped put the decorations up and earnt a reprieve. You look great. At least you'll escape the hideous treatment those who turned up without due effort have been subjected to.' Jay kept his eyes on hers. Looking into her face, as though he too was remembering through the years.

She smiled and blushed. How she wished she'd followed Kate's lead in outfits. She looked round, wondering where the bouncy girlfriend was, wishing she could remember her name. Hoping someone would use it before she had to prove she couldn't remember.

'I disturbed you, sorry. I thought I saw Kit here.'

'He was,' Nick agreed. 'He's gone to dance with the swans.'

'There's more of them?' Isabelle asked.

'A whole flock load,' Nick said.

She grinned at him. Nick was curt and funny in the same breath.

'Flocking hell,' Isabelle quipped back.

'Swans don't flock,' the woman said to her drink.

'Swans will do whatever the flock Kit tells them to do,' Nick countered. He renegotiated the two bottles into one hand, knocked back the martini and swallowed the olive with a grimace. 'Salty little fuckers, can't stand them. C'mon dear, I need to dance. We may not be able to persuade your favourite partner back to the floor, but you do still have me.'

Nick gathered his partner by the elbow and herded her past Isabelle toward the stairs.

'We haven't finished this conversation, Jay.' The woman didn't protest. 'I'm coming back to find you.'

'Great stuff, look forward to it, Leah.'

'You and I are dancing before the end of the night. I won't accept you've quit for good.'

Jay and Isabelle watched her disappear.

'And I'll put on swan legs before that happens,' Jay muttered as she passed out of hearing.

She turned to look at him. He was watching the couple push their way through the crowd with a frown on his face. His shoulders dropped an inch and he turned to her, picking up his drink.

'You saved me, thanks.'

'She seems a bit demanding.'

'Real prima donna,' Jay agreed. 'I don't know how Nick lives with it. Have you met them before?'

'No,' Isabelle said. 'I've met hardly anyone before.'

'Kit's going all out to impress Adele, I'd say.' Jay looked across the room. 'Though, for the record, this is all your fault. If you hadn't burnt him over Christmas, this would never have happened.'

'Oh, don't say that.' Isabelle groaned. 'At least, don't let Kate hear that.'

'Kate's actually here?'

'Yes, and she said exactly the same thing.'

'It's obviously true then,' Jay teased her.

They stood for a moment, conversation run dry. He looked down at her tulle skirt again and grinned. She brushed her hands over it self-consciously.

'Where did you manage to get that from?'

'I made it,' she told him. 'About three days ago. It was a complete nightmare. I'm more used to working with linen these days.'

'I hear you've given up the work in Bollywood since having Indigo?'

Isabelle blinked at the oddity of hearing her daughter's name spoken. Trying to encompass the knowledge he had of her that she was missing of him. His girlfriend's name. His job. Why he wouldn't dance. She could remember Lou dancing in his arms with such pleasure it had even made her want to try.

'Yes,' she answered. 'Though I'm taking Indigo to Mumbai, to visit my friends, hopefully this coming year.'

'Do you still have that map in your hallway?'

'Yes, wow, how did you remember that?'

'A memorable thing to forget.'

Conversation ebbed again.

'How is, ehm...' Isabelle grimaced. 'Your girlfriend?'

'Lydia?' Jay's smile slipped from his face, pulling his features toward his drink.

Isabelle felt awful and put her hand on his forearm. 'I'm sorry, I'm hopeless with names. Especially when I've met people at a party. I always forget them.'

Jay looked down at her hand and blinked. 'Wish I could,' he muttered.

'Sorry?' Isabelle could feel herself warming and removed her hand.

'We separated,' Jay straightened up. 'Earlier this year. Almost everyone here knows Lydia, I've heard nothing but her name all night. I haven't seen most of this crowd since before we split up.'

'That's always awkward. I'm sorry to hear that.' Isabelle

resisted the urge to look for Kate and run for cover. Then a memory slipped into her mind. 'How's your dog, Uggs?'

Jay laughed at her, a deep, full bark of amusement that got cut short. 'Wow, you remember his name, and forget hers, I like that. Umm, well, he's dead.'

'Oh shit,' Isabelle wished herself out of the tulle skirt and out of the house. 'I'm going to stop talking.'

'It's alright, not your fault,' Jay chuckled. 'Losing the dog was harder than Lydia, but at least the memories are happier. Uggs was loyal, at least.'

Isabelle frowned in enquiry.

'Oh, I forget,' Jay said, nodding at her bemusement. 'Kit never talks about his friends, right?'

'You seem to know more about me, though.'

'I've been here for three weeks. Kit had quite a bit to say about you.'

'Oh dear. I'm sorry.' Isabelle felt the desperate need for a drink in her hands. 'So, you split up with Lydia, lost your adorable dog, have been staying with Kit for three weeks and aren't dancing anymore? Anything else I should know before I put my foot in it again?'

'Don't mention Brexit or Trump, otherwise you're about covered.'

'No worries there, I've had enough of both of those too.'

'Do you want a drink?'

'No,' Isabelle shivered at the suggestion. 'I mean, thanks, but I'm driving, Kate's getting drinks. How's Kit been, with all this?'

'He's totally frigging hyper, it's been horrendous. He'll be happy you're here. And Kate, I can't believe she came, he pretty much made a bet she wouldn't come.'

'Of course she came, why would she not?' Isabelle asked.

Jay frowned at her, tilted his chin to one side and didn't reply.

Isabelle felt the silence stretch again and broke it first, 'So, you've been stopping with Kit?'

'Uhm. After you broke his heart, he suddenly remembered his other friends and turned up on my doorstep and kidnapped me.'

'What have you been doing for three weeks?'

'What, apart from putting fairy lights up and distracting Kit from his shattered Christmas dreams?' he quipped.

'I refuse to accept responsibility for all of this.'

'Nice try, yeah, no. It's totally on you.' Jay moved toward the windows with her. 'Either that or he needed a broken enough person to take on the dirty work of reading his mother's diaries.'

'Really?' Isabelle felt a thrill of connection. Rowena's diary entries remained vivid in her mind. 'Wow, I've been reading some old diaries too.'

She saw Jay glance behind her and lose all interest. She turned to see Kate had found them, a tall ice filled highball in each hand. Kate clocked them chatting and moved toward them, the full skirt moving round her body like a sunset cloud.

'Kate, you are stunning,' Jay stepped forward to place a light kiss on her cheek.

Isabelle realising that she hadn't got a kiss.

'Jay, how are you? Wonderful to see you. Where's the insane architect of this mayhem?'

'God knows, he won't stay in one place long enough to pin down. He'll be thrilled you came though, both of you.'

Isabelle noticed how bright Kate's eyes were, her voice

had switched into the old habit of confident host. She wondered how many drinks she'd had already.

'Darling, a nice perky fruit-filled soda for you.' Kate pushed a drink into her hand. 'You can pretend it's got alcohol.'

'Wonderful,' Isabelle said. 'I have the short straw in both outfits and drinks.'

'You deserve it,' Kate told her. 'This is all her fault, Jay, did you know that?'

'I was just expressing the exact same thought.'

'Oh, enough,' Isabelle muttered. 'I'm going to find Kit, are you coming?'

'No, I'm going to stop here and talk to Jay.' Kate said.

'Jay's been reading Rose's diaries,' Isabelle said, glancing past her into the room, wondering where to start looking for Kit. When she glanced back, expecting a retort, she caught a blur of action and Jay had caught Kate's slipping glass before it fell from her hand. Not before it had spilled over the hem of her dress.

'Oh, no, your dress!' Isabelle cried. 'What happened?'

'I don't know,' Kate was fussing with the chiffon, trying to brush the liquid from it. 'Too much ice, made the glass slippery.'

'It's barely noticeable,' Jay reassured her. 'Trust me, no one is going to be looking at the bottom of your dress.'

Kate blushed and looked at him with such crushed gratitude that Isabelle reached out and took her elbow in concern.

'Are you feeling alright?'

'Fine, fine, of course,' Kate laughed it off. 'A little out of practice with parties.'

'I feel you,' Jay wiped her glass against his jeans to get rid of the moisture and handed it back to her. 'I'd have done anything to get out of this, but it wasn't an option. Apparently.'

'So, he finally opened that trunk?' Kate asked.

'Yes, curiosity got the better of him. Except he hadn't got time to read them, so he gave me the task.'

'Wow, you're braver than me,' Kate mocked him. 'You couldn't have paid me to read Rose's inner thoughts. I dread to think what she said about us all.'

'It was fascinating.' Jay looked from Kate to Isabelle and smiled.

'I'll bet.' Kate smoothed her skirt down again.

'I was telling Jay that I've been reading some old diaries too,' Isabelle added. 'It's addictive stuff, though some rather tedious bits too. You can see why they all get published abridged, there's an awful lot of repetition in them.'

'There wasn't much you'd abridge in Rose's diaries,' Jay said. 'If Kit ever runs out of money, he could publish them for a fortune.'

'Jesus Christ.' Kate stared at him in horror.

'Oh, you'll have to tell us more,' Isabelle said. 'I'd love to share Rowena's diaries with you, they were so inspiring.'

'Who's Rowena?' Jay asked.

'My great-great-great-grandmother,' Isabelle told him. 'She was given Riverdell as a wedding present when she made a lowly marriage match. She planted the magnolia in the courtyard, and she was amazing.'

'Riverdell was a consolation prize?' Jay asked. 'I dread to think what she came from.'

'Jesus. I need another drink.' Kate knocked the rest of her drink back 'Anyone else? No? Right, I'll see you later.'

Isabelle and Jay watched her walk away.

'I have no idea what's going on with her,' Isabelle said into the sudden absence. 'She's being truly weird tonight.'

'Really?' Jay asked. 'No idea at all?'

'No.'

They looked at each other with the same quizzical expression on their faces.

'We should go find Kit,' Jay suggested

'Shouldn't we get Kate first?'

Jay looked in the direction Kate had gone. 'No, I think we should leave her to find us. I'll help you hunt a swan, and you can keep me safe from the evil geisha's dancefloor clutches.'

'So, you're not dancing at all?'

'Nope. Not since Lydia left.' Jay glanced out of the garden doors, scanning the garden, looking up to the first floor. He nodded outwards and Isabelle followed him into the garden.

'What a shame, because of her? That's terrible.'

'You're supposed to be backing me up, not falling in with this lot,' Jay told her.

She glanced back to try and get a glimpse of Kate. Instead, saw Hester moving through the thong of people in her direction. A gut shot of anxiety flaring in her.

'Oh crap, Hester's here.' Isabelle took a step further out of the room.

Jay reached for her, saying, 'Right, let's make a run for cover. We'll find Kit, locate a safe space and mount a rescue mission for Kate.'

Isabelle looked down at the hand, back at his face. A timid smile flickered at the corners of his mouth. Doubt trembled in his eyelashes. Her odd eyesight, which could conjure an outfit out of details, realised he was covering anxiety with a veneer of confidence as thin as Kate's chiffon dress. As it had caught her unawares on the front doorstep, to see Kate so out of sorts, it overtook her now. This twisting round of life to a place where she was the confident one. She took his hand and tucked it inside her arm, stepped up beside him and moved toward the patio steps.

OVER THREE HOURS later they were stood on the fringes of the dance room watching Kit prepare for his midnight count-down. Isabelle was tired. Her feet were sore from the constant standing. Her ears were aching from the music. Her neck was cricked from keeping a perpetual eye out for Hester.

Kate, having demanded she not leave her side, had abandoned her for a place in the garden where she had pulled a fan group to her side and was busy working on bookings for her next year's courses. New Year's Eve it appeared was the perfect time to sign people up for her 'New Year, Old You' online course.

'I didn't know you were doing an online course,' Isabelle had whispered when she had managed to push her way through the fan group to her side.

'Neither did I,' Kate winked. 'We start on February 1st.'

'That's hardly New Year.'

'I know, but it only gives me one month to set the bloody thing up.' Kate had beamed at her. Isabelle thought that if she could look this alive and vibrant after an ungodly number of gins in her early seventies, she would be feeling smug with herself. 'And besides, who wants to do self-improvement in January. You feel like shit, and you're broke. No one believes in New Year resolutions anymore.'

Isabelle looked over at Kit. He had barely spoken to her. Dispensing a huge and enveloping hug alongside a torrent of words. Eyes searching for Kate in the background. Then he'd disappeared, leaving a trail of leaking swan feathers and a scent of chemically dosed sweat. She had been left with Jay for the whole evening, watching as people would come over, talk to Jay, the women asking him for a dance. Jay politely declining and sticking by her side.

'It's odd,' she'd said in one interlude, when they were loitering at the bottom of the stone steps from the sitting room down to the garden. 'Kit's been part of my life since I was a kid, yet I know next to no one here, whereas you seem to know the whole room.'

'He's always been pretty protective of his family,' Jay agreed. 'When he invited us up to your place for Kate's do, I felt pretty honoured.'

'Honoured?' Isabelle asked. 'You sure he wasn't keeping you lot safe from us?'

Jay smiled at her.

'We see next to nothing of him since that party.' Isabelle dropped to the step for a moment's respite from standing, hugging her knees, crunching in the tulle. As the cold of the stone seeped through the thin fabric, she remembered the chill that Italy and Moth had left between her and Kit. A chill it had taken Indigo's arrival to thaw. 'He only ever comes to shower Indigo with presents and tell me all the things I'm doing wrong and Kate all the things he's doing better than her.'

Jay, stood three steps below her, leaning on the iron handrail, had not responded. Watching her quietly and sipping his beer.

Now they were stood in a corner of the dance room. The room hot and rocking with bodies. As dancers swirled around them, she could feel his discomfort increase and tried to ease it with conversation.

'Kate has converted the ballroom at Riverdell into her classroom,' she said, nodding at the packed room, straining to hear herself speak. 'Weird to imagine it full of people like this in the past.'

'That would have been worth seeing.'

'I read about it in the earlier diaries. I think it might have been a more subdued affair than this though.'

'Fewer fairy lights?' Jay asked, his teeth gleaming as a disco beam flashed across them.

'I'll say.'

'Jay, at last!' A familiar voice called out, barely audible in the room. Isabelle looked over his shoulder and saw the makeup geisha sliding off the somewhat warmed face of the woman.

'Oh dear,' she warned. 'I think you're about to be collared.'

Jay turned round as the woman came up and snatched his hand.

'Come on, we're dancing, I won't have this.'

Her voice was ragged with drink, her eyes wavering as she said it.

'You're wasted, Leah,' Jay told her and refused to budge, pulling his hand free.

'I'm not having that bitch ruining your life. Yes, she fucked off and humiliated you, big deal, get over it,' Leah nearly shouted. 'Don't give her the satisfaction of ruining your life into the bargain.'

Isabelle wanted to disappear. Embarrassed for Leah's indelicacy, mortified for Jay. She saw his hard-jawed disgust, sucked behind tight lips and glaring eyes as Leah finished her loud and slurred speech. If Isabelle hadn't warmed to her before, now she positively hated her. She reached to catch

Jay's sleeve, putting herself in front of Leah and looking for a path through the bodies away from her.

'You know what, Leah,' Jay said, slipping his hand into Isabelle's. 'You're right. What an idiot am I?'

The geisha smile twisted into lines of smug superiority, thick makeup streaking into folds.

Jay handed her his beer and pulled Isabelle forward, not toward the hall, but onto the dancefloor. Isabelle felt her feet trip over themselves as she realised what he was doing. Saw Leah's eyes widen in outrage as her own flared in shock.

'What? No, wait.' She tried to pull back. 'I can't dance.'

'Can't or won't?' Jay asked as he turned his back to the middle of the room and offered her his other hand, pulling her after him. 'Only, if you could find it in you, I'd be forever grateful.'

'Can't. I mean, honestly, I've never done this.'

'Never danced with someone?' he asked in disbelief.

She thought about dancing with Moth on the lawn at Riverdell and realised it wasn't going to cut it with these professionals.

'Not like this!'

'Like this?'

'Yeah, this, this, together, whirling, thing, proper, stuff,' Isabelle threw out a horrified word with each step that Jay sucked her closer into the middle, her tulle skirt squashed aside by dancers.

'Don't worry.' He came to a stop, holding both her hands. She was aware of how cool his were, how hers were heating up. 'You're in safe hands.'

Isabelle looked down at his hands. 'I thought you didn't want to dance again, ever?'

'I don't. Not like that.' He nodded at the other people swirling past them. 'I'm done with that.'

'What's this about then?'

'I guess... we'll find out?'

She took a step closer to him, threatened by the whirring bodies beside her.

'May I?' he asked, loosing go of one hand and extending his arm to invite her forward.

She took another step closer. Felt his hand cup her elbow, guide her sideways. Isabelle glanced outwards, past dancers, over heads. Leah had her arms closed across her chest. Hester was at the far end of the room, her back turned, Lou peering over her shoulder with a curious frown on her face. Lou had been with Hester all night, keeping as careful an eye out for Isabelle as she was for Hester. Turning them aside when there seemed a danger they might meet. Lou's easy-going smile had hardened into a blank stare whenever their eyes met that made Isabelle doubt her eyesight more than normal.

'Relax,' Jay murmured close beside her. 'Think of it as hiding in plain sight, no one can see you.'

She clocked the number of eyes turning to look at Jay. She saw the nudges, the pulling back of dancers, the calls going out through the hallway and felt her stomach fall to her feet. However long he had been away from dancing, he had been missed. But Jay wasn't looking, he had his eyes down at the floor, listening to the music. His arm encircling her back to hold her elbow, his hand turning hers to extend in front of him. She had been moved, without being aware of it, without thinking, to a place of being held, close and yet removed. Waiting on a beat to see what happened, the moment paused, the next yawning before her.

'Jay, I don't think this is wise,' she said. 'I don't want to make a fool of you.'

'You can't make any more a fool of me than Lydia already did.' He smiled grimly at her, their heads side by side, her cocooned within the power of his shoulder, bicep, hand. 'But we can stop if you prefer.'

Isabelle heard the words taut beside her as she looked back at the room, the other dancers. His pain was tangible. Like the emotions she'd read in the diaries. Years of hopes and cruelly dashed wishes. She could feel it, the sense that each of those people had truly lived, breathed. That their skin had been as solid and warm and alive as Jay's hand. Holding her strong, free to release at any moment. Light and steady. She had forgotten that extraordinary confidence in his hands. Remembered it from the first time she had met him at Kate's housewarming. She squeezed his hand, leant into his arm and gave him permission. The room began to move. Music twirled.

'I'd forgotten about this,' Jay said, stepping round her so that Isabelle wasn't sure if she was dancing or he and the room were moving. 'Beginners haven't asked me to dance for a long time, they get daunted. Got. Daunted.'

'By you?' Isabelle asked as the room moved again.

'Maybe. Maybe by Lydia.'

Isabelle watched him turning, handing, passing her from one hand to the other while she wondered how her feet had ever learned to not fall right over themselves.

'You have good rhythm, and such long legs! Heavens, you have long legs.'

'Is that bad?' Isabelle looked down at her legs and nearly stumbled as they moved again. How was he making her body do this, barely aware of itself and yet dancing? Here. In a room full of people. No wonder Lou had looked giddy that night at Riverdell. It was an extraordinary feeling. Like air and light were moving through her.

'Not bad at all. I have long arms according to...'

Isabelle heard the hitch in his cut-off voice.

'Is this why you don't dance?' she asked. 'Because it reminds you of her?'

He didn't respond, focused on dancing. Time seemed to change when you were counting it in a song. Minutes pushed aside in a breathing flow of limbs. Isabelle could see the crowds had lost interest. Whatever they had hoped for, they hadn't expected this stumbling novice doing a few whirls.

'You know, Riverdell reminds me of Moth.' She let herself be moved until she came closer to him again. 'All the time.'

'Is that hard?'

'I wish he'd come home.' She was turned in a swirl that made her ridiculous dress bulge out in a way that made her feel as excited as Indigo had by the layers. 'He was there for such a fleeting time, yet now the house feels different without him. But I still love Riverdell. Even though it's changed since him.'

They danced in silence again, the rhythm unwinding. Isabelle could sense the song gathering itself. The dancers gearing up to finish it off in style. Jay pulled her in closer to protect her from their big swirls and extended movements. Holding them steady, her back to him, both looking outward across the floor. This close she felt her height again. The height that James and Moth had always dismissed in their own. She didn't fit into the crook of Jay's arm. Her head would never rest easily against his shoulder. But she could feel his strength. Jay would catch her, his hands would steer her clear of danger. Isabelle leant into that safety as the dancers went wild and he held her, protected, an island of calm in the middle of it all. The warmth of his body easing away any tension in hers. His hands supported hers and she felt that cool dryness in his skin that warmed like silk to hers, as familiar and pleasurable as the fibre she most loved. She moved her palm across the surface of his hand to feel the soft pull of moisture that formed between them. Jay lifted his hand to bring her arm closer to them and as she followed the movement with her eyes, she was granted a swift pathway of clear sight to Hester and Lou. As dancers twirled and shimmied across her poor vision, she stiffened in confusion, then doubt, then shock.

She could feel Jay looking over her shoulder to where she stared.

'Did I just see...' she looked back at him in confusion.

'Ah, I did wonder. Apparently so.'

'But, but...' As she tried to grasp it, they heard Adele calling in excitement, jumping up and down with glee and pulling Kit into a great hug and kissing him.

'Oh no.' Isabelle scanned the room in a rush of guilt. 'Where's Kate, it's almost midnight.'

'WHAT THE HELL?'

'What?' Adele asked, pulling away from him. A slight crease between his eyes where Kit's attention had drifted away from their kiss.

He turned and followed Kit's eyes behind his back to where the packed room was closing a fleeting tunnel of vision to Hester, her arms wrapped round Lou's neck, nodding her head and swiping at tears pouring down her face.

'That.'

The vision got swamped by guests. Had he just seen what he thought? He'd been watching Jay dance with Isabelle trying to figure out how that had happened when he'd seen Isabelle freeze and followed her eyes to find Lou kissing Hester. As in properly kissing her. With lips and everything. Then holding out a box. At which point of weirdness, Hester had thrown herself around Lou's neck, wiping away tears, just as Adele appeared and grabbed him.

'What that?' Adele asked.

'Lou, Hester and I don't know what the hell just happened. There was a box. And they were... kissing. Really kissing, kissing.'

'Are you surprised?' Adele joked.

'Are you not?' Kit demanded, trying to see through the guests again. 'Did you know about this?'

'Me?' Adele asked, his smile twisting in delight at Kit's discomfort. 'How could I know something you don't?'

'I mean, I knew they were close, but...'

'... but what, you thought they were sight-seeing in Amsterdam?' Adele snuggled up to him, but Kit held him back.

'Wait, you think that was...'

'Oh Kit, surely you must have guessed by now. They're in love, it's clear as day.'

'Love?' Kit held Adele by the biceps, staring into his face, looking to see if he was taunting him. 'They can't be in love.'

'Oooh, what's this, jealousy?' Adele freed his arm and tickled his chin.

'Jealousy, are you joking me? This is a disaster. I don't need people I love falling in love with other people I love.'

'You don't know that. Maybe you're the one to bring people together.'

'I need to know what that was about.' Kit made to move in their direction. 'I can't have Hester breaking Lou, she'll never recover from another emotional wreckage.'

'Oh no, you don't,' Adele grabbed his arm as he moved. 'You need to leave them alone and focus on us. Your family are not taking New Year's from us too.'

Kit pulled up, caught on a guilt line.

'Right, they're ready, come on. This is the moment.' Adele stepped toward the open doors, waving at the DJ who was stood in the garden looking for them.

Kit tried to fathom the impossible, peering toward the window where Hester and Lou had been stood. What else had he missed tonight, as he tried so hard to avoid the obvious. He heard Adele calling him, turned to see him disappearing down the stone steps. Outside, he could see down to the lawn and the crowd near the heater where he knew she had settled for the last few hours. They were all drunk, loud, laughing. Oblivious to the hour. Kate sat in the middle, a hypnotic chiffon fairy on a rattan pouffe tussock. Avoiding his eyes as assiduously as he was hers.

One look.

That was all it had taken.

The moment he looked up from conversation, his neck hairs prickling a warning, to see her descending the stairs to his kitchen. One hand resting on Isabelle's shoulder. Her eyes scanning. Finding his. Looking away.

Kit had felt it with a punch in his gut, a spasm down his back and a surge against the feathery confines of his black swan legs. His mouth stumbling on the words he was speaking. Adele not the only one to look in the direction of his eyes.

'Sorry, ice stuck in my throat. Anyway...' and he'd hared after the dumb conversation she'd car crashed him out of.

No one had seen bar Adele. Who'd given him a quizzical look and needling moments of insecurity through the night. 'Are you still in love with Isabelle?' 'Are you sure you wouldn't rather talk with Isabelle?' 'Where did she find that ridiculous dress?'

But better Adele think it was Isabelle who had choked him on the ice than the sight of Kate in her Grace Kelly dress. Adele didn't need to know that Kate was wearing an outfit it had cost him a fortune to buy at Bonhams. Or to get into an argument about why he would not be making her put on any of the fancy dress he'd forced the other guests to wear. As far as Adele knew, Kate was coming to keep Isabelle company.

Kit moved onto the top stone step, watching Adele run around in happiness, gathering attention. He'd made plans for days over the words he would say. He hoped his neighbours' kids were up. Because any sleep they were trying to get was about to be blasted out of the sky. Down at the far end of the garden, in front of the safety line, he could see Fred in his high-visibility coat, keeping an eye on the guests. The words he'd been thinking of, heroics, optimism, sarcasm, all slipped from his mind.

An old year ending, a new one starting. Would it be any different? Would there be a time when he didn't stumble like a starstruck teenager at the sight of her? Kit felt the cool breeze rise over the trees and fan toward the house, carrying a tickle of heat from the garden before chilling his nipples into bullets and his arms into goosebumps.

It was Jay and that bloody parcel. That was the problem. He'd been fully on track with the party of all parties until Jay had unearthed that surprise. Sitting on a sofa apiece, long after Adele had gone to bed. Staring at the parcel like a sleeping snake on the table between them. The parcel his mother had sent back from India to a locked postal deposit box. In 1984. Supposedly several months after her death. A locked postal deposit box that someone, somewhere, must still be paying for. The contents of the fancy-dress boxes strewn across the kitchen. Kit thinking he had two days left to achieve brilliance and Jay wanted him to open Pandora's box.

'How can you not open it?' Jay had finally asked, after they'd what-ifed and butted it for hours.

'It's been sat in that post box all this time and life has gone on without its contents.'

'It might be important, Kit.'

'Nothing is more important than the life I've got. What if it changes all that?'

'Maybe your life needs to know what's inside.'

'Well maybe my life can see how it copes a bit longer not knowing.'

Kit thought at least, if nothing else, this trawling through the past had helped the guy find a better focus. Jay, curious, was a step closer to the Jay he knew. It had even nudged him back onto the dancefloor. Though why he'd picked Isabelle of all partners was beyond him, she couldn't dance at all. Kit tried to shake the chill off, took another two steps downward. Adele was moving toward him through the crowd. A mic in his hand.

'Your speech!' he grabbed Kit's arm. 'There's no time left!'

'It's fine, I had more fun writing it than I ever would saying it.' Kit put the mic down on the curling stone newel and pulled Adele close. 'I'm cold. Warm me up.'

Adele was hot, sweaty from herding people outside, their feathers rearing up against each other as he jumped onto the step behind and pulled Kit into his arms. In the kitchen they could hear the DJ turn up the radio. A strained hum ran over the crowd. Kit felt it ripple through them. How many others were wondering what level of life's disappointments would stay in the old year and what would creep forward? He pulled Adele's arms a little tighter. The chimes of Big Ben kicked out, brittle from distance and a country holding its breath.

At the balcony of the dining room, where there were no steps down to the garden he could see Isabelle beside the rail, peering toward Kate, her lips pursed that she hadn't made it downstairs in time. Behind her, holding people back, he could see Jay. Jay was not looking into the garden. Total discomfort in the set of his shoulders as he watched Isabelle. He was probably sick to death of the party, the people, regretting the dancing. He looked how Kit had felt when Jay asked him if he wanted to open the parcel.

It had been one thing hearing the excerpts from those diaries. Toying alongside memories he'd held dear. But that parcel had looked like pure poison to him. To know what her final thoughts had been. To ask the questions he'd left with the therapist.

'I love this bit,' Adele said, nibbling his ear.

Kit looked back down the garden, eyes glancing over the crowd by the burners. She was there. Stood up on her pouffe, supported by hands, peering toward the end of the garden with a glass of champagne in her hand. That bloody dress catching the light from the fairy strings. £11,000 for a dress and here it was haunting him. It was a relief he'd had to skip the speech, sarcasm might have come out strongest.

The crowd gathered themselves together as the countdown started. Five. Four.

Kit felt the surge of muscle at his back and shivering excitement as Adele jiggled on his toes in anticipation.

Three. Two.

He focused on the night sky, willing it into illumination.

One.

All over the country, the city, his house and garden, cheers erupted. Adele roared as the first fireworks erupted in a scream of noise and light, bounding up the stone steps to merge with the crowd jumping for joy at the top. Leaving Kit alone at the bottom. He watched the lights soaring, bursting, cartwheeling across the dark sky. They looked flat to him. Tardy and predictable. While all he felt was the cold and emptiness of the night.

He picked up the mic from the precarious place on the newel where Adele had left it and headed toward the kitchen. The DJ would not be happy if he lost that. And he was cold. Chilled through. A smile plastered on his face as people cheered and hugged him. He hadn't drunk enough, that was the problem. A sober new year. That was a disaster.

At least he could fix that.

He handed the mic over, went to the deserted bar and ordered a large glass of red wine. Knocked half the glass back and told the bartender to hand him the bottle. He tilted the bottle to swig straight from it and darted a glance at the window, conscious of his bad manners. Saw Kate stood there, looking over at him. Empty glass in hand, fixed smile slipping from her face. The crowds behind her. He looked from top to toe. The swinging hem of glimmering chiffon, a slight stain at its edge that made him wince. The swooping neckline that revealed the age crease in her cleavage, making him ache for the years gone by. The gleaming sweep of her hair, adrift tendrils framing her face and needing tucking into place. The same emptiness behind the false smile he could feel slipping from his own face.

New year, same old him.

'There you are!' Adele bounded down the stairs from the hall, grabbing his attention. 'We need to dance, come on!'

Kit glanced back at the window. She had gone. He let the wine flow over the lip of the bottle and took a long swig of its bitterness.

'Yes, let's dance.'

Two HOURS later he could avoid it no longer. He was stood in the main hallway with Adele, saying farewell to guests when Isabelle and Kate came over. Jay talking to Kate, who was leaning on his arm. Her eyes bright, her smile broad. Waving farewell to friends made that night, soon to be forgotten.

'I hear you've bullied my friends into doing an online course?' he greeted her.

'Bullied?' she retorted. 'They practically begged me!'

'Are you going to cope with driving all the way back?' Kit asked Isabelle.

'Fine, I am absolutely sugared up on Coke, I won't sleep for a month.'

'I on the other hand, shall be asleep by the end of the road,' Kate quipped, letting go of Jay and opening her arms to give Adele a farewell hug, stage whispering to him, 'What a rocking party. Could you make him do it more often?'

It was exaggerated, overfriendly, pretend drunkenness. Kit knew Kate drunk and this wasn't it. He on the other hand was feeling the room attempt to trip him up with spinning. Kate and her careful pretences. As bad as Elsa, always making life look good when it was a mess underneath.

'Did you know Jay has been reading my mother's diaries?' he asked Isabelle, feeling Kate freeze to a halt. 'He found the key for that bloody chest Elsa gave me.'

'Yes, he's been telling me about it. It must be fascinating.' Isabelle replied.

Kit looked at Kate, 'Yes, there's certainly a lot of material in there. I'm not sure she ever meant them to be read.'

She widened her smile at him, rocked back on her heels and gripped Adele's arm. 'The car is going to be freezing, I brought a blanket with me though. Honestly, I'll put that seat back and be gone in seconds. Isabelle is such a steady driver. Nothing like yours truly.'

Adele laughed at her. 'I love the way he drives, it's exhilarating.'

'Yes, if you like living with the fear of speeding tickets,' Jay countered.

Jesus, would they ever bloody get on, these two.

'He's even found a parcel she sent back from India, right about the time she died.' It was out of his mouth before he could suck it back in. A bitter secret spat out at the worst of times.

'What? You never said!' Adele cried, releasing himself from Kate's arm and looking at Jay with a frown. 'What was in it?'

'He won't open it,' Jay responded in defence to the looks he got.

A large group of guests headed out, pushing Kit and Kate to one side of the hall, with the others stepping back to give them space. Kit was sick of the farewells, he wanted it to end. To get to bed, where the room could stop surging.

'I didn't say I wouldn't open it,' Kit protested when the crowd had passed. 'Just that I don't want to open it yet.'

'It took you long enough to open the chest,' Isabelle added. 'Surely you must be curious?'

'You should have just opened it,' Adele told Jay. 'I would have.'

'I'm sure you would,' Jay agreed.

While they speculated, Kate watched him back from behind that false smile. Adele turned away to say farewell to the group leaving. Isabelle and Jay drifted after him toward the front door. Kit was left closer to Kate than he had been all evening. Close enough to smell her warmed perfume, a prickling shiver goosing his arms.

'What about you?' Kit asked her. 'Would you open it? You knew her best after all, what might she have sent back home?'

'I dread to think,' Kate smoothed the front of her skirt down. The lights rippled across its surface as it moved, blush and blue glimmering together. Their favourite two colours. That's why he'd bought it. Unable to resist those dancing threads even as the price went up.

By the door he could see Isabelle thanking Jay, who took her coat and opened it for her to slip into. 'Thank you so much for your company.'

'Thank you for keeping me safe,' Jay told her, taking her hands in his in farewell.

They stood in the doorway together, commenting on the stars, the new year, the party, unaware of him and Kate. Kit could feel her waiting beside him. He needed to say goodbye, to go lie down. To sleep. God, how he wanted to sleep. He could recall, in the faint strain of her scent, nights spent together, talking, laughing, falling asleep in a tangle of limbs and closeness of skin. He tried to think of how to say good-bye. How to tell her, it was all gone, over, past. His life was perfect. He didn't need her, anymore than he did messages from beyond his mother's grave.

'That's a stunning dress,' he said.

'I hoped you'd approve.' She adjusted the neckline. 'Though my cleavage is more creased these days than I want to see in a sober mirror.'

Kit glanced down at the crease disappearing into the chiffon folds. A darkening hue where the skin gathered, slipping into the shadows of the neckline. It was hypnotic, catching his aching head, pulling invisible lines inside him tight.

'Kit,' she lowered her voice, reached a hand tentatively out to him. 'Your mother's package, perhaps you shouldn't open it.'

Kit looked at the hand hovering in the air between them. Her nails a nude glimmer. He remembered the feel of that hand on his skin. The first time she had ruffled his hair. The time she had pulled him close when he'd arrived at Riverdell, telling him she was there for him. The first time she'd held her hand out to him and pulled him to bed. The hall was a high bubble of instability, voices and people echoing in its space and his head. He resented that tentative hand more than their noise. It suggested comfort, reassurance, a steadiness he wanted to reach for but couldn't grasp.

'Why not? More secrets we don't need to share?' Kit asked.

She looked at him, a wary frown appearing behind the false drunk sparkle, a crease in the corner of her lip as she considered her response. 'Things left unsaid too long are best left in the past, don't you think?'

'Along with your cleavage?' Kit struggled not to fall over in the rush of bitterness that dredged the words from him. Because there was just too much unsaid that he needed to release. And the urge to take her hand was stronger than he could resist. And the space around him would not stop spinning.

Kate snapped her hand back to her body, where she held it in front of the sweetheart bodice, covering her skin. She looked at him, hurt in the brilliant blue eyes that welled up behind their wounded, fluttering eyelashes.

'Goodbye, Kit.'

He watched her move away, out of the door and into the night, taking Isabelle's arm as they walked across the driveway. The lights from the house catching at the hues of her swishing dress. Kit followed her to the door. She never looked back as they rounded the corner and disappeared beyond the clipped Ceanothus that framed his driveway.

Perhaps that was all it had needed.

Not Christmas at Riverdell.

Not this mammoth event that fizzled out with the fireworks and Prosecco.

Just an unkind word he would have forgotten by morning and life finally moved on. As he stood in the doorway, Adele reached out for him, and Kit pulled his hand close, clinging to his strength.

ACKNOWLEDGMENTS

A writer is the spy amongst you. I am indebted to the many families who welcomed me into their homes and lives and inspired so many of my characters. Riverdell would not exist without that experience. I do hope no one is offended.

Writing and editing the third book of this saga will forever be linked in my mind with both the extended misery of COVID and huge upheaval in my personal life. For sustaining me through those challenges one freezing wild swim at a time, for guilt-tripping me by way of her exemplary standards to adequately nourish myself, and for conversations that enrich us both, I am beyond grateful for the light in this world that is Jennifer Tindall.

To Leila, for sending me outraged text messages demanding an explanation for what I put Moth through in Book 2, I hope this book heals some of those wounds.

To all my readers, you are and always have been my only goal in being a writer. Thank you for returning to Riverdell.

ACKNOWLEDGMENTS

ROSE DE LAVELLE

There is no doubt that the star of this act is Rose de Lavelle, Kit's mysterious mother. Her diaries were an audacious act of writing that constantly demanded I put aside my own fear and be brutally true to the character.

It was not without doubt that I sat down to write a character who has gender dysphoria, who is questioning their place in the world, who is considering their options. Research can only take you so far, at some point you have to let go and feel for the character beneath the subject matter. I hope that readers who feel a connection with Rose in their own journey will know that I wrote from a place of love and support. I did not want Rose to be a case study, I wanted her to be the impossible, intrepid, uncompromising individual that she truly is, stuck in a world that can't satisfy her. To be the mother responsible for making Kit into the person you have come to love and hate. I know it won't please everyone but when writing a character feels this terrifying, I know I am right where I want to be in my work.

RIVERDELL HOUSE

Riverdell House is a fictional house in a real location. It is a love song to all the wonderful houses I was fortunate enough to work in during my wonderful career as an interiors consultant.

When I sat down to write this story, I began not with a sentence but with a line, a stroke drawn on a clean sheet of paper which was the first wall of Riverdell. That line spread, into the two wings of the house and the entrance that nestles in their crook. I expanded upward into the attic bedrooms, downward into the basement and each room was a memory of some other home I had worked or lived in.

I filled in colour charts, selected furniture, chose door shapes, designed window treatments, raised ceilings, widened fireplaces and discarded the trappings of life: clothes, books, cups, sweet wrappings. Only once the house sat before me, a full spread of floor plans and decor schemes, did I let the characters in.

Of course they didn't like what I had done, any more than new owners like what has been left by the former. They tossed out my ideas, presented fresh ones. But Riverdell was strong enough by then to take the new fancies, as many old houses are tolerant of the fads that pass through them. As you can imagine, Kit and I had many arguments long into the night. He won most of them.

Finally, Riverdell and I had to decide where the house belonged. Though we considered options there was only ever really one; the Dinham Green in the magical and quaint rural town of Ludlow. A place reclaimed by the Millennium Trust that was a tired old space of tumbledown cottages and disused tin-roof swimming pool. Now it is a green and glorious space, with a thriving cafe in the old mill buildings and a popular place with both tourists and townsfolk. The cottages are enviable homes. It is also now home to the fictional house of Riverdell and I hope that you get to visit Ludlow and sit on the Dinham lawns and imagine yourself looking out from the windows of the glorious house, as I do whenever I visit. You can walk the weir as Isabelle and Moth did, listen to the town that rises above the river.

Houses are made of empty rooms. Homes are rooms filled with love, memories, souls and secrets. Riverdell is a home. Testament to the love, the commitment, the traumas that many families go through in turning their purchased house into their dream homes. Homes have many stories to tell and I am rather addicted to them.

Marianne, Ludlow, 2021.

ALSO BY MARIANNE ROSEN

Discover where the journey started with Book 1 of

The Riverdell Saga:

The Doors of Riverdell

Followed by:

The Halls of Riverdell

And coming in April 2022...

Book 4, the thrilling conclusion of The Riverdell Saga:

The Children of Riverdell

It's February 2020, the family have endured the winter floods and are looking forward to spring when a phone call from Kit's friend turns Isabelle's life upside down. Kit has gone to India to discover the truth about his mother. With Moth finally ready to return home to Riverdell, the last thing Isabelle needs is a wild goose chase to help Kit, especially when there's an unexplored romance to avoid on the way.

And, at last, hear the past from Kate's perspective as she weathers the family storm and airs her own troubled secrets while waiting to see which of Riverdell's children will get to come home.

Sign up to Marianne's newsletter at www.mariannerosen.com to keep updated with release details.

ABOUT THE PUBLISHER

Oriel Books Ltd is an indie publishing house dedicated to promoting the careers of indie authors.

Combining traditional publishing practice with modern digital vision we work to advance and promote the careers of dedicated, series-based authors at every stage of their journey.

If you have enjoyed this book consider joining us as a beta reader or advanced copy reviewer, working to help develop the stories of new authors in your favourite genres.

If you are an emerging author with a strong idea for a series of books, consider pitching your novels to us.

Details can be found at www.orielbooks.com